A
Teacher's
Heart

Lessons of the Heart ©2020 by Terri J. Haynes
Courting the Doctor ©2020 by Cecelia Dowdy
Schooling Mr. Mason ©2020 by Lynette Sowell
Lessons of Love ©2020 by Lynn A. Coleman

Print ISBN 978-1-64352-428-3

eBook Editions:
Adobe Digital Edition (.epub) 978-1-64352-430-6
Kindle and MobiPocket Edition (.prc) 978-1-64352-429-0

All scripture quotations are taken from the King James Version of the Bible.

This book is a work of fiction. Names, characters, places, and incidents are either products of the author's imagination or used fictitiously. Any similarity to actual people, organizations, and/or events is purely coincidental.

Cover image © Sandra Cunningham / Trevillion Images

Published by Barbour Books, an imprint of Barbour Publishing, Inc., 1810 Barbour Drive, Uhrichsville, Ohio 44683, www.barbourbooks.com

Our mission is to inspire the world with the life-changing message of the Bible.

Member of the
Evangelical Christian
Publishers Association

Printed in Canada.

A Teacher's Heart

4 Historical Stories

LYNN A. COLEMAN, CECELIA DOWDY
TERRI J. HAYNES, LYNETTE SOWELL

BARBOUR BOOKS
An Imprint of Barbour Publishing, Inc.

Lessons of the Heart

by Terri J. Haynes

❧ Chapter 1 ❧

Fort Ward, Alexandria, Virginia
1864

Elim Smith held his breath as he faced his men, a section of the 105th Colored Infantry Regiment, keeping his expression neutral. These were the men he had been promoted to lead. The gold double chevrons of his corporal rank felt like a vise on his arm. His uniform a skin needing to be shed. Then the real Elim Smith would be seen. A failure and a fake.

He took in a deep breath and then bellowed the instruction. "Support arms!"

Only half the men performed the first motion correctly. Even fewer followed through with the second and third motions of the command. A few dropped their pieces, and several men had to duck to avoid being hit with their neighbor's weapon. None of them did anything in the right timing.

Elim's shoulders sagged but only for a second before he corrected his posture. This was the simplest command in the drilling manual. Heaven help them when they reached the harder commands. If they ever—

"Rest!" he shouted. The men almost accomplished it but were still shifting about from the first command.

He worked to relax his expression. His men looked back at him with the same shame that was gnawing at his thoughts. "I think that is enough for the day. Private Holt, a word."

The men dispersed and Private Holt walked to Elim with worry creasing his face. Holt was the youngest and newest member of his squad. He was also the prime recipient of the men's ribbing. They had taken to calling him Private Halt because the young man was a chatterbox. Elim had fought the urge to laugh when he first heard the nickname but recognized the chatter as nervousness. Holt was also the most forgetful and scattered person Elim had ever met.

"Whatever they said I did, sir, I didn't." Holt didn't give Elim a chance to speak.

Elim motioned to the front of Holt's uniform, which was missing two buttons.

Holt looked down. "Oh."

Elim reached in his pocket and produced four buttons and a sewing kit. "I want those buttons on by the next drill. Can you sew?"

Holt dropped his head. "I'm sure I can figure it out."

"Sew them tight so you won't lose them again. Keep the extras in your kit."

"Thank you, sir." He shoved the buttons in his pocket. Elim wondered how long they would stay there.

Elim waited until Holt was out of sight before he dropped his rigid posture. Other battalions drilled around him in the open field. These soldiers were everything his men were not. Skilled, precise, and white. He stood, one colored man in a sea of whites. The story of his life.

Memories rose like fog, and he quickly dispelled them. A lock of his hair had escaped from under his cap. When he tucked it back into his cap, he caught a glimpse of his hands. They were red from being in the sun, and soon he would tan. Thankfully his men didn't resent that he looked more like the soldiers in the white battalions than them. He did though. He was a mutt, a Mulatto, and had told his men right from the beginning. He had been a slave like them, and his color hadn't saved him from any of the horrors they had suffered.

He was one of them. . .except he was taught to believe the lie that he was different. Better.

A private from one of the other squads trotted up to him and saluted. "Sir, Major MacDonald wants to see you."

Elim nodded and pressed his lips into a tight line. No good could come out of a summons from the third in command of the regiment. The man was hard to puzzle out. He had reluctantly allowed Elim's squad, a colored one, to muster under his command. It was clear, however, that he wasn't committed to the arrangement. Elim's men were an afterthought when it came to handing out provisions, and first in line for any unpleasant job that needed completing. While the other men manned the cannons and worked in the armory, Elim's men drove supplies back and forth to an outpost on the other side of Alexandria, and one of his men almost always had night duty.

The officer's quarters, which doubled as their meeting place, sat to the east of the drilling ground. Elim knocked on the door and received a sharp, "Enter," from inside.

Major MacDonald sat at his desk writing something with such force that Elim thought he would tear the paper. He dropped the pen and it clattered on the desk. "Corporal."

"Sir," Elim said with a salute.

"I will be quick as I have other, more pressing matters to attend to. I need to speak to you about your men."

Elim's chest nearly caved in, from both the major needing to discuss his men and his insinuation that colored troops weren't a pressing matter. "Yes, sir." *This is what Holt must have felt like.* Elim would make sure to speak to him later.

"Your men are not progressing. Your drills have been described to me as organized chaos."

Elim clasped his hands behind his back to hide the tremble in them. Major MacDonald had never seen his men drill, which meant someone else had told him about Elim's men. "The men are newly mustered and need time to—"

MacDonald held up his hand. "I don't have time or resources to waste on you or your men. They were more useful to me when they were digging ditches."

"Sir, I'm sure that with a little more time, they will be ready for battle."

The major let out a sharp bark of a laugh. "Slow down there, Corporal. Those are pretty high expectations for colored troops."

"The men are capable of fighting for the Union."

"Doesn't sound like it. Right now, it seems that they are only here to receive benefits from the Union. I have capable men working as teamsters and horsemen while I have a section who can't even get into formation correctly."

"I can get the men into shape."

The major sighed. "I allowed this because I saw potential in you. There are not many educated Negroes around, and I thought you would be a good role model for other coloreds. It looks like I was wrong." He gave Elim a piercing glare. "Am I wrong, Corporal?"

"No, sir." Elim's voice held more confidence than he felt. "I will make sure you don't regret mustering us."

MacDonald leaned forward. "When?"

"Sir?" The question bounced around Elim's mind.

"When will you have the men properly trained and drilling correctly?"

Elim toyed with time frames in his mind. Based on the major's expression, six months was too long, which was probably what the men really needed. Anything shorter than that would be impossible, especially since he didn't know why the men were struggling so much. "Three months." The words stung his tongue. He couldn't do it in that time unless he drilled the men nonstop day and night.

"How about a month?"

Elim sucked in a breath. "Sir, I—"

Major MacDonald stood. "You mean, 'Yes, sir.'"

Elim swallowed hard. "Yes, sir."

The sunlight seemed hotter as he stepped outside the hut. The Virginia heat stuck in his throat as he fought to keep his breathing regulated. *One month.* No matter how much hope he had that his section would improve, it would not, could not, happen in a month. The men would lose their chance to prove that they were worth more than trench digging and supply hauling. So would he.

When the wagon stopped, Adeline Barris wanted to bolt from its confines. Instead she remained on the hard wooden bench for a few seconds more, calming her breathing.

She was back in Virginia, a moment she'd dreamed about for many years.

The trek had lasted three days instead of the weeks it took to run from Alexandria to Philadelphia on foot. The passing landscape was the only thing that had kept her from going mad with her thoughts. Once again, they drifted to Papa as she scooted toward the wagon's gate. He would have been overjoyed to be back in the place where he was once enslaved. Happy to be near dear Florence, Adeline's mother, and her brother, Michael. Both joy and pain swirled in her heart.

Mr. Hunter, a tall man with a broad, dark face, came from the front of the wagon, rubbing a hand over the flank of one of the horses as he did. "That was a long ride. Looks like a long one for you too."

Adeline smiled at her fellow teacher, sliding down from the wagon with as much grace as she could. "Yes, but not too long."

Mrs. Hunter, much shorter and fairer, appeared from around the back of the wagon. She walked with a stiff limp. "Oh my. I am glad to be on solid ground."

The wagon sat in front of a simple wood building, their lodgings for the time being. Supporters of the Society for the Betterment of Colored People in Philadelphia had provided the funding for the trip. The problem of orphaned colored children had been the main topic of discussion in the Society's meetings.

But their trip had put another need before the Society. Illiterate colored troops. Adeline and the Hunters had been dispatched to Alexandria after the chaplain sent a request for someone to teach the soldiers and the orphaned children down in the freedman's village in a town called The Bottom.

A woman sat at a small desk in the entryway of the house. She smiled at them when they entered, introduced herself as Millie, and explained the rules of the house and the meal schedule. "Your trunks arrived a few days ago along with some mail." Millie passed two letters to Adeline. "For Miss Barris."

Adeline's heart thumped. She had left careful instructions for her mail to be forwarded to this location. Any responses to the advertisement she placed in the newspaper could be the linchpin in her success. "Thank you." Adeline's voice squeaked with excitement.

Millie showed them their rooms. Adeline's trunks holding her clothing and books sat next to a small bed. There was also a small writing desk and chair. She shut the door, removed her cloak, and laid the letters out in front of her.

The first letter was from someone she didn't know, probably answering the advertisement. She opened it and found her assumption was correct, but the contents of the letter were not what she was expecting. In a neat hand, the writer stated that he had information about the slaves from Ashton and informed her that some of the slaves had run west to Kansas.

Adeline let out a loud sigh. This was not about slaves from Ashton Place Plantation in Virginia. The writer was speaking of another Ashton in Mississippi.

She flipped to the second letter with a return address from

Baltimore. This letter was from the National Freedom Committee, an organization that assisted runaways who came through the Underground Railroad. The committee collected information and the stories of slaves who passed through Baltimore from the South. She had written to them before she and the Hunters left home. In the letter, a Mrs. Tuttle informed Adeline that she had no information about slaves from Ashton Place, Virginia. Adeline's heart sank even though the letter closed with Mrs. Tuttle's promise that she would continue to look for information.

Adeline folded the letters, her mind racing. This was only one tiny setback. There were still lots of sources of information, especially since she was so near to Ashton Place. Now that she was closer, she had a better chance of finding her family. Then the cloud over her could finally dissipate.

❧ Chapter 2 ❧

*A*nother day, another summons.

The men had finished drilling when Chaplain Thomas walked over to observe them. Elim nearly groaned. He didn't want anyone to see his men struggle. The chaplain was a kind man who freely gave encouragement and support and was one of the few men who actually cared about his people. Still, Elim was unable to meet the man's gaze.

After he dismissed the men to clean their weapons, which wasn't necessary but showed that they were taking their duties seriously, Elim went to the chaplain.

"Can you come to my hut for a moment?" the chaplain said after greeting him.

"Yes, sir." Elim gave his men instructions to continue working until he returned.

To Elim's relief, he and the chaplain traveled the space in silence. Elim's worry was too heavy for him to carry on any kind of small talk.

Chaplain Thomas sat at his desk. "How is the drilling going?"

Why was he asking? He'd seen the disaster himself. Elim swallowed his unfiltered reply: *Disorganized, chaotic, disheartening, frustrating.* "It could be better."

"Have you identified the problem?"

"They are struggling with getting the commands right, despite their manuals." He swallowed. The admission stung.

"Fortunately, I think I may have a solution. I received a letter from another chaplain serving in New York. He wrote of the progress the colored men in his regiment are making."

"I would love to know how they are doing it." He would take all the advice he could get, because a life building fortifications and digging trenches was not much different than the life his men had escaped from.

"He taught the men to read."

Elim raised an eyebrow. "Read? Not sure of the difference that would make."

"You're literate, so you should understand the benefit of it. Many of the other men have not had the privilege of education."

Elim winced. Hard to call knowing how to read a privilege in his case. He had not been taught to read for his own benefit, but so he could be a plaything. His education was a curse. "I understand, but. . ." His words dropped, his argument failed.

"Then why do you disagree?"

"It's not that I don't think the men should learn to read," Elim sputtered, hearing the harshness of his words. Just because he felt uncomfortable about being educated didn't mean the men shouldn't have instruction. "But it will do them no good if they aren't prepared to fight. However, if you think it would help. . ."

"I do. I took the liberty of writing a few letters on your behalf." Chaplain Thomas tapped a pile of papers on his desk. "My chaplain friend recommended the group who helped him, teachers from the Society for the Betterment of Colored People out of Philadelphia. I sent them a request to come and teach your troops along with the runaway orphans down in the freedman's village. They arrived yesterday and will be here today to work out logistics."

Elim kept his eyes straight ahead. "Sir, I wish you had consulted with me before—"

Chaplain Thomas held up a hand. "When this war is over, your men will have to make their way in this changing world. It will benefit them to have as many tools as possible to help them find work and support themselves."

"But they have to survive the war first."

Chaplain Thomas nodded in agreement. "That's true, but they need to survive it with something to live for."

Something to live for. Those words sat in his stomach like hardtack. Most of his men had run from their plantations with nothing but the clothes on their backs. They'd left families and friends behind and had joined the army because they wanted to be truly free. But take away their freedom, their ability to contribute to the victory, and they truly had nothing to live for.

After a quiet breakfast, Adeline and the Hunters left their lodgings for the short walk up to Fort Ward. Adeline fell a little behind the Hunters, her mind still on her letters. Both of these methods of finding her family had only a slight chance to

succeed, but they were a start. It helped her eliminate the possibility that Mama and Michael were no longer at Ashton Place.
She would continue to write to other groups who helped slaves
to see if anyone had seen or heard from them.

It wasn't easy to get information about runaways. She would
have to take advantage of all the ways available to her. She had
asked around about her mother and brother in every location
she'd ever taught. Yes, it was improbable, but the more people on
the lookout for them the better.

The noise of the fort rang out before they reached it. Wagons
rolled past them up the path to a gate that looked like a giant
wooden door. Behind it was a long stretch of open field followed
by rows of tents. There were few trees and almost no grass, probably from the number of feet, hooves, and wheels that traveled
this way.

Fort Ward wasn't as large as other forts she'd seen. It was laid
out with all the tents to one side and six cannons on the other.
Troops marched in the open space in the center of all this. One
of the groups was colored troops. Her heart swelled with pride.
Colored soldiers fighting for the freedom of people still in slavery. She smiled as many looked in her direction.

Maybe the war would free her mother and brother instead of
the meager money in her purse.

As they reached the chaplain's small hut, Mr. Hunter stepped
to the open doorway and knocked on the frame. A voice called
out, "Come in."

Adeline followed the Hunters inside. Blinking, she surveyed
the small quarters. A man sat at a small desk in front of a book-
shelf lined with Bibles and other books. Standing in front and to

the right of the desk stood another soldier. His skin was chestnut, his eyes deep brown, but his softly curled, fine hair gave him away as a Mulatto. He held himself erect, shoulders back, arms at his sides.

His eyes met hers and her stomach did a little flip. She took in his uniform, perfectly pressed, his polished boots, and the cap he held in his hand. The image of a well-groomed solider. He held her gaze for what seemed like forever and she fought the urge to squirm under his scrutiny. Even when she wasn't the focus of his attention, his commanding presence seemed to fill the hut. It made her feel she should do everything exactly right.

"Good afternoon," Mr. Hunter said. "I am looking for Chaplain Thomas."

The man behind the desk stood and gave Mr. Hunter a handshake. "You've found him. How can I help you?"

"I'm Frederick Hunter, this is my wife, Margaret, and"—Mr. Hunter motioned to Adeline—"this is Miss Adeline Barris. We are the teachers sent by the Society for the Betterment of Colored People."

Chaplain Thomas smiled wide. "A pleasure. I'm glad to see you made it safely. This is Corporal Elim Smith. His men will be your students."

Adeline noticed the corporal turn his head in her direction before turning it back to Mr. Hunter. He frowned like he was the unruly student sentenced to lessons. "Good day," he said.

Mr. Hunter seemed to puff up with excitement, something he did at the prospect of new students. "We have secured lodgings and will assess the situation with the children soon. Depending on how many there are, we may split our party."

"I think the children should be the priority." Corporal Smith's words rumbled deep; he obviously was a man used to projecting his voice. "Chaplain, you know how I feel about the lessons for my men, and don't say this because of our difference of opinion."

Adeline tamped down the urge to ask what the difference of opinion was.

Mrs. Hunter waved her hand. "It's not a problem at all. If need be, Miss Barris can teach the men here, and we will instruct the children in the village."

Adeline's attention snapped to Mrs. Hunter, a wave of nausea causing her to press a hand to her stomach. One day, and her plan was being threatened already. Being at the fort would take her away from why she was really here.

"Or the other way around," Adeline said quickly. "I'm better with children." And she was. Most of her students in Philadelphia were twelve and under. She'd taught the occasional Sunday school class and served as an assistant whenever the Hunters taught soldiers, but children were her strong point.

As she turned her focus back on the chaplain, her gaze crossed Corporal Smith's. He was watching her with a raised eyebrow.

"This is an answer to prayer," Chaplain Thomas said, shaking Mr. Hunter's hand and grinning at Corporal Smith, who did not return his smile. "There is an abandoned chapel outside the south gate. I think it would be a good place to hold the lessons."

Mr. and Mrs. Hunter agreed. Adeline and the corporal continued to frown. *At least I'm not the only person unhappy with this arrangement.*

They exited the hut, Mr. Hunter and Chaplain Thomas out front discussing the location of the chapel and when Adeline would come back to the fort for the lessons. Corporal Smith fell in step beside her. "Miss Barris, thank you for volunteering, but I am not sure how effective this is going to be."

She bit back a sigh. The corporal's company wasn't what she wanted right now. If she talked to the Hunters, she could convince them to switch. It would be a disaster if she spent her whole time in Alexandria here at the fort. "Education is a very important part of self-esteem."

"Discipline and practice are what the men need to be better soldiers."

She peered up at him, taking in his profile. Did he ever fully smile? "Learning to read will make them better men."

The little openness in the corporal's face disappeared. "I also wanted to tell you that if you need any assistance, please let me know. I will make sure the men treat you with dignity and respect. You are under my protection now."

Her words jumbled in her brain. The way Corporal Smith carried himself, she would probably be the safest she'd ever been in her life. "Thank you."

He turned to her and gave her a curt bow. "Until tomorrow."

❧ Chapter 3 ❧

*A*deline left her lodging as soon as there was enough morning light to navigate the worn path from Alexandria to the fort. She wanted to arrive early enough to see where they would be holding classes and to plan her lessons. She needed at least one of her schemes to go right. Yesterday had not been the start she wanted. Instead of spending her days in the freedman's village, she was at the fort, away from the runaways, her best source of information.

Even her backup plan had failed. She had talked to the Hunters about letting her teach the children in the village while they went to the fort, but their argument was valid. There were only twenty men in Corporal Smith's section. There were far more children, and two teachers would be better than one. She certainly couldn't ask them to split up.

Another delay. Papa had waited too long, and now he was gone. He died with his dream of reuniting his family unfulfilled. The sweet man who had worked hard and loved equally as hard.

Finding Mama and Michael wasn't only her dream, but his as well.

And here she was, messing things up again.

As the chapel came into view, a figure stood outside. She slowed her pace. The man turned, and she recognized Corporal Smith. He stood with his shoulders back and carriage erect. He looked every part the solider. *Does he ever relax?*

He turned as she cleared the low brush around the chapel. He nodded to her. "Good morning, Miss Barris."

"Good morning, Corporal. You're here early."

"I wanted to have a look at the place before I brought the troops over. I haven't been inside yet."

He motioned her toward the door, which appeared sturdy enough. He pushed it open for her and it creaked loudly on its hinges. It was dim inside, the rising sun starting to brighten the room through the dingy windows. It would warm once the sun fully rose. Chaplain Thomas was right. The pews remained intact, but the place was covered in dirt and dust.

The room was a sad sight that reflected her soul. It had been ages since she felt at peace in a church. She'd gone every Sunday with her father and then, when he passed, with the Hunters. Yet although her body went, her heart remained distant. She went there to find grace but found shame instead.

"This will do," Corporal Smith said from behind her.

"It will, but it needs some cleaning."

"The men are used to being in less than ideal conditions."

She arched an eyebrow at his dismissive tone. "But I am not."

His face flushed pink and he rubbed his chin. "Of course. I will have the men clean it."

"That will give them a sense of ownership of the place."

His expression hardened. "I wouldn't go that far."

She schooled her face into a pleasant look, even though she wanted to tell him to forget the lessons. He clearly didn't want to be here. "Cleaning this place will show the men that something important is happening here."

Corporal Smith turned sharply to face her. "We need to settle something right now. My men need all the time they can get to drill. This"—he waved his hand—"takes them away from that. You will teach them for no more than an hour a day."

His words were hard. He was used to giving orders and people obeying them. "I cannot guarantee that until I get a sense of what the students know."

"You have an hour." Corporal Smith let out a harrumph and turned to the door. "I'll bring them over."

Adeline watched him go and then exhaled. This was a battle she didn't want, especially since she didn't want to be here either.

She looked around the small space. She had taught in a lot of places before, many times in the Hope Street Church. She walked all the way to the back of the room, counting the pews and formulating a plan. Chaplain Thomas said that the class would be around twenty men. There were plenty of pews for that. And enough space that each man could spread out and find his own space to work in. Only one thing was missing.

She scanned the far corners near the front where the daylight hadn't quite reached. *Ah. That's what I need.* A wooden pulpit sat in the corner. It would make the perfect desk. As she got closer, she saw it was sturdy but not too heavy for Corporal Smith to move it. He appeared to be as strong in body as he was in temperament.

The top was covered with dust. She tapped the podium with the side of her foot.

A loud screech cut through the air.

Adeline screamed, scooting backward until she was pressed against the wall. A raccoon scurried from the bottom shelf of the pulpit and raced out the door. Adeline didn't move, hand still over her mouth, until the humor of the moment caused her to chuckle.

The sound of footsteps running thumped outside the chapel. In a flash of blue and gray, Corporal Smith barreled through the door, pistol drawn. "What's wrong?" he panted. He scanned the room, posture tense, ready to fight.

She held up her hands, enjoying seeing him display an attitude other than annoyed. "There was a raccoon in there." She pointed to the pulpit. "He ran out the door. He wasn't interested in learning today." She gave a soft chuckle.

He studied the pulpit, glanced out the door, then holstered his pistol. "I heard you scream."

A blush warmed her cheeks and she ducked her chin. He'd come running to save her. "I am fine."

He shifted out of the way as his men entered with mops and buckets of water. Adeline moved to greet them, her heart warmed by her protector. Maybe he had more emotions than dissatisfaction.

A raccoon.

Elim bit back a grumble. When Miss Barris's scream cut through the morning quiet, he'd taken off running before he realized his feet were moving. He'd barreled into the room like a fool without knowing what enemy he was facing. How did that look to his men?

She stood before him with a smile on her face and what looked like admiration in her eyes. From their first meeting, he suspected that she thought he was the surliest man she'd ever met. Now, her look had softened, humor in her eyes. She had laughed when she explained what happened. A note of jealousy rang in his mind. How nice to be able to laugh at oneself.

He straightened his uniform, which had suddenly grown excessively hot, but Miss Barris stepped around him with a bright smile on her face and addressed his men. "Good morning."

The men came to something that looked like attention. A few of them mumbled a "Good morning" in return. Elim gave them a stern look, and a strong, unified "Good morning" echoed through the chapel.

"Much better," Elim muttered. He might not be able to teach them how to drill properly, but he could teach them to be courteous to a lady.

Miss Barris looked at their cleaning supplies. "Looks like you came ready to work."

Work. The men were very much in danger of doing harder work than cleaning an abandoned chapel. They needed to improve, and quickly. Instead of drilling, however, they were here. Elim removed his jacket, placed it over one of the pails they'd brought in, and rolled up his sleeves. "Where should we start?"

Miss Barris clasped her hands in front of her. "The pews."

The men took their jackets off and moved to the pews.

"Oh my." Miss Barris leaned over the first pew. "This pew is so dusty that someone could write his name in it." With a dainty finger, she traced a line of *A*'s down the length of the pew. When she was done, she motioned to the man nearest to her, Private Howard. "You try."

Howard glanced at Elim, and Elim gave him a slight nod, although annoyance surged through him. The men weren't here to play games. They were already sacrificing precious time with these reading lessons.

Howard stepped up and traced a line of *A*'s under the ones Miss Barris wrote. She moved beside him, giving him gentle instruction and correction. Once he was done, she motioned to the next man to follow suit. Elim watched, realization dawning on him.

She'd turned the pew into a chalkboard. Ingenious, but they would need a whole lot more pews to get the men reading and back to drilling. He folded his arms across his chest.

"Everyone take a turn. Those who have already done it, help your brothers," she called to the men as she moved to stand behind the row. The soldiers covered the first two rows of pews with *A*'s, and she clapped. "Congratulations. You all have learned the letter *A*. Now you can clean these pews."

While they did, she turned and wrote a line of *B*'s on the third row. Now that they understood what was happening, the men lined up and began writing *B*'s.

Miss Barris motioned to Elim to join her at the fourth pew. "Can you help write the letters on the rest of the pews?"

Elim frowned at her. "You assume I can read."

A look of embarrassment colored her lovely brown cheeks. "I—"

He stifled a smile. "I can read, Miss Barris. Just so we are clear, I don't agree with this."

She paused in her writing. "With teaching the men to read?"

"There are many in this fort who can't read, white and colored alike. They will all fare the same under a hail of bullets."

Her posture became stiff and he could feel the heat of her anger rolling down the pew toward him. "So you think it's better for them to die illiterate? Would that make their deaths more palatable?" Her voice was low and tight.

"I never said such a thing. I believe the most pressing lesson these men need to learn is how to fight. To live through a battle and prove their worth."

She moved down the pew toward him, giving him a fine view of the fire in her eyes. "You think all the work that abolitionists and teachers do is worthless in the face of war? That is incredibly cruel thinking, Corporal."

"Or realistic thinking," he challenged. "How will these men benefit if they know how to read if they are captured? You think it will make a single ounce of difference when they are standing on an auction block?"

Miss Barris stared at him, her mouth slightly agape and one hand pressed to her heart. His own chest rose and fell in hard breaths. He licked his lips, not sure of how he'd gotten so worked up.

Miss Barris recovered before him and collected her skirts in a swish that stirred the dust around them. "Excuse me." Her voice was tight as she moved past him to the next pew.

He stood there for a moment, watching her shoulders as she wrote the letter on the next pew. Her posture was so rigid that he wasn't sure how she bent over. Once she calmed down, she would see his point. When she wasn't so mad, he would try to explain to her that he understood the work people like her and the Hunters were doing, but it wouldn't change the troops' lives now. Maybe after the war. And there was the linchpin. If they didn't win the war, then horrors untold would be awaiting educated slaves. The northern abolitionists were convinced that reading and education would give the men hope like some kind of magic. It was good that Miss Barris was here to see how things truly were.

By the time he and Miss Barris lettered all the pews—there were enough pews for *A* through *H*—the men had fallen into a rhythm of tracing the letters and then cleaning the pew.

Miss Barris came to stand beside him, her gaze cold and hard. "I need your help with one more thing. I'm going to use the pulpit as a desk. Could you move it for me, please?"

Elim easily lifted it to the place she'd indicated. "Is this where you want it?"

The fire was back in her eyes. "If this is such a useless endeavor, why are you helping with all this? Why not drop the men off and leave? Or wait outside?"

"Because I don't disobey orders."

She narrowed her eyes, turned her back to him, and began cleaning the pulpit in silence.

Elim felt the dismissal in her movements and left her to check on the troops. They, of course, were enjoying every second of their lesson. Probably because it got them out of drilling.

After the troops had cleaned the pews, she had them write the letters *I* and *J* on the windows before they cleaned them. Then they practiced more with brooms and mops on the floor. When they were done, the place looked like it was ready to be used as a schoolroom and a proper church. It reminded him of the church near his home. He shoved that thought away. Not home, but a place of bondage.

Miss Barris stood behind the newly cleaned pulpit. "Gentlemen, you did well today. Tomorrow we will begin in the primers."

Most of the men beamed, but Elim didn't join them. This was the first lesson, and although it appeared to go well, it could still go poorly from here. He took a look back at Miss Barris and saw the daggers in her eyes. Clearly, as far as she was concerned, things were already going poorly.

∾ Chapter 4 ∾

![A]lthough the lessons had begun well, after two weeks, Adeline's students had started to become restless. *Maybe it's me.* It had become increasingly difficult to keep their attention even though they were progressing well. Several times during the lesson she'd had to call them back to order, winning her a disapproving look from Corporal Smith. That, coupled with her unfruitful search for her family, made it hard to keep a smile on her face.

Options were few and leads fewer. After discreetly questioning Millic and other free blacks in town, she still hadn't learned anything about her family. In her questioning she was careful not to mention that she was seeking information about them. The task of finding them was too important to leave to someone else.

Disheartening. The same downcast mood was reflected in the men's faces. She wasn't alone.

She had a few students who still showed a sparkle of

excitement in their eyes when they arrived, but for most, including Corporal Smith, the enthusiasm had disappeared. Well, Corporal Smith never had it. As a matter of fact, anytime she pointed out the fact that he could read, he glowered at her.

She had hoped that he would provide an example for the men of someone who had bettered himself through education. But he seemed determined to hide his intelligence. And after their little argument the other day, she wanted to stay as far away from him as possible in the small space.

Today the troops shuffled in, their conversation muted. Corporal Smith wore a neutral expression.

"Good morning," she said as cheerfully as she could. She received a halfhearted "Good morning" from the men in return.

I need to change tactics.

For the past couple of weeks, the routine was for the men to come in, retrieve their primers, and begin work until review time. That wasn't going to work today.

She reached into her bundle and pulled out a small tattered book. An old friend. She cracked the cover and began to read out loud.

The words flowed easily. She'd read *Rip Van Winkle* to almost every child she'd ever taught since finishing college. The wonder of the story always pulled them in. She'd thought of the book last night after spending an evening talking to some of the people in the freedman's village. There was such hopelessness there. The dream of freedom had turned into a nightmare. As she listened to others' stories, her own nightmare had filtered into her mind.

She had left Virginia not knowing what she was doing. She had followed her father into the night and thus found her freedom by accident. But it was not the dream she'd thought it would be. It never became that. Mama and Michael weren't with them and Papa was always at work. All alone, she clung to the Hunters, willing to do anything to help them so she wasn't left alone in the room she and Papa lived in.

It was a happy day when she started school. She soon made friends, and that helped stave off the loneliness. But it did nothing for the pain of returning to that tiny room and knowing that her mother and brother were probably still working in the fields. She cooked, cleaned, and made sure Papa could focus all of his energy on working to reunite the family. Some nights she would read to him. He seemed to enjoy knowing that she was learning to read. After she would shut the book, he would place a hand on her head and say in a weary, heartbroken voice, "That's a good girl."

Rip Van Winkle was one of his favorite stories, and he chuckled at the idea that anyone could sleep that long. After one particularly hard day, he looked at her with sad eyes and said, "I wonder what it would be like to go to sleep a slave and wake up free."

Her memories of Papa wove between the words on the page. She didn't realize that the room had grown quiet. She stopped reading and looked up. All the faces in the room stared back at her. Corporal Smith wore a frown.

"Do you want me to stop?" she asked.

A chorus of "No!" and "Keep going!" sounded back at her.

So she kept going, ignoring the deepening scowl on Corporal Smith's face.

When she ended the reading, making sure to conclude at a spot that would keep the men interested in what would happen next, she closed the book. "I hope you enjoyed the reading."

Hoots and cheers went up. But the corporal's expression never changed. He abruptly stood. "It's time to go."

Adeline knew for a fact that they had more time, but she didn't object. A few men let out groans, which only seemed to worsen Corporal Smith's disposition.

Once the men were outside the door, he wheeled around. "Miss Barris, I appreciate what you are doing here, but I do not think it is wise to fill the men's heads with silly stories."

Adeline positioned herself, spine straight and chin up, as if she were handling an unruly student. "Novels are not silly."

"In light of what they are facing, reading a story about a man falling asleep to avoid work is ridiculous. Their lives will be nothing but hard work."

She held her ground. "This story transports them to another place. Novels help them escape their hard lives, even if it is only for a short time."

"Only for them to be cruelly reminded that nothing has changed."

"Spoken like a man who has never lost himself in a good book."

Corporal Smith clenched his jaw and spoke through his teeth. "You don't know anything about me, and I would appreciate it if you don't make assumptions."

"I don't need to make assumptions." She put her hands on her hips. *He will not make me feel like I've done something wrong.* "What you do not seem to understand is that reading an interesting story to the men makes them motivated to learn."

He huffed. "I don't see how reading motivates them when they are facing life and death."

Her anger crested, and she felt as flush as his face was. "Are you certain? A good passage from a book can motivate people in ways you've never imagined."

He folded his arms. "I disagree."

"I'll prove you wrong." She reached to the podium and grabbed the first book her hand fell on. She had been trained to perform dramatic readings, and they had proven over and over again to be a valuable tool.

Without breaking eye contact with Corporal Smith, she let the book fall open.

She glanced down. The book was her Bible, and it had opened to the Song of Solomon.

Oh dear.

She studied the passage, knowing if she broke her stance or turned to a different section, he would take this as a concession. His shoulders were still tense, as if he was bracing for a blow and preparing to return one. She cleared her throat and began to read with her richest, airiest voice.

" 'He brought me to the banqueting house, and his banner over me was love.' " She didn't look up, but she could sense that the corporal's posture had changed, his annoyance cooled.

She continued, trying not to think about what she was saying to him. " 'Stay me with flagons, comfort me with apples. For I am sick of love.' "

Adeline dared a peek at him. His face had changed from a deep red of anger to the hottest pink flush. " 'His left hand is under my head, and his right hand doth embrace me.' " She recited the rest by heart. Which she shouldn't have. Because the minute her eyes left the page, the image of Corporal Smith's hand winding into her hair leapt to her mind.

She inhaled deeply, an attempt to recover her senses. "How can you say that is not motivating?"

He blinked, his expression like Rip Van Winkle's after he awakened to a world he didn't know. Like he too was seeing what she saw. His gaze flicked down to her lips, lingered for a moment, and then down to the Bible. He took it from her hand and snapped it shut. "Good day, Miss Barris."

He left the room with the thudding of boots. Only once he was gone did her heart slow down.

Private Howard shifted his weight from foot to foot as he held the Bible open on his palms. Adeline leaned forward from the front row pew where she was sitting next to Corporal Smith. She gave Private Howard an encouraging smile, although her emotions swirled in many different directions. The men had found renewed interest after a few more episodes of her reading aloud and were now eager to show her how they had improved.

He cleared his throat and began to read. " 'The Lord is my she—' " He moved the Bible closer to his face.

"Shepherd," Adeline supplied.

"Right. 'The Lord is my shepherd; I shall not want.' "

Adeline nodded, encouraging him as he read for the first time in his life. She bit her lip to fight back tears as Howard continued. Hearing learners read for the first time was like watching someone receive salvation. Both opened a person up to a whole new world. Adeline would gladly concede that salvation was far more important, but learning to read was wondrous too.

She was also glad to have a scripture that didn't involve love or romance. She had fought to keep a blush off her face when she saw Corporal Smith this morning.

" 'Surely goodness and mercy shall follow me all the days of my life,' " Howard read more confidently now, reaching the end of the passage. " 'And I will dwell in the house of the Lord for ever.' "

There was a pause before applause filled the chapel. Adeline clasped her hands over her heart. "Very good, Private Howard."

He gave a nervous laugh, his relief showing on his face. "Thank you."

Corporal Smith applauded too, but much less enthusiastically than everyone else. "Good job."

Adeline switched places with Private Howard, a tiny ache of longing making her drag her steps. The room felt cooler as she left Corporal Smith's side. She focused on the group, chastising herself for her silly thoughts. This was a temporary assignment. Once she found her mother and brother, she would be leaving for Pennsylvania. She would probably never see Corporal Smith again. "Anyone else want to read?"

Another private, Holt, pulled out his drilling manual.

Corporal Smith sat up straighter.

"Please begin, Private Holt."

With halting words, he began reading a portion of the drill manual. " 'With the left hand turn the musket to the right so that the lock plate is facing to the front. . . .' " He stopped, but his eyes continued to move across the page.

Adeline stood. "Do you need help?"

Private Holt looked up at her with wonder in his eyes. "No, I—" In a flash, he turned, grabbed his weapon, and rushed outside.

Adeline hurried to the door right behind Corporal Smith. The other men crowded in the door behind them.

"Private, what has gotten into you?" Corporal Smith called out, moving down the stairs. Adeline followed him.

"Sir, I understand this now." Private Holt read a little more and then placed the book on the grass in front of him. " 'With the left hand turn the musket to the right so that the lock plate is facing to the front.' " And then he performed the motion.

Corporal Smith stopped up short and she nearly ran into his back. "Yes, that is correct," he said in such a quiet voice that she wasn't sure if Private Holt heard him.

Adeline let out a cheer, and soon the other men were cheering with her.

Private Holt grinned like a child with his first toy. "Sir, I can do the rest of them."

They all stood and watched as Corporal Smith called out

the commands and Private Holt read the book and then performed the motions. Tears blurred her vision. She had wanted to teach them to read. She had done that and helped them to be better soldiers. Exactly what Corporal Smith said they needed to be.

The other men filed out with their manuals and weapons and got into formation. Adeline took a seat on the chapel stairs. Corporal Smith took them through several rounds of drilling. She couldn't see his face from where he was standing, but she had never seen him stand taller. The men were reading their manuals and trying to perform the motions. Not the neatest drilling she'd ever seen, but they were trying. If someone got stuck on a word in their manuals, Corporal Elim would go over and help him. A few times he took up a weapon and demonstrated the action in slow motion.

He performed each command, his body moving with both precision and grace.

Adeline sat and watched them and for a time forgot about her quest and her mistakes. This was something she had done right. If she did this a hundred more times in addition to finding her family, maybe the guilt would lift.

When Corporal Smith gave the "Rest!" command, Adeline stood and applauded. Every day she'd left the fort with Corporal Smith leading the men straight to the parade field. Often she'd stand off to the side and watch until the sun got too hot. Private Holt had told her that they'd spent hours going through the commands but it didn't seem to make much difference. Today, however, the men had performed better than all the other times she'd watched them.

The men grinned, patting each other on the back. Their smiles were infectious. When Corporal Smith turned, he too was smiling.

Adeline walked over to him. He gave her a short bow. "Thank you, Miss Barris."

She folded her arms. "Oh, are you admitting that you were wrong about the reading?"

"I guess I am."

"Your humility is very becoming," she said, giving him a sassy glance. The problem was that his humility was *extremely* becoming. His pride was palpable and seemed to open up his whole soul to her. He was proud of his men. He cared for them and his joy was for their success.

"I will try to remember that." He tipped his cap. "Now if we can be released from class, I would like to take my soldiers on a parade march around the fort."

She laughed and clapped her hands. "Don't let me keep you."

"Thank you again," he said, his voice lowered. "You did what I couldn't."

"No, but you did your part. You taught them not to give up and got them disciplined to drill. I simply gave them the tools to understand it."

He took in a deep breath. "You are too gracious." His expression shifted from outright joy to something with admiration mixed in. Something she couldn't place. An emotion she could spend all day seeing. One he was directing at her.

Her words choked in her throat. "Well—"

His eyes roamed her face, and just as when she had read the Song of Solomon, his gaze rested for the briefest second on her lips. Her face heated and her mouth went dry.

Then he took a jerky step backward. "We should go."

"Yes, of course." *Especially before you act on that look in your eyes.*

Chapter 5

*E*lim finished his morning routine and stepped outside his tent. The sky had begun its progression from dark to light. If he closed his eyes and imagined, he could transport himself back home. . .no, not home. The plantation he grew up on. It was surrounded with a few low mountains and acres of green forests. He was often up before sunrise to complete his tasks for the household and make sure the other slaves had also started their duties. His early rising had a different purpose now. It was the army ordering him around, but at least he got something in return.

The colored troops' tents sat in the farthest corner of the fort. It was the worst area, but being placed here had an unexpected benefit. Here they weren't subject to staring and ridicule from the other soldiers. Someone on this base had reported his troops to Major MacDonald, because the man had never come to see them drill a single day. Maybe he could use the space near the chapel to drill the men. At least they could fail in private.

A figure trotted down from the main section of the base. It was a small boy about nine years old. He spotted Elim. "G' morn', suh. Do you know Mr. Smith?"

"I'm Corporal Smith."

"The teacher lady told me your right name, but I forgot." The boy gave him a toothy grin. "Miss Adeline says to tell you that she can't come up today. There was a whole heap o' new runaways come in last night and she said she gon' help the Hunters. She said you can bring the men down tuh her for their lesson."

A sad memory bubbled in Elim's chest. He had been tired, hungry, and confused when he'd first come upon faces that looked like his. It was a group of colored workers traveling with a Union regiment. They had graciously fed and clothed him with whatever they had and told him that he could work for the soldiers. Elim had been excited to dig ditches if it meant he wouldn't have to go back home.

"Thank you," he said to the boy, but the child didn't move to leave.

"Are you a real soldier?"

Elim laughed at the question. "Yes, I am."

"With a real gun?" Admiration twinkled in the boy's eyes.

"Yes."

"Ya gon' get us free?"

A simple question, but it boomed in the quiet like the cannons in the fort. He alone couldn't do it, but that didn't mean he wouldn't try. "I'm going to help."

The boy stared at him a little longer. "You coming down? My little brother never seen a soldier up close."

Another round of emotion twisted in his chest. "I would like to meet your brother."

The boy laughed. "You talk like Miss Adeline," he said and then turned, running in the direction he came from.

Miss Adeline would get a dressing down for this. He had thought they had come to some sort of truce, but he was wrong. He didn't care how pretty she was or how much he wanted to kiss her—this was too much. He did not have time to take the men away from the fort. That would cut into their drilling. The days until the inspection were ticking away. He was stuck between two commands, and neither looked to work out well.

Once the men were awake and dressed, he formed them into two neat lines and led them out the back gate down to The Bottom. Elim sighed as his men sang and chatted behind him. Why had he promised he'd meet the boy's brother? He could have sent word to Miss Barris that they would not be coming. Then he wouldn't see Miss Barris either. He increased his pace at that thought. Why did it matter if he didn't see Miss Barris?

The freedman's village didn't live up to the title of *village*. It was rows of huts and makeshift tents around a more substantial wooden building that served as the village center. It was a depressing sight to him but was probably the happiest sight the runaways had ever seen.

Miss Barris stood talking to several people on the front stairs. When she spotted him, she smiled. Her smile was bright and directed only at him. Heat flushed under his collar.

She left the group, and her approach gave him a chance to study her. She wore a gray day dress with a row of buttons down the front. Her hair was twisted up on her head like a crown. His heart thumped and he looked back at his men.

"Good morning, Corporal. I wasn't sure if you were coming. Let me show you where we'll be having lessons today."

She led them to a less populated section of the tents where there was almost a clearing. He could see the children already there and Miss Barris's stack of primers sitting beside a blanket. She turned to Elim. "Will the men mind sitting on the ground?"

He chuckled at her attempt to make them comfortable. "We are soldiers, Miss Barris. We are used to it."

"Doesn't mean that they want to do it."

Elim clenched his jaw. Her statement made it seem like the men had the option to do what they wanted.

She motioned for the men to join the students, stood in front of the group, and began to teach. She was already animated, but when she was teaching, she seemed to beam with energy. Her tone and smiles quickly disarmed the toughest of students, even his men.

Careful, or she'll disarm you. Elim stopped smiling and folded his arms.

As he stood there, he took in his surroundings. Groups huddled together over campfires, all of their belongings, if they had any, piled about them. A woman cradled an infant and a man with a bandage wrapped around his leg sat staring at nothing. The sight both saddened and motivated him. He knew this pain. It was a pain they would all return to if the North lost the war.

After the lesson, Miss Barris walked to him with a smile that set his heart racing. "Thank you for bringing the men down today. With all the runaways, I couldn't leave the Hunters without assistance."

"I understand." He kept his face serious. "I agreed to it this time, but from now on, all the lessons will take place in the chapel. This is too much of a distraction, and coming here takes away from our drilling time. If you can't come to us, we will cancel the lessons."

Miss Barris shook her head. "Drilling, drilling, drilling. All you talk about is drilling. Let me give you some teaching advice," she said, clutching her bundle of books to her chest. "You can't drill these men nonstop. They need a break."

Elim narrowed his gaze. "I don't need you to tell me how to train my men."

"Your students," she replied, her shoulders back.

"They are soldiers."

She let out an exasperated sigh. "They are pupils just the same. All this training is not going to make them learn any faster. They need time to process what they've learned. And it doesn't help that you are putting so much pressure on them."

"Pressure? I'm stressing the importance of them becoming proficient. We only have. . ." He stopped himself. If he finished the statement, she would have a hundred questions, and he didn't want to answer any of them. "They are the only colored unit in this fort, and they need to be as good as the other soldiers."

"I can tell you this. Your plan is going to have the opposite effect you want."

She left him standing in the field. Infuriating woman. He would drill the men until they were perfect. He had to prove that they were better than ditchdiggers. He looked around for his young messenger but didn't see him.

On the way back to the camp, Holt seemed extra quiet. Elim checked the number of buttons on his jacket. All of them were there. He slowed down so he fell in step beside the private.

"Everything all right?"

Holt looked up, a halfhearted smile on his face. "Yes, sir."

"You don't look it."

Holt rubbed his hands on his pants. "It's the children, sir."

"The orphans in town?"

"I'm an orphan too. Ran off after my massa sold my parents to two different farms. It's not easy. Then to get here and still have a hard time. Those children don't even have anywhere to sleep."

Elim patted Holt on the shoulder. "This is what we're fighting for. It is hard, but this is how we can help."

Holt nodded. "I know. But I think we can do more."

As Elim returned to his place at the front of the group, Miss Barris's words bounced around in his head. Was he too focused on drilling? He sighed. He and his men had their part to play in this war, but Holt had a point. They could do more.

Adeline rubbed her eyes as she made her way down to breakfast. Helping the Hunters and other leaders in The Bottom get the new runaways settled had lasted well into the night. There were so many men, so many tired, crying babies and children and their frightened mothers.

As she passed the front desk, Millie handed her a note. "A soldier delivered this before you were up."

She opened the note:

Miss Barris,
  The men will not be having lessons today.
                              Corporal Smith

She sneered at the very neat and graceful handwriting on the paper. Was he still upset about her rebuke yesterday? This proved that it had hit its mark. He was probably planning to make up for lost time and have the men drill all day. She let out a harrumph. No matter. The cancellation gave her more time to help the Hunters. Also, it would give her time to really talk to some of the runaways.

When the large group had arrived two nights ago, her hope was renewed. Maybe someone in this group knew something to help her in her search. She could question them about where they ran from. This close to Ashton Place, there was a chance someone had some information.

A chance, but not a good one. If they came from nearby, there was the possibility that they had run past anyplace that would have put their freedom in jeopardy. Runaways stayed away from plantations and spent the night sleeping in the woods. That's exactly what she and her father had done.

Oh Papa. I wish you were here with me. Her father's death had been a blow she didn't think she would recover from. He had spent years working to save the money to buy Mama's and Michael's freedom. Her returning to Virginia was a fulfillment of his dream to reunite his family. Now they would have to wait until heaven for that. Maybe Mama, Papa, and Michael had already gone and she was the only one left on this wretched earth.

No, she would not accept that Mama and Michael were dead too. They had to be alive, and she would find them.

At breakfast, she informed the Hunters of her change of plans and they readily accepted the extra help. They gathered their things and started out for The Bottom.

This part of Alexandria was alive with activity even this early in the morning. She could hear the clang from the smithy and the bustle of vendors setting up their wares in front of their shops. Such a different scene from the freedman's village.

As they walked, a wagon rolled up behind them.

"Good morning, Miss Barris!" someone cried out.

She looked up to find Corporal Smith driving a wagon holding half his section. The men waved at her and she laughed and waved back. Then another wagon passed holding the rest of the men and they waved too. *So Corporal Smith isn't angry with me.* Private Douglas had told her that they sometimes had to deliver supplies from the fort to an outpost a few miles away. They probably had to make a delivery.

To her great surprise, when she and the Hunters arrived at the place where they had held classes the day before, Corporal Smith and his men were standing by the two parked wagons.

"What is this?" she asked Corporal Smith. "I thought you canceled the lessons today."

"We are not here for lessons." He motioned to the closest wagon.

"I don't understand." She peered into the wagon. Canvas fabric and wooden poles were stacked in the beds.

"I asked Chaplain Thomas if there were any extra tents not

being used at the fort. These are a bit older and may not be in perfect condition, but they are better than sleeping out in the open."

She gaped at him. "These are for the runaways?"

"For the children. We'll help you put them up."

Before she could think about what she was doing, she threw herself into Corporal Smith's arms and squeezed him. "Thank you."

He let out a nervous laugh and stumbled backward. "You don't have to thank me." His arms closed around her, his embrace firm but not stifling. Almost like he was as affected by it as much as she was.

Then he abruptly pulled away. "Let's get to work."

They split into two groups. With her cheeks heating, she avoided being in the same group as the corporal. In no time, the men had the pieces of the tents unloaded and began work. Corporal Smith had taken off his cap and blue jacket and worked in a white shirt with the sleeves rolled up. His arms were quite muscular, but she knew that firsthand.

As they worked, the runaways gathered around them, and when they realized the tents were for them, they joined in to help. A woman and a small boy began arranging tent pieces as one of the men, Private Chase, drove the stakes into the ground.

As they pulled the fabric tight over the tent's frame, the woman put her arm around the boy and admired the tent like it was a real home. "No more sleeping outside," she announced to the boy. He let out a cheer and climbed inside.

The woman laughed. "That was the worst part of the journey. Cold at night and sleepin' in the brush."

Instead of seeing the boy and his mother in front of her, Adeline saw Mama and Michael as she remembered them. Of course they would have changed since the last time she'd seen them twelve years ago.

Her heart ached. "Where did you come from?"

"Westwood Estates."

Adeline froze. Westwood Estates was near Ashton Place. Well, not exactly near. It was about the distance of a morning's walk. Papa would sometimes work there when the estate needed more workers to harvest their fields. "I'm from Ashton Place."

A strange sense of connection flowed between her and the woman as the woman nodded. "Knowed that place well. Went to work there a few times."

"Do you know any of the slaves there?"

" 'Fraid not. Our overseer didn't like us talkin' to the Ashton Place folks."

"Is anyone else in this group from Westwood?"

The woman shook her head. "Only me and my boy. I doubt they be anyone else, since we ran in the night when the Yankees came by." She frowned. "The Union soldiers went to Ashton too, except they didn't just talk. They set it on fire. The massa and his family left in a long line of wagons. Most of the slaves left too."

Adeline's heart sank like a rock in a pond. *A fire?* She closed her eyes and tried to imagine the big house blackened and charred with soot. "My family. . ." She stopped before she continued. This poor woman had braved a run with a small boy. It was clear that she didn't know anything. She didn't need Adeline's sad story too.

"Need some help?" Corporal Smith had moved to her side

without her noticing. He smelled of sun and sandalwood.

Adeline forced tears from her eyes. How was she ever going to find Mama and Michael? "We're almost done."

He leaned in closer. "The young boy you sent for me yesterday wanted me to meet his brother."

Adeline didn't catch her surprise before it went to her face. "Oh, little John."

"Could you take me to him?"

"Of course."

Chapter 6

*E*lim didn't trust himself to walk this close to Miss Barris. Not after that hug she'd given him. She had been soft and warm in his arms. Emotion had threatened to overtake him when she'd pressed her face to his shoulder. When was the last time someone had held him? He shook hands with other soldiers all day long, but a hug? He couldn't remember. His mother was gone before he could remember her. All the other slaves kept a safe distance from him because of his preferred status in the big house.

Elim had never had a hug like that in his whole life. And Miss Barris gave it to him over some tents.

Miss Barris sniffled beside him.

"Are you well, Miss Barris?"

She turned to him, tears in her eyes. "I want to thank you again for the tents. It was very kind."

"As I said, you don't have to thank me. Some of them were in such bad condition that they couldn't be used for the soldiers."

"That still doesn't change the fact that you made these

runaways' lives a little better."

He shrugged. "I remember how it was when I ran. The first people who were kind to me. This was doing for someone else what was done for me."

She hiccupped. "Oh, you're going to make me cry."

He chuckled. "That is not my intention."

She swiped her face. "It's hard seeing such young children who've braved flight with their parents. I remember too."

He slowed his gait, not in a hurry to leave her presence. "I heard you say that you ran from a plantation nearby. How close were you?"

She looked down at the grass beneath her feet. "Two days' walk from here."

"And you managed to go all the way to Philadelphia alone?"

Her shoulders slumped. "I—um—was with my father."

"Oh. Is he still in Philadelphia? He must have great courage to let his daughter travel so close to southern lines."

"Papa was very courageous. But he's dead."

"I'm so sorry."

She hugged herself. "He was the best father ever. I didn't think I could move forward from his loss. He was delighted that I wanted to become a teacher and let me teach him how to read."

"I'm sure he would be proud of you."

Miss Barris sighed. What was it like to love someone, even to lose them? To be honest, Elim hadn't seen this level of love displayed ever before. People desperate to find their loved ones or families taking great risks to keep their children from being sold away. Elim had spent most of his life feeling emotionally detached from others. Especially when he found that his closest relationships were a lie.

Little John and his family lived in the tents on the opposite side of the wooden building. The boy sat playing with a smaller one as a woman Elim assumed was his mother sat nearby. There was also a man stringing a line, probably for laundry.

"John, I brought Corporal Smith to see you," Adeline said. He could hear the pride in her voice.

John leapt to his feet and nudged his brother. "See, I told you he was a real soldier."

Elim's uniform felt too tight at the praise. Coloreds weren't considered real soldiers. Added to the fact that his men were struggling to learn, he felt as far from real as he could get. "What's your name?"

"Nathan," the boy replied with wonder in his eyes.

The man had stopped stringing line. "Right nice of you to come and visit."

"I promised," Elim said. What did this man think of him? Judging by the way the man studied him, he was probably wondering what interest a Mulatto would have in his son. "You know, the fort is always looking for men to work. It's hard work, but they'll pay you. If you come up to the fort and ask for me, I'll show you to the man you need to talk to. John knows where to find me."

The man's expression relaxed. "Thank you."

Elim nodded. "I have to go now. Nice to meet you, Nathan."

Nathan and John waved.

As they walked back to the men waiting by the wagons, Miss Barris chuckled.

"What?"

Her amusement made her eyes twinkle. "I am delighted by the discovery that you have a heart."

He shot her a frown. "I didn't realize the existence of my heart was in question."

"It was, and I'm glad you answered that today." She tipped her head to look up at him. "I would very much like to see your heart again."

He took in a sharp breath. *If you keep hugging me and talking like this, I may give it to you.*

The letter in his pocket sat with the weight of a musket round.

His men chatted happily behind him as they walked the worn path from the back gate of the fort to the chapel. Mail day gave them a boost in morale, no matter what the letters held. They longed for updates from their home plantations, to know that the people they left behind were safe or to learn who had moved on. Elim never wanted to hear from his home plantation again.

Yet there was a letter in his pocket.

Even though he didn't want to hear about the occupants of the big house on Harwood Plantation ever again, there were some from the fields and slave quarters who wanted to reach out to him. When he ran, he knew Ms. Oma and Mr. Walter would worry. They were the closest thing to family he had, even though he had family on the plantation. His mother was gone. His father. . .

Don't think about it.

When they arrived at the chapel, the door was still shut, and there wasn't any sign that Miss Barris was there. He checked inside. The pulpit where she normally placed her books was empty.

"It appears Miss Barris is still on her way," he told the men.

"Can we read our letters while we wait?" Private Howard asked, a wide grin on his face.

Amazement stole over Elim. This was the first time in their lives they could read their own letters. Ones that were most likely written by someone at their home plantations who could write. Elim had fulfilled that task many times for the slaves on his plantation. Before, Elim or Chaplain Thomas normally read any correspondence the men received. Now, thanks to Miss Barris, they could do it on their own.

"Just until Miss Barris arrives." If she didn't come soon, he would drill the men here. He could not afford to waste any more time.

The men filed into the pews, the ones without letters gathering around the ones who had them, wanting to hear anything about the wider world.

Birdsong floated above his head as he took a seat on the chapel stairs. He checked the path on the other side of the clearing for Miss Barris once more before he slipped the letter from his pocket. He took a deep breath and opened it.

The handwriting was messier than other letters he'd received from Ms. Oma, and it was more like a note than a letter. It was postmarked a month and a half ago:

Elim,
 I learned my letters, and I'm writing this with my own hand.

*Things have changed since you left. Me and Mr. Walter
done left the plantation and moved into town. We got our
own place but it is small. We still go up to the plantation
sometimes for work.*

*Massa Wilson ain't doin' so well since most of us done
left. Mr. August is gone and no one knows where he done
gone off to. He left when you did and we all thinks he was
goin' afta you.*

*Please write back, Elim boy. We been hearin' some bad
things about this war and some of the men in town been
killed already.*

May God watch over you,
Ms. Oma and Mr. Walter

Elim fought against the rush of emotion.

August left. Ms. Oma was probably right in the idea that he
came looking for Elim. Elim was, after all, August's property. His
runaway slave.

Despite the upsetting news, the fact that Ms. Oma had written
to him warmed him. Her letters and well wishes from Mr.
Walter were the only expression of care he'd felt since he'd left
the plantation. The men he had joined up with after he'd run
were only concerned as far as his safety was tied to them. Other
than Ms. Oma and Mr. Walter, he was alone.

He had told Miss Barris that the men's focus should be on
living through the war. But what did life hold for them after
all this was over? This was thinking he didn't allow himself to
indulge in often, because there was nothing for *him* after the war.
No family, no sweetheart. Nothing but being a solider. He would

be free. . .and utterly alone.

His mood clouded over, and he folded the letter and returned it to its envelope.

"I'm so sorry for being late." He looked up and Miss Barris was standing before him, almost out of breath with a bundle of books in her arms. "I was helping the Hunters with a task in the freedman's school and it took a little longer than expected."

"Not to worry. Today was mail day, and the men were quite excited about reading their letters."

"Looks like you were too." She pointed to the letter still in his hand. "You got a letter from a loved one back home?"

Harwood was not his home. "A couple who were on the same plantation as I was sent me a letter."

She sat next to him on the stairs. "And all is well?"

He forced a smile and held the letter up. "Ms. Oma and Mr. Walter left the plantation and got their own place. Ms. Oma learned to read and write and she sent me this letter."

Miss Barris grinned. "That's wonderful, Ms. Oma!"

Despite himself, Elim laughed. In her excitement, he almost forgot his troubles. That happened often when she was around. He had fought her about the need for the lessons, but she drew him into a sort of dream. Especially when she was reading to the class. The rest of the men always got transported into the story. He got lost in the sound of her voice and the way her expression matched whatever mood the story took.

"Where is home?"

Nowhere. He swallowed the lump of loneliness. "Virginia. . . . I guess it's West Virginia now."

"Will you go back after the war?"

He studied her face. This was a conversation many a soldier had had since the war began. "No."

She leaned in closer to him, and for a moment he thought she was going to lay her head on his shoulder. "Where will you go?"

He shrugged. "There are too many variables to say with any certainty."

"Where do you want to go?"

His shoulders sank. *Oh Miss Barris, don't make me dream.* "I must admit I haven't given it much thought. I plan to stay in the army. It will be up to them where I go." That would guarantee that he would keep moving.

"I think that is a good idea. You are good at this." She motioned behind her at the chapel door.

This was the first time he'd studied her while she was sitting this close and not fighting with him. While she was teaching, he tried not to notice how beautiful she was. But now, it was all he could see. "Thank you."

She reached over and touched his sleeve, and the skin underneath heated like it was in the direct sun. "I'm sure you'll end up exactly where you're supposed to be."

He nodded and for a moment allowed her hope to be his.

❧ Chapter 7 ❧

When Corporal Smith arrived at the front door of her lodging at first light and said the men wouldn't be at the chapel today, Adeline had stifled a sigh of relief. The men were tasked with other duties today, ones Corporal Smith clearly wasn't happy about. She kept her expression neutral to hide that she was grateful for a day off after teaching for almost a month straight. Not that she minded teaching. But having the day off would give her time to do what she came to do.

Today she would take another step toward accomplishing her goal.

Several of the free blacks in the freedman's village had spoken well of Chaplain Thomas. She had learned that he sometimes came down and held services for them in one of their small huts. They also informed her that he helped runaways who joined the Union lines at Fort Ward.

She arrived at the gate of the fort, and her heart sank when she saw the guardhouse. Would they let her in? She hadn't actually been here since the first day she arrived. Because of the chapel's location, there was no need to come through the front gate. She smiled sweetly at the guard. "My name is Miss Barris, and I was wondering if I could speak to the chaplain."

The guard didn't even acknowledge her with the courtesy of a look. "Do you have an escort?"

She considered telling him that she and the Hunters were allowed in a few weeks ago, but held her tongue. "I'm teaching some of the colored soldiers to read."

That got the guard's attention. "Now that's a waste of time. Everybody knows they are too dumb to learn."

Heat crept up her neck. "Sir, I—"

A hand touched her on the shoulder. She turned to find Corporal Smith standing behind her. "Private, she's with me."

The guard straightened a little, his face broadcasting that he didn't appreciate giving deference to a colored corporal. "Yes, sir." His answer held none of the respect she heard from Corporal Smith's men.

Corporal Smith led her through the gate. "I didn't expect to see you here."

"I wanted to speak to Chaplain Thomas."

Corporal Smith glanced at her over his shoulder. "Come to complain about me to the chaplain?"

Even though his words were in his normal blunt tone, she heard something else in them. Fear. He couldn't be afraid of her. "What if I was?"

He slowed down to walk next to her. "He's already on your side."

She laughed before she could stop herself. "My side?" Did the corporal think he was at war with her?

"He wants the men to learn to read. No need to go in and give him a tongue-lashing like you did with me."

"I did no such thing. You are exaggerating."

He peered down at her from under his cap, one eyebrow raised. His eyes were a warm brown. An inviting place to get lost.

She swallowed, her next words vanishing from her mind. "I—um—"

The corner of his mouth tugged up in the most glorious half smile. Even his eyes brightened. "I'm what?" His voice dipped.

Her heart did a flip in her chest. "A distraction." That word cleared the haze that his smile had caused in her mind. She pushed past him and headed for the chaplain's tent.

"Have a good day, Miss Barris," he called from behind her.

She watched Corporal Smith walk across the field where his men stood in a cluster. When he reached them, his posture stiffened and the men fell into formation. Adeline sighed. Every day the same thing and he couldn't even see the impact it was having on his troops' morale. Why was he so hard-driving with no consideration for how his men felt? She understood that constant drilling was a part of their duties, but she didn't see the other soldiers on the fort drilling as much as Corporal Smith's men did.

Adeline directed her steps to Chaplain Thomas's hut. The door was open and she could see him intently studying a book on his desk.

She cleared her throat. "Good morning, Chaplain Thomas."

He looked up and smiled. "Miss Barris. Come in," he said, standing. "How are the lessons going?"

"Well, and the chapel is the perfect place."

"I'm glad to hear it." Chaplain Thomas motioned for her to sit in one of the chairs in front of his desk.

She tried to still her nerves. "I wanted to ask you about a nearby plantation."

He returned to his seat. "Which one?"

"Ashton Place." Saying the name brought a flood of unpleasant memories. The coolness of the night as she followed Papa through a bank of trees, willing her feet not to make a sound. Her confusion over why he was leaving.

"Seems like I heard about it." He reached back and picked up a weathered notebook. "I keep a record of which plantations slaves run from. I heard that some of the abolitionists in the North do the same, and I thought it was a good practice."

Adeline leaned forward. "Do you keep the names of the slaves too?"

"Sometimes, when I can get them to share their names. Many of them won't tell me for fear that I'll turn them over. Also, most runaways continue running, to get as far north as they can." He returned to the journal. "I don't have a record of anyone from that plantation. I do know that Union solders burned several plantations near here to the ground to make them unusable for the South."

Burned to the ground. The words hit her like a fist, knocking the wind from her. "Would the runaways have come here for help?"

"It's possible, but if the Confederate soldiers found them first, they would have been taken as slaves or leverage in prisoner exchanges."

She pressed her hand over her mouth. What if Mama and

Michael were taken or. . . She let out a soft sob.

He returned his attention to her. "Miss Barris, are you all right?"

She dropped her head so he wouldn't see the tears in her eyes before she could regain her composure. "Yes, I—I knew slaves from Ashton Place Plantation."

"I'm very sorry I can't give you better news."

She managed to smile over the roiling fear in her stomach. Answers about her family might be right in the village where she was staying, or two states away. The latter was a scenario she hadn't considered when she jumped aboard the Hunters' wagon. She thought they would still be where she left them. Once again her impulsiveness had gotten her into trouble. "Thank you."

"I pray God will help you."

If she was going to do this, she would make sure God wouldn't have to save her from the mess she made. The thought of crying out to Him, shedding tears until He directed her to her family, was so appealing, but she couldn't. God should not have to fix what she had done wrong.

The inspection was in two days.

No matter how hard Elim tried to sit still, he found himself fidgeting. The men were doing well with their reading, but they still needed polishing when it came to the drilling. He needed every second he could get to drill them.

He shifted again, and Adeline looked over at him from where she was helping Private Chase. Once she was done, she came to him. "Are you all right?"

"How long is this lesson going to take?" The question came out tighter than he intended.

Adeline took a shuffling step backward. "The same amount of time they've always taken. You know that."

He frowned at her. "The men are doing better. I think we should shorten the time for the next couple of days."

She sighed and lowered her voice. "I told you that this constant drilling is excessive. And now you're trying to take away the one escape they do have."

"And I told you that I don't need you to tell me how to lead my men."

She turned away from him. "I wouldn't call what you're doing leading." She spoke the words like she was talking to herself, but he heard them loud and clear.

He stepped around her and glared down at her. "Excuse me?"

She placed a hand to his chest and pushed, causing him to step back. "I am not one of your soldiers. I said you are not leading the men. You're worrying them. Have you noticed how many of them are exhausted? It's from your constant drilling. You are constantly reminding them that they are not good enough"

Elim squirmed. He hadn't noticed they were exhausted, but now that he thought about it, they had been sluggish the past couple of days. "That's because they are not good enough."

"Would it kill you to give them some praise? Some encouragement?"

"Like you? They are facing harder things than a page of writing. I need to prepare them for what's ahead."

She looked as though she was ready to go to battle against

him. "Let's see. You're teaching them to drill, but they are not making progress. I'm teaching them to read with all my praise and encouragement, and they are. Whose methods are more effective?"

"This is not a game, Miss Barris," he ground out. "If these men aren't ready in a few days, the squad will be disbanded and they'll be digging trenches for the rest of the war."

His voice boomed around the chapel and he realized that all movement behind him had stopped. He turned to find the men hanging on every word.

"We're going to be disbanded?" Private Howard asked.

All his fight evaporated. "Major MacDonald gave me a month to get you all in shape before he disbands us. He is doing an inspection in two days."

There was a rumble around the room.

Adeline stepped around him. "Gentlemen, there is no need to despair. You have mastered something amazing. You've learned to read and write in under a month's time. You've even read from your manuals. You can pass this drill."

Although she was addressing the men, her words zinged straight to his heart. She believed in the men, and he didn't. He was preparing himself for them to fail. She was right. He wasn't doing a good job of leading.

"Put away your books and get your drilling manuals," she said with a sweep of her skirts as she turned toward the door. "We're going to practice both reading and drilling."

The men moved with more speed than he'd ever seen them with the instruction to drill. *She's right.* They followed her out the door with haste. When Elim passed her, she grabbed his arm.

"You should have told me. Told them." There was nothing but compassion in her eyes.

"I know."

"Come. Let's get your men ready for inspection."

For the remainder of their time, Elim drilled the men. At first, Adeline stood observing. Then she joined him. When the men missed a command, she would give them the instruction in a different way. Or she would refer them to their manuals and encourage them to ask questions. She even gave Elim suggestions on how to phrase things differently. At one point, she gathered the men in a circle around him and told him to perform the commands. Things he'd never thought to do.

The sun was hot by the time they stopped. Adeline stood in front of the men. "Okay, let's try one last time."

"Yes, ma'am," Private Chase said with a laugh.

Adeline stood before his troops like she was in command, a sight that sent a swell of emotion through him. She looked over her shoulder and gave him a pointed look. "Come command your men."

He shot her a wry look. "I thought you were in charge."

As he led the men through one last drill, the improvement was evident. He could attribute it to the fact that they now understood the urgency of what they were doing. But he knew it was due to the beautiful woman standing at his side.

When the sun got too hot, Elim ended the drill. This time, instead of hearing a sigh of relief, the men offered to keep going. Elim looked at Miss Barris. She looked wilted like a flower.

"No, that's enough for today."

They fell back into their normal routine and went into the

chapel to collect the rest of their materials, leaving Elim alone with Adeline.

He cleared his throat as she swiped her forehead. "Adeline."

At the sound of her Christian name, she turned with a look of surprise on her face. "Yes?"

He took a step closer. "Thank you."

She dropped her arms and laughed. "Your heart is showing again."

He inched a little closer. "What if it is?"

Her eyes grew wide. "Then I think you should be careful."

She was right. He was being reckless, but couldn't he be once in his life? After all, she had hugged him. "What if I'm not?"

She opened her mouth to respond as the men filed out the chapel. She took a long step back. "See you tomorrow." She darted from him to the chapel.

He was still watching her when the men caught up.

Holt was beaming. "We're going to pass, sir. I just know it."

Douglas folded his arms. "Only after we drill you a little more. Maybe Miss Adeline can give you extra help."

The group laughed. "Let's go," Elim said, glancing once more at the chapel door. Adeline didn't come out.

"Maybe getting Miss Adeline to help me might make me better," Holt said. "She's made everyone better."

Including me.

"I sure hope she finds her family," Private Douglas said.

Elim froze. "Her family?"

"Yes, sir. I heard her asking people about the plantation she ran from. I'm sure she was lookin' for her family."

The revelation sent a cold shiver washing over him. All this time, and she'd never said a word. She listened to all his bellyaching about drilling while she dealt with that level of heartbreak.

How did she manage to stay cheerful under such a heavy weight of pain? He would make sure to talk to her tomorrow. Maybe he could find a way to help.

ᘒᘒ Chapter 8 ᖰᖰ

*T*he day had come, cold and drizzling like the night before. Adeline didn't want to walk up to the chapel, but she wanted to be able to help Elim get the men ready for inspection. His outburst yesterday had taken her by surprise and explained most of his behavior. She had wanted to hug him again but knew she wasn't getting away with that twice. He had looked so forlorn. She knew she had to do all she could to help him.

She dressed and went down to check for letters. There hadn't been any more since the ones she received when she first arrived. But when she reached the bottom of the stairs, Elim stood at the front desk instead of Millie. His jacket was dotted with raindrops and he held his cap in his hand.

"Elim, what are you doing here?" She winced. He had not told her she could call him by his first name. Maybe it was the surprise of seeing him here that made her forget her manners.

"I wanted to catch you before you came up to the fort. The

ground in front of the chapel is a muddy mess. And I wanted to talk to you."

She motioned him toward a sitting room, and Millie bustled past them as they walked down the hall. "Can I get you anything, miss?"

Adeline looked at the drops of rain on Elim's face. "Some tea, please."

They took seats at the small table where she and the Hunters normally took their breakfast. "I'm glad you asked for tea. My hands are freezing."

She reached across the table and grasped both his hands in hers. They were cold, but quite a bit bigger than hers. He flinched at her touch and then relaxed. "What did you want to talk about?" she asked.

"Your family."

She stiffened at his response, one she had not expected. "What about them?"

"Douglas told me you were looking for them."

Her mind went back to the day they had set up the tents. Private Douglas was there when she'd asked the mother and son about Westwood Estates and Ashton Place. "I am."

He leaned forward and shifted so he was holding her hands now instead of her holding his. "You told me that your father died in Philadelphia. What other family do you have?"

She took a deep breath, the pain of the memory threatening to steal the air from her lungs. "My mama and my little brother, Michael."

"But how—" he began.

Adeline let her shoulders sink. "When I was twelve, my

parents decided that my father would run to the North. He was to find work, buy his freedom, and come back for us." She let out a short laugh. "Unfortunately, they decided to keep that a secret from me."

Elim was now rubbing small circles on the back of her hand with his thumb. The intimate motion seemed to be unraveling this story she didn't want to tell. "He didn't make it, did he?"

"He did. And so did I."

He tipped his head. "I thought you said it was a secret."

"I could tell that something was going on. I saw them setting food and other rations aside. My father made himself a sack to carry everything. But the most telling thing was he would leave his boots outside the front door every night."

"And you noticed."

She nodded, her head feeling heavy. "In the week leading up to my father's departure, I would stay awake for as long as I could. Somehow I knew that whatever was going to happen would happen at night. On the night he ran, I heard him creep across the floor, move something, and go out the door. I, however, had a plan of my own. I crept out behind him."

Elim leaned back in his chair and let out a hard breath. "Did you realize what was happening?"

"No." Her voice warbled on the word. Oh, if only she had known. "And he didn't know I was behind him until he was well away from the plantation. He had no choice but to take me with him."

"Oh Adeline."

"I can't imagine how worried my mother must have been. We came across an Underground Railroad station and one of the conductors promised to get word to my mother that I had run with my father. When we got to Philadelphia, my father got a job and I went to school. Once my father died, I came back to find them, but I have no idea where they are. One of the runaways in The Bottom told me that Ashton Place was burned down and the slaves are all gone." She finished the story with an exhale, spent from the telling of it. Her guilt thickened the air around them.

Elim squeezed her hands. "Surely you don't blame yourself. You were a child."

"Being a child didn't make things any easier for my father. He had to work twice as hard to support me too. Sometimes I think he worked himself to death. I complicated his plans to earn enough money and buy all our freedom."

"You'll find them. You are an intelligent, brave woman. I have no doubt you will."

The confidence in his voice nearly brought her to tears. "I pray so."

"What is your plan?" he asked quietly.

"The newspaper advertisements I placed haven't produced any results. Neither have the letters I wrote to several abolitionist organizations. I came here because I would be closer to the plantation and thought that might increase my chance to get information. I have a little money to try and buy their freedom. But I don't even know how long ago Ashton Place was burned down."

He leaned closer to her. "If the plantation burned, there may not be anyone there to accept your payment."

She let out a huff, clearing her head. "What I do know is that Mama and Michael and I will go back to Philadelphia until this war is over. Together."

When Millie brought the tea, she released his hands, noting that they were quite warm now. "We need to cast a wider net," Elim said as he poured tea into her cup then his. "I will write to some of the other colored units and have them ask around. I can also help you question the runaways in The Bottom. Just because you haven't found out any information doesn't mean someone doesn't know something. Maybe we can even take a trip to Ashton Place."

Her jaw dropped in surprise. "You would do that to help me?"

"Yes. There may be something at the site that will point us to your mother and Michael. I doubt your owners simply gave up the land because of the war. They may even have a small crew there still working the land."

"I never thought of that." Of course she didn't, because she never had a solid plan. She acted more on impulse. Like she did on the night she'd run with her father. She looked back up at Elim. "Why are you helping me?"

"Because you helped me and my men."

Real hope bloomed in her mind. Elim was the perfect person to plan with, his methodical mind seeing things that her worried one couldn't. This mission was her own, but it couldn't hurt to accept a little help from him. It was no more unusual than accepting help from the other people she'd questioned.

He talked and she studied his face, enjoying seeing an emotion other than anger or worry on it. He realized she was staring and stopped talking. "What?"

"Your heart is showing again."

Elim lined up the men on the parade field, his nerves jittery. Major MacDonald stood to the left at a perfect vantage point. The men had stayed up late polishing their boots and buttons and putting in a little extra practice. They had done so without Elim asking. They understood how important this was. Not only was their section's status in danger, but so was their freedom.

Although he was ready for this to be over, Elim's mind drifted to how things would change if they passed. They could be sent to another fort, one closer to the fighting. Or into a battle straight-away. He and his men may have to kill or be killed. He looked at each man, knowing how hard it would be to lose any of them to battle. As much as he wanted to add his strength to the fight for freedom, he didn't want this for his men. The alternative, staying out of the battle, was just as undesirable. For the first time in their lives, they could do something about their bondage. None of them was going to give up that chance, even if it came with great danger.

Elim moved to stand in front of his section. The men's faces were serious and concentration furrowed their brows. Good. They were as ready as they could be. Adeline had constantly reminded them that their best was all they could do. He had repeated those words to them yesterday. If they did their best, they would pass with no problems.

A flash of blue to his left caught his eye as he prepared to give the first command. He stole a glance in that direction.

Adeline stood off to the side of the practice grounds with Chaplain Thomas. She was angled half facing the chaplain, but it was clear she was watching them. Elim sucked in a breath. She had come to support him. When their eyes met, she offered him a wide smile and he felt the strength in her faith in him and the men.

"Attention!"

The men snapped into place in one fluid motion and Elim nearly cheered. He took them through each command, keeping his voice strong. The men, in turn, followed each command so well that no one would believe they were the same men as a month ago. He could see their pride. They knew they were getting it right, and their confidence increased with each command.

But they were not safe yet. They reached the harder commands. Elim steeled himself and gave the "March!" command.

The group moved almost perfectly. There were a few who were a half a step behind the others, but they quickly corrected themselves. Elim led them in a short march around the parade field, bringing them back to the starting position.

He wanted to beam. "Rest!" It seemed as if the whole squad exhaled.

Elim left the men in position and walked over to Major MacDonald. The major stood with a surprised look on his face. Elim tipped his head down to hide his grin. "Sir," he said but dared not say more.

"Not bad, Corporal."

Elim relaxed a little more.

MacDonald looked over Elim's shoulder at the men. "You must have worked these men hard. You've all earned a half-day pass. Congratulations."

Elim grinned. "Thank you, sir."

The major dismissed him, and he walked quickly to his men. He didn't want to tell them about the major's praise until they were back at their tents for fear of their reactions. He wanted to jump and whoop. He knew the men would feel the same. But he gave them an approving smile.

Chaplain Thomas and Adeline met them a few yards away. Chaplain Thomas smiled at him. "Your men look good, Corporal."

Elim beamed. "They did well today."

Chaplain Thomas nodded and turned toward the tents. Adeline moved closer. "So?"

"We passed."

He saw the joy bubbling on her face. She was always loud with her praise. "Shh," he said with a chuckle.

"Right." She fiddled with her dress.

Once they were back at the camp, Elim informed the men that they had passed the inspection. They let out a loud cheer, confirming that Elim had done the right thing telling them the news away from the parade grounds. They whooped even louder when they learned they had earned a half-day pass.

As they talked about how they were going to use their passes, Elim already knew how he was going to spend his and who he was going to spend it with. He shouldn't. A relationship between the two of them couldn't be. It could lead to great pain. He knew this, but it didn't change his plans.

๑ Chapter 9 ๑

A knock at her door startled Adeline out of her thoughts. Seeing Elim's pride today had lifted her spirits higher than they'd been in a long time. To see his men succeed and know she helped warmed her. She also felt grateful that she had been able to help someone while she was looking for her family.

She rose from the desk and opened the door. Millie stood there with a wide smile. "You have a visitor."

Adeline frowned as she followed Millie down the stairs. She wasn't expecting anyone, but the children in town sometimes came up to visit her after she was done teaching.

Elim stood at the bottom of the stairs. He wasn't in uniform. He wore a blue striped shirt, a brown jacket, and blue pants. He held a hat in his hands and looked as uncomfortable as a turtle without a shell. Then he looked at her and beamed.

She rushed down the last few steps. "Elim, what are you doing here?"

He shifted from foot to foot. "Major MacDonald gave us a

half-day pass as a reward."

She tipped her head. "And you came here?"

He cleared his throat. "I thought maybe we could have dinner or. . ." He looked around. "Or go for a walk."

Adeline's face heated. "We can have dinner here. Millie is an excellent cook."

He smiled. "I'd like that."

Millie, who had been watching the exchange with a smile on her face, grasped Elim by one arm. "Why don't you go have a seat in the dining room. Miss Adeline, why don't you change into something nicer?"

Adeline rushed up the stairs to hide the blush on her cheeks. She quickly changed into a white blouse with a delicate ruffle and a blue skirt, her best Sunday outfit she had brought with her. She smoothed her hair back and tied a scarf around it to secure it. All the while her heart thumped at the implications of this dinner. Something was growing between them. But what could it be since it was all so temporary?

Elim stood when she returned to the table. "You look lovely."

She smoothed her skirt. "I didn't bring my nicer clothes."

He pulled out her chair. "You're beautiful."

Millie served them a simple meal of roasted chicken and potatoes. Elim let out a nervous laugh. "I can't remember the last time I had real food."

"Eat your fill. It was mighty nice what you did for the people down in The Bottom," Millie said.

Adeline tried to eat, but her stomach was in knots. Was Elim courting her? If she was back in Philadelphia and a man had dinner with her, a man as eligible and handsome as Elim, she would consider it courting. "It's amazing how this war has changed everything."

Elim looked up. "Both for the good and for the bad."

"Good that people will be free, bad because we don't really know what that freedom is going to look like."

"Or how many lives will be lost." He looked at her. "Do you like living in Philadelphia?"

"Very much. There are lots of free blacks there. Schools, churches, places for people to start families."

Elim paused. "Is that what you want?"

She looked down at her plate. "I'm like you, I guess. I haven't thought much about it. My focus is to find my family."

The conversation lightened as the dinner progressed. Adeline marveled at how much her perception of Elim had changed. When she first met him, he seemed like the most disagreeable man she'd ever met. Now she saw that he was disciplined and steady, caring and thoughtful.

Dinner finished, he rose. "Shall we take a walk before the sun sets?"

"Let me get my shawl."

The streets of Alexandria were quiet. Soft music drifted from some of the inns, and all the shops were dark. Adeline fell in step beside Elim and fiddled with the corner of her shawl. He reached over and grasped her hand in his. It was warm and strong.

They reached the tents in The Bottom and stood watching the lights of the campfires. "One good thing about this war, people are still fighting for their families. Love is still winning in all this." Elim squeezed her hand. "It seems like it would be the opposite."

She faced him, looking up into his eyes. "Love is really the only thing worth fighting for."

His expression softened. "Your heart is showing."

He searched her face before he leaned down and kissed her. His mouth was warm and soft, and the kiss was tentative. She felt herself suck in a breath at its tenderness. Elim slipped his arms around her waist and pulled her closer, and she let herself lean into the kiss.

He pulled away, breathless. "I'm sorry."

"Don't be."

"I mean. . ." He rested his forehead on hers. "This isn't for me. Not for the future ahead of me."

She tightened her arms around his neck, bringing his lips back down to hers. "It can be for now."

Elim collected the tattered primers as he watched Adeline explain one last point to a soldier named Andrews. As she talked, Elim's gaze drifted to her lips. Ones he had kissed a few days ago. His own lips still felt warm from the encounter. Not only his lips—his heart felt like a puddle in his chest. Both regret and pleasure flitted through his thoughts. It was absolutely foolish for him to start something with Adeline that he couldn't finish.

The idea of them being something more had taken up camp in his mind since the night they'd kissed. That they could make a home together somewhere in the North. Maybe he'd go to Philadelphia with her. They could purchase a house and live in freedom. She could continue to teach children and he would. . .

That was where the dream faded. He had no idea what he

would do. He imagined he would stay in the army, but that would mean no happy home in Philadelphia. If he got out of the army, what would he do? He might get a pension, but colored soldiers weren't getting equal pay as it was. It would be foolish to expect a pension, free or no. There was no way that dream could come true for him.

Elim cleared his throat and both Andrews and Adeline looked up. "Time to go."

Andrews nodded and thanked her and collected his cap, smiling all the time, and rushed out the door behind the rest of the troops.

Adeline picked up the book Andrews had been reading and placed it with the others.

They exited the schoolhouse and began the walk back to the main part of the fort. He slowed his pace to walk side by side with her. Since they had grown closer, she had taken to walking back to town through the front gate. He tried to keep an acceptable distance between them so the men wouldn't suspect anything. But what he really wanted was to wrap his arm around her waist and pull her close.

The morning air was cool but held the promise of a hotter day. They caught up with his men, who had slowed to watch new soldiers file in. Elim caught up with them. "Keep moving," he commanded, and his soldiers surged forward in the next open gap.

"Adeline." He turned to her, but a face in the group of soldiers snagged his attention. *It can't be.* He leaned forward and trained his eye. The man he was watching didn't turn away. He held Elim's gaze. Both hot and cold washed over him as August raised a hand in a nervous wave.

"Elim?" Adeline's voice cut through the fog, a jarring return to the moment.

He looked down at her and saw that her eyes held a questioning look. "I'm sorry."

"Are you all right?" She turned and looked over her shoulder in August's direction then back at him. How much had she seen?

"Yes, I'm fine." Elim stood taller, willing himself not to look back in August's direction even though his mind screamed for him to watch where August went. To follow him and find out why he was here—

"I was saying I think your men are waiting for you."

Elim looked at his men. They had formed a sort of loose formation. Several of them were watching him. "I will see you tomorrow."

Adeline nodded and Elim walked away from her as quickly as he could without seeming to rush. If only he could get away from August so quickly. Or at least find out if he'd come to take him back.

He waited until the group August had been with filed toward the tents before he walked to the chaplain's hut.

He knocked on the hut's door and Chaplain Thomas called for him to come in. No matter why Elim came to see him, Chaplain Thomas always seemed glad to see him. "What can I do for you, Corporal Smith?"

Elim swallowed, willing his heart to slow. "We have new soldiers at the fort?"

"Yes, the 127th and the 51st."

"Do you know where they were mustered?" Elim asked, even

though he suspected he had an idea of where at least one of the units came from.

"One from Ohio and the other from West Virginia."

Beads of sweat broke out on the back of Elim's neck. "That's good. Always good to have men to join the fight."

His expression must not have been as neutral as he thought, because Chaplain Thomas studied him. "Are you all right?"

You're the second person to ask. "I was simply curious."

"I've been meaning to come and congratulate you on your men's success."

"Thank you. They've worked hard."

"Apparently you made such an impression that Major Mac-Donald was considering mustering more colored men. He was thinking of recruiting contrabands from the town. Maybe you can train them."

"I don't think I could have done it without Miss Barris. Once she leaves, my men will go back to drilling poorly." He let out a nervous laugh, trying to cover his worry. He couldn't take on another squad, because he may have to run away from August.

Chapter 10

*A*deline finished the lesson, and the men bolted from the building like children. Their conversation and laughter echoed around the clearing. The sunshine seemed to make the sounds brighter. Since the constant drilling was over, they seemed to get more enjoyment out of their lessons. She watched them and thought about how they seemed like a family. For some, this was the only family they had.

And if they were a family, today Elim was the moody father.

He helped her stack her books in silence. When she collected them from him, she grasped his hands as well as the books. "What's wrong?"

He seemed surprised by the question. "Nothing. I have a lot on my mind."

"Like the white soldier you were staring at yesterday? You turned quite pale when you saw him. Who is he?"

He released the books into her hands. "It's difficult to explain."

She put the books on the pulpit and sat on the front pew.

"He's my brother."

Adeline gasped and pressed her hand to her heart. "You have a white brother?"

Elim shot a glance to the door. The men were still talking outside, oblivious to her and Elim. "My owner is my father and his father too. We grew up together and were as close as brothers could be. Until I found out that he was my brother."

"You didn't know?"

Elim shook his head. "I found out when my father gave me to my brother for his eighteenth birthday. And then I found out my father sold my mother after she gave birth to me. I was August's slave for a year until we got into a fight, and then I realized I couldn't stay."

"Oh Elim."

He lowered himself to sit on the pew beside her. "I was devastated. I thought I was August's equal. I don't know if it was guilt or what, but my father treated me better. . . ." He exhaled. "And now August is here."

"Have you talked to him?"

Elim let out a sharp laugh. "I'm his property. He could be here to collect me."

She reached over and gently touched his arm. "Your brother is a Union soldier. I doubt he's here for that."

"You don't know that for sure. Not everyone in the Union is fighting for the freedom of the slaves. Some are fighting to keep the country unified."

She leaned closer. "You have to talk to him. He's your brother."

Anger flashed in Elim's eyes, and she knew she had said the wrong thing. "He's my owner. And the owner of other slaves.

What is there to talk about?"

"If that was Michael. . ." She softened her voice.

Elim sprang to his feet. "This is not the same thing! This isn't some happy reunion. He could force me back to his plantation."

Private Chase bounded in the door. "Are we staying, sir?"

Elim quickly turned. "I'm on my way."

Adeline grasped one of Elim's shoulders. "Elim—"

He pulled away and left without looking back.

Elim didn't know where he was going. His anger with Adeline clouded his vision and he walked more on impulse than intent. Her happy thought of him reconciling with August was ridiculous. She had a happy family. His family had lied and owned him. He wasn't even family. He was property. What would he say to August? We should be brothers again? Things had changed since the war started. The world had changed. But with this battle going on, there was no plausible ending involving a relationship with August. Not between a white man and his Mulatto brother.

He was so deep in thought that he didn't even notice that August had stepped into his path. "Sir."

Elim's vision straightened, and his muscles tensed. *My owner is addressing me as "sir."* "Private."

August relaxed, his old playful smile forming on his lips. "You've moved up in the ranks quickly."

It had been three years since he ran away. Two since he joined the army. "Why are you here?" Elim asked through his teeth.

"Same as you. To fight for the Union."

"I'm fighting for my freedom."

August's smile faded. "I'm here for that too."

"But you're talking to the slave you own."

August reached inside his jacket. "Not anymore." He produced a paper and held it out to Elim.

Elim didn't reach for it.

August sighed, his shoulders slumping. "Your manumission paper."

The air in Elim's lungs whooshed out and he nearly doubled over. He took a step back.

"Please take them."

Elim looked up at his brother, the man he'd spent most of his childhood reading and playing with.

"I'm sorry it took me so long to find you." August lowered his arm a little, and the paper trembled. "Daddy forbade me to leave or he would disinherit me. It took me too long to realize I didn't want what he had. So I did the one thing I could to prove I didn't want it. I followed you into the army."

Breathing became harder. "Is this supposed to erase all the pain?"

"No, but at least you will be fighting as a free man like me."

Elim took the paper, unable to hide his shaking hands. "Did our father agree to this?"

August folded his arms. "I didn't need my father's permission. He gave you to me. I'm giving you to yourself."

"Once I ran, I became a free man. This paper doesn't repair what has been broken."

August hung his head. "No. I don't know if that's possible."

Despite wanting to run, Elim couldn't get his feet to move.

The man in front of him was his little brother. He'd spent many days playing and dreaming with him until he found out he belonged to him. That the man he called massa was his father and had separated him from his mother. The same anger simmered now. "No, it's not. Now that I have my freedom, I don't have to talk to you anymore." He needed to leave before his anger got out of control.

August reached out and lightly grasped his shoulder. "Elim."

Elim shook his hand off. "Don't. Adeline—Miss Barris told me to talk to you. I knew it was a waste of time."

"The teacher? Maybe she was right." August splayed his hands out in front of him. "Look, I don't know how to handle this. As far as I was concerned, you were my brother. And I told Father that. I left to find you. To apologize. . ." August's words trailed off.

"For owning me? I don't think there is an apology on earth for that."

"I didn't know," August pleaded. "I thought Father really was going to treat you as a real son."

Elim's anger exploded. "Why did you think that when he owned other slaves? That's all I was to him. A slave. Never a son. I was an oddity for him to show off and humiliate."

August stood quietly while Elim regained his composure. He dropped his head. "That still doesn't change the fact that I love you like a brother."

The confession nearly crumpled Elim. He balled his fists against the rush of conflicting emotions. He had loved August like a brother too, even before he knew. August never treated him any differently than he would treat a brother, which was why it was such a shock when they both learned Elim's status.

"I need time to think about this."

August took a shuffling step back. "I understand. My regiment will be here for a month, I think. I would like to talk to you when you're ready."

Elim didn't respond. He didn't know if he'd ever be ready.

❧ Chapter 11 ❧

*T*he practice field was empty as Elim crossed it with his fellow corporals and sergeants. They had all been summoned to the field by Major MacDonald, and whispers of "Why?" had flown through the camp in a matter of minutes. Elim discarded most of the rumors, fear building with each step. Was this the end? Was he being summoned to be told that his men weren't fit for more than trench work? His fears subsided when he saw all the noncommissioned officers making their way to where the major stood.

August wasn't there. A strange twist knotted in his stomach. He outranked the man he'd been a slave to for most of his life. Private Smith would not have been called to this meeting, although he may be outside right now. Elim had spotted August watching him at the chapel, the mess tents, and the parade field. August was probably waiting to see when Elim would be ready to talk.

Major MacDonald waited until the men fell into something

like formation before he began speaking. Elim took a place near the rear. "We have received word that Confederate troops are marching north attacking supply lines." His voice was steady, but a shudder went through the crowd at his words. "We are sending troops south to support the battle."

The air was still. This was it. The fort had been relatively stationary, mostly drilling. No one had been sent out for battle since he'd gotten here, white or black. The fact that was about to change sobered Elim.

The major called out several units that needed to prepare to be mobilized. Elim held his breath, worry rising. What if. . . He swallowed down the strange mixture brewing in him. Part wanting to be called and part dreading to be called.

Major MacDonald looked at Elim. "Corporal Smith, your men will accompany us to build fortifications."

Horrified shock rattled through him. The men had passed the inspection. He had done what he thought was impossible. But still they were assigned to ditchdigging and fort building. He'd wasted his time. "Yes, sir," he croaked.

Major MacDonald continued giving a few more details, oblivious to the blow he'd dealt Elim, and then dismissed the meeting.

As he arrived back at his camp, he spotted Adeline with his men, a worried look on her face.

"Is everything all right?"

Elim put on a calm face. "May I speak to you in private?"

She nodded, and he led her a few steps away from his men. He lowered his voice. "You should probably go back to Philadelphia soon."

She gaped at him. "Not without my family."

He gritted his teeth. "I'm not saying forever. Maybe for a month or two."

"My family could be caught in whatever you're trying to warn me about. I refuse to leave and go back north without them."

"You don't know for sure that they are here."

Her face shifted to a mask of hurt. "I have good information that they were here. That could lead me to wherever they are. I can't believe you would even suggest—"

"You can't help them if you're dead."

Her face hardened, and he knew he was wasting his time. "Thank you for your concern, Corporal." She flung his rank at him like a stone, and it hit its mark. She spun and left him standing alone. He resisted the urge to go to her, pull her back, and demand that she get out of harm's way. He did nothing but watch her walk away. What could he do? He had no power to help or protect her.

It took her most of the lesson for her anger to dissipate. Elim sat through the lesson, looking at everything but her. Maybe he was being eaten from the inside out with the ridiculousness of his request. He knew how important her mission was to her. How finding her mother and brother was the only thing that would give her real freedom. He could have his danger and warnings. She wasn't leaving Alexandria until she'd found her family.

Even though she had left Philadelphia without a fully formed plan, she had understood the danger of returning to the South.

"Miss Barris?" A voice sounded close to her ear.

She turned to find Private Douglas standing next to her. "Do you need help?"

"No, ma'am. I think I can help you. I wanted to tell you yesterday on our walk, but I wanted to be sure. I think I found out something about your family."

She closed her book and slowly lowered it to the pulpit. "You have?"

Douglas nodded, a smile spreading on his face. "One of the other men said they remembered a boy named Michael who sometimes came to work at the fort. He was here with his mama and said he'd come from a nearby plantation. The boy talked about his father and his sister Adeline in Philadelphia."

Adeline fought to breathe. "And? Is he still here?"

Douglas's smile faded and he shook his head. "The boy hasn't been seen around for a couple of months. But the man said he thought the boy went to work on a farm south of here owned by a free Negro woman. Milton Farm."

Tears sprang to her eyes. "Thank you."

"I even got directions to the farm." He handed her a piece of paper with directions scribbled on them. The paper felt like a stone in her hand. Directions written by a man she had taught to read and write.

A flash of regret cooled her excitement. She had done everything she could to find her family on her own, but she had failed at that. Private Douglas had found them, not her. Would she ever be free from her guilt? She had to get Mama and Michael home to free her from her debt.

A small thought sounded in her head. *What if you don't have to do it alone? What if you need My help?*

She ignored the voice. God shouldn't have to fix her mistake. She was the one who sneaked out after her father. She'd made the trip to reach freedom harder and longer for them. If she hadn't left, Papa could have worked and used all of his savings to buy his family's freedom instead of using the money to support her. He would have seen his whole family free before he died. She never should have left Mama and Michael, so now she should be the one to get them free. She folded the paper and stuck it in the pocket of her dress, where it sat like a smoldering fire for the rest of the lesson. As soon as Elim announced that it was time to go, Adeline quickly gathered her things.

"Adeline," Elim said, after the men had filed out of the chapel. "I wanted to—"

"I'm sorry, but I can't stay."

He took an abrupt step back. "Oh."

She pushed past him, but he lightly grasped her arm. "Can we talk later?"

He stood so close. She could see the apology in his eyes, but she couldn't let herself hear it. If she found her family, she would be returning north to get their freedom. Elim would be here, fighting.

"I must go." She pulled herself from his grip and rushed out the door.

To her surprise, he followed her. "Adeline, please," he called from behind her, but she kept walking. She didn't want to turn around. Because then she would have to acknowledge that she was walking away forever from the man she loved.

He caught up with her and stood in front of her. "Please let me apologize." He was slightly out of breath, and a lock of his hair had fallen on his forehead without his cap holding it in place.

"I forgive you." She moved to go around him.

"Don't go." Her knees turned to jelly at the pleading in his voice. "Don't go. Stay here with me."

"Elim, I can't."

"At least tell me what you are going to do."

She dropped her head, bothered that he could read her so well. "I'm going back to town to help the Hunters. You don't need me here anymore."

He stepped closer. "But I do need you."

She let out a sob. "And then what, Elim? You marry me, and what? I watch you go off to battle, never knowing if you're going to come back? Is that the life we would have?"

He swallowed. "I would marry you today if you would agree to it." His eyes told her that he was speaking the truth.

Now tears flowed freely down her cheeks. "And what of my family?"

"I'd help you find them. We'd search together."

"No, Elim. You are right now preparing to go to the battle lines. I have to find my family. This can't be." She pushed past him, but he grasped her waist.

Without warning, he leaned in and kissed her. There was need in that kiss, overwhelming need. The world seemed to spin around them. She almost got lost, until she realized that this was their goodbye kiss.

⧁ Chapter 12 ⧑

The map in front of her kept blurring. How she had gotten to her lodgings from the fort after she'd left Elim, she didn't know.

Elim who loved her and who said he would marry her today.

She sniffed and focused on the map she'd borrowed from Millie. She needed to find out how far Milton Farm was from the fort. Then she would have to figure out how she was going to get there. The map showed both roads and train tracks. It looked like Milton Farm was a day's walk from here.

A new problem presented itself. It had been a long time since she'd traveled under the cover of night and on foot, but she could relearn it. That would be the easy part. Free or no, there was no way she could travel alone to Milton Farm. She'd heard enough stories about slave catchers prowling about in the woods capturing any colored person they came across.

She folded the map and tucked it into a book sitting on her desk before she went down to breakfast. The Hunters were already seated at the table. Mrs. Hunter looked up from her tea. "Are you going up to the fort today?"

Her heart lurched. "No, and I don't think I will be going back. All of the men know how to read now." At least she could be proud of that accomplishment.

"Just as well. I don't think the men are going to be there much longer. I heard through some of the people in The Bottom that the fort is mobilizing to North Bend. Some of the coloreds are going with them to work as cooks, laundresses, and teamsters."

Adeline's head snapped up, the answer to her problem presented right over breakfast. According to the map, North Bend was less than a mile from Milton Farm. She looked back down at her plate to hide her excitement. She would take work as a cook and go with the soldiers. She would go up to the fort. . . . Her thought screeched to a halt. Elim would be going to North Bend too. She would have to be extra careful not to be seen until she got to Milton Farm. That wasn't impossible if he and his men had duties to keep them busy.

She rose from her chair. "I think I will go up to the fort today, but not for long."

She slipped out the front door as fast as she could without running.

She came to the front gate and crossed the field, pausing only to check to see if Elim and his men were drilling there. When she saw the coast was clear, she rushed to Chaplain Thomas's hut. He was coming out and closing the door behind him. "Miss Barris."

"Chaplain, I heard that the fort was hiring cooks to travel with some battalions here."

He nodded. "They are." He eyed her.

"I was thinking about inquiring about a position."

"I thought you were teaching the men."

Another stab of pain. "They are well on their way and don't need me anymore. This is an opportunity to make a little money." That was mostly true. Once she found Mama and Michael, she'd need more money than she had to get them passage to Philadelphia.

"If you're serious, you can talk to Miss Eve. She's in charge of the cooks."

Adeline caught herself smiling harder than she should at being a cook, especially with all the hard work it entailed. She tempered her smile. "Thank you."

Miss Eve turned out to be a stout, no-nonsense woman who, after questioning Adeline's small frame, hired her on as a cook. "We leavin' in the morning. Be here tomorrow morning before the sun. We got to feed these men before they leave."

Adeline nodded, fighting a grin. This was the most move-ment she'd had in her search. In a day's time, she would be on her way to North Bend and to Milton Farm. To find her family. And she had done all this without being spotted by Elim.

She was so lost in thought that she bumped into someone as she turned to go.

She looked up to find August, Elim's brother, staring down at her. "Good morning, Miss Adeline."

She stood taller. "Good morning."

"Are you here to see Elim?"

Adeline's mouth went dry and no amount of swallowing could moisten it. "No, I had other business."

August looked over her shoulder and then back at her. "Should I give him a message for you?"

Elim had said that August was his brother, and it was never more evident than now, with the way August was reading her like a primer. "Ah, no. I'm sure he's busy."

"We're mobilizing soon."

She squirmed. "I heard. Please be safe."

He gave her a knowing look. "You too. Have a good day."

She nodded, afraid to move. Nothing got past these brothers. Now she'd have to hope he didn't mention what he saw to Elim.

Although he hadn't enjoyed the hard drilling he'd given his men the past month, it had come in handy. His men were conditioned for the long, grueling march and were faring better than some of the other sections. Also, the hard conditions and the effort of taking step after step held another benefit. The pain in his feet was a good distraction from thinking about the fact that he'd left Adeline behind without saying a proper goodbye. He never should have dreamed of a relationship with her in the first place.

At some points in the march, Adeline was first in his mind. At others, August. Elim hadn't said goodbye to him either. If that was even the right thing to say. The miles separating them provided a clearer perspective. August had defied his father and followed Elim into the army. He had given Elim his manumission paper. Elim was free now, and if the war went the wrong way, Elim was still free. The fact that August even found him was amazing. He should have said goodbye, at least.

As the major announced that they would be camping for the

night, Elim let out a long breath. The area surrounding them was green and covered with a dense forest. There was a field in the middle of the trees that Elim couldn't see until they cleared the trees. His men went to work setting up tents. They moved with a speed that he didn't think their tired bodies could.

Elim went to work pitching his tent.

"I would offer to help, but I think you have it under control."

Elim knew the voice and didn't need to look up to know it was August. Something twisted in his chest. As much pain as his childhood had caused, learning that August was here hurt. He was going into battle. August could be injured and maybe even killed. Could he bear that? Knowing August died following him into the Union Army to fight for his freedom? He wanted to hold on to his anger with August, but it slipped from his grasp. "You shouldn't be here." Elim meant in the section of the camp with the colored soldiers, but that statement also applied to the mission they were on.

"There is someone else who shouldn't be here. Your sweetheart."

Elim's stomach churned and his chest tightened. "Adeline?"

"I saw her today and asked her how she got here. She said she is working as a cook for another company. I told her that it was a strange career change, but she didn't say any more."

Elim rubbed his forehead as a memory flashed in his mind. One day after drilling, Douglas had mentioned he had found some information about Adeline's family. Elim had waited for Adeline to say something, and when she didn't, he assumed the information must not have been helpful. "She came to Virginia here looking for her mother and brother." There was no doubt in Elim's mind that she would do anything to get to them.

August frowned. "But the Confederate lines are nearby too."

Dread snaked around his heart and squeezed. "Do you remember which company?"

"No, but I think she's hiding from you. She tried to find out if I was going to tell you that I saw her."

"I need to find her," Elim growled, dropping the tent pole he held in his hand. He started off, but then his steps slowed. And do what after he found her? Send her back to Alexandria all alone?

August grinned. "She's quite a woman. You might want to keep up with her and marry her after the war."

After the war. What a foolish thing to think about as they headed to battle. "I don't know if I can."

He left August to find Adeline. Thankfully there were only a few platoons in the group. He made his way to where the cooks had stations set up. It only took a second to spot her. She wore a big, floppy hat—a poor disguise for a woman he'd watched nearly every day for the past month.

He stood in front of the pot she was stirring. "Adeline, what are you doing here?"

She didn't even respond with surprise, as if she suspected he would find her. "Before you start fussing—"

He stepped around the pot, grasped her arm, and led her out of earshot. "Have you gone insane? This regiment is going into battle."

"I know that, Elim. But they are marching right past where my family could be."

"You could have asked me to look for your family."

Surprise lit her face. "You would do that for me?"

He stepped closer. "I love you, Adeline. I'd do anything for you."

Tears shimmered in her eyes. "You have to understand why I had to do this."

"I don't understand why you feel like you have to do this by yourself. Finding your family is tricky business."

She dropped her head, tears on her cheeks. "I have to find them."

He grasped her shoulders. "We will. Please don't put yourself in any more danger."

She sighed but didn't look up at him. Which meant she was going to do whatever she thought she needed to do to find her family. Including putting herself in more danger. There was nothing Elim could do but pray.

҉ Chapter 13 ҉

*T*he dirt road between the fort and Milton Farm was lined with trees, shielding Adeline from the sun. The shade also gave the walk an otherworldly feel. As she traveled, she would step into a pool of sunlight and then back into shadow. Very much like her thoughts. One moment she was imagining what it was going to be like seeing her mother again. Wondering if they would recognize each other. Michael would be a boy of fifteen, no longer the chubby baby she left behind.

Her eyes smarted at the apology she would give her mother. How she would fall on her knees in front of her and beg for forgiveness. And then she would do everything in her power to get back to Elim and apologize to him. She had bundled all she had and slipped out of the camp before even the cooks rose. She didn't get a chance to say good-bye. At least she knew his unit. Once she got her mother and Michael safely to Philadelphia, she would write to him.

The farm came into view as the sun began to light the tops

of the trees. She heard cows and chickens but no other sounds. There was an open field in front of the house, and she crossed it to reach the front door. It opened before she knocked.

A wiry colored woman stood in the doorway. She had a basket in her hand, probably going to collect eggs. A look of shock formed on her face. "What do you want?"

"I—um. . ." Adeline faltered at the woman's abrupt tone. "I am looking for my mother and brother, Florence and Michael."

The woman's face softened. "You must be Adeline."

Tears sprang to Adeline's eyes. There was only one way this woman could know who she was. "They're here."

The woman smiled and stepped out the door. "In the quarters near the barn."

Adeline thanked the woman as she took off running down the stairs. The quarters were a simple but sturdy-looking log structure. Outside, a woman had a pot hung over a fire. She spotted Adeline and stopped stirring the pot.

Adeline never considered that her mother wouldn't know who she was. In her mind, time was frozen. Michael was still a baby, Mama's face was still without the worry lines of age, and Adeline was still twelve. The woman who stood before her had changed, aged, but Adeline recognized her as soon as they made eye contact. "Mama?"

Mama straightened and let the spoon she was holding drop from her hand. "Adeline?"

Tears blurred her vision. "I found you," she whispered.

She wasn't sure who moved first, but in seconds they were in each other's arms, Mama planting kiss after kiss on her face. "Oh Adeline."

"Mama?"

A voice sounded to their left. Adeline turned to find a tall boy who could have been her father's younger twin. "Michael?"

Michael took one step back. "Who is this, Mama?"

Mama turned Adeline to face him and led her forward a step. "This is your sister, Adeline."

Michael's face went through several phases, first shock and finally amazement. "You came."

She ran to him and hugged him. "I did."

After a long moment, he pulled back and looked up at her. "Where's Papa?"

The way he asked, she suspected he already knew. "He's gone to heaven. He wanted nothing more than to see you again."

"Mama told me all about him. I wanted to meet him." Michael sobbed and returned to her arms. Adeline's heart broke with each one of his heaving breaths. Mama came and embraced both of them, tears on her cheeks.

Once Michael's tears slowed, Adeline turned back to her mother. "I'm so sorry, Mama."

"There are some things we can't control."

"I'm sorry for following Papa. I didn't know." Fresh tears flowed down her cheeks.

Mama pulled her close. "I know you didn't. There is no need for forgiveness. I asked God to bring you back to me, and He did."

Light rippled through Adeline's heart. As much as she'd tried to do this on her own, God had indeed led her back to her family. No matter how badly she thought she had muddled the situation, God had been working the whole time to reconnect her with her family. She threw her arms around Mama and held on.

After a long while, Mama released her. "Let's go inside and talk."

Mama filled her in on how they got from Ashton Place to here. "One night while we was sleepin' we heard a loud ruckus. It was a battle between some Union soldiers and Confederate ones. We were so scared we hid in the woods on the back of the plantation."

Michael nodded. "There were cannons boomin' and men screamin'. It was scarier than when the Confederate soldiers came earlier and took all the horses, food, and menfolk with them. Once the fightin' stopped, Mama told me to get whatever we had left and that we was goin' with the Union soldiers."

Adeline smiled. "I met someone from Westwood who told me the same thing."

"Before long, I was cooking and doing laundry for the Union soldiers. They told us we was free and even paid us for any work we did." Mama nodded. "I didn't much care about the work as long as I didn't have to go back to the plantation. From there, we traveled here and we met Miss Charlotte, who owns this farm. She offered us work here and we stayed. I hadn't seen a colored woman own anything. She also taught us to read."

Adeline's heart was so full that she felt like she was floating. "I am so happy to hear it."

Inside Mama's hut, they sat in chairs at the table. "Now tell me how you and your papa fared in Philadelphia."

Adeline filled them in on her journey north, her becoming a teacher, and Papa's death. Mama and Michael sat with amazed looks on their faces. In her mind, all she could think was that God had done what she never could have done.

As the morning drifted to afternoon, Adeline grasped Mama's and Michael's hands. "We may need to leave soon."

Mama frowned. "Leave? What for?"

"There are Union troops passing by to stop Confederate troops from coming north." Adeline's mind drifted to Elim. "There may be fighting breaking out soon. We should go back to the Union camp."

"Is that where you came from?" Mama asked.

"Yes, and there is someone there who can help us." *If he's not too furious with me for leaving.*

Mama stood. "Right. I hate to leave Miss Charlotte, but it would be safer to get further north, 'specially if we can travel with the Union soldiers."

While Mama went to talk to Miss Charlotte, Adeline and Michael packed up what little belongings he and their mother had. The door opened behind them and they turned to find Mama in the doorway, wearing a worried look. "Looks like them troops done got here sooner than we thought." She shut the door, flipped a table over, and pushed it against the door. "I saw them from the lane when I was talking to Miss Charlotte. We need to find a place to hide. We'll wait a bit and then go hide in the trees."

Adeline's heart thumped. She'd come all this way only to be captured by the Confederates. No doubt her reunion with Mama and Michael would be short if they were captured.

God, we still need Your help.

Elim gathered his men to start their day's work.

As he passed the cooks' stations, he noticed a huge change.

Adeline wasn't in the line of cooks. The men began forming a line for mess. Elim went to the other end of the line to the cook who had been near Adeline yesterday.

"Ma'am, where is the other young lady who was here?" he asked. He presented the question like an official request, even though his heart was thumping. *Adeline, I hope you didn't do what I think you did.*

The woman smiled up at him with a gap-toothed grin. "Your sweetheart?"

Elim blushed. "Uh, yes, Adeline."

"Ain't seen her. Her bed was gone when I got up this mornin'."

"Thank you," Elim said. He rushed to find Douglas, who had sat down on the grass with his plate of beans and pork. "Douglas, I need to speak to you. What did you tell Miss Barris about her family?"

Douglas looked puzzled. "I told her that someone had seen her brother at a farm near here."

Elim exhaled. "Do you remember the name of the farm?"

Douglas stared down at his plate of beans for the longest minute of Elim's life. "I think it was Milton or something like that." He looked back up at Elim. "Is Miss Barris okay?"

Elim looked back at her empty spot in the cook line. "I hope so." He turned his feet in that direction, berating himself as he did. He should have known she would go find her family the first chance she got. A part of him was angry, but another part of him understood. The part of him that was going to leave the camp after dark to go find her.

He asked the cook about the farm and she directed him to another woman who knew all about it.

" 'Bout an hour's walk east. Miss Charlotte is colored and owns it. She's real nice," the young cook said.

That gave Elim a little peace, but not much. He needed to come up with a plan. He could make the walk to the farm and back before anyone noticed he was gone. He nearly groaned at the thought of getting caught. His military career would be over. But he had to go. If the Confederate troops got to the farm before Adeline got back. . . He didn't want to think about it.

He was so engrossed in his thoughts that he didn't see that August had moved into his path. "Where's Adeline?" he asked.

Elim sighed. "She went off to find her family. They may be at a farm near here."

August frowned. "May?"

"That was the last piece of information she received about them. That they were working on this farm."

August nodded. "I'm assuming you're going to get her."

Elim looked away. The fewer people who knew what he was planning the better.

August laughed. "Still the same Elim. You never were afraid enough for your own good. Some people would call it bravery."

"August, I don't have time for this. I need to figure out a way to this farm before nightfall."

"I'm coming with you."

Elim folded his arms. "No, you're not."

"Either you let me come or. . ."

"Or what?" This felt like when they were back home. August would threaten Elim, but he never carried through with the threats.

"Or nothing. All right." August threw his hands up in

frustration. "But I am coming with you."

"I can't let you do that."

"You can't stop me any more than I can stop you."

Elim stood taller. "That's an order, Private."

August gave him an amused look before he grew serious. "You love her, Elim. Let me help you find her so you can have some sort of happiness in all this."

Elim sighed. "I do love her."

August still stood in front of him.

Elim groaned. "Be ready by nightfall."

Chapter 14

The night was cool, but humidity still hung in the air. Elim had waited until most of the fires in the camp had been extinguished before he'd crept out of his bedroll and out into the night air. He took his pistol but left his rifle. Hopefully, he wouldn't need either.

He approached the meeting place he'd arranged with August and saw his brother peeking out from behind a tree. Elim trotted up to him and took cover beside him. "Ready?"

Another voice answered. "Yes, sir."

Standing behind Elim were Privates Chase, Howard, Holt, and Douglas.

"What are you all doing here?" Elim hissed.

"We wasn't about to let you go off and save Miss Barris without us." Private Douglas spoke with mock bravado.

"How did you even know about this?" Elim eyed August.

"You need help," August said.

"If we get caught—" Elim began.

August tugged his arm. "We will if we stay here any longer."

They started off single file, avoiding the worn path the wagons had made and sticking close to the tree line. The night was silent except for their footsteps and the animals concealed by the darkness. The going was slower than Elim wanted, but after what seemed like hours, a building appeared in the darkness. The windows were all dark, and the grounds were as shadowed as the woods.

August leaned close. "Are you sure someone is here?"

Elim's heart ached. "Doesn't look like it."

Before he could formulate a plan for what to do next, a woman's scream rang through the night like a gunshot. Elim motioned for his men and August to take cover. He saw a man in a red coat drag a colored woman by the arm out of the house. Elim held his breath, eyes trained. *Please don't be Adeline.* As the man moved away from the house, other Confederate soldiers lit torches and emerged from the trees on the other side of the farm. The light was so stark in the darkness, it seemed as if the sun had risen over the farm.

The woman thrashed and pulled against the man's grip, but to no avail. "I am a free woman."

"But we know you're hiding runaways here. You belong to us now."

Elim gritted his teeth. He motioned to his men and August. "Holt, go back to the camp and report this." He saw the disagreement in Holt's eyes, but Elim held up a hand. "You're the youngest and the fastest." He may not be able to save everyone's life, but Elim could at least save this young man. For now.

They watched Holt disappear into the night behind them.

August pointed. "There are some buildings on the other side that may give us some cover."

"Douglas and Chase, go around to the other side behind those buildings. We'll catch them in the middle. August and Howard, spread out around the side, and be quick."

The group dispersed. The Confederate soldiers were going through the house and barns with no thought of what was going on around them. Douglas and Chase reached the buildings without being spotted. August moved counterclockwise through the trees. Howard moved in the other direction. Elim stayed where he was, loading his pistol. From his count, there were twelve Confederate soldiers.

Twelve to five. Horrible odds. He would have to use the element of surprise to full advantage.

The soldiers had gathered more people in the area in front of the house. They huddled together, arms wrapped around each other, but still no Adeline.

Movement to his left caught his eye. August was waving his pistol at him. Once he got Elim's attention, he pointed the weapon.

A soldier was leading Adeline to the clearing. She had one arm around an older woman and the other around a young boy.

Elim sighed, pride filling his chest. She'd done it. She'd found them.

"Get all the goods from the house and let's go," the sergeant in charge barked out. The Confederates spread out, and a plan formed in Elim's mind. If the sergeant was left alone, Elim could overpower him. Then the people gathered could run for the trees. Maybe they wouldn't have to wage a battle to rescue these people.

He looked to August, who was staring at him. Elim gave him a brief nod, and once the last of the soldiers disappeared around the side of the house, leaving only the sergeant behind, Elim sent up a quick prayer and charged.

Running full speed, he'd crossed half the space before the sergeant turned and saw him. The man raised his pistol at Elim. He wasn't going to make it.

Suddenly, a figure tackled the sergeant from the back, knocking him off balance. The shot went high into the air. The sound of the shot echoed around the field.

"Run!" Elim screamed, and the people in the clearing sprinted. They only had a moment before the other soldiers would come running. As the freed captives ran for the trees, he spotted the figure who had knocked the sergeant down.

Adeline. She grabbed her mother and brother and ran for the trees.

The sergeant was trying to get on his feet. Elim pointed his pistol at him. "Stay down."

The sergeant lifted his hands.

Elim nodded. This man would go along with the rest of the Confederate soldiers being held for prisoner exchange.

"Call your men back," Elim said through gritted teeth.

The sergeant stood slowly. Elim took a step back, not liking the look in his eye. "You're outnumbered, Corporal."

"Call your men or take a bullet." Elim cocked his gun.

Two Confederate soldiers appeared from the house, their expressions showing their shock. They pulled their weapons, and the sergeant said nothing to stop them. The first two shots whizzed past Elim like flies buzzing. Both he and the sergeant dove to the ground. Elim rolled, hearing return fire coming from beyond the trees. The two men near the house went down and August emerged from the trees, his pistol still smoking.

More shots rang out and Elim got to his knees, looking in the direction they were coming from. August glanced in the direction that Douglas and Howard went before he trotted over to Elim and helped him up from the ground. "You all right?"

"Yup. We need to do something with this one."

But when he looked in the direction of the sergeant, he went cold at what he saw.

The sergeant raised his pistol and aimed directly at August.

Elim was moving before he realized it, shoving August hard. His brother went down and the bullet that was aimed at him slammed into Elim's shoulder. The pain exploded, knocking the wind from his lungs. He fell to the ground and thought he heard a woman scream his name.

Adeline.

Another shot went off close, and Elim gripped his shoulder and scooted backward, pain turning his stomach and blurring his vision. August stood, pistol still aimed at the air. The sergeant, however, was lying on the ground screaming in pain.

August rushed to Elim's side. "Lie down."

"We've got to get the other men and get out of here."

"I'll get them. Don't move."

The instruction wasn't needed. His arm throbbed with pain every time he inhaled. The world went fuzzy and his arm grew warmer and warmer. He glanced down at his sleeve and saw that blood had soaked his coat. At least he'd managed to save the two people in the world whom he loved. He closed his eyes against the pain. Soon he wouldn't feel any pain at all.

Adeline knew she should run with the others, but she lingered at the tree line. Elim stood, pistol pointed at the Confederate commander. He watched as August fired shots at the two soldiers coming from the house. Those shots, and some others whose source she couldn't identify, bounced around the trees.

Then, as if time slowed down, the solider nearest Elim and August raised his pistol. Adeline wanted to scream, but the sound caught in her throat. Elim saw the raised gun at the same time and pushed August out of the way. She watched as the Confederate soldier fired and Elim fell to the ground. She screamed for Elim.

Adeline scrambled to her feet, but Mama grabbed her arm, pulling her back. "No, Adeline."

Adeline looked at her mother, the woman she'd searched so long to find, and tears filled her eyes. She'd found them but now needed to leave them. Elim needed her. "Mama, I can't leave him."

"Girl, you best come on. You can't tackle every solider out here."

Her eyes went to Elim lying on the grass. August had left him there and had run in the direction of the house. "He's hurt. He came to save me. I can't leave him. Take Michael and go with the others. I'll meet you back at the camp."

Mama watched her for a second longer and then leaned down and kissed her on the forehead. "Come back to us." Then she and Michael disappeared into the trees.

Adeline checked the clearing for more soldiers and, when she saw none, crouched down and ran across the grass. When she reached Elim, he was lying still, his breathing shallow. His whole left side was soaked with blood.

"Oh no. Elim."

His eyes fluttered open. "Adeline, go," he managed, his voice weak.

"I'm not leaving you." She needed to stop the bleeding. It looked like the bullet had hit him high on his arm, but she couldn't tell with all the blood. She pulled the scarf from her head and wrapped it around his arm. "Take a deep breath," she said.

When he had filled his lungs up, she quickly looped the fabric around his arm and tied it tight. He cried out with the breath he had taken in. She wrapped it again and tucked the edges under to secure it. "That should stop the bleeding."

His head lolled to one side and his face grew pale. Lights flickered in the trees, and Adeline saw more soldiers on horseback coming up the path, but they were Union soldiers. They quickly spread out, some of them coming to Elim, others going to the Confederate soldier in the grass. The medic dropped down beside Elim and she gave him space to examine him.

"Looks like this is all taken care of for now. I'll see if we can remove the bullet once we get back to camp."

Elim looked over at Adeline, his expression showing both amusement and pain. "Teacher to cook to nurse. How do you know all this?"

She smiled down at him. "I read it in a book."

And to her heart's delight, he chuckled.

☙ Chapter 15 ☙

$\mathcal{E}$lim shifted against the sling.

"Stop fidgeting," Adeline said from beside him. She wore a bright smile as the wagon lumbered along. Her mother and brother sat across from him, chuckling at the admonishment.

"It itches," he grumbled. But the discomfort of his healing wound didn't compare to the joy he felt.

He was on his way to Philadelphia with Adeline and her family. August had been given a month's pass for his bravery and to escort Elim north. Once Elim healed he would return to the war, if it was still going.

"We're almost home." Adeline patted his arm.

Home. He hadn't been able to call anywhere home in his life, and now he was about to start a life with the woman he loved.

They had talked every day while he was recovering. Talked about him staying in the army after he healed. Talked about where they would live. Even though August assured him that their father would accept him back as a free man, Elim preferred to leave his memories in the past. Maybe one day he'd go to see his father, but not until the war was over. Adeline suggested they go to Baltimore or Philadelphia. Her mother, however, told them she wanted to go to Philadelphia to see where Adeline's father was buried, and that settled that.

They would search for somewhere to live and get his family settled.

He grinned at the thought. His family.

Adeline frowned at him. "What are you smiling about?"

He leaned against her. "Just thinking."

They had made all these plans but hadn't talked about marriage. It was almost as if it was a given. But he still needed to ask.

They arrived at the boardinghouse where Adeline and her father had lived. None of them had much to unpack, so the process didn't take long. They met back downstairs for dinner. Elim watched Florence and Michael grow more and more comfortable with August as the trip progressed. It had taken a good deal of convincing for Florence to let down her guard around August, but she had made progress since the trip started.

After dinner, Elim cleared his throat. "Adeline, how about a walk? I need to stretch a bit from that long ride."

She gave him a concerned look. "A short one, right?"

"Of course."

She took him outside and they walked down the sidewalk. Philadelphia was busier than Alexandria, and Elim had to adjust to seeing coloreds and whites walking together like there wasn't a war going on.

"You know, we've talked about everything but getting married."

She tipped her head. "Do we have to?"

Elim laughed. "Get married? Yes. There is no way I'm going back to the war without making you my wife first."

She blushed, a sight he hoped he would be able to see for the rest of his life. "No, talk about getting married. You told me you would marry me months ago."

"But I never asked, and you never gave me an answer."

She stopped walking and turned to face him. "Okay. Ask."

"Adeline, will you—"

"Yes." She waved a hand. "There, it's done."

Elim threw back his head and laughed. "Not much for romance, are you?"

She gave him a sassy look. "I already decided I was going to marry you. You're the one caught up on formalities. I am ready to be your wife."

He reached out and pulled her close. "Are you truly okay with me going back to the war?"

She sighed. "No. But if God helped me find my family, reconciled you to August, and brought us together, He can protect you. Besides, the war may be over before you heal."

"If not, I will have you and my family to keep me going." He pressed his forehead to hers. "I love you. I'm looking forward to living a long life with you."

She stood on her tiptoes and kissed him. "Your heart is showing."

Terri J. Haynes, a native Baltimorean, is a homeschool mom, writer, prolific knitter, freelance graphic artist, and former Army wife (left the Army, not the husband). She loves to read, so much that when she was in elementary school, she masterminded a plan to be locked in a public library armed with only a flashlight to read all the books and a peanut butter and jelly sandwich. As she grew, her love for writing grew as she tried her hand at poetry, articles, speeches, and fiction. She is a storyteller at heart. Her passion is to draw readers into the story world she has created and to bring laughter and joy to their lives.

Terri is a 2010 American Christian Fiction Writers Genesis contest finalist, and a 2012 semifinalist. She is also a 2013 Amazon Breakthrough Novel quarterfinalist. Her publishing credits include *A Cup of Comfort for Military Families*, Crosswalk.com, *The Secret Place* devotional magazine, Urbanfaith.com, Vista Devotional, and *Publishers Weekly*.

Terri holds a bachelor's degree in theology, a master's degree in theological studies, and a certificate in creative writing and graphic design, meeting the minimal requirements for being a geek. She and her husband pastor a church where she serves as executive pastor and worship leader. Terri lives in Maryland with her three wonderful children and her husband, who often beg her not to kill off their favorite characters.

Website: www.terrijhaynes.com
Blog: www.inotherwords.terrijhaynes.com

❧ Courting the Doctor ❧

by Cecelia Dowdy

❧ Chapter 1 ❧

Pennsylvania, 1870

eborah!"

Deborah winced as she slammed her book shut and shoved it into the wooden crate. No way could she let Ma see what she was doing. The last thing she needed right now was a lecture. "Deborah!" Oh, Ma's voice was loud as a cat during mating season. She winced at the sound of her mother's approaching hard footsteps. She scooped up an armful of hay and scattered it over the crate, hiding her precious book. The barn door slammed open, the loud sound causing Susie, her black barn cat, to scurry toward her. She scooped up the cat and smoothed her hand along the animal's shiny dark fur.

"What are you doing in here?" Her mother scanned the barn as if searching for a long-lost secret.

It was hard to keep anything from Ma, but she just couldn't, just wouldn't, tell Ma about her secret, at least not yet.

"I'm petting Susie." Well, at least that wasn't a lie. She'd been petting Susie since her ma had stormed into the barn.

Ma placed her hands over her ample hips and sniffed. "Smells like peppermint. Have you been making your peppermint oil?"

Deborah pushed her spectacles up on her nose and pointed to the small open satchel. "Yes. I need to have some on hand to sell." She'd been making it shortly before she'd started. . .well. . .doing what she didn't want her ma to know about. She'd sold out of the last batch. Her peppermint oil was known to help folks with runny noses and fevers.

Susie squirmed, so Deborah stood and released her cat before focusing on Ma again.

Ma shook her head. "You're always thinking about making money selling peppermint oil. Deborah, you've been focusing on the wrong things. That's why you're not married."

"Ma, I'm sure you didn't come out here to talk about that." Honestly, her ma made her feel downright sick and unsettled at times. Before her fraternal twin sister, Eve, passed away, Deborah had thought about finding another place to teach—a place far away from her folks. She'd never been away from them, and yes, it would have been hard. But after Eve passed, she found that her goals had changed. She just couldn't leave Ma and Pa alone, so she'd come up with another plan, a better plan—a plan that would make her feel happier and more content. However, she wasn't sure if her plan would work. Only time and a lot of prayer would help her to figure that out.

"I've been calling you for the longest time." Her mother sighed before fingering the white bonnet on her head. Her smooth, pudgy brown face softened as she gazed at her daughter. "It's time for you to go to the train station to pick up Timothy and Lily."

Deborah turned away from Ma and focused on the barn floor.

She didn't feel like fetching her brother-in-law and her niece. Well, that wasn't totally true. She didn't mind fetching Lily, but Timothy, now, getting him made her a bit nervous. Was he still considered her brother-in-law since his wife—her sister, Eve—was dead? She gulped. Her gut still burned with sadness, dread, and something else she couldn't quite decipher, since the death of her sister a year ago.

"Can't Pa go get them?"

Ma placed her arm around Deborah's shoulders. She grabbed her satchel just as her ma gently led her out of the barn. "Deborah, we've been through this. Your pa's working the fields. I've got an order of hand pies to make."

Her ma made apple hand pies and sold them to the folks in their small Pennsylvania Negro community. Their farm included a small apple orchard, and harvest season was about to start. Her mouth watered for one of her ma's pies right now. Her ma removed a brown paper sack from her pocket. The delicious scent of cinnamon and apples wafted toward her. "I made these for you to eat on your trip."

"Thank you, Ma." Just knowing she'd have a treat to enjoy during her trip made her feel a little bit better.

Ma squeezed her shoulders. "I've got to make sure all the food is prepared for our dinner with Lily and Timothy. They'll be starving after that long train ride. So that's why I can't come with you." Ma stopped walking and firmly took Deborah's chin, forcing her to look directly into her eyes. "You don't have to be scared of him. I know you took a shine to Timothy and he married your sister instead. But that was eight years ago. He's probably forgotten all about that, and he's sad, grieving over his wife while trying to raise Lily all by himself. He's going to be the town's doctor now, so you've got to get used to being around him." She pointed to the small cabin just a short distance from their house. Since old Doctor Smith had retired and moved, Timothy and Lily would be living nearby in Doctor Smith's old house. "It'll be right nice having Lily around." Her ma gave her a sly look. "Doesn't look like you'll ever be getting married and giving me some grandbabies, so I'm glad Timothy has agreed to be the new town doctor. It'll give me a chance to spend time with my granddaughter."

Deborah blew air through her lips. She honestly didn't know what to say about that. She'd overheard some of the womenfolk at church complaining about their husbands. Were they honestly happy? She sometimes wondered if she was better off alone with Susie for company while she studied her books.

"You got your lesson plan done for the first day of school tomorrow?"

"Yes." She didn't need to have much of a plan for the first day. It took the kids a day or so to get back into the routine of school. Lily would be in her class, so that was a blessing. After Eve and Timothy had moved away, she'd only seen Lily a few times. She longed to get to know her niece better and hoped Lily would take a liking to her. She got into the wagon, took the reins, and flicked them, and the horses started off at a gentle trot. Ma waved to her as she drove the team of horses down the wooded path. Shouldn't take too long to get to the station since she was getting an early start.

As she steered the horses, she removed the paper sack from her pocket and bit into one of the apple hand pies. Apples, cinnamon, sugar, and flaky crust exploded in her mouth with sweetness. Filling drizzled at the side of her lips. She quickly licked it away. Simply delicious. Her ma had been making hand pies for the last few years. Deborah had helped her to develop a great recipe using a secret ingredient. After Ma fried the pies in hot lard and served them, Deborah had a hard time waiting for the little pies to cool before enjoying them. Now that the apples were ready for harvest, her ma would be making more pies, as well as applesauce and apple butter.

She sighed as she popped the last bite of pie into her mouth. Ma. She shook her head as she glanced at the oak trees in the distance. Sometimes when Ma spoke to her, she felt like a little kid instead of a twenty-five-year-old woman. Plain spinster. She inwardly winced as she spotted a patch of chicory growing at the side of the road. Maybe she'd stop and pick some on her way back. She was used to the townsfolk in their small Negro community secretly commenting about her plain looks and her shy nature. Well, she wasn't really shy. She loved being around children and she enjoyed being the town's schoolteacher.

It was adults she didn't take a shine to. *Lord, please forgive me for my unkind thoughts.* The long ride to the station went by quickly since she focused on the plants that she spotted along the side of the road. She named them as fast as she could. Just looking at the plants and naming them soothed her. Plants had a way of making her feel better. She figured if she focused on them during her entire journey, she wouldn't be so nervous about seeing Timothy for the first time since her sister's death.

She breathed deeply as she reined in the horses at the train station and pulled the brake lever. She removed the pocket watch from her reticule. The train should be coming in soon. She took her satchel and strolled over to the station, scanning the dusty platform as she wiped sweat from her face. There sure were a lot of folks waiting for the train. She eyed several benches around the station. All of the seats were taken, except for one seat on a bench. An elderly white lady and a little boy sat on the long, pew-like seat. The little boy ate a bar of chocolate and wore a fancy black suit. Deborah's leather shoes echoed on the floorboards as she strolled toward the bench. Taking her chances, she plopped down beside the twosome. "Good afternoon, ma'am."

The woman narrowed her eyes. The boy simply grinned at her while he enjoyed his candy. She swallowed. She needed to do what was necessary to come up with the money to fulfill her dream. "Ma'am, I see you have a little one with you. I'm a schoolteacher, and I know how little ones can get runny noses." Quick as could be, she opened her satchel and removed a bottle of her peppermint oil. "This is peppermint oil. Folks in the town where I live use this regularly for colds and stomach ailments."

"We don't need anything like that from *your* kind." The lady pointed a bony finger at Deborah while she stood and forced the little boy to get down from the bench. The youngster waved at her, giving her a huge smile. The chocolate candy had smeared on his chubby white hand. "Don't wave at her. Never wave at a Negro." The elderly woman leaned in close to the child, her loud voice echoing in the train station. She squeezed the boy's wrist and he cried, dropping his candy onto the ground.

Deborah shook her head. Foolish woman. It was a terrible shame that just because of her brown skin, the woman didn't want to talk to her about peppermint oil. She scanned the platform. A young Negro man reading a newspaper stood nearby, and a few groups of people congregated with one another. Should she approach somebody else? Maybe the Negro man might be interested?

The echo of the whistle from the approaching train pierced the air. She slammed down the lid of her satchel and turned the clasp. She pushed her spectacles up on her nose. The entrance exam for the female college could prove daunting, and if she made it into the college, she'd need enough money to pay her tuition. She still couldn't believe she was studying to take the entrance exam. She'd thought and prayed about it for over a year before making her final decision.

If Timothy had been in town when she'd made her decision, she may have shared her news with him. Being around other folks made her bored; her mind was so cluttered with ideas, questions, and thoughts. She supposed that's why she enjoyed teaching children. She always encouraged questions from her pupils.

She'd spent time with Timothy when she was seventeen, and she hadn't gotten bored. Actually, the opposite had happened. Timothy made her think. Timothy questioned a lot of things, just as she did, and their discussions and debates proved long and fulfilling. The train whistle echoed in the air once more. She again eyed the folks standing on the platform. The Negro man had closed his paper, and he smiled at the approaching train. He was obviously anxious for the train to pull into the station. She sighed and stood up and leaned against the wall. As white puffs of smoke from the train exploded into the warm humid air, she pressed her hands together, trying to calm her frazzled nerves.

She squeezed her eyes shut as the acrid smell of smoke filled the air. She sniffed. *Lord, help me.*

She kept her eyes shut, silently talking to God, as she listened to the cadence of pounding footsteps, probably travelers rushing by and folks exiting the train. She sniffed again. *Lord, please help me to calm down.* Sweat trickled down her brow, irritating her skin. She whisked the moisture away with her hand. It sure was hot out today.

"Deborah."

She knew that deep voice, rich and slow as the molasses she'd used on her flapjacks that morning. She forced herself to open her eyes. "Timothy." She was so nervous, his name barely squeaked across her lips. It was a wonder she could speak at all. But something was wrong. His chocolate-brown eyes were laced with worry.

"Daddy. . ." Lily stood beside Timothy. The pretty seven-year-old child looked just like Eve. With Lily's smooth brown skin and pretty face, Deborah predicted Timothy would have no problem finding a husband for his daughter when she grew up. Lily tugged on her father's pants. Her mouth quivered and tears slid down her cheeks.

Deborah's stomach curled with dread as she gently rubbed Lily's back. "Lily, what's wrong?"

"I don't feel—"

The child vomited right onto Deborah's newly polished leather shoes. The sour stench sickened her stomach. Looked like it had been an awful trip for her newly arrived relatives.

Chapter 2

Timothy's heart pounded with shame as he lifted his daughter into his arms. He quickly carried her to a patch of grass at the side of the station and set her down just as she vomited again. The awful stench filled his nose as his heart pounded with fear. *Lord, please help my Lily.* He needed to give her some medicine, maybe some ginger for her upset stomach. After Lily had stopped vomiting, he focused on Deborah, who stood right beside him. He vividly recalled her calm, quiet nature with little ones. She touched his shoulder. "There's a water pump out back. Let's take her there." The command flowed from her mouth softly, like a cool dose of spring rain. Beside himself, he needed someone to tell him what to do. Yes, he was a doctor, but when it came to his daughter, he found the dread of worry overshadowing him.

He didn't want to make a mistake when treating his daughter like he'd done with Eve. He still blamed himself every day for the sudden death of his wife. Guilt raged deep within him. He'd tried to pray away the worry and fear that consumed his entire being, but to no avail. And now with Lily sick, he had no way of knowing what would happen next.

He threw the unwelcome thought from his mind as he focused on Deborah again. He needed to clean up Lily. Deborah could help him. Finally, in the midst of this sudden emergency, he managed to find his voice. "Lily, can you walk?"

Lily nodded. She clutched her stomach while Deborah held her shoulder, and they made their way over to the water pump. Deborah repeatedly pumped the handle until water gushed from the spigot. He removed his handkerchief from his pocket and together they cleaned off Lily's dress. Deborah removed her own shoes and held them under the spigot. She washed off the awful stench of Lily's sickness, and then she lifted first one stockinged foot, then the other, under the flow of water. He focused on her slim ankles and slender feet. Their eyes briefly met and he winced, embarrassed that she'd caught him staring at her ankles. Well, no harm done. He was just a bit beside himself with Lily being sick and all.

After she'd cleaned up and placed her drenched shoes back on her feet, she tapped Lily's shoulder. "Hold out your hands." The girl cupped her hands under the spigot and Lily pumped water into them. "Drink some water, but don't drink too fast." His daughter's mouth quivered as she sipped water from her cupped hands. She cupped her hands again for more water. Deborah shook her head. "No, just wait a bit." She offered her a vial. "This will make you feel better."

Memories, sweet as candy, swept through Timothy's mind. He recalled how Deborah used to make peppermint oil in the wooden shed behind her pa's barn. The time they'd spent together years ago, talking about plants, reading books. . . He couldn't stop the next word that popped out of his mouth. "Peppermint."

"Oil."

"Heals colds and stomach pains." As they spoke the sentence together, his heart skipped. Back before he'd started dating Eve, he'd spent a lot of time with Deborah. They'd been good friends. He'd loaned her several books about science and plants, and she'd once confided that he was one of the few men whom she'd befriended in her life who didn't bore her to tears. They'd had a game where they'd memorize herbs and how they were used as remedies. They always started their game by reciting the use of peppermint, probably because they used it so much in their small town. He recalled that after he and Eve married and moved away, Eve told him that Deborah had started selling her peppermint oil to the townsfolk.

"Daddy, I want to go home."

"We'll be home soon, Lily. We'll be riding in Deborah's wagon to your grandparents' house."

Lily shook her head. "No, I want to get back on the train and go home."

Well, he couldn't argue with her. Since he'd announced that he'd be taking old Doc Smith's place and they'd be moving to Eve's hometown, his daughter had been moody and upset. She was simply too young to understand that she needed a ma. Eve was gone, and he was sure that Eve's mother, whom he fondly called Mama June, along with Deborah, would be a strong female influence in Lily's life. He didn't know how to be both mother and father to his daughter, and he hoped that Lily would thrive on the extra attention that her female relatives would bestow on her.

After Deborah directed them to her horses, he found an old blanket in the back of the wagon. He made a bed for Lily and helped her up into the wagon bed. "Lily, I want you to lie down." He kept his voice gentle as he pointed to the blanket. He then opened up his medicine bag and pulled out his stethoscope. He plugged the device into his ears and placed the base of the stethoscope to Lily's heart. Her strong heartbeat sounded fine. He removed the device and felt her forehead. Burning hot. He focused on Deborah. "She has a fever. I'm worried."

"I have a canteen with me. I'll fill it with water and give her some more peppermint oil later. She can rest while we journey back to my house." Deborah was always so practical and smart. He'd always admired that about her and had missed the camaraderie they used to share.

He felt Lily's forehead again, then spoke to Deborah. "When we arrive at your home, you or your ma can give Lily a hot bath if her fever hasn't broken."

"You want her to sweat, right?"

"Yes. If she starts sweating, that proves her fever has broken." After Deborah filled her canteen with water and returned to the wagon, he gestured toward his daughter. "Please stay here with her while I tend to our baggage." He jumped down from the wagon and quickly found two young, dark-skinned porters. They hoisted the baggage onto the back of Deborah's wagon. They didn't have much to bring with them, except for his doctoring supplies and a few clothes. The community here had a small pharmacy downtown as well as a mercantile. He'd have to order the supplies he needed based upon his new patients' health concerns. He'd not needed to bring a lot of his household supplies with him. Mama June had assured him that Doc Smith had left his furniture and cooking utensils in the cabin. He'd sold or given away most of their belongings before he and Lily moved.

He got into the driver's seat of the wagon and eyed Lily, who'd fallen asleep. The child looked so much like her ma that his heart tugged. He missed Eve. If she hadn't died, they wouldn't have had to make such a drastic change in their lives. If only he'd known what to do to save her. Her death was all his fault.

"Are you all right?" Deborah touched his shoulder, her cool fingers making his heated skin feel good. She'd removed her wet shoes and now sat in her wet stocking feet. The faint scent of peppermint surrounded her, again bringing to mind the times they used to share together, studying herbs.

"Yes, I'm all right." He gestured toward Lily. "Just worried about her is all. I don't want her to get sick during the trip home." He took a deep breath. "What if she's seriously ill?"

Deborah's eyes widened. "Of course she'll be all right. You of all people should know how children get sick sometimes."

"Not Lily."

She tilted her head, staring at him behind her spectacles. "What do you mean?"

"Since the day my daughter's been born, she's never been ill."

Her mouth dropped open. "Never?" The disbelief was evident in her voice.

"Never. She's the healthiest child I've ever known in my entire life." He again glanced at Lily. "Her sudden sickness makes me wonder if the Lord's trying to tell me something."

Folks bustled around them, hoisting baggage into nearby wagons and carriages. A gentle breeze blew as a loud bird squawked from the sky. He looked up and spotted an eagle swooping through the clouds. He focused on Deborah again. She seemed to be thinking as she toyed with the strings of her bonnet. Memories, sweet as honey, again filled his mind. He recalled Deborah's kind and compassionate nature. She was one to think and measure her words. She never wanted to hurt another person's feelings. Now, Eve, she was completely different. Deborah's twin could prove to be conniving, often thinking of herself before others. Yes, he'd loved his wife, still grieved for her. But he needed to be honest with himself. He knew Eve had a few faults—faults he'd often mention to her when they had one of their spats.

"What do you think the Lord's trying to tell you?"

"Maybe I shouldn't have moved back here. Lily is sick for the first time in her life, right after we've moved. Don't you think the Lord may be telling me that I should not have returned?" He looked at her, the ache to know her opinion burning in his gut like a strong fire. Deborah had always been intelligent; with her strong mind and gentle spirit, he figured she'd tell him if she agreed with him.

Heaven help her, she couldn't believe that Timothy was asking her opinion about such a huge change in his life. Of course the Lord was *not* trying to tell him that he should not have moved. Didn't he realize that? He stared down at the reins he clutched in his hands. His full, comely lips were mashed together in apparent anger. He appeared to be carrying the weight of the world on his broad shoulders, and the urge to make him feel better swept through her like a strong wind. He was so handsome, a right nice-looking young man. Since he was thirty, and the town's doctor, she imagined he'd be courting an attractive female within weeks. Eve had been dead for a year, so it would be proper for him to remarry now.

She knew he wanted her and Ma to help with Lily, but once he got married again, she wouldn't be surprised if he decided to move away and become a doctor somewhere else. No, that wouldn't surprise her one bit. But he'd asked her a question, and she had an answer for him. He was being downright silly. She needed to voice her opinion. "Look, Timothy, the Lord is not trying to tell you anything. Lily is obviously upset. You've taken her away from the only home she's ever known. She's not used to living here."

His brown eyes pierced her with a long look. Gracious, she could stare into his long-lashed, intense eyes for a good long while. His skin reddened, and he looked away. Goodness, she *had* been staring at him. She didn't want him to think that she actually *enjoyed* looking at him. She cleared her throat. "Folks get sick riding on a train sometimes, especially if, like Lily, they're not used to it. She's going through an upsetting emotional time right now, and she just needs us to be patient and kind. Eve always told me that Lily was a good child, so we just need to give her some time to get used to her new home." There, she'd said what she could to make him feel better. He appeared to be feeling guilty about moving here, and he shouldn't feel that way at all.

"All right, I trust your judgment." He trusted her judgment? Was her opinion really that important to him? He touched her hand and her skin sizzled from his brief touch. She swallowed, ashamed that she enjoyed sitting here in a wagon with him. Ashamed, because he was her dead sister's husband. "Thank you, Deborah."

Before she could even speak, he flicked the reins and started their journey home.

✒ Chapter 3 ✒

On the drive home Timothy kept eyeing Deborah while Lily snoozed in the back of the wagon. His daughter had always been a hard sleeper, and the bumps on the path didn't seem to disturb her slumber. Deborah's wet shoes still sat on the floorboards and he found himself peeking at her slim ankles. Tall and slim, with that bright red bonnet covering her dark curls, she'd been easy to spot at the station. He'd initially hesitated before approaching her, since her eyes had been closed. She looked lovely. He recalled a few of the gents at the station eyeing Deborah.

He'd always wondered why sweet, kind Deborah had never married. The few times he'd asked Eve this, she'd gotten angry. Why, he never could understand. He'd always sensed that Deborah had a bit of a brooding nature and that she needed a certain sort of man as a husband. Right now she appeared to be looking at the plants at the side of the road. Again, he recalled the time they used to spend together. He'd caught her staring at him right before they left the station. But since they'd started their journey, as far as he could tell, she'd not looked at him even once. "I noticed you had an entire satchel full of peppermint oil back there. I could smell it."

Her stiff shoulders softened and she looked at him. "I was going to try and sell it to folks at the train station, but I didn't have time."

"I see. So what do you do with the money you earn from selling your peppermint oil? I figure with your teaching salary and your earnings from your oil, well, you must have quite a stash, since you live on the farm with your folks."

She pushed her spectacles up on her nose and her shoulders stiffened again. "What I do with my money is my affair."

The irritated tone of her voice startled him. He'd obviously offended her. He hadn't meant to do that. Well, if he was going to be living right across the field from her, sharing meals with her family each day, it wouldn't be wise to put her on edge. She had to understand that he wasn't the enemy. He was simply curious. He stopped the wagon. She frowned. "What are you doing? We're almost home."

"Look, Deborah, I just don't want you mad at me is all. You're angry because of my question. I obviously asked you something that was none of my business. Can you forgive me?"

She looked at him with her wise, pretty eyes. Her hands were pressed together, almost as if she were nervous. She was probably just anxious to get home to do whatever it was she needed to do. "I forgive you."

He decided traveling alone with him must be a bit awkward for her, since they weren't actually a couple. Deborah probably wasn't used to taking such a long journey alone with a man other than her pa.

He regripped the reins and thought of his new living quarters, right near Deborah's home. Mama June had written to him, stating that he and Lily were to share meals with them each day since he didn't have anybody to cook for him.

As he continued to drive the horses, memories exploded in his mind. He recalled when he'd first come to this town to study medicine under Doc Smith. He'd lived with the elderly, widowed doctor. After church one day, he'd spotted Deborah. A lot of the womenfolk had broken off into groups, talking about. . .well, whatever womenfolk talk about. Deborah, however, had gone off by herself. Apparently she'd been waiting for her ma, pa, and Eve to finish their conversations. He'd approached her, wondering what she was looking at in the bushes. She'd been excited about finding some goldenseal and had excitedly shown him the plant with healing properties.

She was the first woman he'd met in this town who knew more about plants than just the basics. Once he'd discovered her interest in them, he'd offered to loan her some of the botany books he had on his shelf. Her bright smile and sparkling eyes were evidence that he'd excited her. She'd started asking him questions and sharing how fascinated she was with what she was learning. She'd even showed him how she dried the plants she found and sometimes used for cooking as well as curing simple illnesses. His vivid memories continued as they pulled up to the familiar house, right where he used to spend time with Deborah and Eve.

It had been a few years since he'd visited, and just seeing the house where Eve grew up comforted him. A bench as well as two wooden chairs crowded the small porch. He remembered sitting on that porch drinking tin cups of cold water.

"It sure took you all long enough to get back from the train station." Eve's mother, June, and father, Daniel, came out of the house. Mama June peeked into the wagon. "That child looks plumb tuckered out."

He got out of the wagon and was about to go and assist Deborah, but she scampered out of the wagon so fast he didn't have a chance to help her down. She looked away from him toward the house. She was acting downright skittish. He needed to let her know how much he appreciated her help. "Lily got sick at the train station. Deborah helped clean her up and gave her some peppermint oil. Having Deborah's help today was a real blessing."

Her pretty eyes widened at his compliment. "Thank you, Timothy."

"You're welcome." He carried Lily from the wagon. He felt his daughter's sweaty forehead. Her fever was gone, and he sighed with relief. But even though she didn't have a fever now, he wanted to be sure that he watched her all night, just in case something else ailed her.

"Come bring Lily back here." Mama June beckoned him toward the spare room in the rear of the house. He laid Lily on the bed and Mama June covered her with a quilt. She also removed Lily's shoes.

They returned to the kitchen and he shook hands with Deborah's father. "Good to see you again, Papa Daniel."

The bald old man grinned before pulling him into a hug. "Lily looks just like Eve. I felt like I was looking at my little girl all over again." His voice wavered and he took a deep breath before wiping his suddenly wet eyes. "I still miss her."

Timothy touched Papa Daniel's shoulder. "So do I. I think about her every day, especially when I see Lily."

Deborah stood to the side, watching them, but she didn't say a word. She finally gestured toward the kitchen. "Dinner's ready. Ma wants you to come and eat." The scent of cooked meat and herbs filled the air. The table was laden with all kinds of food. He spotted the roast beef, swimming in gravy. Mashed potatoes filled a large bowl, and biscuits were piled high on a plate. There were also bowls of vegetables as well as a small crock of butter. He eyed the plate of Mama June's apple hand pies for dessert.

He eased into a chair and Deborah sat to his right. As soon as Deborah's parents were seated, they joined hands. It was a tradition in Eve's family. Deborah's hand felt warm and soft, and the light scent of peppermint wafted toward him.

Papa Daniel cleared his throat. "Lord, thanks so much for this lovely day. Thank You also for this wonderful food to nourish our bodies. Also, Lord, I want to thank You for allowing Timothy and Lily a safe journey. We've missed our family, and we're oh so happy for the blessing of seeing them again. Please help Lily heal from her illness. Please be with Timothy as he becomes acclimated as the town's doctor. Amen."

"Amen." Everybody uttered the word before they started to eat. When Timothy tasted the rich, tender meat and the creamy whipped potatoes, he felt like he was eating a slice of heaven. "This is delicious, Mama June."

"Thank you, Timothy."

He eyed his father-in-law as he spread apple butter onto a

biscuit. "How have you been, Papa Daniel?"

"*Humph*. Busy. Apples are about ready for harvest. I've a lot of chores to do. I might hire a couple of folks to help pick the apples." He glanced at Mama June. "June will be storing lots of apples in our root cellar, and she'll be making applesauce and apple butter."

"Sounds like your farm is doing well. I'm glad to hear that you're having such a plentiful season."

After they'd eaten their dinner, Timothy stood up. "If it's okay with you, Mama June and Papa Daniel, I want Lily to stay in the spare room here tonight. I don't want to move her home. I'm going to sit up with her."

Deborah looked at him. "Lily is fine. Why don't you go to your new home, and Ma and I will stay up with her?"

He shook his head. "No, *I* want to sit up with her. I can't. . .I can't leave her, not when she's sick." He refused to allow them to argue with him.

Lily had a simple stomach upset. Why was Timothy acting as if she had some kind of dreaded disease? She'd probably be fine in the morning. These thoughts twirled through Deborah's mind like leaves scattered in the wind. It had been two hours since dinnertime, and Pa had gone up the road to Doc Smith's cabin, which was now Timothy and Lily's cabin. Timothy wanted Pa to bring back the box of medical notes for all of Doc Smith's patients. He had explained that he needed to start his doctoring duties right away, so he wanted to go through the files while he sat up with Lily.

He had pen and inkwell in the room too. He'd set up a workstation, claiming he'd start making trips to his patients the following morning, and that he also needed to go downtown to the pharmacy. Eve had been dead for a year. Perhaps it had been awhile since a woman had given him advice. She pulled a chair into the room where he worked. Lily continued to sleep, her soft snores filling the small space. Deborah plopped into the chair as Timothy mumbled to himself, reading through the files. "Timothy."

"Hmmm?" He didn't even look up from his task.

"Why don't you get some rest tonight? We have a mattress we can bring in here so that you can keep an eye on Lily."

He still didn't look at her, just kept looking through his files. "No, I have to get started making patient visits tomorrow." He speared her with one of his intense looks. "I told you that earlier."

"But you're tired. Lily is sick. You've had a long journey. Some of the neighbors probably saw us when we were driving home. I figure everybody knows you're back in town, so they know where to find you if they need you."

He shook his head. Stubborn, that's what he was. Would it hurt to lie down and get some rest for a few hours? Well, she wasn't going to sit and try to reason with him. Perhaps Ma or Pa could talk some sense into him. "Why is it so important for you to do this *now*? You can always do this tomorrow."

He speared her with another look, his lips mashed together. He sighed and finally put his pen aside. "Deborah, the answer is obvious. I don't want anybody to *die*."

∾ Chapter 4 ∾

Timothy's fervent words haunted Deborah as she stood on the top step of the schoolhouse the following morning. She'd tried to talk to him about getting some rest. However, he'd told her to leave him alone so he could work. Both Ma and Pa had approached him as well, and they'd not been able to get him to sleep either. He'd been like a machine of a man, on a mission, not listening to any of them.

She shook her head. How in the world did Eve ever reason with him? The intense way he'd focused on his task had worried her, so she'd stayed up with him, making tea and helping with Lily, who awakened a few times throughout the night.

About an hour before her ma and pa had gone to bed, she'd had a customer come to the door. One of their neighbors had twin toddlers with runny noses, and they purchased two vials of peppermint oil. Deborah had been glad to get the money from the sale. Timothy was unaware of the visitor, he'd been so intent on his task. She hadn't mentioned it to him, because that might cause him to pry and ask questions that were none of his business.

Still thinking about Timothy's overly strong work ethic, she held the school bell tightly in her grip and blinked her eyes. She yawned, exhausted. *Lord, please help me stay awake on this first day of school.* She breathed deeply before enjoying the soft rustle of the multicolored leaves as they fell from the surrounding trees. A gentle wind blew as she took another deep breath. Children congregated around the schoolyard. Some of the older ones stood in a group, laughing and talking. Those were her eighth graders, and it would be their last year in her school. Once this school year was completed, they would probably be helping their parents on their farms year-round. The younger children had joined hands and were skipping in a circle, and their loud laughter sounded joyful on this beautiful late-summer day.

A loud scream rippled through the air quick as a whip, interrupting the children's banter. Deborah's heart skipped as she dropped the school bell, and it clanged on the steps as she rushed down the stairs. Another scream pierced the air as she ran, fast as she could, to a child lying on the ground, crying and holding her arm. The girl couldn't have been more than five years old—a child new to her classroom. Tears streamed from her large, chocolate-brown eyes as she screamed again.

"Let me see your arm, honey." Deborah sat beside the child and made sure her voice was gentle and soothing. The girl was obviously hurt and frightened, so she needed to help her as best she could. But she couldn't help her until she could determine what was wrong.

The child started shaking. "No, it hurts too much."

"I'm going to help you, honey." She rubbed the child's hand until she released it from her arm.

A bee sting. The poor child's dark skin swelled with the venom. She needed to take fast action. "Hold her down." The command flew from Deborah's mouth. Quick as could be, two of the older girls held the child as Deborah removed the stinger. The little girl's scream of pain pierced the air. Deborah's gut churned with dread. _Lord, please help me._ She eyed a patch of wild basil nearby. _Thank You, Jesus._ She tore the leaves from the plant and stuffed them into her mouth. She gestured to the children who held the hurt girl to release her. Deborah chewed before spitting the leaves into her hand and smoothing them over the poor child's arm. Miraculously, in a few minutes, the girl stopped crying. "What's your name?" Deborah kept her voice soft, low, and hopefully compelling as she took more leaves, shoved them into her mouth, and chewed again.

"Abigail." The child had relaxed, which was a relief.

Again Deborah spit the leaves into her hand and pressed them onto the girl's injured skin.

"I hear the new doc came to town yesterday. Maybe one of us can go fetch him." One of the older boys made the suggestion.

Now that was a good idea. However, it was a bit of a walk, and she figured it would be best if one of the children simply took Abigail over to Timothy instead. Thankfully, the child seemed better. Deborah focused on her. "The new doctor is at my house with his daughter." She needed to be sure they went to the right place. "Lindsey, you take Abigail over to my house and tell the doctor what happened." Lindsey was one of her older students, and she had proven herself to be trustworthy.

Twelve-year-old Lindsey scrunched her nose. "Who's the new doctor?"

"His name is Doctor Washington. Now go, take Abigail on over to my house. After that, take her home, and then you can come back to school." Within minutes, the twosome slowly strolled down the wooded path toward her home. Abigail was speaking to Lindsey, so it appeared that the child would be fine. But now it looked like she'd be missing two students for the first day of school.

The children had started talking again, their mumbling filling the air. She needed to bring some order to these restless students. It was the first day of school and she needed to get started. She quickly marched over to the steps and found her bell lying on the ground, right where she'd abandoned it when she'd gone to assist Abigail. She needed to get the children's minds off of the bee sting and back onto school.

She pushed her spectacles up on her nose then raised her bell and shook it back and forth. The loud, familiar clang made her heart skip with joy. The wonderful sound echoed all around them as the children quickly gathered their dinner pails and other belongings from the ground and scampered into the school. One of the younger boys stopped and tugged at her skirt. "Miss King, we don't need no new town doctor. The way you fixed up Abigail, they should make you the new doctor."

Deborah stifled her laughter, not even bothering to correct the child's grammar. She highly doubted they'd take a female doctor seriously in this small town. Each child greeted her as they entered the building. A few of the female students even hugged her. She knew the boys wouldn't want to share a hug—that was no surprise. She'd seen a lot of the students during the summer, but a number of them who lived a bit farther out, and who seldom attended church, she'd not encountered since school let out last spring. The echo of the children's footsteps surrounded her as they entered the schoolroom. As soon as the last child had entered, she closed the door and walked to the front of the room. She set her bell on her desk and scanned the children who sat on the wooden benches.

The benches, the floor, and even the windows gleamed from the sunshine spilling into the room. The tangy scent of lemon oil tickled her nose. She mentally thanked the church ladies who'd volunteered to clean up the room before the first day of school.

Well, it was unfortunate that Abigail had gotten stung by a bee, but one good thing had come of it. The incident had left her wide awake. She was no longer exhausted from her long night of sitting up with Timothy and Lily. "Good morning, everyone."

"Good morning." The echo of the students' voices filled the room. It sure was nice to be back into the routine of school.

"For those of you who don't know, my name is Miss King." Taking a piece of chalk, she wrote her name on the blackboard. "Does anyone remember how we start our day?"

Several of her pupils raised their hands. "Rebecca."

The young girl grinned. Looked like she'd lost a few of her baby teeth over the summer. "We start the day with the Lord's Prayer."

Deborah smiled. "That's right." She wanted to instill a deep faith within all of her students, and reciting the Lord's Prayer every day was important to her. "As I say to you every year, if you don't know what to say to Jesus and have a hard time finding the right words, just say the Lord's Prayer. Jesus knows what's in your heart." She knew that sometimes it took time for the children to learn to be honest with God in saying their prayers, so she hoped knowing this simple prayer would help them with their prayer life and faith as they grew older. She focused on the few new young pupils sitting in the front row. "I realize that some of you may not know the Lord's Prayer by heart."

One of the youngsters raised her hand. "What's 'by heart' mean?"

Deborah smiled at the girl. "From memory." She then focused on the entire class again. "So let's begin by reciting the Lord's Prayer together. I want all of you to bow your heads and close your eyes."

She bowed her head.

"Our Father which art in heaven, Hallowed be thy name. Thy kingdom come, Thy will be done in earth, as it is in heaven. Give us this day our daily bread. . ."

The smooth, gentle cadence of young voices raising a prayer to God lifted her spirits. As they finished the prayer, Deborah felt renewed. She'd been a bit tense and uneasy that morning due to Timothy and Lily's recent arrival and from Abigail's sudden bee sting. As she opened her eyes, she felt right nice, almost as if angels were smiling down on the classroom. Her eyes teared with happiness. She quickly blinked them away, not wanting the students to see her get emotional.

She smiled at her students. "Doesn't that feel nice, speaking to Jesus first thing in the morning?"

"Yes, ma'am," the children responded.

"When's Abigail coming back?" One of the younger students,

sitting in the front row, voiced the question.

"Abigail should be fine after she sees the doctor. I suspect she'll be back to school tomorrow." She paused and took a deep breath. "Could all of you in the back come up here to help the new students, please." The eighth graders in the back of the room came to the front of the classroom. She gave them the primers for the younger students. "I want you to start going over the alphabet with the new students who've not yet been to school." She wanted to be sure her young pupils could read simple words before the school year ended.

As the eighth graders obediently started working with the youngest students, she gave assignments to the next few groups of students to work on. She then focused on the middle grades by showing them how to do long division. The children stood at the blackboard while she outlined how to solve an equation. She patiently answered their questions. She realized it was tough for some students to learn adequately since a lot of them missed school during harvesttime or if they were ill.

After the students had been working for a while, Deborah clapped her hands. She knew it would be hard for them to concentrate for long periods of time on the first day. Realizing the new students likely didn't know all of the children in the classroom, she thought it was best to rectify that.

"Why don't we go around the room and introduce ourselves? If you'd like, you can tell me what you did over the summer." She figured the suggestion would help the children ease into the routine of school again.

As the children introduced themselves, she sat at her desk and tried to listen to them as best she could. *Lord, forgive me for my wandering mind, but I'm just worried about Timothy.* Timothy had slept in a chair beside Lily's bed. It had been strange, having somebody sleep in Eve's bed. Since her twin had gotten married and moved away eight years ago, her bed had remained empty.

Earlier that morning, Timothy had woken up, looking relieved when he noticed that Lily seemed much better. Ma had told him to stay for the day while she helped care for Lily.

Timothy. . . She still didn't understand his strange reaction to Lily's illness. Why would he react so strongly, almost fearfully, because Lily had a simple upset stomach? Kind of hard to believe that her niece had never taken ill before, but he'd been so upset. The urge to rub his strong shoulders and tell him that everything would be okay had swelled deep within her.

"Miss King, are you all right?" John, the oldest student in her class, asked the question from the back of the room, and she realized the children had gone quiet, waiting for her to call on the next child.

"I'm fine, John." She gestured for the children to continue their introductions as she continued to dwell on the previous night's events. She'd wanted to comfort Timothy but knew it wasn't a good idea to do so. Heaven help her, she still found him as attractive now as she had when she'd been seventeen and he'd been an apprentice to Doctor Smith. His beige skin and expressive light brown eyes, his strong shoulders, and his voice. Comforting him was *not* something she needed to think about.

Besides, Timothy was interfering with her thoughts in a negative way. Since Timothy had arrived and Lily had gotten sick and they'd unexpectedly had to spend the night at her house, she hadn't taken time to study for her college entrance exam the previous night. She studied for that exam *every* night. She just *couldn't* fall behind with her studying routine. She was a twenty-five-year-old spinster, and these children in her classroom would be the closest she'd ever come to being a ma. Since she'd never have any kids of her own, nor ever have a husband, she could do what she wanted.

She wanted to earn a botany certificate from the women's college in Pennsylvania.

Being a Negro woman, she knew it would be hard for some folks to accept that she had an education, but she didn't care. Learning was what she did best, and her active, inquisitive mind had discouraged the few suitors she'd ever had in her life.

"Miss King?" John spoke up again. She eyed the classroom and noticed the expectant look on their young faces. Oh goodness, she'd been daydreaming about Timothy again and had completely forgotten to pay attention to her classroom. They'd obviously finished their introductions and were awaiting her next words. Gracious, Timothy was already wreaking havoc in her life, and he'd been in town less than a day!

After she spent the rest of the morning going over some of the basic lessons that each group of students had learned the previous year, her stomach growled for dinner. *Thank You, Jesus.* Time to stop teaching for an hour while the children enjoyed their midday meal. She could eat the cold fried chicken and apples she'd packed for her lunch while she studied her botany book. She'd tucked it away in the top drawer of her desk so that she could catch up on her studying. She stood up. "Dinnertime."

The students scampered from their desks to retrieve their dinner pails for nooning. Some of them got into groups—she'd noticed last year that some of them traded dinners. She placed her food on top of her desk and opened her drawer to retrieve her botany book. She blinked as her stomach curled with dread. The book was gone, and she knew she'd left it there this morning. Where was it? She closed her eyes and balled her hands into fists. Anger, thick as the pea soup her ma made every spring, bubbled within her. She scanned her classroom. All of the students were gobbling their dinner. Some sat at their desks while others were outside in groups.

"He that is slow to wrath is of great understanding: but he that is hasty of spirit exalteth folly." Proverbs 14:29 popped into her mind. She stared at the cold fried chicken and apples laid out on her desk. Since her precious book was missing, she'd lost her appetite. Which of her students could've taken her book? Was this some kind of prank to pull on the teacher on the first day of school?

ᘉ Chapter 5 ᘊ

imothy strolled toward Deborah's house, holding Lily's hand. He'd managed to get settled into his cabin that day and Lily had made a full recovery from her stomach illness. It was suppertime, and he and Lily were on their way to Mama June and Papa Daniel's for their meal. As they continued toward the house, he thought about his first day back in town. He'd gone through all of the patient files that Doc Smith had left behind and even visited a few of his elderly patients.

He'd been thorough as he questioned his new patients, making sure he understood the full breadth of their illnesses. He was determined to make this town as healthy as possible. Smells of apples and cooked meat filled the air. His mouth watered as they approached the door and opened it. Mama June had mentioned to him earlier that he was family and did not need to knock when coming over for supper.

Mama June and Deborah barely spoke to them as they bustled around the kitchen. They set the food on the table, but he noticed that Papa Daniel wasn't around. "Where's Papa Daniel?"

Mama June grunted as she set a bowl of potatoes on the table. "He's sick. I think he got that stomach illness from Lily."

Timothy's mouth dropped open. "Why didn't you come get me?" Fear seeped into his gut. What if Papa Daniel were seriously ill?

Mama June shooed away his concern. "We know he'll be fine come tomorrow morning. He couldn't do the barn chores, so Deborah and I will have to do them after supper."

Timothy left Lily in the middle of the kitchen and rushed back to his home. He returned with his medical bag and rushed into Papa Daniel and Mama June's room. "Papa Daniel?"

The older man slowly opened his eyes. Sweat beaded his brow. "Hello, Timothy."

"Mama June said you're sick. I'm going to examine you."

Timothy removed his stethoscope and checked the older man's heartbeat. He then checked his eyes and made him open his mouth. "Are you thirsty?"

"Yes."

A pitcher of water rested on the table. Timothy poured a cupful and the old man took a few sips. Timothy nodded. "That's right. Drink it slowly. You don't have a fever. I figure you'll be fine tomorrow or the day after that. If you need me, just send Mama June to come get me."

"Thank you," the older man grunted before falling back to sleep. Timothy touched his shoulder, then squeezed his hand. *Lord, please help Papa Daniel to heal. Amen.* He loved both Papa Daniel and Mama June. They were like a second set of parents to him. He'd lost both of his parents to illness when he'd been barely a teen, and that was when the desire to become a doctor bloomed within him. His folks had been wealthy, so he'd used his inheritance to attend college and study medicine. When he moved to this town and was mentored by Doc Smith, he'd gotten to know and respect Eve's parents. If they ever needed his help for anything, he wanted them to be sure they could ask him.

He finally entered the kitchen again, and his mouth watered when he eyed the food. As they sat for supper, he glanced at Deborah. Something was wrong with her. Her pretty mouth drooped and her shoulders were tense. She barely spoke during the entire meal. He needed to find out what was wrong. Perhaps there was something he could do to help. Today was the first day of the school term, so he wondered if the children had misbehaved. After supper he stood up and focused directly on Mama June. "Mama June, I'm going to leave Lily here with you to help clean up the supper dishes. Deborah, I'll help you do the chores, since your pa is sick."

"Thank you, Timothy." She didn't look at him or speak to him during their quick trek to the barn. After he carried the water to the house so that Mama June and Lily could start the dishes, he focused on the barn chores. He helped Deborah feed the horses, stealing glances at her the entire time. She then milked the cow and fed the chickens. She barely paid him any attention as they fetched water for the horses. While he'd visited patients around town that morning, he'd heard talk that Deborah had been selling a lot of her peppermint oil. He took a deep breath, anxious to figure out what was making her so sad this evening.

"Deborah, what's wrong?" He set his pitchfork against the wall and focused on her.

She bristled. "What makes you think something is wrong?"

"I can tell by the way you look. You're upset. Why don't you tell me what's wrong? Maybe I can help."

She shook her head as she set her watering pail on the ground. "I'm not sick, so I doubt there's anything you can do to help me."

Stubborn woman. He figured she just didn't want to tell him what was wrong. From what he'd been able to gather on his first day back, it appeared that Deborah was still a loner. He'd not heard of any of the female folk in town being close friends with her. Her ma was fussing about that earlier in the day while he'd been at her house. She said Deborah spent too much time by herself and that's why she'd never gotten married.

"I know you're not sick. Deborah, we used to be friends back before I—"

"Before you married Eve?" The words tumbled from her mouth like hard pebbles. She sounded angry, and for the life of him, he couldn't understand why.

"Yes, before I married Eve." He paused and looked directly at her. "Why don't you tell me what's wrong? Did something happen at school today?"

Her mouth dropped open as she pushed her spectacles up on her nose. She took a deep breath and closed her eyes. She was probably praying, wondering if she could trust him. She finally opened her eyes and beckoned him over to the adjoining room. He recalled that was where she kept her peppermint oil. She pulled out a couple of wooden crates. She touched his hand. "I'm sorry, Timothy. I'm very upset right now. I'm acting angry toward you and you're just trying to help. Please forgive me."

"I forgive you. But it might help if you tell me what's wrong."

"All right." She gestured toward the crates. "Please sit down." Her voice sounded tired and weary. He sat on an empty crate, and the old wood creaked beneath his weight. She eased onto the crate beside him. A black cat scurried into the room. "Come here, Susie." The cat scampered onto her lap, and she stroked the cat's shiny dark fur. The animal's gentle purr sounded soothing. He stared at her long, slim, gentle-looking hands while she petted her cat. "Remember when you were asking me what I did with my teaching salary and with the money I was making from my peppermint oil?"

"Yes?"

She sighed. The urge to take her hand bubbled within him. No, he couldn't do that. He reached over and scratched the cat's neck, and the animal purred even louder. Maybe if he showed some kindness to her cat, she'd confide in him. Deborah smiled, just a little bit, when he touched her pet. "I've been saving my money for a while now. I want to go to the women's college and get a certificate in botany."

"Deborah, that's wonderful." She was one of the smartest women he'd ever known.

"Do you really think so?" She actually grinned, as if pleased that he agreed with her ambition.

"Yes. I know some men are against women learning at college, but not me. I think you'll do well there."

"Oh Timothy!" The joy in her voice filled the small room. She jumped up, forcing the cat to scamper away, and hugged him.

Have mercy, she couldn't believe she'd hugged Timothy. His muscled arms were hard as rocks, and when he hugged her back. . . It was the first time a man had ever hugged her, besides Pa. Wait, she couldn't make a fool of herself. She didn't want Timothy to know she still found him attractive after all these years. She quickly plopped back onto the wooden crate and folded her hands.

He touched her shoulder, apparently wanting to put her at ease. "Deborah, it's all right that you hugged me. I can tell you're excited about going to the women's college." Every time Timothy spoke in his deep, strong voice, her insides turned to mush. She figured she didn't have the same effect on him, but that was all right. She needed a friend in whom to confide right now, and if that person happened to be Timothy, then so be it. Perhaps that was why the Lord placed him in her path at this time. "I don't understand. Why does your going to the women's college make you upset?"

Oh, just being around this man was hampering her ability to think clearly. She'd failed to tell him what had happened in her classroom earlier that day. "One of my students stole my botany book for the exam. I need it to study."

He narrowed his eyes. "Are you sure somebody stole it?"

Was she sure? What kind of question was that? Sure, she'd been a bit on edge since Timothy and Lily arrived, but she knew for a fact she'd taken the book with her to school that morning, and she needed Timothy to understand that.

She pulled her crate from underneath the table, removed the loose hay from the top, and lifted a thin book from it. "This is the study manual for the women's college. It outlines what I need to review for the exam. Most of the science that I need to know is in my botany book. I usually keep the book in this crate and study out here. I find it nice and peaceful, being out here while I study about plants. I took the botany book with me to school this morning and left it in the top drawer of my desk." She put the book back in the crate. "I know when my students have been up to mischief." She paused and licked her lips. "I talked to them about the value of honesty and truthfulness this afternoon. I told them that Jesus doesn't take kindly to stealing, even if it's a prank. Hopefully what I said will have some impact on them, and the guilty person who took my book will return it."

"So when do you think one of your students could've taken the book?"

She pressed her hands together. She'd been thinking about this since dinnertime, and she had a good theory as to what had happened. "Did Abigail come see you earlier?"

"You're talking about the little girl with the bee sting? She sure did. You did an excellent job of removing the stinger from her arm. I smelled the basil on her skin. I gave her some ointment before sending her home. Lily was here, and she started chatting with Abigail." He paused before looking directly at her with his kind brown eyes. "I haven't heard Lily talk so much since Eve died. She seemed quite taken with Abigail." He shrugged. "Hopefully they can become friends in school."

"That'd be a blessing for sure." She paused. "The reason I mentioned the bee sting is I was thinking that one of my pupils may have taken my book as a prank while I was tending to Abigail. Most of the class was focused on helping Abigail, as was I. It would have been easy for someone to take the book then."

"Deborah, let me help you. I can talk to your class—"

Was he serious? "Timothy, I appreciate your offer to help. Honestly I do, but I can handle my own classroom. I've been teaching school for years, and I know how to make the culprit come forward soon enough." At least she hoped her book would turn up soon.

"What's the matter? You're frowning again."

"I don't want to fall behind. I feel like this is my calling, deep in my gut. As clear as the sun shines in the sky and the birds sing from the trees, I think the Lord wants me to attend the women's college. Not having my book is affecting my calling, and that bothers me."

"I understand. Let me help you study. Remember how we used to spend time together, looking at my books about the healing power of plants, and then we'd go look at the plants in the fields? You have a quick, active mind, and we work well together."

She winced. Now how in the world would she manage to do that? If she started spending time with Timothy, studying plants, well. . .she'd probably end up falling in love with him all over again, and she just didn't think that was a good idea, not at all. He'd never fall for a plain woman like herself. Sure, she was probably a great match for him as a study partner. She could probably even help him while he tended patients sometimes, just like she used to help Doc Smith occasionally, but she couldn't imagine spending time with him without getting emotionally involved. . .or could she?

He lifted the study manual out of the crate and flipped through it. "This is a good women's college, and since it's only a few miles away, you wouldn't need to leave home to attend." He took a deep breath. "I know some of the professors over there. One of my old classmates teaches there. I think I may have a good idea what the exam will be like. Let me help you study, Deborah."

Oh Lord, what have I gotten myself into now? "Let me think about it, all right?"

His mouth drooped and he narrowed his eyes. He was upset that she hadn't accepted his offer. Did he really want to study with her that badly? He stood up and gestured toward her house. "All right. I need to fetch Lily. It's getting late, and she needs to go to bed."

They were quiet as they walked together toward the house. He barely skimmed his fingers on her back as he opened the door for her and let her enter the house first. Her skin burned from the brief contact of his fingers. Lily sat at the kitchen table, reading one of the primers Deborah used to teach her younger students. Her ma was putting away the clean dishes. "About time the two of you got back from doing the chores. Lily should be ready to go to bed soon."

Timothy smiled at Lily before focusing on Ma. "I was just trying to convince Deborah to allow me to help her study for the entrance exam for the women's college."

Deborah whipped her head around to glare at Timothy just as her Ma dropped a dish. It clattered to the floor. She dropped her head into her hands. How awful. She'd been so enamored of spending time with Timothy that she'd completely forgotten to tell him that her ma and pa didn't know about her future plans. Her ma would probably do everything she could to prevent her from attending college.

She just couldn't stay in this room right now. She opened the door and rushed outside.

"Deborah." Ma called her name so loudly Deborah reckoned just about half the town could hear her. She ignored it. She just didn't feel like talking to Ma tonight about her dream of attending college. Hard footsteps pounded behind her. Someone grabbed her arm and she whipped around and looked into Timothy's gorgeous eyes. He reached for her hand.

"Why didn't you tell me your ma didn't know?"

She couldn't tell him that being alone with him in the barn, just seeing his handsome face and caring nature, made her forget her common sense. "I forgot to tell you it was a secret." Heaven help her, she wished that this one time she hadn't been so infatuated with Timothy's nearness that she lost her presence of mind. If being around Timothy made her forget to tell him about the secret she'd hidden from her ma and pa, then maybe studying with him for the exam was a bad idea. What if she was so distracted by his handsome face that she couldn't memorize the information?

"Deborah, I'm sorry. If there's anything I can do. . ." He frowned as he finally released her hand.

Her hand felt warm, and she didn't want him to let it go.

She blew air through her lips. This just wouldn't work, not at all. "Timothy, I've made up my mind. I don't think it's a good idea for you to help me study. This is something I need to do on my own."

Chapter 6

*D*eborah pulled the pan of hot biscuits from the oven. Her ma set the jar of molasses and the plate of butter on the table. The oatmeal was about done and Timothy and Lily were due for breakfast soon. "Deborah, let's sit and talk for a minute." Her ma frowned as she pointed toward a kitchen chair. When Timothy had left with Lily the previous night, he'd been confused. She remembered the way he used to look whenever he was trying to figure something out. He was probably wondering why she'd turned down his offer to help.

Well, she wasn't sure if it was a good idea to explain her reasoning to him. His light brown eyes had been intense and sad when he'd said good-bye. She glanced at Ma and shook her head. Her ma would never understand what she was going through. How could she? "Timothy and Lily will be here for breakfast soon."

"We have a few minutes. Sit down." Deborah plopped into the seat and her ma sat beside her. Two tin cups of hot coffee rested on the table in front of them. The chicory smell of the brew soothed her. She took a sip. The hot coffee felt good going down her parched throat. Thank goodness Pa was feeling better this morning and was still out doing chores. She didn't think she'd have the energy to discuss this with both of her parents at the same time. Her ma didn't really sound angry, but she didn't sound happy either. Deborah closed her eyes. *Lord, I love my ma. Please give me the right words to explain this to her. Help her understand why I need to do this. Amen.*

Ma folded her hands together. "Now, would you care to explain to me why you want to go to the women's college? You know it's best if you simply teach school. You should know that a smart woman can make a man feel uneasy."

Tell the truth. The words filled her gut, her soul. She needed to let Ma know how she felt. *Lord, please don't let Ma get angry with me.* "Ma, I don't believe I'll ever get married. I'm twenty-five, I'm smart, and I want to help people. Not all people are called to get married. Remember the Apostle Paul spoke about that in the Bible?"

"This has nothing to do with the Apostle Paul."

"Yes, it does. You know how I try to live my life by following Jesus. The Apostle Paul talks about not being married. I'm an unmarried woman, and when I read Corinthians, I feel like God is giving me advice about being an unmarried lady. Ma, I'm not pretty like Eve. I know you're ashamed of me. You're proud that Eve got a husband and had a child, and it bothers you that I didn't do either of those things."

Ma grabbed her hand. "I'm not ashamed—"

Deborah pulled her hand away. "Yes, you are." She wiped

her suddenly sweaty hands on her dress. She just couldn't sit. She stood up and paced the kitchen. She just *had* to make Ma understand how she felt. She stopped walking and turned toward her mother. "Ma, I'm tall, skinny, and plain. I hear what folks in town say about me. I can't help it if God made Eve beautiful and talkative and He made me quiet and plain. I think God wants me to study botany. I love plants. I made the decision to attend the college a year ago, shortly after Eve died."

"Oh, you know I love you, Deborah. I'm *not* ashamed of you. You made this decision right after your sister died? Honey, maybe you should pray about this."

She rushed to her seat and sat back down. "But Ma, I *have* prayed about this. Please, listen to me." She swallowed another sip of coffee. "I've been hoarding my teaching salary and the money from my peppermint oil so that I can go to college. I've been studying out in my room behind the barn. That's the secret I've been hiding from you."

"Oh Deborah." Oh no, Ma was crying. She swiped her tears away. "I just don't know what to say."

"This news isn't sad. It's a joy. I help people with my plants. You know this. It's my calling. I can feel it deep in my bones." She paused. "Think about all the folks I've helped so far. Just think about what I could do, what the Lord could allow me to do, if I went to college to study about plants."

"Honey, I don't know about this."

The door swung open, the rusty hinges creaking. Timothy stood in the doorway, holding Lily's hand. The sunlight splashed onto him, highlighting his good looks. She certainly could get used to seeing him in her kitchen every morning.

His eyes pierced right through her. She gulped and pressed her hands together.

"Good morning." He spoke the words to both her and Ma, but he looked directly at her.

"Good morning." Thank God she didn't sound as nervous as she felt.

"Daddy, aren't we going to go in?" Lily tugged at her father's hand.

"Come on over here, honey." Ma beckoned to Lily. The girl hugged her grandma before hugging Deborah.

He glanced at her and her ma. It wouldn't surprise her if he realized they'd been in the middle of a serious discussion.

Pa strolled through the open doorway and they all took a seat at the table. After they'd said grace and enjoyed bowls of hot oatmeal laced with milk, butter, and molasses, and had consumed the hot biscuits and coffee, Timothy wiped his mouth with a napkin and stood up. He looked at Deborah, surprising her with his warm smile. "Since this is Lily's first day at school, I thought I'd walk the two of you to the schoolhouse and make sure she gets settled in properly."

Whoa, she didn't want the students to see them strolling together to school. Some of her students would mistakenly think he was her beau, wouldn't they? She pushed the thought from her mind. Timothy was Lily's father, and it wouldn't raise suspicion for him to accompany his daughter to class for her first day of school. She was worrying for nothing. "Fine. Let me get my things." After she'd gathered her dinner pail and placed her schoolbooks in her satchel, she tied her bonnet on her head and stepped outside.

Timothy strolled down the wooded path beside her. The strong scent of soap and hay wafted from him as they walked down the path. Lily skipped ahead of them. Timothy turned and looked at her. "Is your ma still upset?"

"Yes." She took a deep breath as he focused on the trees for a few seconds. The sun splashed from the vivid blue sky as puffy white clouds moved in the heavens. A right beautiful day, but she'd enjoy it more if she didn't have so much on her mind. "She wasn't mad, but a bit sad because she doesn't understand." She didn't want to confide to Timothy all that she'd discussed with her ma that morning.

"But you're still going to college?" The urgency in his tone made her pause. He really wanted her to fulfill her dreams. She could hear it in his voice. She finally nodded as they approached the schoolhouse.

"Yes. Even if Ma and Pa object, I'm still going. As long as I pass the entrance exam and I have enough money, I'll go."

He stopped walking. Lily had run toward the schoolhouse when she spotted her new friend Abigail. The twosome held hands as they picked wildflowers. "Then let me help you study," he said. "Do you think the folks in town will gossip if they discover that we're spending time together? Are you afraid that it may be upsetting for you and your family since I'm Eve's widower?"

Truth be told, she did feel a bit unsettled about spending so much time alone with her sister's husband. Every time she looked at Lily, she was reminded of her sister's beauty and charm. She sighed. She was highly bothered by her attraction to him. She didn't want him to know the real reason she hesitated. She liked him, plain and simple, but she couldn't let him know that.

"No, I don't think the folks in town would gossip."

"Well, from what I've heard, most college entrance exams are hard. I know mine was. Let me help you. I've often heard that some folks have to take the exam multiple times before they are admitted to college." She widened her eyes and pushed her spectacles up on her nose. She hadn't realized that the exam would be that hard. Could she really ignore her strong attraction to Timothy while he assisted her in studying for the exam? *Lord, can I do this? Should I do this?* She glanced at the children playing in the schoolyard.

"All right."

He grinned, giving her a nice view of his perfect white teeth. Heaven help her, Timothy was even more attractive when he smiled. She needed to be sure he understood something. "We can study together for a little while. If I find that I study better on my own. . ."

His eyes sparkled with warmth. "Deborah, if my studying with you causes a problem, then we can stop. Deal?"

"Deal." They shook hands. Her slender hand was dwarfed in his large one, and he continued to smile as they strolled toward the schoolhouse. Surprisingly, he walked up the steps with her into the building. He even escorted her to her desk. She then opened the top drawer of her desk and saw her book.

"Timothy, look! My book is here!" She pulled the book out of the drawer and found a note of apology tucked inside. The crudely scrawled note had obviously been penned by one of her younger students. There was no signature, but she didn't care. She was just glad that she had her book back.

"Deborah, that's wonderful. We can start studying together tonight after supper."

As she watched Timothy walk away from the schoolhouse, she hoped she was making the right decision.

๑ Chapter 7 ๑

"Class is dismissed." She grinned when her pupils whooped as they retrieved their dinner pails and the rest of their belongings. She was so glad it was Friday evening and the first two weeks of school were officially over. She'd spent the afternoon teaching the children arithmetic by splitting them into groups for a game. Each group took their turn at the chalkboard, and the one in the group who figured out the answer to the question first won the round. Then the winners from each group competed against each other. It had proven to be a great way to spend a Friday afternoon with her pupils. They'd been restless, anxious for the weekend break.

She'd also encouraged them to start studying plants, if they wished. She had some old canning jars on the windowsill. She'd filled the jars with water, and the children could bring in any plants they thought were interesting. She would then find the names of the plants in her botany book. It would be good for the children to know the names of the different plants that grew around their town.

"Are you ready?" Timothy entered her classroom and gave her a warm smile.

She smiled back at him. "Yes, just give me a minute to gather my things."

"Hi, Daddy." Lily hugged her father.

Over the last couple of weeks, Lily had been shy but was slowly making friends. So far, she seemed to get along well with Abigail, and that was refreshing. Deborah had been worried about her when she'd initially started school, but now she seemed to be settling in quite well.

"Hello, Lily." He kissed his daughter's cheek before approaching Deborah at the desk. Oh, how she wished he'd kiss her on the cheek, or the lips for that matter.

She tried to calm the fluttery feeling in the pit of her stomach. "I brought the wagon with me, just as you asked me to." He gestured behind her desk. "You received a lot of pumpkins from your students."

She eyed the pumpkins that had been given to her over the past week. Some of the farmers grew pumpkins on their farms, and each year they gave her some of the bounty. She and Ma would be canning pumpkins and making pumpkin pies this weekend. Just thinking about eating the pumpkin treats made her mouth water. She made the best pumpkin pie, and she longed to share one with Timothy and Lily.

"Yes, thank you. I'm grateful that my students give me pumpkins, since Pa doesn't grow them on the farm."

He chuckled. Oh, how she loved to hear Timothy laugh. They'd been studying every night for two weeks and had gotten into a slow, easy routine of studying. She'd found that having him help her really did prove beneficial to her learning. They'd been steadily making their way through the study manual, and come exam time, she'd be more than ready to take the exam, Lord willing. "Why are you laughing?"

"Because I have more pumpkins back at your house. I gave them to your ma this morning."

She raised her eyebrows. "Really?"

"Yes. Folks have been paying me for my medical skills with pumpkins and other squashes."

In their town, a lot of the folks didn't always have money to pay the doctor. She recalled that Doc Smith used to accept payment in the form of livestock, fruit, and vegetables.

After they'd loaded the pumpkins into the wagon and she and Lily had gotten settled in for the short ride home, she thought about all that had occurred since she finally agreed to let Timothy help her study for the entrance exam. Her ma continued complaining about her plans to attend college, but Deborah had learned not to focus too much on her ma's negative words. Her pa, usually quiet and reserved, had actually given her his blessing. And then Ma had gotten mad at Pa for encouraging Deborah. Even though her decision caused disharmony between her parents, she still felt that the Lord wanted her to attend college.

Deborah's home life had been very different since Timothy and Lily came to town. Seeing Timothy every day for meals with her family while she bonded with her niece had added some joy to her life.

As Timothy guided the horses, she thought about other things that had happened over the last two weeks. The first evening she'd studied with Timothy in the room next to the barn, with her cat Susie as company, her ma had had a conniption. "It just isn't right for you to be alone with him for so long in the evening. If you're really going to pursue this foolish notion, then you and Timothy need to do your studying right here in the house, at this kitchen table."

Deborah had been hurt that her ma referred to her college degree as a "foolish notion." However, she agreed. She needed to study with Timothy at the kitchen table. Since her aspirations were no longer a secret, she didn't have to hide out in the barn to study.

As Timothy steered the wagon toward her home, he cleared his throat. "Unless a patient needs to see me, I should be able to accompany you and your parents to church this Sunday." For the last couple of Sundays Timothy had been treating patients and had been unable to attend church.

"That sounds nice. We have a wonderful pastor. I'm sure you'll enjoy the sermon." She'd attended church with Pa, Ma, and Lily over the last couple of weeks. The thought of attending church with Timothy excited her.

Eve shoved the dishes into the tub of hot, soapy water. She shook her head, her movements quick with anger as she washed the dishes. "How could you be smitten with Deborah? My sister doesn't want to marry. Besides, if it weren't for your incompetence, I'd be alive right now. It's your fault that I'm dead, Timothy." Her loud voice exploded in the kitchen right before she pushed the tub of water toward him. "Get away from me." Her dark eyes sparked with

anger and she stomped out of the room.

Timothy jerked awake. He pushed off the sweaty, tangled mass of sheets and rolled out of bed. Groaning, he poured a cup of water from the pitcher. The cool liquid slid down his parched throat. He'd had the dream. . .again. It was the same as always, except this time Eve had mentioned Deborah. Just hearing her accusations, her pain, sliced right to the core of his heart. *Lord, are You trying to tell me something? Why would I dream about this now?* In his dream, Eve had looked just as she always looked whenever they had an argument. They'd done a lot of arguing during their tumultuous marriage. Her angry words had been hurled at him like the stone that David had slung toward Goliath.

He lamented about the terrible dream as he donned his clothes for church. He pulled his recently polished shoes onto his feet. "Are you ready, Lily?" His daughter got dressed herself, but Mama June and Deborah would usually check to make sure her hair looked presentable before she left for school or church.

Deborah. She'd been dominating his mind lately. And now his dream about Eve. . . He didn't know if he should give the dream further thought, but it was hard to forget Eve's cold, cruel anger in the dream.

"Yes, Daddy, I'm ready." Lily's voice interrupted his thoughts. His daughter grinned, showing a gap where she'd recently lost a tooth. After they ate some cold biscuits, they exited the house. As they walked toward Deborah's home, he thought about how his life had changed over the last couple of weeks.

He'd been studying every night with Deborah. He'd also seen Mama June's open disapproval regarding her daughter's educational goal. He'd wanted to try to reason with Mama June, but he sensed that Deborah didn't want him to interfere in her relationship with her parents. It bothered him whenever she frowned, upset about her ma's disapproval. He sighed as he continued walking toward Deborah's house. With startling clarity, he realized that he enjoyed spending time with Deborah. They'd developed an easy camaraderie while they worked together. She always smelled nice too. Sometimes she smelled like peppermint. Other times she smelled of basil or wildflowers. Whenever she was concentrating, trying to figure out an answer, she'd bite her lower lip and scrunch her eyebrows together.

Heaven help him, whenever she came up with the correct answer or got excited about learning something new, the urge to kiss her consumed him. He liked working with her, but he also felt guilty. Eve had been dead for a year. Was it wrong for him to have feelings for her twin sister? Was Eve looking down from heaven right now, frowning because he was falling for Deborah?

"Hi, Timothy." Deborah greeted him from the door, giving him a smile as warm as sunshine. She looked fetching in her yellow bonnet and brown dress. He resisted the urge to take her hand and hold her in his arms.

"Good morning."

She frowned. "What's wrong? You look upset."

Was it so obvious? He mentally sighed. No way could he let her know that the dream he'd had the previous night was haunting him. "Just had trouble sleeping last night. Are all of you ready to go to church?"

"Yes, we're ready." After he, Lily, Mama June, Papa Daniel, and Deborah had settled in the wagon, he flicked the reins to steer the horses toward the school building. The town was so small that the schoolhouse doubled as the church. As they got out of the wagon and made their way toward the steps, he again resisted the urge to hold Deborah's hand. She walked beside him, her gentle peppermint scent wafting toward him.

"Excuse me, Doctor?" a loud voice called from behind him. He turned around and spotted one of the most beautiful women he'd ever seen in his entire life. Her long dark hair curled and shimmered in the sunlight, and her light brown eyes were fringed with long lashes. She wore a fancy brown dress and carried a parasol. He couldn't imagine why she'd need a parasol on this cool autumn morning.

"Yes?" Before focusing on the beautiful lady again, he quickly glanced behind him and realized that Deborah, her parents, and Lily had already gone into the school.

"I'm Clara Blue, and this is my ma, Mildred Blue." He then noticed the short, becoming woman standing beside Clara. He shook both of their hands and dipped his head. "Pleased to make your acquaintance. I'm Timothy Washington."

Clara giggled and fingered his shirt. "Oh, we *know* who you are, Doctor. I haven't seen you at church since you came to town. I was wondering why you hadn't yet shown up to serve the Lord." The slight disapproval in her voice made him pause. Taken aback by the comment, he didn't respond.

"My daughter is eighteen, Doctor, and is still learning how to converse well with others. I'm afraid she sometimes forgets her manners."

No harm done. He really needed to get inside the church. "Again, I'm pleased to meet both of you. I need to go into the church to sit with my family."

"Oh Doctor," Clara whined. "Why don't you sit with me and my ma? We'd love to have you sit with us, and maybe you can come over for dinner afterward. We're having fried chicken, apple pie, and buttermilk biscuits."

Fried chicken and apple pie sounded nice, but he honestly didn't think he could stomach sitting beside Clara for an entire afternoon and hearing her whiny voice. Plus, she smelled like a perfume bath. The smell proved almost too much for him to handle. She didn't have the nice gentle smell of peppermint and wildflowers like Deborah. He mentally shook his head. Now why did he have to go and compare Clara to Deborah?

Well, he had to be a gentleman. He escorted Clara and her ma into the school. He glanced around the crowded room. Deborah and her parents and Lily sat on a bench near the front—no empty seat for him. He frowned. Why didn't Deborah save him a seat?

"Doctor, come sit with us." Clara issued the command before patting the empty spot on the bench beside her. Well, it appeared he didn't have a choice. He sat beside Clara and her ma while the pastor began the service.

After the congregation sang a few hymns, he struggled to listen to the pastor as he preached about Christian charity. He mentioned that Stephen advocated for the widows and children, making sure they had enough food. Timothy enjoyed the pastor's message. He'd not yet formally met the preacher, so he needed to be sure to do so after the service was over.

In spite of the preacher's eloquent message, he eagerly waited for the sermon to end. He felt sick. It was Clara's strong perfume, he was sure of it. The pungent smell was making him ill, and the urge to get away from her consumed him. After the sermon and prayer, Clara tugged on his sleeve. "Doctor, I have a headache. Could you please come this afternoon?" She then told him how to get to her home.

"Clara." Stark disapproval tinged her ma's voice. Why was her ma so upset?

Taken aback, speechless, he looked directly at Clara. Now he understood why her ma sounded so angry. Clara's eyes sparkled with good health, and he highly doubted she had a headache. No way was he falling for this woman's shenanigans. "Perhaps you should lie down when you arrive home."

Clara sniffed as if she had a runny nose. "Please, Doctor?"

"Clara." Mildred Blue glared at her daughter.

What could he do? He'd just met Clara. What if she really was ill? He squeezed his eyes shut. *Lord, please help me.* Folks were slowly filtering out of the church. He overheard them talking about rushing home to eat their Sunday dinner. He figured Deborah and the rest of the family would be waiting for him at the wagon. He focused on Mildred Blue. Somehow, that seemed like the safest thing to do. "I have to go and get my bag. I'll be there as soon as I can."

◈ Chapter 8 ◈

I just can't believe I'm being courted by the new doctor."
Clara's strong voice resonated in the mercantile. She obviously
wanted everyone to hear what she had to say. Deborah pursed
her lips and rolled her eyes. Clara's voice was so loud, she
sounded like a town crier. Deborah highly doubted Timothy
was courting Clara, but he had quickly fallen in love with beautiful Eve, so she could imagine his being smitten with pretty
Clara. Clara was in the back of the store, probably talking to
one of her friends. The woman loved socializing—she reminded
Deborah of Eve so much—and that was probably why Timothy was attracted to her.

He'd spent the last two Sunday afternoons at Clara's house.
The first time Clara had had a headache, of all things! The second
Sunday, Clara's ma, Mildred, had been ill. Deborah had known
both ladies for years. Mildred really had been sick. Apparently,
Timothy had given her some medicine and Clara had served
him dinner. Since Mildred had to stay in bed for a few days

because of her illness, Timothy had had to go to Clara's home to treat her ma. She'd hardly call *that* courting someone.

Deborah had continued studying with Timothy, and they were making progress. However, he'd been reserved and quiet, and not nearly as friendly as he used to be. She had so many questions to ask him, but she just didn't have the courage to do so.

"Can I help you?" An unfamiliar woman spoke to her from across the mercantile. She looked to be about the same age as Deborah, and she smiled widely.

"Good afternoon. I don't believe I've met you before?" She approached the woman, curious. She'd known the owners of the mercantile for years, and she'd not heard that they'd sold their store.

"I'm Lucy. The owners recently hired me to work in the store."

"I need help," Clara commanded from the counter. Looked like she'd finished her conversation with the woman she'd been speaking to earlier. Clara nodded at Deborah. "Hello, Deborah."

Deborah returned the nod. "Hello, Clara. Nice weather we're having."

"Well, it's been a mite too cold for me." There'd been a definite cool autumn snap in the air, hinting at the forthcoming winter. Deborah loved the cool autumn mornings, but she didn't think it was wise to tell Clara that she enjoyed the changing weather. At times, when someone disagreed with Clara, the woman had a fit and wouldn't stop arguing until everyone agreed she was right.

Lucy approached the counter to help Clara select fabric, and Deborah continued browsing the shelves. She needed coffee, more chalk for school, flour, oatmeal. . . Her ma needed so many things. It had been a good long while since they'd been to the mercantile, and she'd been so unsettled lately, an outing seemed like a nice idea for a Saturday afternoon. After Clara had taken her exit, Lucy again approached Deborah. "Did you need help finding anything?"

"No, thank you, I think I've found everything I need." She placed her items on the counter. "My ma goes through a lot of flour when she makes her hand pies."

Lucy grinned. "I've heard about your ma's delicious hand pies. I'll need to try one."

"You should. They're the best pies I've ever tasted."

Lucy gestured toward Deborah's merchandise. "I'll get somebody to carry that to your wagon." The woman hesitated and bit her lip. "How about sitting with me for a spell and having a cup of coffee? I'm new in town and don't know anybody yet." Deborah paused, mentally sighing. She really wanted to get home and get some studying done this afternoon. She wanted to be ready when Timothy quizzed her after supper. "I don't mean to keep you. Just being friendly is all."

Well, why not? There was nothing wrong with being friendly. Her ma was always chastising her about spending too much time alone. She was sure Ma would be thrilled that she'd shared coffee with the new mercantile worker. "Yes, I'd love a cup of coffee." She and Lucy strolled to the back of the store where Lucy settled into the seat across from her. Deborah sipped her coffee. "So, where are you from?"

"Maryland. Just arrived almost a week ago. My husband died in the war."

Deborah set down her cup. "I'm so sorry." Her town had lost a number of men in the war against slavery.

Lucy waved the comment away. "It happens. I still miss him. We never had any little ones, so I'm sad about that. I'm thirty, and don't take kindly to the men who've courted me since my Stanley died. I'll probably never marry again." Lucy sipped her coffee. "How about you?"

Lucy seemed so open and friendly. The urge to tell her about Timothy, Eve, and her dream of going to the women's college swelled within her. For some reason, she liked that Lucy was thirty, a little bit older than she, and was unaware of her reputation as the town's spinster schoolteacher. Unable to resist, she told Lucy about her history with Timothy, Eve's death, Timothy's return to town, and his apparent "courtship" with Clara. Lucy listened intently, in spite of the fact that they were interrupted by customers. After she'd finished talking with Lucy, Deborah felt better. Sharing her feelings, her dreams, with someone felt refreshing.

Lucy poured them fresh cups of coffee. She appeared to be weighing her words, pondering. Even though she'd just met Lucy, Deborah sensed that she was wise and sensible. She pulled out her pocket watch and realized that she'd been sitting there talking to Lucy for two hours! She honestly couldn't recall the last time she'd had such a long conversation with someone. Truth be told, the last time she'd spoken to anyone at such length was with her ma, pa, or Eve.

"So, Deborah, your twin sister, Eve?"

"Yes?"

"Was she a kind person?"

Such an odd question. Deborah paused, unsure of how to respond. "Eve was just. . .Eve. Talkative, friendly. Like I mentioned, we were not alike at all."

Lucy touched her hand. "Just think about it. When you told me about how you used to spend time with Timothy and then he started courting Eve, I felt the need to ask you that. You don't have to answer the question if you don't want to." She frowned. "You mentioned that Timothy has been quiet lately?"

"Yes."

"He might be feeling guilty about his feelings for you because of your sister, Eve. He might feel that he's being unfaithful to her." She shrugged. "I know that seems strange since Eve has passed away, but I'm familiar with such feelings because I'm a widow myself. Even though I never had particularly romantic notions for the few men who've courted me since Stanley's death, I still felt like I was doing something wrong when I was courted by a man. It might take Timothy some time to get used to feeling romantic for somebody other than Eve."

Oh, Lucy must not have understood everything she'd just said. "But he doesn't have romantic feelings for me—"

"I think he does, from what you're telling me." Lucy shrugged. "Of course, I could be wrong, but. . ." She shrugged again. "I think he likes you, and that's one reason he wants to help you. He knows that going to college will make you happy, and he wants you to be happy."

Deborah raised her eyebrows. "Lucy, I don't know about that."

"You mentioned Clara." Lucy changed the subject. "He's not courting her. I don't think he even likes her, not romantically. Clara has been coming into this store every day for the past week. She usually waits until another woman shows up in the store, and then she starts boasting about the doctor being her new beau. She wants attention, and I think she's stretching this out to get as much attention as she can. I think she knows that in a matter of time folks will realize the doctor is not courting her."

Now that was no surprise. "Even though they're not officially courting, I think he still might find her attractive."

Lucy took a sip of her coffee then said, "Yes, he might. Most men would find Clara attractive, but that doesn't mean they'd want to court her." She tapped her fingers against a nearby barrel of pickles. "My advice to you would be to simply ask Timothy."

Deborah blinked. "Ask him what?"

"Simply ask him about why he's been so quiet lately. Sometimes you've got to just come right out and ask a man what's wrong. Do your ma and pa always listen in on you and Timothy when you study in the kitchen?"

"Yes. They're right in the next room."

"Well, take him out on the porch. Serve him some of your ma's hand pies. Have a nice chat alone and ask him if something's bothering him. Tell him that you're concerned and would like to help him—same as he's helping you. Do that and see what he says."

Deborah pondered Lucy's words as Lucy got a delivery boy to help load her supplies into the wagon. Right before she flicked the reins, she paused. "Lucy, would you like to come to my home tomorrow for Sunday dinner?" She'd just made a new friend, and it would be nice to have someone to converse with during the family meal. Besides, if she wanted to be honest with herself, she wanted her new friend to meet Timothy. She appreciated Lucy's insight, and she loved being able to talk to someone about all that had been bothering her lately.

Lucy grinned. "I'd be much obliged, Deborah."

ᕽ Chapter 9 ᕽ

*T*imothy clutched his bag as he strolled toward the schoolhouse. He'd been dreaming about Eve almost every night for the last two weeks. In spite of his bad dreams, he still craved spending time with Deborah. They were three quarters of the way through the book for her exam. If their pace continued and if Deborah continued learning as well as she had, he thought she'd be ready to take the test.

He'd been shocked the previous day when Deborah's family had a guest for Sunday dinner. No, not Deborah's family—Deborah had a dinner guest. Lucy, a new worker at the mercantile, was now Deborah's friend. It had been strange but refreshing to see Deborah talking companionably with another female. She seemed happier, not so worried about the exam. She'd been studying so hard, it was possible her confidence was built up and she was no longer fearful about not passing the exam. For some reason, Deborah and Lucy seemed to get along superbly. Lily also seemed to take to Lucy. She showed Lucy her doll and told her about her friend Abigail.

Deborah had been full of surprises. When Lucy had gone home after Sunday dinner, Deborah said she wanted to walk him and Lily home. On the way to his house, she'd asked him to come and speak to her students about his medical career the next day. She said she wanted her students, especially her female students, to study and perhaps go to college if they could. She was trying to let them know that it was all right to be intelligent. She'd even hinted that she might want to start a lending library in town. She said they might be able to keep spare books in the back room of the schoolhouse. Seeing her enthusiasm warmed his heart. When they reached his home, he'd again been tempted to kiss her, but of course he didn't act on his feelings. *Lord, what am I going to do?*

He approached the schoolhouse. It was unseasonably warm for a late October day, and he spotted the partially open door of the schoolhouse. He stopped for a few seconds, thinking. He wiped the sweat from his brow as he made his way up the stairs. Deborah's voice, sweet and clear, drifted from the room.

"So, class, what is this plant called?"

"Goldenrod," one of her pupils answered.

"How about this one?"

"Queen Anne's lace," another pupil responded.

She continued quizzing the children about the plants. Her science plant project had been a huge success, and he was glad the children seemed enthusiastic about it. Should he go in and interrupt them? He gently pushed the door, and the squeaky hinges announced his arrival. Deborah looked up from the chalkboard, directly into his eyes. "Class, Dr. Timothy Washington is here.

Say hello. He'll be talking to us about what it was like for him to become a doctor."

"Hello, Doctor Timothy," the children chorused. Lily gave him a small, gap-toothed grin and waved. He waved back at her and gave her a quick wink.

He smiled at the rest of the class. "Good afternoon." He strolled toward the front of the classroom. He resisted the urge to kiss Deborah's smooth brown cheek as he set his medical bag on her desk. "Miss King asked me to talk to you about my job as a medical doctor. I thought I could show you some of the things in my medical bag." He grinned at the class as he opened his bag. "You can ask me questions if you wish."

He removed several vials of powders. "I use these powders to help patients with pain. Some can heal illnesses."

One of the older children raised his hand. "Which one of them powders do you use the most?"

Deborah cleared her throat as she focused on the child who'd asked the question. "Remember to use proper English. Which one of *those* powders do you use the most."

The boy nodded. "Sorry. Which one of those powders do you use the most?"

"White willow bark. It's an excellent remedy for headaches."

"Is that what you gave Miss Clara for her headache? I heard her tell you she had a headache one time at church." One of the youngest female pupils, sitting in the front row, asked the question.

His eyes widened at the bold question. Deborah narrowed her eyes at the girl. "Now, Sarah, you know you should raise your hand before asking a question. And it's not polite to ask people personal questions."

Sarah raised her hand. "What's a personal question?"

He eyed Deborah. She folded her slender arms across her chest and tapped her booted foot. She looked annoyed, and he suddenly had even more respect for schoolteachers. He figured it wasn't an easy job to teach a roomful of children every day. She kept her eyes on the student who'd asked the question. "A personal question is a question that most folks might not want to answer."

"But—"

"Does anybody else have a question?" She didn't seem to want to give nosy Sarah any opportunity to ask another question.

One of the older students in the back row raised his hand. "How did you become a doctor?"

Good question. He looked at the student. "What's your name, young man?"

"John, sir."

Timothy smiled at him. "I'm glad you asked that, John. My parents. . ." He paused, unsure how to address the fact that he was a Negro who'd had wealthy parents. Well, he'd be truthful without boasting. "My parents owned a business. After they passed away, they left me with enough money to go to school to study medicine. I'm sure some of you remember Doctor Smith?" Several of the children nodded. "After my schooling, I studied under Doctor Smith as an apprentice." He paused for a few seconds and removed a few more items out of his bag. "After studying with Doctor Smith, I got married and moved away and started a practice. I returned here with my daughter, Lily"—he gestured toward his daughter—"after my wife passed away."

The children were respectfully silent. He took the rest of the items from his bag. "This is my stethoscope." He focused on the younger children. "Does anyone want to listen to a heartbeat?" All of the children's hands shot into the air like bullets. He laughed and glanced at Deborah, who also smiled. He ached to touch the cute dimple on her left cheek. "Is it all right if I show them? I don't want to impose on your teaching time." He asked her the question in a low voice.

"It's fine, Timothy." When she said his name, it sounded sweet, like golden honey. He quickly focused on the stethoscope again. He didn't want the children to see him ogling their pretty teacher. He spent the next hour patiently letting each student listen to each other's heartbeat. Afterward, he showed them his magnifying glass. He then showed the class another item. "This is a lancet."

"Do you cut people open with that?" One of the younger children boldly asked the question without raising his hand.

"I use it to draw blood."

"Why?" another child asked.

"Sometimes I have to draw blood to make a person feel better." He then showed the rest of the items in his medical bag to the students. His stomach growled. It must be dinnertime. He didn't realize that he'd spoken for so long.

"Class, it's dinnertime. I want all of you to thank Doctor Washington for speaking to us."

"Thank you, Doctor Washington." The entire class echoed their appreciation.

"You're dismissed for dinner," Deborah announced. The class scurried toward the door for nooning, grabbing their dinner pails.

Timothy placed the items he'd been showing the class back into his medical bag. "Timothy?" Deborah approached him with her dinner pail.

"Yes?"

"Would you like to sit on the front steps with me? I had a few questions about some of the material in my botany book."

"Of course." He escorted her to the front steps. He thought it would be best to sit in plain view of the students while they talked since the schoolmarm wasn't allowed to have a beau.

They sat on the bottom step. She looked a bit nervous. . . nervous and rather fetching in her yellow bonnet and brown dress. The subtle scent of peppermint wafted toward him.

A breeze blew, tossing multicolored leaves through the air. The echo of children's voices and laughter floated toward them as Deborah opened her botany book. "The floral formula. It makes sense to me, I think." He smiled at her. She probably understood the formula perfectly; she just needed someone to study it with her.

Abigail and Lily ran toward them, swinging their dinner pails. Abigail stopped and grinned while she traced the sketched flower in the book. "What are you doing?"

Lily quietly stood beside Abigail. She seemed quite happy that he'd visited her class that day. "I'm helping Miss King study the floral formula."

Lily leaned toward the book and touched the drawing of the flower. "What's a formula?"

Deborah squeezed Lily's shoulder. "That's a good question, Lily. A formula represents something." She pointed to the letters and symbols in the book. "These letters and symbols tell us about the different parts of a flower. For example, the formula for a rose would be different than the formula for a tulip. Both of those flowers have different scents, different petals. . ."

Abigail continued staring at the page. "I don't understand."

Lily smiled. "I think I do."

Abigail looked at Lily. "You do?"

"I don't know. . . ." Lily looked toward an oak tree in the distance. His daughter was still so quiet. It was refreshing to hear her speak her opinion about something.

He smiled at her. "Go ahead and finish what you were going to say."

"I don't understand what's in the book, but. . .I think I understand that this"—she pointed to the formula—"will be different for another flower."

Abigail stood up straight. "Well, I'm hungry. Let's go eat, Lily." The twosome rushed toward the large oak tree in the schoolyard.

Timothy grinned and looked at Deborah, who was smiling as well. "You're setting a good example for Lily. Maybe when she grows up, she'll want to go to college too. I'm glad you're her teacher."

Deborah grinned as she pushed her spectacles up on her nose. "Thank you, Timothy." She pointed to the book. "Can we study this for a few minutes?"

"Of course."

While they went over the formula, they were interrupted a few times by the younger students. Once they were finished, she shut the book and placed it on the step between them.

"Doctor!" A young man stormed toward them. Timothy

recognized him as one of the Thompson brothers who lived on a farm near the school with their widowed father. "My pa needs your help really bad. He's sick something awful. He's got spots all over him. He's real sick, Doctor."

Timothy's heart pounded with fear. The man's condition sounded serious. "Deborah, I have to go." He quickly grabbed his medical bag. Minutes later, the two men sprinted onto the Thompson property. The young man ran into the house with Timothy behind him. "My pa's back here."

Timothy eyed the older man lying on the bed moaning. His speckled skin and red eyes made Timothy's heart lurch with dread. He opened his medical bag. "Where does it hurt?" He made sure his voice was gentle as he asked the question.

The man coughed. "My throat. . .hurts bad." Timothy touched the man's forehead. He burned with fever.

"Open your mouth." The white lesions in the man's mouth made Timothy wince inwardly. The man closed his eyes and moaned. He was obviously not in any shape for conversation. He turned toward the man's son. "How long has he been sick? Has he traveled anywhere recently?"

"He took a long trip. Was gone to Philadelphia for a couple of weeks. He got back a week ago. Been sick for five days."

"Why didn't you come get me when he started feeling ill?" He couldn't help the urgent tone of his voice—people's lives were in danger.

"My pa don't like seeing the doctor. He said it would go away. But it didn't. It got worse. When I saw them red spots, that's when I went to get you. Someone told me you was at the school, so that's why I rushed there to get you."

"Has he been in contact with anybody besides you and your brothers since he's been back?"

"I'm not sure."

"Well, think." Timothy's loud voice echoed in the room. The young man's eyes widened and his Adam's apple bobbed as he swallowed. Timothy needed to be sure the young man understood the severity of the situation. "I need to know who your father has seen since he's been back. Who has he visited? I need to know if you and your brothers have visited or seen anybody since your pa's been back in town."

"Why?"

"Because your pa has the measles. I don't want you or any of your brothers to leave this farm for any reason—unless you need to get me if your pa gets worse."

The young man hesitated, paced the room. "Come to think of it, he went to the store a few times. My pa's got a lot of friends. He's visited a lot of farms since he's been back."

Well, it appeared he didn't have a choice. He focused on the young man. "This entire town is going to be put under a twenty-one-day quarantine."

~ Chapter 10 ~

*D*eborah!" Timothy's strong voice echoed from outside the classroom, interrupting her long-division lesson. Something was terribly wrong. Mr. Thompson must be drastically ill. *Lord, please be with Mr. Thompson. Help him to heal.* "Children, stay in here and continue with your work." She rushed outside the building and slammed the door. Timothy stood in the schoolyard. "Deborah, wait, don't come closer, not yet."

"What's wrong?" She stood at the bottom of the steps.

"Mr. Thompson has the measles. We need to quarantine the town. Ask the children if any of them have been near Mr. Thompson or his sons. Let me know if any of them have. You need to send the children home, and we need to let everyone know that they need to stay on their own property for twenty-one days."

Deborah rushed back into the school. She needed to hurry and do what Timothy had asked. *Oh Lord, we really need Your help right now.*

Deborah quickly gathered all of the dried and fresh herbs that she could fit into her case. Timothy stood right behind her. "Deborah, we have to hurry. We can come back to get more if needed."

She couldn't argue with him. She got into his wagon, mulling over how much had happened since their noontime chat on the school steps had been interrupted earlier that day. After Timothy had made his announcement, it had been discovered that five of the children had been in direct contact with the Thompson family. Three of the children had said that their ma or pa had been feeling poorly the last few days. She'd noted their names, and all of the children had left in chaos. Some of them had been frightened, and some had been ecstatic about their twenty-one-day hiatus.

Timothy flicked the reins as they made their way to the first home on their list, and Deborah continued to think about all that had occurred. For once in her life, she thanked God for an illness she'd had in the past. She, Timothy, and her ma and pa had already had the measles.

They'd caught them when Eve insisted that they travel to Philadelphia for her wedding. Eve had always been one to put on airs. They'd contracted measles during that visit and all of them had survived. Deborah knew they could not catch the dreaded disease again. However, Timothy was concerned about Lily. Although he knew that he was immune, he was unsure about his treating other victims and then coming into contact with his daughter. Could Lily catch the disease if she were around him?

He needed to make sure he protected her.

They decided that Lily would stay with Ma, quarantined on their farm. Deborah and Pa would stay with Timothy, since Timothy would need Deborah's help while treating the victims. She knew it would be downright awful if it were discovered that the unmarried schoolteacher was staying with the town's doctor, which was why Pa would be staying with them. Pa and Timothy would share a room and Deborah would sleep in Lily's room.

They returned to the Thompson farm first, because one of the brothers sent word that he was feeling sick. When they entered the room, Deborah paid attention as Timothy checked the young man's eyes, ears, and mouth and listened to his heartbeat. The man did not yet have a rash. However, he did have a fever. "How do you feel?" Timothy's deep, kind voice echoed in the room.

"My throat hurts and my eyes hurt."

Timothy touched the man's forehead and felt his throat. "You probably caught the measles from your pa. I'll be praying for you. You'll be seeing a red rash on your skin within the next few days." He removed a packet of white powder from his bag. "You need to take this white willow bark for your pain." He told him how much he needed to take. "Make sure you drink lots of water."

Deborah placed a cool cloth over the man's eyes. "I made a mixture of peppermint oil, lavender, salt, and some of my herbs. If your skin itches, you can put the mixture on your skin. It might help you."

All they could do was keep the patients comfortable. From what Timothy had told her, the disease had to run its course.

She recalled the itchy red rash she'd endured shortly after Eve's wedding. *Lord, please help them feel better.* Hopefully, everyone would survive without aftereffects. They made sure the rest of the brothers knew how to care for their two patients.

They visited several infected homes throughout that first night, Timothy giving instructions to the families. When they returned to Timothy's home, Deborah yawned. She'd never felt so tired in her entire life. The sun was just starting to rise, and Pa had left hard-boiled eggs on the table for them. Too tired to eat, Deborah fell onto the mattress in Lily's room and fell asleep.

Over the next twenty-one days, Timothy and Deborah worked side by side, visiting the homes of the infected and treating the illness as best they could. As they worked together, she focused on leaving her herbs for the patients and explaining how they could use the herbs to relieve their painful, itchy skin.

After two weeks the rashes began to fade and the fevers broke. The townspeople wanted to break the quarantine, but Timothy had let them know in no uncertain terms that the afflicted were still contagious.

Since most of their patients had healed, Deborah finally felt that she could relax for a few days. She'd prepared a special dinner for Pa and Timothy. After the food had been laid on the table, Pa entered the kitchen. "Looks good. I'm hungry. Where's Timothy?"

"He's in his workroom. I'll go get him." Timothy had a workroom adjoining his house. As she walked outside, she recalled that Timothy had told her he needed to take stock of his supplies.

She stopped walking as soon as she heard his deep voice spilling from behind the closed door. To whom was he speaking? "Lord, thank You. I don't think I could've stood another person mercilessly dying because of me. Amen." Shocked, Deborah didn't know what to think about Timothy's prayer. He was a good, strong, caring doctor. Working with him over the past three weeks had made her see what a wonderful, godly man he was.

She thought about Timothy's prayer over the following day. Should she talk to him about it? The day before the school reopened, Deborah sat with Timothy on his porch. Pa was in the kitchen drinking a cup of coffee. Timothy glanced at her house across the field. "I miss Lily."

"So do I." She paused, biting her lip. "Actually, I miss all of my students." She took a deep breath, needing to speak what was on her mind. "Timothy, I want to ask you something. When I went to your workroom to fetch you for dinner the other day, I heard you praying." She took a deep breath. "I feel bad that I heard your private prayer to God, but I just feel that I need to ask you about it. When you prayed that nobody would die because of you, what did you mean?"

He sighed. His jaw tensed and he pressed his hands together as if he were in pain. She touched his shoulder. "Are you all right?"

"Yes." He paused. "I never told you about what I've been going through. . .with Eve."

She blinked, her heart skipping a beat. "You say that like Eve is still alive." She couldn't believe the words that had just come from his mouth.

He sighed again. "I've been having dreams."

She leaned toward him. "What kind of dreams?"

He told her about Eve's accusations in his dreams. "When Eve got sick. . .well, she'd been quiet, not been herself for a few days. She didn't tell me about her illness. By the time she told me, it had gotten worse. I tried to treat her, but it was too late. She died." His voice broke. "If I'd treated her sooner, I may have been able to save her."

She took a deep breath and touched his broad shoulder. "Timothy, I'm sorry." She stroked his shoulder while he swiped away his tears. She closed her eyes. *Lord, please be with Timothy. Help him understand that Eve's death was not his fault.* She pressed her hands together, tried to think of what to say. She thought about the conversation she'd had when she first met Lucy in the mercantile a few weeks ago. She'd asked her if Eve was kind and had told her to think about it. Deborah had been so busy with patients, assisting Timothy, that she hadn't really had time to give much thought to Lucy's question until now. "You know, Eve could have told you that she'd been feeling ill. It's not always up to you to guess the way a person is feeling, especially if the person is able to speak and has a clear mind."

"But I'm a doctor." He pointed to his chest with his index finger. "I should've known. She probably didn't want to tell me she was sick because she didn't want to bother me since I'd been working so hard."

Deborah shook her head. "Or she could've said something. Timothy, as a doctor, you know that people will die."

"But I don't want folks to die if I have the means to prevent it. I know I'll lose some patients, but if there's anything I can do to prevent them from dying, then I'll do what I have to do to keep that person alive."

Deborah sighed. She doubted she could convince Timothy that his reasoning was wrong. All she could do was hope and pray that somebody would be able to make him understand that he needed to stop blaming himself.

⊗ Chapter 11 ⊗

Deborah plopped down at the kitchen table, exhausted. Timothy and Lily had just left, going back to their home. School had started that day. She'd loved being in the classroom, and it had been nice to see the children again. After supper, Timothy had again helped her study for the exam. It would be given in two weeks, and even though they'd lost study time during the quarantine, she still felt ready to take it.

As she put her study manual and botany book away, she recalled the conversation she'd had with Timothy the previous evening. What he'd told her bothered her deep within her gut.

Again, she thought about Lucy's question, about Eve being kind. Had her sister been kind? She'd often thought of her twin as being self-centered. She'd thought Eve was like that since she was so beautiful, the same way Clara acted. But was she kind?

"Why are you looking so serious?" Ma came into the kitchen and settled into the empty chair beside her. "I'd think you'd be happy. You and Timothy worked hard to help care for the quarantine victims. Nobody died. You should be praising Jesus instead of looking sad. Are you upset about the exam? Deborah, just forget about that test."

"Ma, you know how I feel about going to college." She took a deep breath. Perhaps it would just take some time and patience for Ma to see reason and to really understand why she wanted to do this. "Ma, I wanted to ask you about Eve."

"What about her?"

"Do you think she was kind?"

"Kind? Deborah, why are you asking me this?"

She told her mother about her conversation with Lucy. Ma sighed. "I think Lucy asked you that question because you told her that you'd spent time with Timothy and then he started courting Eve."

"I never understood that. I really liked Timothy. He's so smart and handsome. I could have a long conversation with him about plants and science and not get bored. Then he just started courting Eve and didn't have time to spend with me anymore. It was so abrupt and sudden. . ." She jerked back, her eyes widening. "Ma, was Eve jealous because I was spending time with Timothy? Did she start flirting with him like Clara did? Ma, did Eve want to court Timothy simply because *I* was spending time with him?"

"Honey, we'll never know for sure—" Her ma looked away, toward the floor.

"Ma. . ." Deborah sighed. "That's why Lucy asked if she was kind. Eve only thought of herself. If Timothy hadn't been spending time with me, would Eve still have wanted him to court her?"

"Deborah, you know your sister," was all Ma would say.

After her ma had gone to bed, Deborah couldn't stop the thoughts tumbling in her head just like the leaves falling from the trees. If Timothy had truly had feelings for her eight years ago, then he shouldn't have been so easily swayed by Eve's charms. Lucy had said that Timothy wanted her to be happy. Maybe he felt guilty not only about Eve's death, but also about his actions eight years ago. Did he *really* enjoy spending time with her, or was he simply helping her to study for the exam to relieve his guilty conscience? *Oh Lord, if ever I needed Your help, it's now.*

Timothy eyed Deborah as they walked toward the tall redbrick building at the women's college where the test was being held. When they entered the building, they saw several women slowly strolling the long hallway, their footsteps echoing. Other ladies stood alone, open books in their hands. A lot of women had shown up to take the test.

Deborah was the only Negro.

Several of the women openly stared at her. Timothy ached to put his arm around her and let them know she had his support. He didn't know if his showing his affection right before the exam would bother her or not. He certainly didn't want to distract her right now.

"I can't believe a Negro is taking the test," one of the young ladies said, obviously wanting Deborah to hear her. This women's college had just admitted its first Negro students two years ago.

Deborah ignored the comment. She'd initially wanted to come alone, but Timothy wouldn't let her. Since the quarantine, she'd been quiet and reserved. He'd thought they were growing closer when they assisted the patients during those weeks, but it appeared things had changed since he'd told her about his dreams of Eve. He figured that was why she'd been quiet and moody. As she made her way into the testing room, he touched her hand. "I'll be praying for you."

"Thank you." She looked directly into his eyes. It almost seemed as if she wanted to say something else. He touched her cheek, and then she went into the room with the rest of the women who were taking the test.

Several of the women openly glared at her as the proctor handed out the test booklet. Choosing to ignore them, Deborah closed her eyes while she clutched her pen. *Lord, please help me do well on this test.* When the signal was given and she began reading the first question, Timothy's face popped into her mind. She recalled how he'd helped her study. For each question on the test, she thought about their studying at her kitchen table. She recalled his deep voice asking her some of these same questions from the book. She loved seeing the joy on his face whenever she got an answer correct. Knowing he was praying for her, even now, she continued through the test, finishing just before the proctor called out that time was up.

When Deborah exited the room after the test, she bit her lower lip, looking nervous. Timothy approached her as other women spilled out of the room. "What's the matter?"

"I hope I did well."

He touched her soft cheek again. "I'm sure you passed. Next year you'll be a student at this college. Don't let those ladies' comments about your being a Negro bother you. God is behind you." He took a deep breath. "If they give you trouble, share your faith with them. I don't know if they'll listen, but they need to know that you're following your calling and that they are acting in an ungodly manner."

"I'll remember that if I attend this college." She took a deep breath. "Thank you for escorting me to the test, Timothy."

"I was happy to do it." He'd had to reason with her so she would allow him to accompany her. He again recalled how she'd initially rejected his offer to help her study. He figured Deborah was used to being a loner and not always open to accepting help from others. Hopefully, she was learning that it was all right to allow others to assist her. After they'd exited the building, he gestured toward the restaurant across the street. "Would you like to share dinner with me?"

She shook her head, fingering the strings of her pretty red bonnet. "I'm not hungry. I want to go home."

"Deborah, you haven't had anything to eat since breakfast." He touched her shoulder. "You might get hungry once you're in the restaurant and smell the food."

He breathed with relief when she finally nodded and agreed to his invitation. He gently touched her back as they entered the small restaurant. The scent of meat and vegetables filled the air. He wiped his sweaty palms on his pants before pulling out Deborah's chair for her. She sat down, pushing her spectacles up on her lovely nose. He sat down across from her as the waitress approached the table. "We're only serving stew and biscuits this afternoon. Would you like to order some?"

He'd heard they only served one meal each day. He smiled at the woman. "It smells delicious. Yes, we'll order the stew and biscuits."

She returned soon with tin cups of water. "I'll be bringing your food shortly."

Maybe now was the time to tell Deborah all that had been on his mind. Or maybe he should wait until after the meal? He honestly wasn't sure how she'd react to what he had to say, so perhaps he should wait. He didn't want to spoil her dinner by asking the question that had been burning in his mind like a hot biscuit.

The waitress returned to the table with tin bowls of stew as well as two spoons. He took Deborah's lovely hand and they bowed their heads. "Lord, please be with us as we enjoy our meal. Thank You for allowing me the pleasure of having Deborah's company today, and Lord, please let us hear positive results from Deborah's exam. Amen."

"Amen." She gave him a small smile and squeezed his hand before releasing it. The stew was delicious. The roasted meat, potatoes, and vegetables were swimming in thick salt-and-pepper gravy. Even though he was nervous, he managed to eat the entire bowl of stew, and Deborah appeared to enjoy hers as well. She dabbed her mouth with a napkin.

The waitress returned to the table. "We have cake for dessert. Did you want some?"

Deborah smiled. "I'd love some."

Timothy looked toward the waitress. "Yes, please bring us two slices of cake."

The yellow cake was served on a tin plate with a shiny, slightly lumpy frosting in a separate bowl. He sliced into the cake and popped a bite into his mouth. He then tasted the frosting. The sweet and tangy lemon flavor went well with the cake. When the waitress returned for their dirty dishes, he gestured toward their empty plates. "That cake was amazing. I've never tasted frosting like that. Usually you can't find lemons around this time of year." He could seldom get citrus fruits at any time.

"That's lemon curd. Isn't it good?"

"Yes, it's wonderful."

Deborah grinned. "It was delicious."

Thank goodness she'd enjoyed her meal. Now he could focus on Deborah. She looked at him. "I guess we need to go home. I want to tell Ma and Pa about the exam." She frowned just a bit.

"Your ma still doesn't take to your going to the college?"

She shook her head. "She still doesn't. I tried to make her understand, but Timothy, sometimes it's just plain hard to reason with Ma."

Unable to resist, he took her hand. Her eyes widened at their joined hands on the rough wooden table. "Deborah, I think your ma will understand eventually. You know that I understand what you are doing, and I think it's wonderful that you're following God's calling." He took a deep breath. "I spoke with your ma and pa last night. You were out in your shed making peppermint oil."

"What did you speak to them about?" Curiosity tinged her lovely voice as she looked at him.

"I wanted to know if it was all right if I courted you. I sensed that we were on our way to being a couple when we were working together during the quarantine."

She pulled her hand away. Oh no, that was not a good sign,

not at all. *Lord, please help me say the right words to Deborah. I'm falling in love with her, and I don't think she realizes just how strongly I feel for her.*

"Timothy. This is just so hard."

What was she talking about? "What do you mean?"

"Well, I'm a teacher. I'm not allowed to have a beau."

He sighed. "Well, I believe you'll get into college. I highly doubt you'll be renewing your teaching contract."

"Well, that's true." She bit her lower lip and looked away.

"What's the matter?"

"There are a lot of things that bother me."

He widened his eyes and leaned back in his seat. He had a feeling this was going to be a long conversation. "Do you mean there are things about *me* that bother you, or are you speaking about something else?"

"There are things about you that bother me. It would be difficult for me to be courted by you if I know you have guilty feelings about Eve's death. Do you still feel guilty about that?"

He sighed. If he'd never told her about his guilty feelings, would she have been more open to being courted by him? "Yes, I do, but—"

She grabbed his hand and squeezed it. "Talk to somebody about it. It's not right for you to feel that way. Maybe talk to the pastor or. . .somebody. My pa is pretty easy to talk to. Tell him. Feeling guilty like that will make you sad. I don't know if I'd want to be courted by you if you're still dreaming about my sister. Maybe you're still grieving for her and you're simply not ready to court somebody else yet."

He looked into her wise, honest, kind eyes. He'd not thought about how confessing his guilty feelings would affect Deborah. "Is there anything else about me that bothers you?"

She released his hand and gripped the handle of her reticule, seeming nervous. Well, he needed to hear all she had to say. The urge to court her swelled within him like a wave, and he figured if courtship ever happened between them, it would take some time and a lot of prayer. "Yes. I've been bothered by something since you returned to town."

He frowned. This didn't sound good at all. "What's been bothering you?"

"Remember when I was seventeen and you were an apprentice to Doc Smith?"

"Yes, I remember."

"We used to spend time together. I liked spending time with you. I even learned a few things from you about plants and medicine. You were so smart and kind. . . ."

He blinked, still unsure as to what bothered her. "I enjoyed spending time with you too."

"If you enjoyed spending time with me, then why did you marry Eve?"

He winced. That was a question he wasn't expecting.

Chapter 12

There, she'd asked the question that had been burning in her mind like a hot pot of porridge. From the shocked look on his face, he hadn't been expecting it. He needed to answer her question if he ever wanted to court her. He sipped from the tin cup of water that still rested on the table. He looked nervous. Well, he needed to be sure he told her the truth.

"I enjoyed visiting with you. I was even starting to be smitten with you." He paused and took a deep breath. "One day when I was coming to visit you, Eve met me on the path. She flirted with me and kissed me." Sweat rolled down his brow. He swiped the moisture away as he told Deborah what happened. "She continued doing this, stopping me from visiting you. One day, you and your parents were gone and. . .Deborah, I'm so ashamed."

She took a deep breath. "Ashamed of what?"

His face reddened. She gasped. "You had relations with my sister and were not married to her?" The question squeaked from her mouth. "How could you?"

"As soon as it happened, I went to your parents and told them we had to get married."

"Did my parents know what you did?"

"Yes, I even told the pastor. Deborah, I'm not perfect. The first thing I did after it happened was beg God for forgiveness. After we got married, I changed. After your sister and I moved to a new town, I went to church and got baptized."

She took a deep breath. "But you always went to church before you married Eve and when you visited me."

"I did, but I'd never accepted Christ as my Savior. I never told the Lord that I accepted His gift of salvation until after I married Eve."

Tears slid down her cheeks. She swiped the moisture away. "I guess I didn't know you as well as I thought. I just assumed you were a Christian when we were. . .visiting together when I was seventeen."

"Oh Deborah. It makes me sad to see you cry. I was struggling back then. I was going through a lot. Questioning a lot. I was angry with God about my parents' deaths. It was a rough time for me. I'm so sorry."

She shook her head. "Timothy, it's not just you. It's my sister. I didn't realize that Eve was so. . .so. . ." She struggled to come up with a proper word to describe her sister.

"Conniving?"

She blew air through her lips. "Yes. I mean. . .I guess maybe deep down I knew, but I just didn't want to admit it to myself." She sniffed and wiped her wet eyes with her napkin. "My friend Lucy asked me if Eve was kind." She sighed and placed her napkin on the table. "Why would Eve want to hurt me like that?"

"I don't think she was thinking clearly. She was self-centered. I think she saw that you were happy from spending time with me, and she wanted some of that happiness for herself. It's possible that she mistakenly thought that being with me would make her happy. She considered her own feelings but didn't think about how much her actions would hurt you."

Deborah vividly recalled the day she'd accepted Christ. She was fourteen, and a week later the pastor baptized her in the river on the edge of town. Folks had congratulated her for accepting Jesus into her life. She winced, recalling that Eve had accepted Christ a week later. Had her sister had a real relationship with Jesus? Or had Eve accepted Christ because she'd been jealous of the attention her twin had received?

"Deborah, what's wrong?" Timothy's deep, gentle voice interrupted her thoughts.

"It's Eve."

"What about her?"

"Did she know Jesus? Did she truly accept His gift of salvation?" She told him about how Eve accepted Christ shortly after she herself had accepted Him as her Savior. She swiped away the sudden tears that spilled down her cheeks.

"Deborah, I hate to see you so upset. I think Eve was a Christian. After Lily was born, she began reading her Bible more. She often read the Bible with a group of ladies at our church. I honestly don't know how she felt when she was fourteen. I do know she said she wanted to make sure Lily loved Jesus." He sighed. "Our marriage was difficult and full of arguments. We didn't always agree on everything, and it was hard, but I do believe that Eve was saved."

What a relief to know that fact about her sister. But this new knowledge didn't change the way she felt. She needed to let Timothy know what she was thinking. "Timothy, we can't court, not now. I need some time to think and pray about this." She paused. "It will be difficult seeing you at meals each day at my house. I need some time alone."

"That's all right, Deborah. Don't worry about that. I won't come to your house any more for meals. I can cook for Lily and me, or send Lily to your house to get our meal. The only reason I dined with your family is because your ma insisted. She wanted to spend time with Lily, and I think she's still sad about Eve's death. Take as much time as you need, and when you're ready to talk about this again, please come and see me." He paid the waitress for their meal. He then took Deborah's hand and they exited the restaurant.

So, she had to think about his request for courtship? The question had been spinning in his mind ever since he'd shared dinner with Deborah a few days ago. He peered into the Kings' barn and breathed a sigh of relief when he spotted Papa Daniel feeding the horses. He figured Deborah's pa would be out doing chores in the barn while Deborah and her ma fixed supper. He'd already sent Lily into Deborah's house to fetch their supper pail. He'd told Lily that her grandpa would come fetch her when it was time for them to walk home. This would guarantee that he had ample time to speak with him.

"Papa Daniel."

The older man looked up from his chore. "Timothy. I'm surprised to see you."

He strolled into the barn and helped Papa Daniel toss hay into the horses' feeding trough. They worked together silently. Once the feeding trough was full, Timothy assisted with hauling water for the horses. The nip in the November air felt good against his heated skin as he performed the chore. After they'd finished in the barn, he gestured toward Deborah's wooden crates in the adjoining room. "I have to talk to you. Do you mind if we sit down for a bit?"

The older man nodded. "Let's rest for a little while." They made themselves comfortable on the crates. Susie scampered into the barn. Timothy lifted the cat and stroked her silky black fur. When the cat wiggled in his arms, he released her. He watched the animal run out of the barn before he focused on Papa Daniel.

"I guess Deborah mentioned that she needed some time to think about my offer of courtship."

"Yes, she did mention that. My Deborah is not one to rush into anything. She thinks and prays about it. She has to seek God's guidance."

"Yes, she does." How could he broach this emotional topic? "Actually, Deborah told me to come and speak with you."

He raised his gray eyebrows. "Really?"

Taking a deep breath, Timothy told Papa Daniel all that he'd discussed with Deborah when they shared dinner after she'd taken the exam. "I know it hurts Deborah to discover what I did with Eve. I also know she's upset about how Eve...well...how

Eve approached me. Sir, I wasn't a Christian at the time. I have a relationship with God now." He took another deep breath. "I'm sorry about what happened. I really am. I just wonder if Deborah will ever forgive me for what I did years ago. I also wonder if she can forgive Eve—even though Eve has passed away, I don't blame Deborah for being upset about what happened."

"What about you, Timothy? Are you upset?"

"Yes, Papa Daniel. I'm upset that my actions hurt Deborah. I'm also upset about Eve's death." He told the older man about Eve's illness and about the dreams he'd been having about her. "I feel awful. Since I've returned to town, I've felt conflicted. I like Deborah." He figured he could even grow to love her the way a husband loves a wife, but only the good Lord knew if that would ever happen. "But she's Eve's twin sister. It seems wrong for me to be with her, yet I want to see her. She's smart and pretty, and I enjoy spending time with her." He took a deep breath. "Then I feel bad about Eve's death. Was there anything I could've done to save her?"

Deborah's pa clapped his large hand on Timothy's shoulder. "Son, you need to forgive yourself for all of that. Jesus forgave you when He died on the cross." He paused for a few seconds. "If Jesus were here right now, what would He tell you to do?" Surprised at the question, Timothy looked into Papa Daniel's wise, kind eyes. "Jesus wouldn't want you to feel guilty about something that wasn't your fault. Son, you need to get on your knees and pray to the Lord about this. Ask Him to lift away your feelings of guilt." He leaned back against the wall. "Ask Him if Deborah's the right woman for you, and then, if it's His will, to open up her heart so she'll accept your courtship. I'll be praying for you and Deborah too. You hurt her when you married Eve. Sometimes it takes folks awhile to let go of pain. Pain can run deep, and your returning to town and then both of you studying and treating patients together. . .well. . .she probably was hoping you'd ask to court her. Now that you have, she doesn't know what to do about it."

After they stood, Papa Daniel hugged him hard. "You're like a son to me, Timothy." He released him. "I'll send Lily out for you."

Timothy thought about Papa Daniel's advice as he trekked home with Lily. After they'd feasted on dinner and Lily had gone to sleep, he went into his room. He dropped down on his knees, steepled his hands, and bowed his head. "Lord, I'm struggling. I brought Lily here to live close to Eve's family. Now I'm dreaming about Eve. I still wonder about her death. I feel so bad about it. Please take away these bad feelings, Lord. Please be with Deborah. Please help her to see that I'm sincere about wanting to court her. I like Deborah. I could even grow to love her. Lord, I need help with so many things. My life is full of guilt and bad feelings. Help me, Lord. Help me so that I can be a better father for Lily. Help me to be the best doctor I can be for this community. Lord, please help me to feel happy and not full of guilt." He paused. "I thank You for all You've done for me, Lord. Amen." After his prayer, he remained on his knees, his eyes tightly closed. The tense feeling in his shoulders lessened as he took a few deep breaths.

He finally stood up. For some reason, he didn't feel sleepy. He lit his lantern and lifted his Bible from the shelf before making himself comfortable at the kitchen table. He opened the Bible to

Romans 3:23-24. *"For all have sinned, and come short of the glory of God; being justified freely by his grace through the redemption that is in Christ Jesus."* He stared at the verse before touching the words with his fingers. He continued reading his Bible until the weak, early morning sunlight streamed through his window.

◈ Chapter 13 ◈

Over the following month, Deborah spotted Timothy only on Sundays when he attended church. He sat at the back of the church and allowed Lily to sit with Deborah and her family. Pa would occasionally bring meals over to Timothy and Lily and he'd also fetch Lily so that she could walk to school with Deborah.

The cool autumn days turned colder as December arrived. Christmas was coming. Most of her students were excited about the upcoming holiday since school would be out for a few weeks and many of her pupils would receive Christmas gifts. As she strolled downtown on a cold Saturday afternoon, Deborah wondered what she should purchase as gifts for Pa, Ma, and Lily. She also wondered about Timothy. Should she purchase a gift for him? She sighed as she strolled into the post office. She eyed the small square holes built into the wall. Many were stuffed with letters while some were empty. She approached the counter. "Good afternoon." She smiled at the postmaster.

"Good afternoon, Deborah. Expecting mail?"

"Yes, actually, I am."

The postmaster searched the cubbyholes before he pulled a letter out and slid it across the counter to her.

The letter was from the women's college.

"Thank you." She barely breathed as she exited the post office and stood on the street. A red wax seal, embossed with the women's college logo, was emblazoned on the back of the envelope. She broke the seal and slid the piece of paper out of the envelope.

Closing her eyes, she opened the letter. *Lord, please let this be good news.* She opened her eyes and read the letter.

She'd passed the test with a high score. She blinked as she read the rest of the letter, which invited her to attend the women's college. Her heart pounded as she folded the letter and slid it back into the envelope. She closed her eyes and leaned against the post office building. Timothy popped into her mind. She thought about him helping her study at her kitchen table. His quick, agile mind and his friendliness had helped her reach this goal.

She missed him. She ached to rush over to his house and show him her acceptance letter. Well, she wouldn't tell Timothy right now. However, she could share her good news with someone else. Taking the letter, she strolled across the street to the mercantile. Thankfully, it wasn't very busy and Lucy met her at the door. "Good afternoon, Deborah. Looks like you have a lot on your mind."

"I do have a lot on my mind."

They hugged and Lucy led her to the back of the room near the stove. Without asking, she made coffee for them and then plopped into her seat. "So what's wrong? I've been seeing Timothy sitting in the back of the church. I know you've been thinking about letting him court you." Deborah had told Lucy about her conversation with Timothy. "So what's on your mind?"

She shared her good news. "I was accepted into the women's college." She waved her letter in the air.

"Deborah." Lucy's voice echoed through the mercantile. "We must celebrate." She jumped up from her chair and pulled a package of English biscuits off the shelf. She opened the box and placed the treats onto a tin plate. "I'll tell my boss to dock the price of these biscuits from my wages. This is my treat. Eat some."

Deborah bit into one of the vanilla biscuits and sipped more coffee. "Thank you, Lucy."

"I got these biscuits to put a smile on your face. Stop frowning, Deborah. Isn't this what you wanted, to get accepted into the college?"

"Yes, but Timothy helped me to study."

"And?"

"And now I'll have to go talk to him and let him know I was accepted into the college."

"Well, talk to him. You haven't said a word to him for a month. Clara has been trying to get him to come to Sunday dinner every week after church. Of course, he declines her invitation, but how long do you think the man will wait?"

"But there was so much we discussed the last time I spoke with him. Remember all that I told you about Eve. . .about what happened between them?"

"I understand, Deborah. You needed time. But we all make

mistakes. We're all sinners. Timothy made that mistake before he accepted Christ. He's trying to do right. The whole point of courting is getting to know the person. Timothy is a Christian and he likes you. Give him a chance."

Deborah asked Lucy how things had been going in the mercantile. As they chatted, they finished the biscuits and sipped coffee. After she purchased the supplies she needed and got them loaded into her wagon, Deborah continued to think about Lucy's advice as she steered the wagon toward home.

After her visit with Lucy, Deborah continued to focus on her pupils. Since Christmas was coming, a lot of her students had a hard time concentrating on their lessons. They were restless, ready for the holiday to begin.

She also purchased gifts for her family. A pretty coffee cup for Ma, a tie for Pa, a doll for Lily.

For Timothy. . . She'd hesitated about what to purchase for him. She'd finally decided on two pairs of socks. Knowing how much he loved her ma's hand pies, she decided to make a batch just for him. On Christmas morning she packed the hand pies, a few fresh eggs, and some ham into her dinner pail. She scooped up her Christmas gifts and walked out into the cold, frigid morning. As she strolled to Timothy's house, snow fell from the sky. She leaned her head back and opened her mouth. A memory, pure and sweet, filled her mind. She remembered when she and Eve were children and they'd stand out in the yard when it snowed. They'd open their mouths to catch snowflakes. If they had a big snowfall, they'd bring in a bucketful of snow and her ma would add molasses to it, making a cold, sweet treat for them to enjoy.

Still grinning about the vivid memory, she knocked on Timothy's door.

"Deborah." The surprised tone of his voice made her smile.

"Merry Christmas, Timothy." Oh my. He looked so handsome. He wore his overalls and his beige shirt. He smiled back, showing his beautiful milky white teeth. He gently pried the food bucket from her fingers and set it on the floor as she came into the house. Then he hugged her and kissed her cheek.

"Merry Christmas, Aunt Deborah." Lily entered the kitchen. "Why did you bring the dinner pail this morning?"

"Because I'm going to make breakfast for both of you."

The girl smiled. Her dark brown eyes sparkled like jewels. She looked so much like Eve that Deborah's heart tugged with joy. She hugged her niece. "You brought Christmas presents?" Lily asked when she spotted the gifts. She jumped up and down, clapping her hands.

"Yes. This is for you." Deborah pressed one of the gifts into Lily's hand. Lily unwrapped her gift and squealed when she saw her new doll.

Deborah then focused on Timothy. "Merry Christmas." She gave him his gift.

"Thank you, Deborah. Merry Christmas." He offered her a small package.

Excited, she accepted the small, beautiful gift. The delicate scent of roses and lilac wafted from the rose-patterned paper. Carefully, she peeled off the paper and admired the fragrant bar of soap. "It's beautiful, Timothy." The soap was too pretty to use.

She sniffed the soap as Timothy opened his gift.

"Deborah, thank you. I needed new socks."

She touched his hand. "I also made you a batch of apple hand pies. We can enjoy them with breakfast if you like."

After they'd enjoyed their delicious meal, Lily went into the adjoining room to play with her new doll. Deborah and Timothy made themselves comfortable at the kitchen table. "Timothy," Deborah said, "I want to share some news with you. I passed the exam and was accepted into the women's college."

"Deborah, that's wonderful. I'm so proud of you." When he hugged her with his strong arms, she sniffed his wonderful scent of soap and hay.

He released her. "Thank you." She took a deep breath. "I've given your offer a lot of thought over the last month. I'd love for you to court me."

"Hallelujah!" He pulled her into his arms again and kissed her lips.

Epilogue

"$\mathcal{D}$eborah Washington." Her name was announced. She stood up, holding her pregnant stomach as she walked across the stage to receive her botany certificate. As she accepted the certificate, she glanced into the audience. Lily and Timothy were front and center, her ma and pa sitting right beside them. Timothy looked so proud. *"I love you."* He mouthed the words.

"I love you too." She mouthed the words right back to him. She settled into her seat and listened as they called the rest of the graduates' names, thinking about all that had happened since Timothy had asked her to court him two years ago. Right after she'd agreed to his courtship, she'd started her term at the women's college, and they were married six months later. The town had had to find another teacher, but she continued helping Timothy with his medical practice. They worked well together. She figured both of them could fulfill their true callings more when they worked as a team.

Her ma had finally accepted that she was going to be a college graduate. When she'd seen her interacting with the other students and realized how happy she was, Ma had learned to accept that going to the college was part of her calling—part of what she wanted to do to serve Jesus, as well as others.

Her baby kicked. She rubbed her swollen stomach. In about a month, Lily would have a new brother or sister. Again, she looked to her family in the audience. Yes, she was truly blessed. She bowed her head and closed her eyes. *Thank You, Jesus, for all of Your blessings.*

Cecelia Dowdy is a world traveler who has been an avid reader for as long as she can remember. When she first read Christian fiction, she felt called to write for the genre. She loves to read, write, and bake desserts in her spare time. She also loves spending time with her husband and her son. Currently she resides with her family in Maryland. Visit her website at ceceliadowdy.com.

❧ Schooling Mr. Mason ❧

by Lynette Sowell

Prologue

June 29, 1895

My dear brother,

I hope my letter finds you well. I have heard that your Stephen has had success in his employ as an educator. I have a position for him at the academy, should he be interested. Wickham Academy could use a straight and steady teacher like your son, and I believe he is ready for the opportunity.

I am getting on in years, and after Mr. Wickham's passing, I find I am wanting to travel more while I still can. Please do not speak of it to Stephen, but if all goes well this year, he may find himself at the helm of Wickham's. I need someone I can trust, and who better to trust than family?

If it is agreeable to you, I shall write to him and invite him to visit me in Northampton.

I do plan to see you at Christmastime, should the weather be pleasant enough to travel.

I remain your devoted sister,
Marjorie Wickham

*M*arjorie placed her pen on the desk and looked at the letter. There. It was done.

Her best teacher, Caroline Parker, would not be happy about the letter if she knew its contents.

But then, perhaps she might be happy for a different reason after Stephen Mason's arrival in Northampton.

Time would tell.

Stephen had sown his wild oats and the grace of God had sheltered him from certain ruin, but Marjorie was certain the serious young man she had encountered last Christmas at her brother's home would be an ideal addition to the staff at Wickham Academy.

Marjorie Wickham had a way of knowing things, and in this situation, she had a good hunch the upcoming school year would be an eventful one for all of them.

҈ Chapter 1 ҉

Northampton, Massachusetts
September 1895

*A*ll Caroline Parker could think was that her right little toe ached inside her best boot. When Mrs. Wickham had summoned her to the office, Caroline made sure she wore her best. She kept her shoulders squared and her chin up as Mrs. Wickham continued speaking. She sat straight in the chair, facing Mrs. Wickham at her desk.

The older woman's voice held an even tone punctuated by the regular *tick-tock* of the cuckoo clock on the wall.

A new sound tickled Caroline's ears—a fly, buzzing at a nearby windowpane.

Listen to her or you'll miss something important, and if Mrs. Wickham dislikes anything, it is having to repeat herself.

Caroline's mind fought to focus even as her eyes stung. A lady should not be given to tears, not at a time like this. Tears ought to be saved for the privacy of her room. Her resolve won, and the tears dissipated before they overwhelmed her eyes.

"I hope you understand, Miss Parker," Mrs. Wickham was saying. "It was not a decision I came to easily, nor lightly."

Caroline nodded. "I do understand." She wanted to reach for the handkerchief in her pocket but resisted the urge. She had work to do before the term began and students returned to the academy.

Mrs. Wickham rose from behind her mahogany desk and moved to stand directly in front of Caroline. She tilted her head.

"Caroline, you are more like a member of my family than a teacher on my payroll. I assure you, your position is secure. I realize that others, including you, expected me to select you as my replacement this summer."

"I'm very happy here at Wickham Academy. I've always considered teaching to be my calling, and I'm very grateful for your seeing my potential years ago, when I thought I knew so much but really knew so little." Caroline ceased her words before a croak could betray her.

Mrs. Wickham, the owner and headmistress of Wickham Academy, had operated the school in Northampton for more than two decades after teaching school herself for more than ten years. When she married Mr. Wickham, he had indulged his wife by opening the school for young ladies.

Caroline had applied for an open position eight years ago, fresh out of her teacher training with her certificate, and felt like she'd walked into a home she'd never known existed. The position had helped her family in nearby Holyoke and put some money in her pocket. She lived simply, and happily. As other teachers left for other positions, Caroline stayed on and the years crept by, a succession of bright moments, uncertainty, long days, and triumphant accomplishments of her students.

With the soft brushing of her skirt on the handwoven carpet beneath their feet, Mrs. Wickham continued her journey to the window and the frantic fly. She raised the window and the fly escaped to its freedom.

"That, my dear Caroline, is the mark of a good teacher, realizing there is still something to learn." Mrs. Wickham stopped herself. "No, a great teacher."

"Thank you, Mrs. Wickham." Even as she wrestled with disappointment, Caroline's cheeks flushed with pride.

"You may go now."

Caroline rose to her feet, and her toe pinged yet again inside her boot. She made a swift yet dignified retreat from the headmistress's office and entered the hallway with its long shadows of the morning. Somehow she found her way to her room in the ladies' dormitory, which, thankfully, was empty. The three summer boarding students were at a picnic with one of the town girls who attended the academy during the year.

The three girls would likely return by suppertime, full of exciting stories about their day, which Caroline would listen to. She'd never experienced the life that most of them had, a life free from want and worry about food on the table and whether enough of Papa's wages would remain to pay the rent.

A breeze wafted through the window, and Caroline took a seat in the soft chair she kept facing her window. Its cushioned comfort took away some of the shock from Mrs. Wickham's announcement.

She'd found the chair discarded in the hall one day, likely headed for the curb, and Mrs. Wickham had permitted her to keep it. Caroline had covered the chair with a pretty pink cotton, replacing the drab oatmeal fabric. The result had been an unusual bit of upholstery, but she liked it. She spent time there reading a favorite book, or writing a letter on her small lap desk, or using her watercolor kit to paint the maple trees outside as the seasons changed.

There would be no announcement that Caroline would take over as headmistress of Wickham's. She kept repeating the main point of the conversation she'd just had with Mrs. Wickham.

Disappointed? Yes, of course she was.

Her mama's words came back to her.

"If you get knocked down and it hurts, cry for a moment, but don't lie there in the dirt. Pop back up and show 'em you've got some fight in you."

Caroline raised her chin. She'd let herself cry for a moment, but she wouldn't be down for long. A new school year would be starting soon, and she had students who needed her. Feeling sorry for herself wouldn't help them, not at all.

Plus, Mrs. Wickham hadn't said Caroline would *never* be headmistress. She said she wouldn't be naming a replacement now. But that didn't mean never. So, Caroline told herself, there was still a chance.

She scanned the bright morning outside and watched a male figure, clad in a suit, striding purposefully along the path that wound through the buildings of the academy. She didn't recognize him. A new teacher, perhaps? There had been male teachers at the academy who worked under Mrs. Wickham's watchful eye. None had stayed long.

Perhaps it was a young father, seeking information about enrolling a new student. But then, if the man was a parent, where was the mother?

Caroline decided to forgo thoughts of whoever the man was and, instead, see to her mending. Tomorrow was Sunday, and she had plans to dine with her best friend, Elizabeth, and Elizabeth's family, who lived in town. The time away from the academy would be good.

Stephen Mason knew if he bungled this moment with Aunt Marjorie, it could very well be his last great opportunity to make something of himself.

The old lady had terrified him when he was younger, with her tall frame, sharp features, and narrow-eyed look.

This morning, while she poured tea in her office, she didn't look so tall, nor her features so sharp. Her narrow-eyed gaze held kindness when she looked in his direction.

"You certainly have accomplished much in your almost thirty years," Aunt Marjorie mused aloud. "Working your way to Europe, then back again. Then out west, I understand?"

"Yes, Aunt Marjorie." He hoped she wouldn't pry as to how he'd occupied himself. He took a sip of tea.

"A professional gambler of sorts, from what I hear?"

He nearly choked on his sip of tea. "Was. I was."

Was, until he'd lost everything, then ended up with two

black eyes after getting in a fistfight and being accused of stealing a horse. He'd borrowed the horse—it had simply been a misunderstanding after imbibing more liquor than he ought. Everything had worked out, just as it always had. Yet the brush with jail time and worse had made him head home again, broke and disgraced. His family had shown him grace, but none of their money. What little he had now was everything he'd earned for himself.

Silence hung between them. He knew this kind of silence, the one during a poker game when another player was deciding whether to raise or fold.

Of course, Aunt Marjorie would raise, and he'd have to meet whatever she asked in order to stay.

He wanted—no, needed—whatever she was offering him. His throat tickled, so he cleared it.

"Yet here you are."

"Here I am, because you asked me to come."

She looked over her spectacles at him. "So, when you are under my employ, you will keep a strict curfew. No venturing out after sunset, and you will attend church on Sundays. You will not frequent billiard halls nor other establishments which could besmirch the name of Wickham Academy. We have a reputation to uphold in our city."

He nodded. "Understood, Aunt Marjorie. I have no desire to go to any of those places, and I'm well aware of the good name the academy holds here in western Massachusetts."

"You will reside in the guest room in my private residence, of course, and take your meals there as well, along with me." She strolled the room, her footsteps muffled on the carpet.

"Every third weekend, you may leave the premises, but you are expected to maintain the same decorum as if you were here."

"Understood." He nodded again.

"As I explained in my letter, I require a mathematics teacher, along with an assistant. You have big shoes to fill, and at the school year's end, I am considering retiring from running the school altogether." She turned to face him.

"Retiring? Does that mean you plan to close the school?"

"No, certainly not! I mean to find a replacement to run the academy without me. I have plans to travel. It's been a long time since I last did, and I would like to enjoy some of the days I have left on this earth, without having to mind a calendar."

Stephen tugged at his tie. Running the academy as the head-master? This was more than he imagined. He was grateful for the teaching job, but headmaster?

"I see your hesitation." Her dark eyes sparkled. "If you don't wish to consider a headmaster position, I do have someone else in mind."

"I see. And who might that be?"

"Miss Caroline Parker. She has taught here for many years and has proven herself to be an excellent teacher and a fine example of how a lady ought to conduct herself."

"Part of the woodwork now, is she?" The woman was probably an old maid, getting on in years. "Well, why don't you just hire her then, and be done with it?"

The edge to his voice surprised even him. His words weren't the way to gain her respect and confidence in him.

Then her chuckle surprised him further, a merry sound to his ears and entirely unexpected, coming from the elderly woman. "You remind me so much of Mr. Wickham, with that manner of speaking. Very well, we shall see who will run this academy at the end of the school year. Whether it is you or Miss Parker, I will be the winner either way."

ᗢ Chapter 2 ᗢ

*C*aroline hurried from the carriage stop. After spending the weekend at her parents' apartment in Holyoke, she was a little sad yet excited to be returning to the life she knew at the academy.

She glanced at the small watch pinned to her best blouse. She'd be late for the first staff meeting of the upcoming new year. But Mama had begged her to come for the weekend before the term began and she became too busy to visit regularly as she had during the summertime.

The buildings that made up the academy came into view as her feet carried her closer to the front gate. The clock at the church on the square began to chime the hour. She had but eight chimes before she was deemed late.

This was *not* a way to show Mrs. Wickham that she was up to the job of headmistress and director of Wickham's. Her eyes stung with perspiration that trickled from her brow, and she brushed the liquid away with her free hand while she tightened the grip on her satchel with her other hand.

Caroline crossed the threshold at the stroke of eight. A few more paces and she'd reach the great room where Mrs. Wickham and the other staff likely had already assembled. She forced her steps to slow as she drew closer to the open doorway. She tucked her satchel into a corner of the snug little bench in the hallway, sucked in a deep breath, and willed her fluttering heart to slow to a steadier pace.

Chin up, shoulders square, she took determined steps into the room, her traveling shoes making sharp clicks on the parquet flooring until she reached the edge of the carpet.

Seven heads turned in her direction and seven pairs of eyes regarded her, as did Mrs. Wickham, who stood before an unlit fireplace. Her hands were clasped together just below her waist.

Her fellow teachers had returned, but there was another pair of eyes she didn't recognize in the room. They were brown and owned by a gentleman likely around her age. The one she'd seen the other day, walking along the courtyard and taking in the sight of the academy grounds. He had a thin mustache and spectacles that perched on the end of his nose. He pushed them up with one finger and continued to stare at her.

"Very good." Mrs. Wickham's voiced filled the room. "Now that we are all present, introductions all around." She nodded in the direction of the man, who now had his focus on her.

He cleared his throat. "My name is Mr. Stephen Mason, and I shall be teaching upper-level mathematics and assisting Mrs. Wickham with administrative duties as required. I taught previously at the Armstrong Academy in Cambridge."

The other teachers took their turns, and then all attention was on Caroline. The man's gaze on her contained more than curiosity about meeting a new colleague. Why?

She cleared her throat. "Miss Caroline Parker. I teach English composition, all levels, and art. I have taught at Wickham Academy for eight years."

She didn't miss the surprise in Mr. Mason's eyes. Yes, she had been straight out of teacher's college in Westfield, and Mrs. Wickham had hired her right away. But she was a good teacher, and she would continue to prove that to them all.

"Now that introductions have been made, let us venture to the main hall where I will unveil our initiative for the 1895 to 1896 academic year." With a sweeping gesture, Mrs. Wickham waved them toward the hallway that Caroline had hurried through not fifteen minutes earlier.

Caroline's curiosity was piqued, not so much by the new gentleman—the only gentleman—in the room, but by the prospect of what Mrs. Wickham would share with them. What change was to come? Whatever it was, Caroline imagined it must be a big one if it was a yearlong venture.

They assembled in the front hall at the foot of a wide, grand staircase that led to the upstairs rooms. Something flat, covered with a cotton cloth, hung on the wall. The large framed painting of a landscape of Mount Holyoke had been taken down, and whatever this was had been hung in its place.

Caroline and her fellow teachers exchanged glances. No one else seemed to know what this was about either.

Mrs. Wickham paused. She was good at the pause, which made others listen more intently. It was something Caroline had picked up on after years of dealing with sometimes impetuous and unruly students. Instead of growing louder and demanding attention, she would simply engage the "Wickham Pause," which Mrs. Wickham was now demonstrating.

"As most of you know, or I hope you know, the Games of the First Olympiad will be held next April, in Athens, Greece. This is an international event that brings together competitors from all over the world." Mrs. Wickham looked at each of them in turn. "I thought it appropriate that we should have our own First Olympiad here at Wickham Academy."

Olympiad? What did that mean? Would they hold footraces and other types of contests? What could young ladies learn from that?

Caroline held her tongue and waited.

"Yes, Charlotte?" Mrs. Wickham nodded in the direction of Miss Huckabee, who taught grammar. She'd been at the academy far longer than Caroline.

"Will the students be competing in games? How will we play games and get our studies completed as well?"

"A very good question." Mrs. Wickham tugged on the cloth, and it fell away to reveal a large square board, painted white. A long black line divided the white space in half, top to bottom. At the top of the left side, printed in black lettering, was the name MASON, and at the top of the right side was the name PARKER.

Listed to the left were subjects of study.

Caroline swallowed hard. Her name at the top of the board? And Mr. Mason's?

She had so many questions they nearly threatened to suffocate her.

"I see you are all wondering what this means, and of course I will explain." Mrs. Wickham pointed to the board. "Our Olympiad will be academic in nature for this school year. We will have two teams, captained by Miss Parker and Mr. Mason. Quite simply, your students will determine the winner for the year. The winning students will receive a special prize. The winning captain will also receive a prize."

A prize. The directorship of the academy. It had to be the prize for the teacher. Whoever had the best students would win.

"Each student will draw a name for a team, either Miss Parker's or Mr. Mason's. In turn, Miss Parker's and Mr. Mason's success will depend entirely on how their students perform." Mrs. Wickham's voice sounded matter-of-fact. "The losers will not suffer consequences or have to endure a penalty. However, they will not get to enjoy what the winners will receive."

Her team's students could make—or break—her chance of becoming the headmistress of Wickham Academy. If they did well, she would do well. If they did poorly? Well, the majority of the students at Wickham did not do poorly. There were some who struggled with subjects, such as mathematics or grammar, but given time and tutoring, most succeeded in their studies. But what if a student was unhappy with Caroline, might one of them try to sabotage her efforts? In the end, the winners would be the students, and ultimately, the academy.

She tried not to glance at Mr. Mason but at last gave in to the urge. He wore an expression nearly as perplexed as the one she knew she wore herself.

Stephen's collar felt like a shackle around his neck as he stood in the front hallway of the academy's main building. He wasn't sure if he was up to this challenge. He'd been prepared to teach and assist his aunt. But now, adding a competition to the mix? He felt like he'd tumbled into the deep end of a swimming hole and was kicking his way to the surface.

Now that Aunt Marjorie had finished making note of which students were on each teacher's team, Stephen cleared his throat.

"Mrs. Wickham, if I may?" he asked. His aunt nodded in response. "I understand the students competing against each other for this competition. But the faculty competition?"

"I'm glad you asked. For the students, we will not have individual scores on the board. Instead, we will compute an average of all students' scores who are assigned to your team. In addition, the faculty will be grading you on your leadership for each quarter of the year."

"I understand." He glanced toward Miss Parker, who wore a puzzled expression. She caught him looking her way and her features softened. Then her face bloomed pink.

Stephen blinked. Here he was, brand-new, and he was already being assessed like this? Well, if he was to lead an academy, then he would need to know how to command a staff of faculty, some of whom were likely more expert than he. Such as the older woman who taught grammar. Miss Huckabee, was it? She appeared to be close to his mother's age.

"Teachers will report grades regularly to their captains, who will then calculate the averages and submit them to me for approval before the average is posted above. The average will be updated every quarter."

Another teacher raised her hand and Aunt Marjorie nodded in her direction.

"So, if I may ask, how did you arrive at the decision for team captains? Mr. Mason is new, and Miss Parker is not the most experienced teacher. I believe Miss Huckabee is our most senior member of the faculty." The woman looked at Stephen suspiciously and then at Miss Parker, as if Miss Parker did not meet with her approval.

"Miss Dunham, I selected the two I thought might be likely candidates for my replacement someday."

Several of the women gasped. "You're leaving us?"

Aunt Marjorie laughed. Stephen did not ever remember hearing her laugh before. His interactions with his father's sister had been limited over the years, and quite frankly, when he was a child, her teacher's demeanor did not endear her to him. He hadn't been the best student as a child, and yet he had managed to complete his education near the top of his class after his father dared him that he could not.

Father's bluff had worked, far more than he had likely imagined at that time.

"No. Not yet. But there will come a time when I won't be here. Wickham Academy shall always be my home. Yet I find myself wanting to step away from time to time, and I need to know I will have someone running it well for me."

Having that conversation with Aunt Marjorie in her study and then hearing the same words in a faculty meeting were two different things. This could really be happening. He wanted to win. If he lost this, he wasn't sure what that would do to his position in the family, as precarious as it was at the moment.

Nothing more was said as his aunt let that bit of information sink in. Stephen could hear only the *tick-tock* of the grandfather clock at the end of the hallway.

"Here we go. Each of you, except for Miss Parker and Mr. Mason, pull a name from the bag." Aunt Marjorie held another bag up, shaking it as she did so.

Each of the remaining six teachers pulled a slip of paper from the bag. Miss Huckabee, Miss Dunham, and Miss Brock drew Miss Parker's name, and Mrs. Benoit, Miss Webster, and Miss Duggan selected his name. So he had the French teacher, the history and geography teacher, and the manners teacher reporting to him.

"Does anyone have any questions?" Aunt Marjorie paused, scanning their faces as she did so. "None? Very well, I leave you to prepare your classrooms. The term starts in one week, immediately after breakfast." She smiled at them all, then strode toward her study.

Miss Huckabee chuckled, then shook her head. "And here we are, the lot of us, standing in her wake. Should we expect any different?"

Mrs. Benoit, who taught French, wore her hair short and spoke with an accent. "This way of thinking, I do not understand. Questions I have, yes, but I am sure they will be answered in due time."

She stepped toward Stephen and extended her hand.

"Jacqueline Benoit. I am widowed and live here in town. I have been teaching for fifteen years and my husband is deceased for five. I have no need for entanglements and always ensure that my students perform at their best."

He shook the woman's hand. "Pleased to meet you."

In turn, he met each of the other teachers. Miss Webster, at first glance, looked dour but had kind eyes. Her specialty was geography. She, like the French teacher, lived in town. She took care of her elderly mother. Miss Duggan was the spinster daughter of Reverend Duggan, who presided over one of the local churches. She taught Latin as well as manners. Charlotte Huckabee taught grammar to the younger students along with penmanship. She reminded him of his older sister, who had a brood of children and whose husband was a shopkeeper.

They took their leave of him, and at the same time so did the teachers speaking with Miss Parker. Her now-underlings wished her well as they left, one of them giving Stephen a grin that bore a challenge. Clearly, Miss Parker had the advantage after being here for so long.

And now, here was Miss Parker.

"Well," she said. "I believe this will be an interesting year."

"I quite agree with you," he replied.

"I hope and pray that the best teacher wins." Her eyes held a sparkle he couldn't miss.

"As do I. I warn you, I don't like to lose."

"Neither do I." She raised her chin ever so slightly. "But as long as the children succeed, it will be worth it to me."

"I quite agree with you on that as well."

"So what made you decide to teach here at Wickham Academy? Mrs. Wickham did not mention until now that a new teacher would be joining us."

"She's my father's oldest sister, and this summer she decided she no longer wished to teach mathematics and offered me the position."

"I see. So I believe you have an advantage, being family."

"An advantage for what? Winning? We have no idea, yet, how the students will perform."

"But surely you know that by the end of the school year one of us will be the head of this academy." Their gazes locked. Her eyes were a curious shade of green with brown flecks at the center.

"I assure you, I had no idea she was going to spring that on me after her offer of employment."

"I didn't believe I was a sure thing for the position either. But. . ." She raised her hands, palms up.

"But you've been here longer and probably deserve it more than I do."

"Probably." She chuckled. "I'm sorry to laugh. But I want this to be a pleasant year for all of us."

"As do I."

"So, Mr. Mason. If I'm to beat you, I should know my adversary. How many years have you been teaching?"

"I have taught for one year."

She blinked at him, incredulous. "One year. At the school in Cambridge."

He knew she probably would have added, *You're already on the way to running an academy at the end of your second year of teaching?*

"That's right. I taught upper-level mathematics to the boys preparing to attend college."

"Oh my. Wickham Academy is very different. We have a handful of young ladies preparing for college, but the majority of your students will most likely be from the younger set, learning their basic sums and such."

"Yes. Aunt Marjorie informed me as much when we discussed my employment. I think the break from upper-level mathematics will be a welcome change for me. I find that with older students, if they do not have firm building blocks of education and mathematics basics, it is much more difficult for them to achieve the higher level work, particularly if I find myself having to reteach basic principles they should have mastered already."

"Then I'm sure this position will be very fulfilling for you."

"And what about you? You said you've been teaching for eight years at Wickham."

"Yes, I've truly enjoyed my time teaching both composition and literature to the older students, and art. Fortunately, my students have had Charlotte teaching them their basics, and I can delve into advanced composition and literature. But I find myself looking forward to the possibility of having an administrative role here."

"Perhaps I should have asked for Miss Huckabee to be on my team."

"You could have, but she is one of my friends here, and I have her loyalty." At first he thought her comment was serious but then he caught the twinkle in her eyes.

"It's good to have loyal friends." He wished he had a

few. He'd burned some bridges along the way, and he suddenly realized that he valued what someone like Miss Parker thought of him. He trusted his aunt's discretion that nothing would be said of his life before his time teaching at Armstrong Academy.

Chapter 3

*T*he voices of excited students filled the halls outside the classrooms at Wickham's. The old routine came back, of breakfast, then morning classes, then lunch, followed by a walk around the courtyard or a hike to Wickham pond, followed by quiet time and a few more classes prior to dismissal in the late afternoon. Mrs. Wickham kept a rather unconventional schedule, but it worked for her students and her teachers, and it was a schedule Caroline approved of very much.

In the afternoon she would set up her easel, as would some of her art students, while her composition students would assemble to write the papers that Caroline had assigned in the morning class. As she painted, students would stop by her side to ask questions. They would fill the large drawing room from one end to the other.

She enjoyed the freedom, and so far the students' papers reflected that their skills were back up to par and even above where they were before the break from school over the summer.

With the return of the students had also come tales of summertime frolicking that had never been a part of Caroline's life when she was their age.

"I was able to stay in Newport, with my cousin, for an entire week," exclaimed Eugenia Ware. "Oh, the fun we had at the coast."

"Much more fun than being here and working on sums and compositions and things like that," said Celeste Monroe.

The two students were also drawing this afternoon. Caroline tried not to chuckle at the remarks. There were a great many things that were more enjoyable than sums and composition, but she believed a young woman would be served well if she were skilled at both.

Yet another reason she valued being at Wickham's. The young women who completed their studies were well prepared for whatever came next, whether it be attending college, getting married, or simply returning to their families. Some of those decisions were entirely up to the young women, but some were not.

She glanced over to where four of her other students were either reading or writing, and smiled.

"And then I heard she was locked in her room because she didn't want to marry the man her parents, or her mother rather, had chosen for her." Eugenia, the older of the two students painting, was talking about one of the young women who'd been part of her circle that summer.

"Goodness!" Celeste shook her head. "I can't imagine."

Neither could Caroline. Her own interest in the life of high society couldn't be denied. Northampton had some of its own bigwigs, but nothing compared to the Vanderbilts, who divided their time between their home in New York City and their summer "cottage" on the coast.

She continued to sketch a landscape that included Wickham's pond that was fed by a small spring over which someone had constructed a footbridge. It was a passable piece, something she was creating as she instructed the girls.

"So, Miss Parker? Do you think you're going to win?" Eugenia asked.

"I would definitely want to be ahead at the end of the first quarter."

"We will know soon. I can't wait for the quarter to be over, because then it's on to the next quarter." Eugenia nodded emphatically. "I do wish school terms were shorter."

Sometimes Caroline did too, but she didn't let on to Eugenia.

"I'm to have my scores averaged and submitted to Mrs. Wickham, so we will know by the end of the week."

"I hope you win. I could even get a few of my mathematics problems wrong on purpose."

"*Eugenia!*" Caroline nearly dropped her charcoal pencil. "That's cheating, and it is wrong. I would like to win, but not that way. I want to win fair and square, in a way that pleases God. And not by cheating."

"Yes, Miss Parker." Eugenia looked crestfallen. Even her curls seemed to droop. "I'm very sorry. I would not really do that to you. I was only making a joke."

"I appreciate that you want me to win. All I ask of you, any and all of you, is that you do your best, regardless of the subject, and even if you are not on my team. That's all I ask. You might not have many years here at Wickham's, not compared to the rest of your life, and I want them to be good ones."

"What about your years, Miss Parker? Have they been good ones?" Eugenia asked, arching an eyebrow.

"They have, indeed. You young ladies have helped make them good years." Eugenia and a handful of the older girls would have their studies finished by the spring, and after that, who knew where they would go and what they would do?

"Why do you want to run Wickham's? Don't you want to have a family someday?"

"Hush, Eugenia." Celeste poked her friend in the arm. "Of course spinsters want to have husbands someday. Sorry, Miss Parker. I'm not trying to say you're old or anything of the sort."

"No offense taken, Celeste. Maybe someday, but not now." Even if a gentleman caller showed up at the academy, she couldn't just court someone. It was forbidden by the terms of her employment agreement with Wickham's. She could not marry during the school year. It had never come up in eight years. But yes, she was a spinster, for lack of a better term.

"What about Mr. Mason?" Eugenia asked.

"What about him?" Caroline decided it would be best to let Eugenia ask her question and then they'd be done with it.

"He's not married and he's not very old, and he teaches too."

Caroline laughed. "Please, Eugenia. That is absolutely out of the question. I've known him less than two months, and besides, I am not giving up my position for any man."

As she spoke the words, she felt herself hesitate. If she lost out on the director position for the academy, what could she do? Stay on, despite the loss? Or find somewhere else to go? As much as she enjoyed Wickham's, it was all she knew in the realm of education. Maybe she could teach somewhere else, or direct another academy. She didn't want to think about that just yet. Right now, she needed to make sure the literature students completed their reports on *The Adventures of Huckleberry Finn* and that her other students practiced their penmanship and learned new drawing techniques.

Stephen heard the girlish chatter and giggles inside the space that Miss Parker used as a study and workroom. It was a stark contrast to the way his classes functioned. Inside his classroom, the students were quiet as they sat at desks, lined up row by row. The assignment of the day was already on the chalkboard when they entered the room. After a brief explanation of the present subject, whether it be addition or subtraction or higher level mathematics, he would expect them to sit and practice the equations. If there were questions, he would answer them. As students completed their work, they would bring it to his desk for checking and assistance.

Those who mastered their work could go ahead with the next assignment, and those who needed help received a little extra assistance. It seemed to work for him, and them.

But there was none of the relaxed chatter and giggles he heard now. He cautiously peeked into the room. At one end were some older upholstered items, upon which three girls sat, reading. A fourth sat at a desk, a book open before her as she wrote on a tablet.

Miss Parker stood at an easel, as did a pair of older students.

He could just make out a line of trees framing a small lake on the canvas. It was quite a good painting. He knew he'd never be able to sketch something of the same quality.

"Miss Parker, Mr. Mason is here to see you," a soft female voice said.

At that, all of the ladies in the room turned to stare at him.

"Ah, good afternoon," Stephen said as he stepped into the room. "I was merely passing by."

"Please, come in." Miss Parker wore a quizzical expression. "Where are your students?"

"They will be in class in about ten minutes. We have a test today," he explained. As if he needed to, and why he was explaining himself, he didn't know.

"Oh, I see."

"What are you working on here? Is this a class?"

"Yes and no," Miss Parker explained. "The composition and literature students will test in the morning, tomorrow. Today they are finishing their review and practice, or finishing their themes."

"So different from what I'm accustomed to seeing in my classroom." He could tell the atmosphere was far more relaxed than in his classroom, yet learning was still taking place.

She nodded. "This is what I've found works for my students."

"We like how Miss Parker runs our classes." One of the older girls, with brown hair and light blue eyes, spoke up.

Miss Eugenia Ware, if he recalled correctly. She was one of his upper-level students, and she struggled with mathematics more than the other students did. Enrolled at Wickham's since she was ten years old, Miss Ware would be completing her studies in the spring.

He wanted to talk with Miss Parker about Eugenia, to see how he might best help her. She had not improved beyond the fall term, and middle-term exams were around the corner along with her next section test.

"Miss Parker, may I have a word with you outside the room?" He really needed to head to his own classroom, but decided he ought to seize the chance to speak with her now, even if briefly.

"Of course." Miss Parker set down her brush and headed in his direction. He couldn't keep from staring at the smudge on her right cheek as they exited the room, and he lifted his finger and brushed his cheek, raising his eyebrows at her.

She reached up and wiped her cheek, but the smudge, in fact, deepened. "Oh, there's something on my face. Is it gone?"

"No. In fact, I think you just made it worse."

She rubbed her cheek a bit harder. "Better?"

"Yes." It was a little better, but the smudge still remained. He wasn't about to wipe it off himself, not with inquiring eyes within the room that could likely see around doorframes.

"So what did you need to speak with me about?"

Somehow, he sensed the young ladies inside the room were listening, waiting to hear the discussion. "Come with me, please."

They stepped along the hall to the entrance of the building. He stopped a careful distance from the room.

"It's Miss Ware. I'm a bit concerned about her mathematics grades and how she applies her knowledge. I'm puzzled, because when I present the information, she acts as if she understands. But when we get to the review and application of what she's been taught, it's as if she is seeing it all for the first time."

Miss Parker frowned. "That's not good. She hasn't mentioned

anything to me about it."

And, he mused, scores would be calculated before the end of the week and posted. Of course he wanted to get to the top of the scoreboard and stay there. He didn't think she'd mind knowing about her student not doing so well in another subject, even if it was a subject she didn't teach and a subject that didn't win her points in the competition.

"Yes. I'm not sure exactly where the problem lies. I've tested her on basic, primary mathematics operations, and those she understands and has mastered very well." He raised his hands. "But I'm stumped."

"If she needs more assistance, I would rather her attend a class with you than spend time here, drawing, if she needs the help."

"I'm not trying to overstep. This isn't about the contest."

"No, it's not, and I understand what you mean," she said. "The first set of averages hasn't been posted yet."

Stephen released a deep breath. "Good. Tomorrow, before testing, we could meet with her together."

"How about right after breakfast?"

He nodded. "That is agreeable to me."

"We'll see you then."

He hurried away from her, back toward his own classroom.

The following morning, both Miss Parker and Miss Ware came to his classroom. Miss Ware looked nervous, and Miss Parker looked concerned.

"Am I in trouble, Mr. Mason?"

"Not at all, Miss Ware." He sat at his desk, and the two of them sat at student desks. "I have your grades from yesterday's test, and, I'm sorry to say, you barely passed."

"Eugenia, Mr. Mason is concerned that you're struggling with mathematics, when in the past it has not been a problem for you." Miss Parker gazed at Miss Ware with an intense expression on her face. "Please tell me it's not anything like we discussed yesterday."

The young woman's face paled. "No, not at all, Miss Parker. I believe that I might, ah, need more help."

Miss Parker shook her head. "Well, I will make sure you have the help you need. I'm sure Mr. Mason will do the same."

He nodded. "Instead of drawing in the afternoon, please come to my primary class in the afternoon and I will give you some additional assistance. And maybe you might be able to help the younger students too."

"A–all right, I will." The young lady's cheeks bloomed crimson.

Stephen and Miss Parker exchanged glances across the desk.

Miss Parker spoke first. "Very well, Eugenia. You will report to Mr. Mason's classroom until your scores are at least ten points above passing."

Miss Ware rose to her feet, nodded, then zipped from the room.

After the sound of her footsteps in the hallway disappeared, Stephen spoke again. "I thank you again for permitting her to have some additional help for mathematics. I'm not sure, even if I sent work for her to complete in the afternoons, that she would be successful."

"Whatever do you mean by that? If you sent some additional assignments, I would ensure she completes them."

"I'm afraid the more casual format would not help her, in this case."

At that remark, Miss Parker's lips sealed into a thin line, unlike the easy smile he had grown accustomed to seeing.

"Mr. Mason," she said at last. "I have had many successes over the past years, with many students, due to the format of my classes, especially in the afternoons. I'll thank you kindly to keep your opinion to yourself as you provide help for Eugenia. Now, if you'll excuse me."

She rose from where she'd tucked herself behind the desk and marched from the room.

Well, he might not have bungled the directorship position, but he'd certainly just bungled things with Miss Parker.

⚮ Chapter 4 ⥁

The entire student body and faculty of Wickham Academy had assembled in the great entryway in front of the Olympiad scoreboard, now covered again with a cloth.

Caroline stood in a row with her fellow teachers. Of course, not all of the students could fit into the space, but others filled the hallway and the parlor beyond the hall. She knew Mr. Mason was probably just as nervous as she was about seeing the team averages so far.

The murmurs rippling through the gathered students ceased as Mrs. Wickham raised both hands as if to summon the students closer. "I have verified the averages for each of the subjects in the Olympiad for the first quarter of the school year. Mind you, there are but three more two-month quarters for the school year, so we are how far through the year?"

"One-fourth, Mrs. Wickham," a quiet voice said among the group.

"Very good, Miss Bardway, very good." She turned to face

the cloth and gave a soft tug, and the cloth came away from the scoreboard. The room fell silent as they all took in the sight of the team averages.

Caroline scanned the numbers below her name: Mathematics 82, Grammar 95, Literature 88, French 88, Latin 79, Geography 91, History 90, Art 98, Sciences 84. The Latin score made her wince and wonder who needed more help. The other scores were relatively strong, except for Mathematics.

She compared her numbers to those of Mr. Mason's, with his being: Mathematics 92, Grammar 93, Literature 83, French 90, Latin 84, Geography 92, History 85, Art 92, Sciences 84.

Who had the best average of all the grades so far? She glanced toward Mr. Mason, whom she hadn't really spoken to since the morning talk in the classroom about Miss Ware.

"So, we took an average for both teams and found it quite surprising," said Mrs. Wickham. "In fact, it is so surprising that we will give the team with the highest average this first quarter a special prize, right now."

Excited whispers echoed in the hall. Caroline smiled. Of course she wanted to be ahead, but she also wanted all the students to succeed.

"As I said, it was a surprise to me," Mrs. Wickham continued. "To celebrate, the winners will be treated to an autumn festival, complete with caramel apples, candied popcorn, a hayride, and a bonfire before we release for Thanksgiving."

Cheers went up, but subsided as the students realized they might not be the ones participating.

"The average for Miss Parker's team is eighty-eight point three. And the average for Mr. Mason's team is also eighty-eight point three." Mrs. Wickham sounded triumphant. "Of course, there is room for improvement, but I trust that both Miss Parker and Mr. Mason, and the teachers on their teams, can help you students to continue to do well through hard work and perseverance."

So they were all getting a celebratory prize? Yes, Caroline had known the averages for her own classes. But to have the same overall average as Mr. Mason's team?

He ambled up to her as the students were rejoicing with each other. "Yes. I checked the math. My overall average is the same."

She smiled. "I have a hard time believing it myself."

Stephen extended a hand in her direction. "Please, accept my apologies for the other day. I wasn't trying to suggest your way is faulty. It's very different from mine, but I can see you get results and your students are succeeding."

Caroline shook his hand. "Of course I accept. You too have had students succeed with the way that you teach."

"I do believe we can both be a resource for each other, to help students who don't respond to our best teaching method."

"I agree with you." She looked down. They'd stopped shaking hands and stood there, hands gently clasped. She slid her hand from his grip.

"So, Thanksgiving is soon," Mr. Mason said. "How do you plan to spend the occasion?"

She swallowed hard. "I plan to stay here. We have a meal with the students who remain at the academy throughout the school year. I usually make pies."

"Really? Well, this year, I plan to stay at Wickham's as well. My parents are hosting a supper at their home in Connecticut, and they understand it's a way to travel. Christmas, now, we may all gather here at Wickham's."

"That will be a pleasant gathering for all of you, I'm sure." She looked forward to a break and to seeing her family, but not to the trappings that went with the holiday.

"Yes, I'm hopeful it will indeed be pleasant this time around." He looked pensive.

"This time around?"

Before he could respond, Charlotte came swooping in. "Can you believe that? Same average? You two didn't plan this, did you?" She wore a wide smile.

"No, we certainly did not." Caroline couldn't help but be free with her own grin. "I'm already planning for how we can do better for the next quarter. It will be a challenge, with thoughts of Christmas in their heads, but I'll do the best I can."

"I'm here to help you however I can." Charlotte's enthusiasm bubbled out. She glanced at Mr. Mason. "You, sir, may fend for yourself."

Mr. Mason looked taken aback, and at that, they all laughed.

The academy held the promised celebration of autumn, which involved a bonfire, apple cider, and homemade doughnuts, after several days of examinations that ended on a Friday. Caroline suspected that the celebration was more about the examinations being completed than the upcoming holiday. It was a time for the teachers to rejoice as well.

Caroline stood in the front doorway holding a platter of doughnuts sprinkled with sugar, still warm. She inhaled the sweet, spicy aroma. As she did, she glimpsed Mr. Mason preparing the bonfire, placing short branches and sticks and scrap wood into a growing pile.

The pile seemed to be growing very large indeed, perhaps due to Mr. Mason's enthusiasm about the whole affair. His cheeks were flushed, and the hair brushed back and spiking from his forehead lent a boyish demeanor to his expression.

He paused when he saw her enter the courtyard. She grinned at him, and his grin in return made her glance down at the doughnuts. Not a one had slipped out of place.

Caroline strode toward the pile of wood. "The students will be here soon. You'd better grab a doughnut now, while you still can. I'm not sure how many more Cook will make."

"Don't mind if I do." He wiped his hand on his trousers before taking a doughnut from the plate.

She set the platter down on a small table, where bottled cider—apple juice, really, that the girls had made themselves—had already been placed.

"I think I'll have one too." She helped herself to a doughnut and took a bite. Her mother would make doughnuts like these, tasting of apple and spices, but the sugar coating the tops of these bits of doughy fried goodness was a luxury.

"After the testing, I believe I could sleep the entire weekend away," Stephen commented.

"So could I, it feels like. I'm encouraged by their scores, I think—although scores are only one indication of how a child learns."

"I share that sentiment with you." Mr. Mason downed the last of his doughnut.

They fell into an easy discussion about the weather, predicting when they might have the first snowfall, and Caroline found herself enjoying the conversation. She did like talking with her other fellow teachers, but this conversation felt different.

She realized it was because she didn't speak with men much, if at all. She couldn't recall the last real conversation she'd had with her father, but figured it must have been during the Christmas season last year. Her exchanges at church services on Sunday were mere pleasantries, greetings to the reverend and other men in the church, most of whom had wives.

"Why did you decide to become a teacher?" she heard herself asking.

Mr. Mason inhaled slowly. "I covered a long road of bad decisions, long story short, and decided I'd had enough. I didn't want to join my father in the family business. We haven't always gotten along. I figured teaching is an honorable profession and something I could do. So I studied for my examination and passed it on the first try. Then I secured the position in Cambridge, and now here we are. . . . And you—what about you?"

Caroline swallowed her bite of doughnut. "My mother wanted better for me than she had, and I was always a good student, if a bit distractible, so she encouraged me to become a teacher. So I did."

It had always been a simple, logical choice for her.

"I'm glad we've both ended up here, no matter what the outcome, Caroline." Mr. Mason nodded slowly. "May I call you Caroline?"

"Why, yes, if I may call you Stephen—after school hours."

"Of course you may."

Caroline found herself smiling as the sounds of young laughter filled the courtyard.

"Look! Miss Parker has *doughnuts!*" a girl shrieked with delight.

All too soon, the school closed its doors for Thanksgiving, giving students the following day as a break as well, so those who lived close enough could visit their families and have a long weekend.

The others, a handful of students who lived farther away than a short carriage ride, as well as Stephen and Aunt Marjorie and Miss Parker, were staying at the academy to have a meal together for Thanksgiving.

Without school in session, there was little for Stephen to do other than act as a helper while Miss Parker made pies. He watched her expertly trim the piecrust edges. She was at ease in the kitchen in a way he'd never seen a woman other than the cooks in his family's kitchen.

"Can you please fetch more eggs for the buttermilk pie?" she asked him. Today she wore her hair back in a simple braid instead of in a twisted knot pinned to her head. The look made her appear younger. Not that she appeared old to him, but. . .today he felt as if he were seeing a glimpse of not just Miss Parker, the teacher, but Caroline, the woman.

"What did you need again? Eggs? How many?" He found his voice fumbling, cracking as if he were an adolescent.

"Six, please. I believe Agnes, Cook's assitant, gathered enough yesterday. They should be in the bowl at the end of the cutting board." She gestured with her head, then winced. "Ouch."

She lifted up one hand, her index finger bearing a stripe of red that began to run down her finger. Stephen immediately stepped in her direction. "Let's get a towel on that, quickly."

"There are towels in the butler's pantry."

Stephen took her by the elbow and guided her away from the counter, leaving the piecrusts behind them. Inside the butler's pantry off the kitchen, he opened a drawer and found a small cloth. Before he clamped it onto the cut, he examined it. He'd given aid to people with a bloody nose and busted lip here and there over the years, so this cut wasn't much of an incident. But Miss Parker's face had paled at the sight of the blood that ran down her finger.

"Here." He wrapped the edge of the towel around her finger. "This will take but a few moments."

As they waited, he stared down at the cloth covering her hand while she stared at the pantry drawers. Footsteps alerted them that someone was entering the kitchen.

"Well, she was here a moment ago." It was Aunt Marjorie. "Caroline was preparing to make pies. Ah, it's just as well. Did you see my nephew?"

"No, not since he brought in more wood for the fire." The second voice was Cook's.

"So what do you think of my nephew and Miss Parker? Do you think they are getting along?"

"About as well as I would think they might. They are both young, intelligent individuals."

Miss Parker looked up at him, questions in her eyes. She moved to pull away from him, but he stopped her, putting his finger to his lips.

"I will not listen and eavesdrop," she whispered.

"This is unintentional. What do you think they would say if they found us here?"

"That you are tending to my cut."

He glanced over her head toward the kitchen.

"I believe they might make a good match. But then, I'm not entirely sure." A pause, then the swishing of long skirts on the wooden floor. "Perhaps she's upstairs. Although I don't see why she'd leave a crust only partly rolled out."

Cook murmured something about the facilities before the two women left the kitchen and it was silent once again.

This time, he let Miss Parker's hand go. She peeled back the towel. The bleeding had stopped, mostly. He wasn't sure where they had bandages, but he imagined there was something in a cupboard nearby.

"A good match? Did you hear your aunt? She thinks we might make a good match?" Miss Parker shook her head. "Why would she think that?"

"Caroline—"

"Stephen. I have a job here, one that I have enjoyed for years. I refuse to give it up."

"No one has asked you to do that. I've never asked to court you, or seen you in any fashion other than related to the school."

"Except today."

"This is a holiday on which we give thanks to God for His blessings, and all come together."

"Yes. But I'm not about to put my job in jeopardy. Your aunt has rules, and they are in place for a reason."

"Take a deep breath—relax. You are my fellow teacher and, I

hope, a friend. We can be friends, can't we?"

She nodded. "I don't see why we can't be friends." Then she smiled.

He smiled back. "Good. Because I'll enjoy besting my friend's team in the Olympiad."

ᘓ Chapter 5 ᘔ

𝒯he days after Thanksgiving became a blur of studying and testing, whispers and secrets, and planning for a gift exchange at a Christmas tree to be set up in the entryway hall. Caroline's finger healed nicely and they'd enjoyed her pies—with new piecrusts—at Thanksgiving and for the days after.

Caroline still couldn't believe that Mrs. Wickham had considered her and Stephen to be a good match. She never would have imagined such a thing. Was the woman playing matchmaker by hiring her nephew at the academy?

True, Mrs. Wickham seemed more relaxed now that she no longer had to teach mathematics classes. But having her nephew come here and work, to meet Caroline? The idea of courting, right now, seemed like a far-fetched one. And what an idea! What if Caroline and Stephen hadn't gotten along? To be sure, they had differing ideas on education, but he had settled into the routine here and had become a part of the staff.

On a Sunday afternoon before Christmas break, Elizabeth

mentioned that perhaps Caroline ought to meet her brother's friend, an attorney moving to Northampton, where he planned to open an office.

"I know you are a dedicated teacher, but if—and when—you become director of the academy, surely the courting rule doesn't apply to you anymore."

Elizabeth and Caroline, covered in lap blankets and wearing their winter coats, rode along in the carriage that would drop Elizabeth off at her home and Caroline back at the academy. The first real snowfall had come to the area, and Caroline was happy for the chance to be relatively warm and snug instead of walking six blocks in the cold.

She pondered Elizabeth's words. "I don't know. Quite frankly, it hasn't been a priority for me. I hadn't thought to ask Mrs. Wickham if a possible new position for me would have an effect on that rule." What was in the air? First Mrs. Wickham, and now Elizabeth wanting to play matchmaker. She had never heard such talk of matchmaking and introductions during her years at the academy.

"So you'll consent to meeting Mr. Thomas?"

"No, I will not. Not now, anyway. What if he doesn't want to meet a teacher?"

"Future director of an academy, you should say."

"There's no guarantee I'll have that position."

"No, but it's a real possibility."

They came to Elizabeth's home and stopped at the curb. "Well, I'll see you soon."

"Yes, see you soon!" Elizabeth popped out of the carriage and Caroline continued along the way to the academy. After a last-day-of-school celebration before the break, which would include an updated score for the second two months of the school year, Caroline would head home to Holyoke.

She looked forward to the holiday and seeing her mother, but seeing her sister and possibly her father, not so much. She had their gifts ready to bring with her, along with a quantity of money that should help their situation for a while.

Why would a man consider courting a woman who supported her family who somehow scraped by barely above the edge of poverty?

Certainly not a man like Stephen Mason, and definitely not an attorney.

The carriage brought her into the academy's courtyard, and Caroline climbed out carefully. There would be a warm meal of stew and bread, and possibly a dessert, the cook had said. Caroline's stomach growled as she headed toward the main building, where her room was. At one o'clock, they would sit down to a meal at the Wickhams' dining table. Typically, she did not dine with Mrs. Wickham, but ever since Thanksgiving, Mrs. Wickham had made it a point to include Caroline in her weekly Sunday supper invitation.

She well knew the reason why, especially after the conversation she and Stephen had overheard on Thanksgiving Day. Caroline quickened her steps as a gust of wind blew through the courtyard.

"Oh Caroline, there you are!" Mrs. Wickham called out into the courtyard. "Please, come inside. This chill is piercing to the bones."

Caroline complied, changing her direction to head toward Mrs. Wickham's home. She tried not to slip on the cobblestones, which still had a light covering of snowflakes that had fallen since the morning.

"I've had sixty-two winters, and each of them has been colder than the last." Mrs. Wickham led her from the entryway into the sitting room, which had a glowing fire that lit up the piano in the corner of the room. "I'll take your coat."

Caroline unbuttoned her coat and slipped out of it, giving an involuntary shiver as she did so. "Thank you."

"Please, sit down. We will dine a little earlier today. Stephen is out running an errand for me. There is a feeling of ice in the air today. I suspect we will have to salt the sidewalks and paths for walking."

They sat in the sitting room, which looked out onto the courtyard. Silvery-gray clouds hung low in the sky, the bare trees swaying from gusts of wind. In spite of her warm surroundings, Caroline shivered again.

"Salting the walks is just one of the tasks one must think of and attend to, as director of the school. Many things must happen behind the scenes so things in the forefront appear to run smoothly, without incident." Mrs. Wickham rose from her chair and strolled to the window. "My Mr. Wickham was good at that. He knew what had to happen on the grounds, and more. There is the matter of food and lodging, and upkeep of the buildings. Without him, I could not have done this, and without him, I learned to do this."

Caroline nodded. "I hadn't thought of it like that before, but it's true. From making sure the walkways are swept to providing enough food for the students who live and eat here at the academy."

"Then there are the matters of recordkeeping, tallying tuition payments, accepting prospective student applications, meeting new families, and conducting interviews. Not to mention ensuring the classroom supplies are purchased. It never ends," Mrs. Wickham said. "Goodness, I am wearing myself out simply thinking and talking about it. For me, it is my life. It is every day of the week, of the month, of the year. There are no holidays, for even when the students are not in class, there are other matters at the academy that must be attended to."

"I understand."

Mrs. Wickham laughed softly. "My nephew said the same thing. But you are both young and up to the challenge, I believe. If you execute the procedures and plans I have already developed, you should do well in the position. Either of you."

Caroline smiled at the older woman's words. "Thank you for your confidence in us, in me." Today she found herself wanting the position very much. But Mrs. Wickham was right—it would be a lot of work, far more than teaching one class and overseeing a team of teachers. Far more than a few would depend on her, if she won the job.

Stephen hurried back to the academy as fast as the horse could pull the cart safely. He was running late for their meal, but it was unintentional, as Aunt Marjorie had let him know at the last possible moment that she'd forgotten to order the salt to spread on the walkways prior to the bad weather that even now was threatening to let loose upon their area.

He had a notice in his pocket, one he was unsure how to

handle. The opportunity wasn't meant for him, but was ideal for someone like Caroline. He had carried it since yesterday, after receiving his personal mail.

It was for a teaching job at Madame Tetreault's Finishing School in Winchester, not so far from where he used to teach in Cambridge. A friend of his who also taught at the school had written to him, asking if he knew of anyone who could teach art and music, as Madame Tetreault would find herself in want of a teacher for both next school year.

He had immediately thought of Caroline. It had nothing to do with the Olympiad and their mutual quest to land the director's position at the academy. If she won, she won. If not, she could very well leave.

The thought of her leaving did not please him one bit. But if this was a better opportunity for her, it would be wrong of him not to share it with her. He was not looking for another position and could not paint, nor could he sing or play an instrument. But Caroline could do all three. He'd seen her take a turn on the piano, she was quite adept at it, and her voice was lovely.

He reached the academy and unloaded the bags of salt into the shed, where the groundskeeper could access the salt to spread along the walkways. If needed, Stephen would assist the man. Aunt Marjorie had had a pointed conversation with Stephen at breakfast that very morning about the full responsibilities of directing the academy. He told her he understood and would do what needed to be done, should he get the position.

Once inside the house, he heard women's voices coming from the parlor. It was Aunt Marjorie and Caroline, chatting about Christmas.

"Yes, ma'am, I'm looking forward to seeing my family. My mother and father have been well, thank you." Caroline's voice trailed off when she saw him enter the parlor.

"Salt has been picked up, Aunt Marjorie. Let the clouds shower ice on us, and we will not slide, not at Wickham Academy." He tugged his scarf from around his neck. "I beg your pardon, Caroline. I did not mean to interrupt."

"Not at all." She inclined her head in his direction.

Aunt Marjorie rose from her chair. "I shall see if the meal has been set out. Pardon me." She left the room.

"So where will Christmas find you with your family?" he asked, settling into the chair his aunt had vacated.

Caroline shifted in her chair. She swallowed hard and stared at the fire. "Holyoke."

"That's not too far of a trip. Close enough to make it there and back again in a day, with a driver." He wondered why she didn't visit her family more often. In fact, he couldn't recall her ever having left to visit them, not since he'd first met her at the school.

"My father works at a press and my mother keeps house. My sister is a seamstress. They are all very busy," said Caroline, as if in explanation to his unspoken query. "But a visit at Christmas will be nice, I'm sure. My mother always made it special for my sister and me as children. We would walk together to a Christmas Eve service, then walk home and wait for my father to get there."

"It sounds like you had an enjoyable upbringing during the holidays," he said.

"My mother made the most of it for us. What we lacked in some things children might have received, we knew the reason for Christmas and we cherished every gift, no matter how small."

He thought of the letter in his pocket. Would now be the best time? He didn't want to hand it to her in front of his aunt. It would be poor form. He wasn't trying to get rid of her by any means. But the directorship was a big load to carry.

"Stephen, what is it?" She searched his face. He shook his head. "You looked like you were about to say something."

"Nothing. Not now," he said, as Aunt Marjorie rounded the corner. "Maybe another time."

"Dinner is served," Aunt Marjorie announced.

ॐ Chapter 6 ॐ

C aroline lugged two satchels up the last step to the door of her childhood home, the third-floor apartment in one of a row of houses in a Holyoke neighborhood. There were no decorations to show that it was Christmas, save a small crèche atop a table beneath the front window. But something delicious was cooking, judging by the aroma wafting from the kitchen.

"Mama, I'm here!" Caroline called out.

Her mother burst into the parlor. She wore the same apron that Caroline remembered from childhood. Yet her mother seemed shorter and more tired, and there were lines on her face Caroline hadn't noticed until now.

"I'm so glad you're home."

Caroline was wrapped in a slim yet tight embrace. "Where's Eleanor?"

Mama released her, yet still held her shoulders. "She'll be back right before supper. She's delivering her sewing. Come to the kitchen with me. You can unpack later. Your bed is all ready."

Caroline set down the satchels and followed her mother to the kitchen area, where a small table with barely room for four chairs had been tucked into one corner, with one wall having room for a stove and an icebox, along with a small countertop with a few cabinets.

"I've made us a chicken pie tonight. I hope you're hungry." Mama turned to the stove where a coffeepot perked. "Coffee?"

"No, thank you, but I'm looking forward to the pie." Her stomach grumbled. "Will Papa be here for supper?"

Mama's shoulders drooped as she poured a cup of coffee. She joined Caroline at the table. "I don't know. I hope he will. Told him this morning, before he left, that you'd be home tonight. But I imagine he'll be down at the Cloverleaf on High Street."

Things had changed for Caroline, but as she suspected, not much had changed at home. "Well, I'll be here until the morning after Christmas, so I'm sure I'll get to see him."

The front door burst open, and along with a blast of cold air, in came Eleanor. She wore a scarf over her head. It also wrapped her neck and was tucked into the front of her coat. She held a cloth bag that swung freely, empty.

"You're here!" she said, looking at Caroline. Without waiting for a response, she pulled a small bag from her pocket. "Look, Mama. Plenty of cash and coin for Christmas dinner. Mrs. Brickman paid me an extra dollar for the dress alteration, she was so pleased with it."

Cheeks flushed, Eleanor marched into the warm kitchen. She set the small bag of money on the table, then tossed the empty bag into the corner, atop a pile of clothing. Mama poured a cup of coffee for Eleanor and set it in front of her.

"I'm bushed. Is the pie ready yet? It smells good." Eleanor took a sip of the coffee. "Thank you, Mama. So, Caroline, how was your trip from Northampton?"

"Cold, but I'm glad to be here." She braced herself for the thinly veiled remarks from her sister about her position. Nearly every time she went home to visit, Caroline would hear from her sister in sometimes not-so-subtle terms about Caroline's apparent putting on airs and becoming too good for the likes of living in Holyoke. She supposed if she taught in Holyoke, dealing with Eleanor might be more tolerable. Eleanor seemed to resent that Caroline had taken a position teaching at a "fancy" academy training spoiled rich girls instead of remaining in her own city.

"So how has the school year been for you?" Mama asked. "Your last letter seemed a bit hurried."

"I wrote it very quickly to post it before classes," Caroline admitted. "It has been a good year so far. In fact, my team is leading in the academy's Academic Olympiad. We're ahead of Mr. Mason's team, 91 percent to his 90 percent, for grades so far at midyear."

She couldn't help but grin at recalling the look on Stephen's face when Mrs. Wickham had unveiled the updated scores. Her team had greatly improved their Latin scores, and they'd made improvements in mathematics as well.

"Who's Mr. Mason?" Eleanor asked.

"He's a new teacher this year. He's Mrs. Wickham's nephew, who came to teach mathematics." She tried to resist the urge to fidget by clasping her hands in her lap.

"Is he married?" Eleanor glanced at her sideways as she sipped from her coffee cup.

"No, he's not. He and I are actually in the running for the director position at the academy. Mrs. Wickham is considering both of us as her possible replacement. We'll find out who wins it at the end of the Academic Olympiad." She watched for their reactions.

"Why, that's wonderful." Her mother clapped her hands. "How long have you known this? I can't tell you how proud I am."

"We found out at the beginning of the fall term. I didn't want to say anything because, well, I don't know if it will happen."

"She'd *give* the school to you?" Eleanor looked shocked, her face reddened.

"No, not the academy itself. But I would run it and manage the teachers and students. She says she's ready to travel more, while she still can."

Eleanor rolled her eyes. "Well, that must be nice." She snatched the bag of money from the table. "I believe I'll go lie down until supper. I have a bit of a headache from being out in that cold this afternoon."

Caroline opened her mouth to respond, but Mama gave an almost imperceptible shake of her head as Eleanor strode away from the table. She disappeared around the corner to head to the short hallway and one of the two small bedrooms.

"She was so proud of how her taking in sewing has been keeping her busier and busier."

"I didn't mean to sound like I was bragging." Caroline frowned. "I'm home, happy to see you all, and sharing how things are for me at the school."

"Of course you are. I'm proud of both of you, as different as you are. Eleanor was never one for book learning, despite how I tried to show her."

"But she is an excellent seamstress. You have to know mathematics and measure to do what she does. It's not something everyone can learn." Caroline glanced toward the front of the apartment and the hall. "I hope she at least considers applying for a position at a dress shop. The work would come to her, and one day she might run a shop herself."

"Now wouldn't that be grand?" Mama nodded. "I don't know if she believes she could do it."

"I'm certain she could. It would be difficult, but not impossible."

"This Mr. Mason, being unmarried and teaching there. . . What do you think of him as a prospect for yourself?"

"Now, Mama—"

Mama waved at her. "Don't 'now, Mama' me. If he's a prospect, you should think of him. You're not getting any younger."

"Mama, I'm hardly getting old. I just don't want to settle, if only to be married. I don't want. . ." She'd nearly said, "I don't want to struggle like I've seen you struggle all these years."

Mama sighed. "I know your father and I aren't a good example of a marriage, not one like I believe God intends for those of us who marry. It wasn't always like this. But since you and your sister have been grown, it's easier for me to see. I don't know how to fix it other than taking care of him and loving him. He doesn't abuse me, and I promise you he never has. But I don't want you to not step into something beautiful for yourself because of me and your papa."

She had to admit to herself that her mother's words were, in fact, true. She hadn't wanted anyone to come calling, in case he turned out to be like her father. Yes, her father was a hard worker, but he drank and often would not come home until late after being at a pub with friends. Caroline could remember her mother pleading with her father to come home in the evening, to be home at night to spend time with her and two little girls who loved him.

"You're right, Mama. I don't want that to happen to me, or to Eleanor. How do I know, though, if it would be something beautiful?"

Mama patted her hand. "I don't know, because I wasn't able to judge that for myself. But I had no one to guide me. Jimmy Parker was the first man to pay me some kind attention, and for me he was a way out of where I was. I could have waited, but I didn't. You, though, don't wait too long. I know that God has guided you so far, and that He will guide you in this too."

"Thank you, Mama."

Her mother embraced her where they sat at the table. "I can't give you much this Christmas, but I want you to remember how much your papa and I do love you. He wants the best for you too."

Christmas was dull this year, especially without Caroline at the academy. Stephen, of course, had never spent Christmas at the academy, but even so, he imagined it would be anything but dull with Caroline there. His parents came, as did his sister and her lineup of cherubs, two boys and one girl, from oldest to youngest. His niece, Betsy, played the Christmas carols she had recently learned, and from morning until they shooed her away from the piano, the sitting room and the entire first floor of the house were filled with music.

The boys made snowmen, short little blobs of snow built from the scant snowfall they had not long after school dismissed. The academy was empty, save for the Wickhams and the staff, with the boarding students having gone to spend Christmas with classmates who lived in town.

Aunt Marjorie lavished a feast on them this year, with a pair of roasted geese filled with chestnuts and bread stuffing, turnips and potatoes on the side, and fresh rolls. His father contributed a thick slab of beef, roasted until so tender it fell apart.

He had never paid attention to the warmth of his family. Last year, a returning prodigal who was proving himself, he'd been so caught up in trying to convince them he'd changed that he hadn't enjoyed himself much.

This year, he had no one to convince, but he didn't find the enjoyment he thought he would.

He sat in one of the parlor's wingback chairs, in front of the crackling fire. He liked the fire, but coal was what kept the whole house warm after Aunt Marjorie made the upgrade several years ago.

He was nearly dozing after the large meal. Aunt Marjorie ran a tight ship with tight purse strings, but at Christmastime, she felt free to indulge a bit more than usual. He liked the change.

His Christmas would be complete if only Caroline were here. He realized he wanted her to meet his family, the rest of it, his parents and sister and brother-in-law, the whole brood. She would enjoy his niece and nephews, or he hoped she would. This was something new for him. He'd never met a woman he wanted to introduce to his family. Yet he knew she needed to be with her family.

"Why so gloomy looking, little brother?" Victoria took the chair across from him. His parents, along with Aunt Marjorie and his brother-in-law, were playing a game of charades with the children. Or they were trying to play, judging by the many explanations punctuated by the laughter of children in the room across the hall.

"Not gloomy. I'm tired, after all this eating." He smiled at her.

"Well, it looks as if something is on your mind. And has been, ever since we arrived yesterday. You've been quieter than usual." She studied his face intently. "Are you sure?"

"I'm sure. I wish you had been able to meet Miss Parker. She's spending Christmas with her family."

"Oh, the teacher you're trying to beat in the Olympiad."

He nodded. "She's ahead right now, but only by a little. I think you'd like her."

She reached out and nudged his arm. "What are you telling me? Are you sweet on her? Doesn't Aunt Marjorie have rules about things like that?"

Stephen chuckled. "She does. But still, whether or not I'm sweet on her, I think you'd like her if you met her."

"Maybe I'll get the chance to, eventually. I'm surprised we're here at all. Richard wasn't keen on traveling this year, but the children were excited to see their grandparents, and you, and their great-auntie Marge."

"Great-Auntie Marge. She'd never let us call her that."

"No, she wouldn't," Victoria chuckled. "But you didn't answer my question. Are you sweet on her?"

He shrugged. He didn't want to say. "I could be. Right now, though, I don't think it's a good idea to pursue. I don't have much to offer her, or any woman."

"You've come a long way from where you were before, and that's saying a lot."

"Thank you." He hoped so. Where he was now was so much better than where he'd been.

Maybe next Christmas dinner, there would be another seat at the table, for her. Was it an unrealistic thought right now? Perhaps it was.

"Hey, you two! We need some help with these charades." His mother's voice sounded a little harried.

Stephen and Victoria exchanged glances. "We'll be right there!" he called out.

∾ Chapter 7 ∾

Christmas had been put away, or at least its decorations had been until the next season. The students returned to the school the third week of January, after cold temperatures caused Mrs. Wickham to reconsider opening as early as usual after the New Year. Caroline had remained in Holyoke for two weeks after Christmas, which was far longer than she had expected to stay.

But by the time she had departed, she had coaxed her sister to take some samples of her sewing to a dressmaker. The two of them had been walking home from the market and had spied a sign in a window advertising a seamstress position. Eleanor had balked—again—at the idea.

"What if I'm not good enough?" She would barely look at the sign.

"Oh, but what if you are exactly who they are looking for? What then? Eleanor, it doesn't matter how fancy or not the home we go to at night; it's how we present ourselves. They are looking for an excellent seamstress, and I believe you are her."

Eleanor's face had flushed. "Well then, let's go in." And so they did.

Caroline had yet to receive word if Eleanor had been hired, but at least her sister had tried something new that she hadn't before.

On this particular chilly afternoon, instead of walking the courtyard outside, the students were permitted to amuse themselves by playing games indoors. It made for a rather raucous display, but so long as no one broke anything or was injured, Caroline didn't mind so much.

However, she could practically see the ends of Stephen's mustache twitching from all the noise. More than seventy girls ages ten to eighteen made for quite a bubbly gathering, and even Caroline felt a tad overwhelmed by the noise and chatter. The younger students were playing games like checkers, and someone had set up hopscotch in the front hallway beneath the Olympiad score sign.

The older students decided it would be fun to play hide-and-seek, with Eugenia and Celeste leading the way. Classrooms and more making up the big old building would have perfect hiding places for the creative child, both younger and older.

Eugenia volunteered to seek first. Caroline watched as they all scattered with a clatter of boots on the floor. Eugenia began counting backward from fifty—they had had a bit of discussion that starting at one hundred would take too long—and Caroline crept out of the room, joining in the fun.

She headed to the hall, then tiptoed into the mathematics room, where Stephen appeared to have taken refuge. His eyebrows shot up when he saw her.

"Shhh, I'll be right behind the door."

"As if they could hear you, with all the commotion out there." He looked at her with an amused expression as she slipped behind the open door. He continued at his desk, writing notes and looking at a book.

At last, she could hear Eugenia shout, "Ready or not, here I come!"

Then came tentative footsteps in the hall. Stephen rose from his desk and headed to the blackboard, where he began to write out sums with parts of the equations removed. She had suggested the idea of a math race, requiring the students to fill in the correct missing number to complete the problem. She was glad to see he was taking her advice for a little more informal instruction.

Caroline glimpsed Eugenia through the crack in the door. She kept her breathing even and slow as the girl tiptoed into the classroom. Caroline had nearly decided it was a good time to make a run for it when something made her pause and watch Eugenia continue her stealthy progress. She was heading toward Stephen with her hands outstretched. He had his back to the doorway.

A few more paces and she'd reach him. Caroline stepped from behind the door. "Hey, try to catch me!"

She allowed herself a glimpse of Eugenia's surprise along with Stephen's startled face before she ran back down the hall. Just as she figured, the girl followed her. She let herself be tagged right before getting back to the home spot.

Eugenia, breathless from the dash down the hallway, was laughing when she caught Caroline. "Got you!"

Caroline chuckled. "So you did."

"You're the first one I tagged."

"It appears so," she said. "However, you did look as though you were preparing to tag someone else, such as Mr. Mason."

A flush of red crept up Eugenia's neck and suffused her face. "I might have been."

"Well, he was not playing the game, so it wouldn't have counted." Caroline kept her smile in place. "Go catch some of the others. But not someone who is not playing the game."

With a nod, Eugenia scurried off in the direction from which they'd both just come.

Although they'd had a little chat about Mr. Mason some time ago, Caroline wasn't so sure Eugenia's pursuit of the man during the game hadn't been with another motive. Was she, in fact, sweet on her teacher? That could cause problems. Today's action during hide-and-seek ignited Caroline's suspicions. The first chance she had, she would look at Eugenia's grades and also speak with Stephen about the matter.

After the loosely controlled afternoon of high jinks, Stephen breathed a sigh of relief when dismissal time came. If—or when—he became director of the academy, he would see to something a bit more structured in the way of indoor recreation. Certainly none of the running and chasing in the halls. The only casualty was a box of chalk that someone had knocked onto the floor, the contents of the box shattered. That, and a skinned knee of ten-year-old Judith White. She endured the pain without so much as a flinch, to her credit, when Caroline cleaned the wound.

The bearer of the name that crossed his mind now stood in the doorway. She frowned, glancing over her shoulder as she did so. "All your afternoon students have gone?"

"Yes, they're gone. Is something the matter?"

She marched over to his desk and stood in front of it. "I have a concern about a student. I'm not quite sure if my concerns are founded—or if it's anything at all."

"Who is it?"

"It's Eugenia Ware. I believe that, well, she has, ah, some kind of feelings for you. That is to say, I believe she, either now or in the past, feigned having problems with mathematics so she could see you more."

Her face bloomed red. She was always a proper woman, save for the time he'd seen her shout and then run out from behind the door of his classroom this afternoon.

He looked down at the papers on his desk to allow her to regain her composure. "Her grades have improved since the start of the fall term, and she's making progress. Her improvement should also help my team's average, so it's a plus for both her and for me."

Then he stopped and considered Caroline's words for a moment. Come to think of it, he did consider it a bit odd and startling that Eugenia would come after *him* during the afternoon game of hide-and-seek.

Caroline had announced her presence and he had turned to see Eugenia right behind him. Eugenia hadn't known Caroline was behind the door.

Aloud, he said, "What should we do about it? She's but a child."

"She's turned eighteen, Stephen. In her society, she is ready for courting, for marriage."

"Oh. I didn't realize that." He set his chin on his hands. "She hasn't seemed quite as eager to study as she was last fall."

Caroline nodded. "Some students are not so keen about studying, especially during the second half of the school year. Perhaps she has prospects and is waiting for her parents to make a decision. Some of these girls go on to higher education, but for others, Wickham's is but a stepping-stone to the next part of their life—marriage and running a household."

"Would you sit down with me, and we could speak to her?" He shifted in his chair.

"Yes, of course I would." Voices in the hallway made her look over her shoulder. "I wouldn't be surprised if that is Eugenia with some of her classmates. I'll check."

She strode to the open door and looked into the hall. Sure enough, there was Eugenia, arms linked with two of her friends. "Eugenia, please come with me for a moment." She gestured toward the classroom.

"Yes, Miss Parker." Eugenia left her friends and headed in Caroline's direction.

"Come, sit down with Mr. Mason and me."

Eugenia followed Caroline into the classroom and took a seat at a desk. She clasped her hands on the desktop and glanced at them both.

Caroline smiled at the young woman. Yes, she truly was a young woman, her hair piled on her head and a bit askew, her cheeks flushed red, her smile wide. Caroline knew little about Eugenia's background other than her father was a businessman and her mother a former teacher. She had an easy life, relatively speaking, and would likely marry well someday.

"Do you remember the conversation we had in the fall, about your mathematics studies?" Caroline asked.

"Yes, Miss Parker, I do."

Now what to say? *Are you improving just enough to help your average and give me points for the Olympiad, but holding back so that you can claim you need extra help from Mr. Mason?*

No, that wasn't quite the thing to say.

Caroline cleared her throat. "It seems to me that you are doing well enough that you don't need the additional help from Mr. Mason." There. That was the easiest solution. As it was, he did not meet with students by themselves, but in small groups.

"But I enjoy the mathematics group very much." Eugenia's lower lip protruded. "I know it has helped me immeasurably."

Caroline looked at Stephen and nodded. "Mr. Mason?"

"Miss Ware, I agree with Miss Parker. You've made excellent progress. I don't see the need for you to come back to the mathematics help group. This is your final year at the school, and I believe you'll continue to improve as the year goes along."

"But I want to do more mathematics."

"Whyever would you want to?" Caroline asked. "As long as you have been my student, you have never had much enthusiasm for mathematics and figures. Perhaps Mr. Mason's time might be used more wisely for a student who faces more mathematics challenges."

Eugenia frowned. "I suppose you're right." She looked almost wistful.

Stephen decided to end the conversation. "I'm flattered that you have done so well in this class thus far. But as Miss Parker says and I've said, I believe you've accomplished much this year. You really don't need my help anymore."

"Thank you very much for your help." Eugenia stood. "May I go now?"

He and Caroline exchanged glances. "Yes, you may go."

With that, Eugenia nearly bolted from the classroom, her boots loud on the wooden plank floor.

Caroline let out a soft sigh—of relief, Stephen presumed. "I suppose that went as well as we could expect," she said.

"I believe it did." He regarded the woman sitting across from him. "Thank you. I think it was a wise action, and not something I would have thought of, because I wasn't paying attention to it."

She nodded, then smiled at him.

Stephen blurted out, "Would you like to take a walk with me after supper this evening? After the bonfire?"

He couldn't believe it. What had he done? They'd taken to having a small bonfire in the courtyard for the few resident students on Fridays after the sun went down. It was too cold for outdoor activities and some of them had cabin fever during the wintry months. He didn't blame them.

He waited for her response.

"Yes, I would like that very much."

"I'll see you then."

ᘏ Chapter 8 ᘐ

Caroline had prepared with a little more care than usual for the weekly bonfire. She and the handful of students had already gathered sticks, having kept them dry under the porte cochere until it was time to light the fire.

The girls chattered and giggled as Mrs. Wickham stood nearby. Stephen worked on the fire and was able to coax sparks from a flint and steel. Soon the fire roared before them. One of the girls started off with a song and they watched as the flames licked at the night sky.

Oh, to have had such an upbringing as these girls. But she found herself now among them through her own hard work and the encouragement of her mother.

"Do better than I did," Mama had told her before sending her off to teacher's college on a scholarship.

"You look pensive this evening," Stephen said at her side.

"Oh, I'm thinking of my mother." She wanted to explain more, but decided against it. He probably wouldn't understand.

"Is she all right?"

"Oh yes, she's fine, thank you."

Mrs. Wickham's voice nearly made Caroline start. "Well, you two seem to be getting along quite well."

Caroline wasn't quite sure how to respond to her employer's comment, other than nodding. She dared not glance at Stephen.

"Yes, Aunt Marjorie, we are. I get along quite well with all my fellow teachers." He turned his focus to his aunt, on the opposite side of Caroline. "We have quite an amicable staff here at Wickham Academy."

Amicable was a good word for it, Caroline had to agree. Yet, she realized, she'd been looking forward to the bonfire, not so much for the weekly diversion it provided, but for the chance to spend more time with Stephen when it didn't concern classes and students.

Amicable meant only a friend, or having a spirit of friendliness. But she didn't look forward to spending time with her other fellow teachers, not in the same way as she did Stephen Mason.

The night seemed to drag on, even with the songs and hot chocolate that made them all feel a bit merrier. If she let herself, she could be quite smitten with Mr. Mason. But it wasn't a good idea, not with so much on the line for both of them.

At last the night came to an end, the fire dying down. Mrs. Wickham ushered the students from the fire, leaving Caroline and Stephen to walk on their own. Although they were in plain view of anyone who might look out a window, Caroline felt as if they were completely alone. She shivered, nearly slipping on a slick patch of the courtyard.

Stephen grasped her elbow, steadying her. "Careful. There, that's better."

"Thank you." Words failed her at the moment. What was wrong with her?

They stepped carefully across the courtyard, pausing beneath the Century Oak, barren in winter.

"So," she said aloud, "should you win the headmaster position, are you ready to stay here permanently?"

"That's the idea. I don't plan to go anywhere, especially if I'm going to run this school."

"*If.*" She punctuated the word with a chuckle. "I'm just teasing you. I consider you a formidable opponent. You've done good things with the students here. I have to admit, I was a tad skeptical of Mrs. Wickham bringing in her nephew. Nor was I entirely happy about it. I've been here a long time."

"That you have." He chuckled.

"What is it that amuses you so?" she asked.

"When she first mentioned my fellow competitor and that she'd been at the academy for a long time, I pictured someone a little longer in the tooth." His grin made him look boyish in the pale light from the moon above them.

"I'm sorry to disappoint you."

"Oh Miss Parker, you have not disappointed me. Not at all." His breath made puffs in the chilly air.

She shivered again, and his hand moved from her elbow as she stepped closer. What was she doing? She needed to think.

If Mrs. Wickham happened upon them, she could and perhaps would fire them both, despite her matchmaking scheme.

But right now, she wanted him to kiss her, an even worse infraction than him having his arm around her waist in a partial embrace.

They both took a half step back.

"What just happened?" she gasped.

"I don't know. I'm sorry if it wasn't what you desired."

She clasped her arms around her waist. "I did, and that's the problem. I value my position here. You are Mrs. Wickham's family. If she came upon us, perhaps she would go easier on you, her nephew, than me."

"Oh Caroline, I understand. But this place is pretty much my last-ditch effort to make something of myself." He pulled something from his coat pocket. "Here. I was going to share this with you before, but I'd forgotten until now."

It was a folded piece of paper.

She opened it and scanned the first lines. "It's a letter addressed to you."

He nodded. "Go ahead, read it."

She headed for one of the gas lamps that gave some light to the courtyard.

It was from a friend, informing Stephen that Madame Tetreault's Finishing School in Winchester would be in need of an art and music teacher next year, and asking him if he knew of anyone who might be interested, to have them write to Madame Tetreault and inquire about the position.

Another position, away from Northampton and her family? It would likely pay more than Wickham Academy. If she didn't get the position here, she had thought about leaving the academy, but it was only an idea. She had no prospects. And now it seemed like an opportunity was literally at her fingertips.

"Thank you, I think." She folded the letter and handed it back to him. "I'm not sure what to think about that. It almost seems as if you're trying to get rid of me."

"No! I'm not trying to get rid of you. Not at all." He rubbed his forehead. "I immediately thought of you when I saw this opportunity. I wasn't thinking about the outcome of the Olympiad. The position alone is a good one, Olympiad aside."

"Yes, that it is." She smiled up at him under the gaslight. "I should go now. Good night."

She left him standing there. One moment she had almost kissed him, and then in the next moment he was referring her to an upcoming position more than ninety miles away. Suddenly she was glad they hadn't kissed after all.

The moment he entered the main house, he knew Aunt Marjorie was waiting for him in the parlor, which conveniently overlooked the courtyard. She likely saw their whole encounter, from their walk to the oak, to the moment he pulled her close, to when Caroline walked away from him to read the letter under the gaslight.

"In here, Stephen," came Aunt Marjorie's voice.

"Yes, Aunt Marjorie." He removed his overcoat, hat, and long scarf, then gave an involuntary shiver. Yes, the night was getting colder, and they'd ended the bonfire just in time.

His aunt was seated in a wingback chair in front of a roaring fire. He joined her in a matching chair.

"So, I see you've been chatting this evening with Miss Parker," she said.

"We were. I assure you nothing improper happened." Maybe he shouldn't have said that, but the words came right out. "We both understand the rules for teachers."

"Of course you do. But what will happen after the school term is over?"

"One of us will be the head of Wickham Academy." He stretched out his legs toward the fire and crossed his ankles.

She tapped the arm of his chair. "Sit up straight. It's bad for your posture to slouch like a sack of flour. *Perhaps* one of you will be the head of the academy." She chuckled. "No, one of you will. I promised that I would choose one of you. But have you considered what you will do if you are not the headmaster?"

"No, I haven't." He nearly told her about the position at the finishing school that he'd just shared with Caroline. "I think I would likely stay here. I like it. And it's good to be near family."

"You've finally realized that, have you?"

He nodded and watched the fire crackle.

"And Miss Parker?"

"What are you asking me about Miss Parker?"

"Do you fancy her?" She regarded him over the top of her spectacles.

"I suppose I do." Her winsome smile, her easy demeanor, the way she worked with the students, so differently than he did. What was not to like about her?

"But you know the rules of this academy."

"I do, as does she." He looked at his aunt. "We will not violate the rules of the academy. It wouldn't be right, nor fair, to shrug away rules that all of us must follow."

Oh, but how he had changed, going by the response he'd just given his aunt. The old Stephen would have figured out a way to make things work his way and no one be the wiser. Thank God he wasn't the man he used to be. He wouldn't have deserved someone like Caroline Parker.

"That's what I thought you'd say. Very good, Stephen. Very good. I did see the two of you out there this evening. I know you'll keep the rules." In spite of her serious tone, her eyes sparkled. "We shall see what the end of the spring term brings us."

⟋ Chapter 9 ⟍

The sound of banging on the bedroom door jolted Caroline from her reading. The afternoon was quiet, and she'd been enjoying it, especially after the long weeks of the term behind her.

The book in her hands fell to the floor.

"Caroline, are you there?" Charlotte Huckabee's frantic voice sounded slightly muffled through the door.

"Yes, what is it?" Caroline sprang to her feet and crossed the room to let Charlotte in.

"This came for you." She extended a folded piece of paper in Caroline's direction.

Caroline unfolded the note.

Caroline, we need help. Mama's sick and we can't pay the rent. Don't know what you can do at the fancy school, but maybe your rich friends can help.

Eleanor

Rich friends.

Caroline shook her head. She didn't think more about that. Mama, sick? Her heart began thudding faster.

"What's wrong?"

"My mother is sick. I need to help her."

"As you should."

"I won't be long. I must see about a doctor." She thought of the can that held her savings. She could bring money home as the family needed it.

And now, it seemed her family did.

Charlotte laid her hand on Caroline's arm. "Pack and go. I'll inform Mrs. Wickham."

"My classes. I intend to return as soon as possible, but my classes—"

"They shall keep for a day. If anything, I can have your younger students in my class to complete their work. All I'll need is your lesson book." Charlotte waved her hands. "I shall order a carriage to take you."

"Please don't tell anyone else where I'm going. Other than Mrs. Wickham." She couldn't let Stephen know, not about her family. She wasn't ready for that. Not yet.

"I'll say nothing. You have my word." Charlotte departed, shutting the door behind her.

Caroline immediately swung into action. She took her can of money. Thankfully, she wouldn't have to pay for the transportation to Holyoke. She'd make sure she had enough to return home on Monday.

She pulled out her satchel and in went a couple of books and a change of clothes. She changed her shoes to her sturdiest ones, should she have to do extensive walking in town when she went home.

Home. But the walk-up apartment wasn't her home. It hadn't been for a long time.

How bad had things gotten, that her parents couldn't pay the rent? Why hadn't anyone told her?

She'd have answers soon enough. She wanted to get away from the academy before Stephen saw her and asked questions. She'd managed to avoid responding to questions about family, or at least giving him specific details.

She grabbed her satchel and her coat and headed downstairs. She hoped the carriage came quickly.

Caroline left the girls' dormitory and scurried to the courtyard, to the porte cochere. She didn't have long to wait before she heard the sound of hoofbeats on cobblestones. *Thank you, Charlotte.*

She glanced around the courtyard as she hurried to the carriage. No one around. She scanned the windows of the buildings. No one there either, as far as she could tell.

"Your bag, miss?" The driver hopped down, and she handed him her satchel.

"Thank you."

Careful not to catch the hem of her dress on the step, she climbed into the carriage and shut the door herself.

She tried not to borrow trouble, as her mother would say. She glanced out the carriage window one more time and looked toward the house where the Wickhams lived. A figure, standing at the window. A man in a shirt and tie.

Did he see her? Certainly, if she could see him, he hadn't

missed the carriage leaving.

Maybe he didn't know she was the one inside.

As the carriage swayed along, the memory came back to her of the almost-kiss they'd shared under the large oak in the moonlight last Sunday evening. Their little meeting under the tree never should have happened, as anything hinting at courting was against the rules of teaching at the academy. No gentlemen callers, and teachers must remain unmarried during the term of their contract.

Until now, she hadn't had a problem with that. She'd managed to keep their conversations light and dealing strictly with school and classes, all week long. They'd had no more moments of being alone together, and it was just as well.

Especially with her family's state now, she couldn't risk losing her employment. If word got out, even if she left the academy for some reason, she might have difficulty securing another job.

No, anything further with Mr. Stephen Mason was entirely out of the question. She doubted Mrs. Wickham would approve of them embracing under the tree at night. She might not dismiss family, but she would likely send Caroline packing, if she knew.

She pushed thoughts of Stephen away as the carriage took her closer to Holyoke. It would not take long to go the ten miles or so. But it may as well have been ten thousand miles, as different as it was from the life she left behind.

She said a prayer for her mother, for the situation that lay ahead of her. For Eleanor to summon her, things had to be very grave indeed.

Stephen didn't miss seeing Caroline wearing a wide-eyed and worried expression as she hopped into a waiting carriage, which then shot away from the academy. She'd handed a satchel to the driver. Wherever she was going, it wasn't for long. Or so he hoped.

He recalled their embrace beneath the old tree during their walk after the bonfire. He'd known the attraction wasn't just on his part—she felt the same way as he gently held her waist. She had willingly leaned on him as he inhaled the scent of the light, flowery perfume she wore.

It could never happen again, no matter how much he wanted it to.

Once they'd acknowledged the rivalry between them, it seemed as though something else had taken over. The academy directorship was within both their grasps. Aunt Marjorie had made it clear that the cream always rose to the top, and the two of them would decide the winner.

But now? What was happening with Caroline? This hurried trip didn't appear to be a mere whim on her part. Something had happened. He hurried out to the street, his only thought concern for her.

The moment they'd both agreed to call each other by their first names had opened the door to a familiarity that was more than just comfortable. He didn't ever want to be this com-fortable with anyone else. Yet she still had a guarded manner about her.

He hailed the first carriage for hire he saw and asked the

driver to follow Caroline's carriage wherever it was going. His curiosity had gotten the better of him. If she was in trouble of some kind, he wanted to help.

The journey took them away from the town and along the road that led to the river crossing and to Holyoke. He had been to the city a few times, a mill town nestled along the Connecticut River, south of Northampton.

They rolled along narrow streets until the carriage drew up to a row of three-story homes, simple wooden affairs that had been divided into apartments. He asked the driver to stop a discreet distance from where Caroline's carriage had stopped to let her out.

Caroline hopped from the carriage, almost stumbling in her haste. As she tugged her scarf more firmly around her neck, she glanced up and down the street and caught sight of the other carriage. That, and Stephen looking at her.

Her worried look was replaced by embarrassment, then consternation. He left the carriage now that she'd seen him and the idea of remaining hidden was no longer a viable one. He quickly approached her.

"What's wrong?" He looked up at the house, then at her.

"This is. . .this is where my family lives," she said. "My mother is ill, and I've come here to check on her."

"How can I help?" Immediately he thought of money, anything he could do.

"No, thank you. I don't need help. Please, go." She waved him away. "I don't know why you came here."

"I'm concerned. You left so quickly. . . ." He should have waited, should have minded his own business.

"My family needs me right now. I'll thank you to go back to the academy."

She dismissed him and the carriage she'd just arrived in. She reached for the satchel and, without a backward glance, headed to the set of stairs attached to the side of the building.

Stephen shook his head. He didn't understand why she seemed almost ashamed for him to see her there. His shoulders drooped. From this point on, he would keep things strictly related to teaching only. They could not have a friendship, not at this moment.

❧ Chapter 10 ❧

*T*oday, the first Thursday in March, only Eugenia and four of the older girls sat with their books open as Caroline stood before them in the classroom. The other students were home, ill with fevers.

Her mother had had a fever as well, but now was much better, according to word Caroline had received from her family. The money she had saved had gone not only to help pay the family's rent, but for visits from a local physician. Something they could not have afforded without her.

The classroom held fewer than half of the usual students who would normally be seated at their desks, ready to discuss *The Adventures of Huckleberry Finn*. The rather controversial selection had caused a bit of a to-do when Caroline proposed reading the book for the older girls' class. Now, however, the students couldn't wait to read and discuss the latest adventure in the book.

This morning, Caroline tried to keep her teeth from chattering. For some reason, she couldn't stay warm, though she wore her extra petticoat beneath her skirt, the woolen one she saved for the coldest weather.

The warmth from the fire didn't seem to reach her desk. Caroline strode closer to the fireplace.

"Please open your books to chapter 8. If you remember, we stopped there at the last reading. For this coming weekend, we shall read chapter 9 and discuss it next week." She paused, then glanced at Eugenia, who had raised her hand while she was speaking. "Yes, Miss Ware?"

"Miss Parker, you appear quite peaked this morning. Are you all right?" The girl wore an expression of concern. Her concern had to be genuine, for this was the first conversation Eugenia had initiated since the conversation that she and Caroline and Stephen had had weeks ago.

"I feel a bit chilled this morning." Caroline rubbed her arms. "Perhaps we'll have another late winter or early spring snowfall."

The last snow they'd had was two weeks ago, and a rain shower had washed it away.

"Now," she said, opening the book she held in her left hand, "let's discuss chapter 8. What, to you, was the main point of the action in the chapter? What purpose did Mr. Twain intend for the story?"

An invisible wave shook Caroline. She reached out for her desk, which was paces away from her. Her peripheral vision blurred, turned brown. She heard gasps as she struck the floor. It was her turn to gasp. She fumbled to put her hands on the floor, in an attempt to push herself up to a seated position. She managed to prop herself up on one elbow. Her book lay several feet away, where it had slid as she collapsed.

"Miss Parker!" Eugenia reached her before the others. "Are you all right?"

Caroline's head continued to swim as she contemplated exactly how to get herself to her feet. She reached up for Eugenia's offered hand.

"Oh, your hand is on fire, Miss Parker!" Eugenia's voice came out as a muffled shriek. "You must have the fever too! I'll fetch Mrs. Wickham!"

As if from a distance, Caroline heard Eugenia's voice as the young woman stumbled from the room.

In less than thirty minutes, Caroline was tucked into her own bed while Cook dabbed cool compresses on her head and neck. Mrs. Wickham had already sent for the doctor.

"There you go, Miss Parker." Cook's voice was soft and low, the cloth applied to Caroline's forehead equally soft. "Don't you worry about anything. The doctor is on his way. Mrs. Wickham has declared classes closed for the next week. Another student has gone home ill. So all you have to do is get well again."

Caroline nodded. Her first thought had been of the children. The blanket covering her held her down and made her feel even sleepier.

Just as she drifted off, her thoughts went to Stephen. How was he? During the prior week, she had barely seen him. And now, her eyelids heavy, she found herself wishing he was right here, right now, beside her.

Yet she didn't deserve that, not after the last encounter they'd had.

She'd said some terrible things to him the day he'd followed her to her parents' home in Holyoke. He'd flinched, and her words had hurt him. But she couldn't bear that he'd seen her meager beginnings. She could never be the type of woman he deserved. She had no background to speak of, while he had known nothing but privilege.

The coolness of the cloth on her forehead began to disappear as the heat from her body absorbed it. She struggled to say something, but all she wanted to do was sleep.

"Rest now. I'll check on you soon and see if you are up to having some broth." Cook gave her one more glance, then left the room, closing the door behind her.

Caroline surrendered to the sleep that claimed her.

Stephen paced the hallway. He wanted to enter Caroline's room, but propriety demanded he stay outside. Long shadows told him nighttime would fall soon. It wasn't yet spring, and the darkest days were behind them. He hoped that was true in more ways than one.

It had become about far more than who would take the reins of Wickham Academy. It was much more than that now for him.

He'd regretted his decision to follow Caroline to her family's home every day since he'd returned to Northampton. He wanted to tell her, so many times, but she'd avoided him.

He leaned against the paneled wall and waited. Surely someone would come and check on her. He dared not go in by himself.

"Oh Mr. Mason." Charlotte approached him. "You need to take care of yourself, that you don't fall ill as well."

"I'm doing my best. I hope the school won't be closed for

long." He watched her stop at the closed door.

"I share that same hope." She nodded toward the room. "I'm going in. Would you like to come with me?"

"I'm not sure that I should, but I want Miss Parker to know I'm here."

Charlotte gave him a reassuring smile. "I'll tell you what. I'll go in, and if she's up to it, I'll let you know, and we can visit with her for a moment together."

"Thank you."

The teacher entered Caroline's room and shut the door behind her.

Stephen waited and tried not to resume his pacing as he did so. A few moments later, Charlotte peeked out the door. "Come in, she wants to see you."

He stepped into the room, leaving the door open as he entered.

Caroline lay, covered with blankets, on the narrow bed. Her room was a bit plainer than his, but still boasted a cushioned chair and ottoman beside the window. There was a small shelf of books. He took in his surroundings then ignored them all, save for the woman lying on the bed.

"Hello," she said.

"Hello," he replied. "I, ah, I wanted to check on you. I've been praying for you, and for all who have fallen ill."

"Thank you. That means a great deal to me."

Right now, nothing else mattered save that she got better. "You just concentrate on resting."

There was so much he wanted to tell her, but he realized now wasn't the time. Instead, he sat while Charlotte spoke in low tones to her friend about the school being closed for the time being.

"It's just a precaution," Charlotte continued. "Mrs. Wickham believes if the school closes for now, the fever will have less of a chance to spread among the students."

Stephen rose from where he'd been sitting on her cushioned chair. "I'll come check on you tomorrow."

Caroline nodded, giving him a slight smile.

That smile made his heart do a somersault. *Please, Lord, let her get better soon—let all of them get better soon.*

๛ Chapter 11 ๛

*T*hen just like that, the fever vanished from the school, much to everyone's relief. Stephen felt the weight on his eyelids as he prepared for classes to resume. He'd spent as much time as possible at Caroline's side. Once she regained her strength and health, he knew he was determined not to accept no for an answer to the question of courting her.

Surely, no matter who won the competition and the top position at Wickham Academy, Aunt Marjorie might make an exception to the marriage rule.

For now, they all tried their best to get back into a class schedule and make up for the time they had lost. There were but a few weeks left to the term, and at that time, they would all learn who had won the position of headmaster—or headmistress—of Wickham Academy.

At the last count, before the fever and temporary closure of the school, their averages were again very close. But Stephen knew whoever's group of students had the best average didn't matter as much as the unfinished business between him and Caroline.

Charlotte rapped on the doorframe to Stephen's classroom. "Mrs. Wickham has asked that we gather at the scoreboard this morning."

He jerked his head up in surprise. "That's early."

"Yes, it is." She scurried off toward the front of the building.

They gathered again in front of the board for this unexpected moment. Stephen scanned the room to see the familiar faces of his students. There she was. Caroline entered the hallway. Her face had more color than the last time he'd seen her, her head on her pillow and hair streaming past her shoulders. She gave him a smile, and that gave him some hope.

The murmurs continued and echoed off the entryway walls, but ceased when Aunt Marjorie clapped her hands. "All right, all right. I know you are all wondering why I've called you here now. It's early, I know. We're not finished for the term. Not yet."

She fell silent, then glanced from Stephen to Caroline. "I know you have all worked very hard during the fall term, and this spring term. I realize some of you may have felt some pressure and high expectations with these scores. I am a firm believer in setting high standards and giving you each a chance to reach those standards.

"But recent happenings, the fever and temporary closure of the school, have led me to realize that while the scores are important, there are other things that are more important. I've summoned you to let you know that I have made my decision as to who will become the head of this school."

Stephen swallowed hard. He wanted to run the school, yes,

but he wasn't sure how Caroline would take the news if he were to be given the spot. After this entire school year, to lead and then fall short? But then, if he didn't get the position himself. . .

He'd be disappointed, for sure. He had learned much this year and was a better teacher, thanks to learning from the others. He didn't want to say so, but each of his fellow instructors had taught him something.

And Caroline, what had she taught him?

He stopped his thoughts and fixed his gaze on the scoreboard, covered with the familiar drape of cloth.

Again Aunt Marjorie clapped her hands. "Behind this drape is not only the most recent average, but the name of the new head of Wickham Academy."

He glanced toward Caroline, and their gazes locked. He couldn't read her expression. He was never good at things like that, save during a poker game. If he'd been across the table from Caroline, he wouldn't be able to tell what kind of hand she had. But this morning he saw kindness in her eyes, and maybe something else?

"Without further ado, here is the new head of Wickham Academy." Aunt Marjorie nodded, and Charlotte draw back the cloth.

There, written in chalk, was the name CAROLINE PARKER.

Stephen heard a gasp. He wasn't sure who it came from, or where. Cheers went up from some of the girls, but there were a few disappointed looks, if only for him. He felt himself grinning despite the sting. Aunt Marjorie moved to stand beside him.

"It was a difficult choice, my dear nephew," his aunt murmured. "Yes, I looked at the scores and how all of the students performed. But because I did not choose you does not mean I do not have a role open here for you."

He figured he would get to keep his position at the academy. He couldn't think about what was next, not right now. The students began to scatter, some headed home for lunch, with the boarding students remaining at the academy.

Stephen started to head toward the Wickham family home, but a soft voice caught his attention.

"Stephen, Mrs. Wickham, I would like to meet with both of you, privately, if I may." Caroline glanced from one of them to the other, her green eyes soft and glowing.

"Yes, we can meet in my office in ten minutes."

Puzzled, all Stephen could do was look at Caroline. What was happening?

Caroline's knees still felt a bit weak after her recent illness, but somehow she found the strength to step carefully to Mrs. Wickham's office. Stephen touched her elbow, and the gesture warmed her to her toes.

Inside Mrs. Wickham's office, the older woman settled behind the desk. "Please. Sit, sit. What is it you wish to discuss with both of us?"

The fact that she would be the headmistress of Wickham Academy, come the fall term, still hadn't settled into Caroline's head yet. A headmistress. So many details, things to keep track of.

"Mrs. Wickham, first I would like to say thank you—thank you for choosing me."

"You have the experience and you have shown good sense in

the face of many things this school year." Mrs. Wickham steepled her fingers beneath her chin. "I feel confident that I can leave the academy in good hands."

"Thank you, Mrs. Wickham. I simply want to continue what you started here so many years ago."

During this part of the conversation, Stephen wore a puzzled expression. He settled into a chair across from Mrs. Wickham's desk, with Caroline taking the chair beside him.

Of course he was confused. He'd lost out on a great opportunity. But she had determined one thing after she'd recovered from her illness, and that was if she became headmistress of Wickham Academy, there were some things she wanted very much.

She hoped Mrs. Wickham appreciated her direct approach. This possibility had entered her mind when she'd seen her name on the scoreboard. But now that she was sitting face-to-face with Mrs. Wickham and Stephen, her courage wavered for a moment.

"Well, Miss Parker? What did you want to speak with us about?"

"Yes, Miss Parker."

She glanced at Stephen. No, he wasn't teasing her. He was concerned.

Caroline took a deep breath. "As I said a moment ago, thank you for choosing me." She turned to face Stephen. "Also, I owe you an apology. I was very unkind to you when you encountered me with my family. For that, I am truly sorry."

He nodded.

All she could think of was that tender moment in the moonlight, when she'd given in to the idea that there could possibly be more between them, more than a camaraderie between teachers at the same academy. She'd fought the idea, and rightly so. She didn't want to lose the position she'd worked so hard to attain.

"I'm not ashamed of my family. But I didn't want you to think less of me." She swallowed again, fighting the lump in her throat. "I was doing the very thing I'd admonished my sister for. . .assuming someone would look at me differently if they saw my upbringing, my family. I have been able to keep things separate, my life here and my family in Holyoke. It is so very, very different."

She dared not look at Mrs. Wickham. The woman was proper, yet not critical of open, frank conversation. She hoped Mrs. Wickham didn't mind the leaning of the conversation.

"You are very correct, Caroline, that it is so very, very different." Stephen's voice was soft. "My life here, my life at the academy where I used to teach, has been very, very different from how I used to live. But, like you, I realized that I deserve to be here. I can't let anyone else determine that I shouldn't be here. Well, only Aunt Marjorie here can determine that."

At that, Mrs. Wickham inclined her head, ever so slightly, in his direction. Her expression was serious, but her eyes twinkled.

Caroline nodded. "You are right. Which is why I am truly sorry. So I am looking forward to taking the role you've chosen me for. But I do have one condition, Mrs. Wickham."

"And what is that, Miss Parker?"

"I realize that teachers must remain unmarried during the school year while they are under contract at Wickham Academy. I believe in that standard, and I have upheld it the entire time I've been in your employ."

Mrs. Wickham's eyebrows shot to the top of her head, but she remained silent.

"That being said, I would like to inquire, of both of you, what you would think about me courting someone."

"Courting?" Stephen blurted out the word.

"Yes. Courting." She smiled at him. "If I could go back to our conversation months ago, I would tell you something differently. I was afraid. I didn't want to put my job in jeopardy."

At the recollection of their almost-kiss, she felt her cheeks flush. She dared not look at Mrs. Wickham. But she'd considered this possibility and knew what she wanted in her deepest heart of hearts.

Stephen smiled back at her. "Courting, you say?" He glanced at his aunt, who, much to Caroline's relief, was beaming.

"I need a co-director of the academy. I need a headmaster here. I need someone to keep things steady and in order. But I don't want to keep on as we have these past months. It's been horrible."

Her heart leapt as he reached his hand into the space between them. "Miss Parker, I agree with you wholeheartedly."

She reached her hand toward his. "Good. I'm glad."

His hand was warm, soft yet firm as he held hers and squeezed. For a split second, she wondered if, had they been alone, he might try to steal a kiss. The idea made her smile.

Mrs. Wickham stood, her smile widening as she did so. "At last, at last. I'm pleased to announce that my plan has succeeded far more than I had hoped."

They both looked at her, then laughed.

Caroline, still smiling, glanced at Stephen yet again. Mrs.

Wickham had played matchmaker, and Caroline couldn't be happier about the outcome.

"Stephen, I believe we will have the most interesting summer."

He raised her hand to his lips. "I quite agree, Miss Parker."

Epilogue

May 29, 1896

Dear Brother,

I hope my letter finds you well. I could write you volumes about the past school year. Suffice it to say, your son has performed admirably in his position here. I could not be happier about it.

You should know that he has begun courting Miss Caroline Parker, who will be my new headmistress for the next school year. I would like to say that it might be good to plan a trip to Europe for next summertime.

However, it would not surprise me to find ourselves planning for an early summer wedding next year.

It seems as though Stephen and Miss Parker will likely be announcing an engagement in the fall. This is highly irregular, but as headmistress, exceptions may be made for Miss Parker.

All in all, it seems as though everyone has won, in this case.

If I do not make a trip to the shore this summer, I hope to see you this fall, or at Thanksgiving.

I remain your devoted sister,
Marjorie Wickham

Lynette Sowell is an award-winning author with New England roots, but she makes her home in Central Texas with her husband and a herd of five cats. When she's not writing, she edits medical reports and chases down stories for the local newspaper.

❧ Lessons of Love ❧

by Lynn A. Coleman

❦ Chapter 1 ❧

Warren, Tennessee
1899

*H*elen's hand paused as she read the fine print. "You're asking me not to court or marry during the entire school year?"

"Yes, Miss Jones," the head of the school board, a tall man with a long, narrow gray beard answered, "that is our standard practice. Once you marry we would be obligated to replace you. A woman's first duty is to her husband."

"Would a male teacher be asked to refrain from courting?" A hesitant nod came from the oldest of the six men on the county school board. "Then I shall not sign the contract."

All six jaws went slack.

"But you are our only candidate," a balding gentleman said while wiping his brow with a handkerchief.

Helen suppressed a smile. She was aware. Which, she supposed, allowed her to be more brazen than normal. She understood culture, but she also understood the times were changing. It was 1899, and the world was about to enter a new century. Women were standing up for their rights. And while teaching came naturally to Helen, she didn't want to be trapped in the role. She had no prospects for a husband, but she also had no intention of being restricted from courting. "If you wish," she said, smiling politely, "I will rescind my acceptance."

"But you would leave us with no teacher."

They had her there. While some of her unorthodox teaching methods had rattled more than one professor as she was finishing her degree, she was their only candidate, and they all knew she would put the children's needs first. "I do not want to put you or the children in such a terrible position. I am willing to teach without the contract until you can find a replacement." Which she knew probably wouldn't be until next fall. At least she hoped so.

The six men huddled together. The chairman cleared his throat. "We accept your offer, but we'll lower the pay."

Helen stood, picking up her valise as she did. "Good day, gentlemen. You shall have my prayers for a new teacher."

"But you can't expect us to pay your full salary without a guarantee—"

Helen cut him off. "You already pay women only a third of what you pay your male teachers. It is hard enough to survive as a single woman on such a meager salary. But for you to offer me even less. . . Well, I can see that the education of your children does not hold high regard in your community."

"Miss Jones, I resent that accusation!" huffed the gentleman to the left of the chairman, who was perhaps the youngest of the grandfathers in the room. "I serve on the board of Irving College, and I can assure you we are quite concerned with the education of our community's children."

"Very well. I apologize for such a broad statement," she replied. "Thank you for your time, gentlemen. I will be returning home on the next train."

Helen left the room, walked out of the building, and headed toward the train station. She shouldn't have lost her temper. But she was tired of people—men—telling her what she could and could not do. It was time for change in this country. She knew it, and so did most women.

Father, forgive me. I know I should sit and wait upon You. But those old men are living in the past!

She stomped her way past the storefronts at a brisk pace, heels clicking loudly on the sidewalk. She would have enjoyed living here. Friends from college had gone on to be doctors while she stayed focused on teaching. She felt it was more than a job; it was her calling.

"And who is it that needed to be taught just now?"

Helen sighed and closed her eyes. "I did, Lord. I'm sorry."

Her eyes opened in time to see a man's shoulder inches from her face, too late to avoid. *"Uff!"*

"Pardon me. Are you all right?" The kindest brown eyes she'd ever seen searched her own as the stranger held her steady by the shoulders.

"Yes, thank you. I'm sorry."

"Forgive me as well. I bolted out of the store without looking. Fortunately, you hit me and not the door." His eyes sparkled at her from a handsome face framed by a full head of brown hair and a neatly trimmed beard, unlike the modern young men in her home of Virginia who shaved daily.

"Yes, yes, I suppose that is true," she stammered, and took

a step back. "Thank you." She looked down for her valise and slipped her hand through the leather handles. "Have a good day, sir."

He tipped his hat and smiled. "And you as well, miss."

Helen continued on to the train station, determined not to look back. She definitely would have loved living here, especially if it meant getting to meet the man with chocolate-brown eyes that pulled her in. She'd never been drawn to anyone like that before. She paused and turned around. He was walking away in the opposite direction. *I wonder who he is?*

Daniel brushed off his ruffled coat and watched the fiery woman head toward the train station. Wisps of reddish-brown hair escaped from beneath her hat as she walked away. But the green eyes that had met his in wide-open surprise—more vibrant than the greenest pastures in springtime—were forever etched in his memory.

He placed his hat upon his head and headed back toward the college. There was a late-afternoon class to teach before his day was done. Today's lesson in biology was always the most difficult to teach. Young men would snicker, others would be red in the face, and a few could even be crude about the fertilization of plants and animals. A necessary topic, especially for those going on in their agriculture studies, but also a core requirement for graduation, which meant several students attended who didn't really want to be there. However, there were always a few students who were serious about the science, and they were the reason he loved to teach.

He glanced back over his shoulder and watched the woman head toward the train station. Who was she, and why was she in such a hurry? Daniel shrugged and continued on to the campus.

An hour and a half later, class was done. The students streamed out of the classroom and Mr. Markle, a member of the school board, approached. "Mr. Moore, I'm wondering if you can take on a local teaching position for our elementary age children."

Daniel cocked his head. Hadn't they hired a teacher? The woman with red hair and green eyes who ran into him earlier flooded his mind. "I don't understand. My schedule with the school—"

Mr. Markle raised his hand. "I have spoken with some of the school board members, who agreed that we can adjust your schedule."

Daniel placed his hands on his hips. He'd been teaching at the college for two years now. He taught young adults, and some in their teens, but not little ones. "I am not the man for such a position. I am not good with young children. They tried my patience on more than one occasion when I was first entering my profession. My professors and I both agreed it was not the place for me."

"Oh." Mr. Markle sighed. "You were my last hope."

"What happened with the woman you hired?"

"She refused to sign the contract. And then, when we agreed to her terms of working without a contract, she refused our pay reduction."

"You reduced the pay more than you already had?"

Shock or possibly dread ran across Mr. Markle's face.

No wonder she refused. "I'm curious," he said. "What was in the contract that made her refuse to sign?"

Mr. Markle coughed to clear his throat. "We asked that she not engage in a courtship during the school year."

"Does she have a suitor?"

Mr. Markle shrugged. "Not that I'm aware." He paused. "It isn't right for a woman to teach and be married."

"Ah, but that is your mistake, is it not? You said she couldn't court. How is a woman to get to know a man for possible marriage if she does not take the time to court?"

"That isn't my concern."

"Apparently, it is. You are left with no teacher for the children. And if I am your last hope, you are in a serious situation. You shall have my prayers." Daniel placed his lecture notes and the students' papers in his briefcase.

"Thank you for that."

"Why don't you teach?" Daniel asked. "Weren't you a teacher in the past?"

"Yes, but, like you, I found I did not have patience for young ones."

Daniel smiled.

The train whistled, signaling it was nearly six o'clock. "Perhaps you should reconsider the young woman's offer. If she's agreed to teach without a contract, the least you could do is offer her a reasonable salary. I understand you offered a third of what you offer male candidates, and she was still willing to come. That says something about her desire to teach. Not to mention what it says about her character, that she was not desperate enough to accept those terms. You might be missing a good opportunity for the children of this community."

Mr. Markle rolled his shoulders back and nodded. "I shall speak with the board members." He glanced up at the clock. "We have two hours before she departs on the eastbound train." Mr. Markle headed out the classroom door.

Warren, Tennessee, was an interesting town, Daniel reflected. Besides the college, whose presence was good for the region, most of the town consisted of farmers who probably didn't have as much use for education as those who were in the education field. However, several of the professors here at the college had young children of their own. If the community didn't offer adequate education, they would move on to another teaching institution where their children's education was treated as a priority. He understood the budget issue, but didn't agree with the rationale that a woman should be paid less than a man simply because she wasn't the head of a household. It was especially ridiculous to his way of thinking in the case of a single woman who was the head of her household and had to provide for all of her own needs. "Mr. Markle," Daniel called after the departing board member. "You might want to reconsider her status as 'head of the household.' After all, who pays for her food, clothing, and other expenses without a husband to provide?"

"I can see you are of the more modern opinion."

"Perhaps, or perhaps I'm simply being practical." Daniel closed the classroom door with the parting assurance, "I shall be praying, Mr. Markle."

Helen stood and stretched her legs, walking back and forth on the platform. She'd been sitting in the slatted wooden chair for the past three hours. The westbound train had stopped to allow a few passengers to exit, but only a few. She understood from the station manager that the eastbound train would be arriving in another forty-five minutes. Then it would be another eight hours of sitting before she arrived at her hometown in Virginia.

Her father would be happy for her return. He hadn't been excited about the job offer she received from the school board in Warren. Nevertheless, he'd given her his blessing, making sure she understood she could always return home. Of course, that meant she would have to begin the process of finding a suitable husband. The prospect of gentlemen callers was limited back home, and most of those men weren't interested in continuing their education. Michael, case in point, had put it bluntly. *"I know how to farm, raise the crops and livestock. I don't need no book learning. My pa taught me all I need."*

That put an end to her interest in him and his interest in her. He married Mary Jane Allen six months later, and the last Helen knew they had two children already and another one on the way. Personally, she was happy for Michael and Mary Jane, and would love to have children of her own someday. But she wanted more from life than what her hometown had to offer.

As Helen continued to pace, the air filled with the sweet fragrance of apple pie. She sniffed, closing her eyes to take in the fresh aroma. Her stomach gurgled, and she looked around, embarrassed, hoping no one had heard. She hadn't eaten since early this morning. Lukewarm coffee and Danish didn't last long.

She leaned out past the train station's loading area to see where the delicious aroma was coming from. Was there enough time to venture out and possibly find a meal? She glanced up at the clock hanging over the loading area. If the eastbound train was on time, she had forty minutes. If it was early, she might risk staying in town overnight. And while she had the money, the idea of spending a night just for a bite to eat seemed foolish. She sighed in frustration and disappointment. The limited salary she'd been willing to accept could have been boosted by picking up some extra income tutoring college students. She shook her head. To think a college town would care so little for the children. Sure, the college was situated in an out-of-the-way farming community, but still. . . *Enough!* she warned herself. *Don't keep dwelling on what might have been.*

Helen picked up her valise and followed her nose toward the enticing apple pie. She took her place in a line of men—both young and old—gathered outside a small cottage near the station. By the time Helen arrived at the door, she had learned that Mrs. Miller was a widow whose baked goods were a favorite of the students from the college. "Hello," Mrs. Miller said.

"Hello! May I have a slice of apple pie and a couple of rolls for my trip on the train?"

"Of course." Mrs. Miller cocked her head. "You wouldn't be the new schoolmarm, would you?"

"Ahhh," Helen stammered, "I came for that position, yes. But it didn't work out."

"Why?" Mrs. Miller placed her hand over her mouth. "Beg your pardon, miss. I don't mean to pry. Well, I suppose I do, but it ain't none of my concern."

Helen liked Mrs. Miller immediately. "I couldn't sign the contract. It stated I could not be courted. I understand not wanting me to marry, but to not court. . ." Helen shook her head. "They were already offering a lower wage than they would a man, and when I suggested a compromise, they wanted to lower the pay even more. I have a bit of a fiery side and, well, I simply walked out after I made the mistake of saying that they didn't care for the education of their children."

Mrs. Miller giggled. "You ruffled more than one gray hair, I imagine."

Helen chuckled too. "I'm afraid so. I'll be heading back home to Virginia on the eastbound train."

"Nonsense. Spend the night in my spare room, no charge. You must be exhausted, riding in on the train today. I know my old bones get tired riding those iron horses. Although I'll admit it is a lot more comfortable than riding a wagon for miles and miles."

"True. But I couldn't impose."

"Nonsense. It's no imposition, and I'd love the company. My Alfred has been gone going on six years, and the children are grown with children of their own now. I'd love the company. I have the room. Please stay. You can catch the train tomorrow."

Helen wouldn't mind a night in a comfortable bed. "Are you certain I would not be an imposition?"

"Positive. Come inside." Mrs. Miller opened the door.

Helen stepped inside as Mrs. Miller leaned out to say, "I'll be right with you gentlemen. Let me get this young lady settled in."

"Yes'm," rang out from the men.

"Thank you," Helen said as she followed Mrs. Miller to the back of the cottage. The room was neat, with handmade quilts and pillows covering the bed and a large upholstered chair, and handmade curtains framing the windows. "Oh my, this is gorgeous."

"Thank you. As I said, my Albert's been gone for a while now. So I have a lot of time on my hands. Sewing and cooking help me pass the hours and support myself. Now, you settle in. The washroom is over there." She pointed to the door down the hall. "I'll finish serving the young men and we can have dinner together. How about some ham and eggs with a serving of hash brown potatoes?"

Helen's stomach flipped. "Thank you. You are most kind."

"Nonsense. It's what any good Christian would do." Mrs. Miller waved as she headed back to the front door. No question the woman had quite a business going. Who wouldn't want Grandma's sweets while away at college?

Helen plopped her valise on the floor then sat down on the overstuffed chair. Her heart went out to this community. She'd been praying for months about this position and had felt the Lord leading her here. Why had the interview gone so poorly? Granted, her attitude was partly to blame, but their attitudes. . .

She closed her eyes as if to shut off the train of thought. She couldn't keep blaming others for her reactions. No one had forced her to apply for the job. There was no call for her condescending attitude toward the board members, even though they appeared to have a lack of compassion for their students. She wondered how many candidates they had approached and turned down. Even for a man, the salary was low. The salary they offered for a woman was downright ridiculous, and yet she had felt confident the Lord would provide. Why couldn't she have kept her mouth shut and prayed before turning them down on their lower offer?

Because she was forever repeating the same fault of speaking before she thought. "Help me, Lord. I'm trying, but. . ." Helen sighed. She'd blown it again. "Forgive me, Lord."

After a few minutes, she removed her hat and went to wash the day's dirt and grime from her face. She brushed her hair and pinned it back into place. Smiling at her reflection, she said, "I'll try to do better next time, Lord."

Helen exited the washroom and joined Mrs. Miller at the doorway. A half dozen men were still lined up eagerly awaiting their treats. "I'm almost done, dear. Have a seat and get comfortable."

The entrance to the home opened into the front parlor, so Helen took a seat in a thickly cushioned chair and looked around. The parlor wasn't formal like her father's parlor back home. It was cozy and comfortable, accented by still more quilted lap blankets draped neatly over some of the stuffed chairs. Mrs. Miller's cheery interaction with her customers drifted in.

"Good evening, Mrs. Miller."

"Good evening, Professor Moore. I was hoping you'd stop by today. How was your day—the usual?"

"Good, but one of your pies will make it sensational."

Helen turned to see the strikingly handsome man she'd bumped into earlier. His chocolate-brown eyes sparkled, and their eyes met. He smiled. "I see you have a guest, Mrs. Miller."

"Yes, yes, I do. This is. . .was to be our new schoolteacher."

His eyebrows lifted and he stepped back half a pace. He gave a polite nod, pulled a coin from his pocket, and handed it to her.

"Have a wonderful evening, Mrs. Miller."

"You too, Professor."

Helen's mind spun as her heart pounded in her chest. Perhaps she should try to catch the train. No sense staying where you weren't welcome.

◈ Chapter 2 ◈

*R*eading the note Mrs. Miller had passed on to him, Daniel hustled back toward the college and tried to locate some school board members. Her note demanded a meeting with the school board. If anyone in this town could help change that board's mind, it would be her. What surprised Daniel was why he was hoping the board would reconsider.

Naturally he found them in the one-room schoolhouse. "Gentlemen," he called out. He scanned the room and gestured at the overall disrepair of the school. "Are the community's assets this low?"

Mr. Markle stepped forward. "We haven't had a teacher for a year," he said defensively. "We were just discussing the status of the schoolhouse."

Daniel walked farther into the schoolhouse. Harry Burgess's sour face confirmed the schoolteacher's opinion. "I come to represent Mrs. Miller, who has asked me to request a meeting with the school board. She was quite insistent." He handed over the note.

Harry groaned.

"I may be out of place speaking with you, but you men are showing great disrespect for the children of this community by offering such meager salaries and allowing the schoolhouse to fall into such disrepair. You have a broken slate for the blackboard," he said, pointing, "a couple of broken desks and chairs—"

"Now stop right there!" Barry Williams fumed. "This schoolhouse has been vandalized."

"Pardon me." Daniel forced himself to relax. "Speak with Mrs. Miller. I happen to know she convinced the young woman who was to be your teacher to spend the night at her place. You have an opportunity to make some changes for the better." He scanned the room again. "Mr. Markle, doesn't the college have excess supplies and unused furniture in storage that could be used to refurbish the schoolhouse?"

Mr. Markle's face brightened. "Yes, yes, it does."

"Excellent! Well, gentlemen, I'll bid you good night. Oh, and one more suggestion, if I may. Seriously reconsider your salary offer. A woman alone has just as many expenses as a single man. Good day, gentlemen."

Daniel didn't wait for a response. He understood and appreciated the different era these men represented. But the new schoolteacher wasn't local, and therefore had no family to rely on. She would have to provide for herself. And as for the school board's concern over the possibility she might attract a suitor partway into the school year, well. . . He had to admit she was rather beautiful. Perhaps suitors would create a distraction from her job. Daniel grinned as the flutter of an idea of courting her came to mind. He shook it off and headed out the door. Working on his doctoral thesis left no time to entertain even the thought of courting.

The next morning he found himself behind his desk at the university, interrupted from his class preparation by a polite knock at the open door. "Good morning, Professor Moore."

Rusty Burger stood in the doorway. He was one student who had a knack for learning yet put little effort into it. "Good morning, Mr. Burger. What can I do for you?"

"Can I have an extension on my paper?"

"No. You've had extensions on all your papers, and I told you the last time I could not grant another."

Rusty's shoulders slumped. "Very well, here's what I've done so far. Hopefully this paper will be acceptable enough so I won't fail." He stepped into the room and placed three pages on Daniel's desk.

Daniel picked up the pages and scanned them. "I don't understand what the problem is, Mr. Burger. Your knowledge of the subject is quite good."

"I have trouble writing down on paper what's in my head."

"Explain, please?"

"I can see the words in my head, and I know what I want to say, but my hand has difficulty writing it down."

Daniel examined the writing more closely. The letters were well constructed, but it was obvious the words didn't flow naturally and easily. Daniel put the papers down. "You're saying you know the information but that you can't write it easily."

"Yes, sir. It has always been a problem for me. I like science, but I didn't realize I'd have so many papers to write."

"I see." Daniel stood up and pointed to a student's desk in front of him. "Please sit down." Young Mr. Burger did as instructed.

"Please take a few minutes and recite your paper to me."

"All of it, sir?"

"Yes, just tell me what it says, from the beginning."

Rusty cleared his throat and began. "Understanding the cellular structure of a plant begins with. . ."

Twenty minutes later Daniel smiled. "Excellent job, Mr. Burger. Your next assignment you can dictate to me, and for this one you will receive an A. It would have been an A-plus, except you confused the smooth ER with the rough ER." Daniel went on to explain the difference.

Rusty smiled. "Thank you, Professor Moore. I really appreciate this."

"You're welcome. What is your major?"

"Agriculture. I'm interested in developing increased production for farmlands without depleting the soil. I'm curious about applying the seventh year of rest that the Bible speaks about, and what effect that would have on the land."

"Interesting. I always regarded the Sabbath year as simply an extended holiday that the Jewish people prepared for in the six years prior, while the olive trees and other perennial plants were for the poor to harvest for food. But you might have a point about the land needing a break."

"Father alters his fields. He's divided them up into sevenths, and every year one section is not planted. Instead, the waste products from the other plants are tilled into the soil on that section. He's done well, and the Lord has provided, but I still want to know about the science and why that process works."

Daniel understood the simple answer wasn't what this young man was looking for. Rusty liked science, and he had a keen mind but a slow hand. He'd seen this before. Daniel tossed a pencil toward Rusty. He reached up and caught it with his left hand. "I think I know your problem."

"What?"

"You're naturally left-handed. I assume when you were being taught to write you were told to use your right hand."

Rusty nodded. "Everyone uses their right hand."

"Not everyone. When you go to your dorm tonight, start teaching yourself to write with your left hand. It will take time, and constructing the letters will be different than using your right hand. Nevertheless, I believe after a while you will become fluid using your left hand. In the meantime, I'll be accepting your oral reports."

Rusty stared down at his left hand. "You think that's all it will take for me to write as quickly as I think?"

"No one writes as quickly as they think, but I do believe it will improve your speed. Have a good day, Mr. Burger."

"Good day, sir."

Rusty leapt from his seat and darted out of the classroom. Daniel smiled, glanced up at the wall clock, and returned to the notes on his desk. Only ten minutes remained before his first class of the day began.

Helen couldn't believe the turn of events her life had taken in the past week. First, she had been hired by the school board for one year. She was given the full salary, and the issue of courting was removed, providing any such activity didn't interfere with her teaching. She was now renting a room from Mrs. Miller, who seemed to be a key player in her being offered the position again. She and some volunteers had cleaned the classroom. Last night she had the opportunity to meet the parents and students, and she felt ready for the students to arrive in the morning.

She had sent her father a letter explaining all her good fortune. Mrs. Miller's rent was far less than she anticipated paying, and in addition, she had a meal waiting for her every night when she finished her day. Which for the past few days had proved very handy since she'd spent so much time cleaning and preparing the classroom. She loved cooking and had helped Mrs. Miller prepare some of her tasty treats, but she loved coming home to a home-cooked meal, something she hadn't had in years.

"Something smells wonderful tonight, Mrs. Miller," Helen said as she stepped into the warmth of the small cottage.

The older woman stood about five feet tall, with white hair that glistened in the sunlight. Her girth was a bit round, but she was light on her feet. She smiled, her apron covered with flour. "Lamb stew," she replied, "cooked like a potpie."

"Yum."

"I made enough to share with the students. They have to come with their containers though."

Helen placed an apron over her dress. "Can I help serve tonight?"

"Thank you. Don't serve that casserole dish," she said, pointing. "That is our supper."

Helen chuckled. "I'll guard it with my life."

Mrs. Miller laughed as she brought a tray of sweet rolls out to the front where she served the students who came by. The sweet rolls were twice the size of any Helen had seen before, and five cents for a roll seemed a very fair price. "We'll charge twenty-five cents for the lamb potpie," Mrs. Miller said.

"What else are we serving tonight?" Helen asked.

"I have a couple pumpkin pies in the kitchen. But those were special ordered for Mrs. Billings. I also made some pumpkin and raisin muffins. Those we'll sell for a nickel as well."

"Sounds good." Helen carried the large casserole dish to the front of the house using potholders. The line outside was building and they hadn't even opened for business yet. Helen smiled. There were many repeat customers, but Professor Moore hadn't returned since that first night. Mrs. Miller said he'd played a part in her reinstatement as the schoolmarm. She wanted to thank him. She also wanted to ask Mrs. Miller about him but didn't dare, out of fear her landlady would get the wrong impression. Her interest, of course, was purely platonic. *Perhaps I should pen him a note? That would certainly be appropriate in this modern time.*

"Well, my gracious, gentlemen!" Mrs. Miller exclaimed. "You've come with your bowls and mugs. How wonderful."

"Anything you cook is wonderful, Mrs. Miller," said the first in line. "I'll have the lamb potpie, a sweet roll, and a pumpkin raisin muffin. No, wait. . ." He paused and looked over the array of fresh baked goods. "You had better make that two sweet rolls and two muffins tonight. I'm famished." Chad Avery winked his baby blues at Mrs. Miller.

Helen lowered her head to hide her grin. She'd been learning to put names to the faces of the regular students.

"I'll have the same, Mrs. Miller," the young man standing behind him said.

"Me too," another replied.

"What on earth were you boys doing that made you all so hungry tonight?" Mrs. Miller asked as she scooped out the potpie.

"Professor Moore had us exploring, walking around outside for nearly ten miles," Freddy Silverman answered. "Saw some interestin' stuff, but we're hungry."

Mrs. Miller chuckled and started serving the young men. "What about dinner on campus?"

"Ain't enough." The young man grinned and held out his small bowl.

Helen couldn't help herself. "*Ain't* is not proper English."

"Huh?" The young man with reddish hair paused. "Oh wait, you're that new schoolmarm, ain't ya?"

Helen gave him a reproving look.

"Sorry, *aren't* you?" he replied, drawing out the correct pronunciation.

"Yes, I am, and I'd be happy to tutor anyone who needs help with English and grammar."

All the young men straightened up and said, "No, thank you," with chuckles and grins.

After thirty minutes they had no more food to sell, and the men left standing in line empty-handed pouted but wished Mrs. Miller a good night.

Helen sat down for a quiet meal with her.

"How was your day, dear?" Mrs. Miller asked as she placed

her cloth napkin on her lap.

Helen was tired, though she did not want to admit it, and had decided to turn in early tonight. However, she was also excited, anticipating her first day of school, and wondered if she would sleep at all. "Fine," she said. "The classroom is in excellent shape, and I'm looking forward to the students coming tomorrow morning."

They folded their hands and said a prayer of thanksgiving.

"How'd you have so much lamb to make all of this?"

"Oh, the butcher gave me a fair price on a leg of lamb. I couldn't resist. Tell me about your classroom."

"The large slate in the front of the classroom has been replaced and all the desks and chairs have been repaired or replaced. The school board has put in a lot of effort."

"As well they should," Mrs. Miller said with a twinkle in her eye.

"Just what did you say to those men to make them reconsider?"

Mrs. Miller shrugged. "Nothing much, just reminded them about a time or two when they were young men and courting their wives."

Helen shook her head. "I really don't have time to be courted. I just didn't like being told what I can and cannot do."

"I truly understand, dear." She reached across the table and patted Helen's hand. "I've ruffled a feather or two in my lifetime."

Helen chuckled. "I can't imagine it."

"Oh, phooey!" Mrs. Miller laughed.

Daniel passed the schoolhouse on his way to the university and waved to Helen Jones as she greeted each of her students parading through the doorway into the classroom. She nodded but kept her focus on the children. He'd been hearing good reports about the new schoolteacher. The praise coming from some of the school board members was especially surprising.

Daniel headed toward the university with briefcase in hand. Unfortunately, he had two students in danger of flunking. It pained him knowing that within a few short weeks their grades, if not dramatically improved, would be beyond salvaging. Mike and Pete were struggling. Their test scores were below fifty and their papers were what might be expected from someone in the fourth grade. It definitely was not college material. Today he planned to meet up with some of their other professors to see if the two boys were having as much trouble in the rest of their classes.

"Mornin', Professor," Judson Reeves said as he walked toward him.

"Good morning, Mr. Reeves. How are you today?"

"Fine."

Judson was one of the few students who actually grew up in town and lived off campus. Most of the students came from other places and lived in the dormitories. "How's your first school year progressing?"

Judson shrugged. "Good, I guess."

Daniel paused. "What seems to be the issue?"

"Oh, ain't noth— Sorry, it isn't nothing, really. Pa says I might have to stop classes in order to help with the farm. My uncle fell and hurt himself. He'll be unable to work the fall harvest."

"Perhaps we can work out a solution where you could take a leave of absence for a week, help at home, but still stay enrolled."

Judson smiled. "I'd like that. So far, my grades are good. It's hard work but I'm keepin' up. Which, given that I didn't have a teacher for the past year. . . I'm just proud of what I've been able to do."

Daniel reached over and put a hand on Judson's shoulder. Perhaps Miss Jones was right in her assessment that the town's school board had not made education a priority. "Which proves you're self-motivated. Let's see what we can work out."

After his early morning class, he and Judson worked out assignments for the week with his other professors that he would complete at home while working the farm with his father. Hopefully he'd be able to keep up with all the reading and writing assignments in addition to the long, hard hours of harvesting.

Daniel finished his day by spending a couple of hours in his garden. He had rented the small lot to provide the data needed for his doctoral thesis on planting and the different nutritional needs for various plants. This garden was separate from the one that he and his students had put in last spring next to the Agricultural Building. In this garden he had three of each crop, using either organic materials or the best new fertilizers on the market.

Now he was faced with an abundance of winter squash, far more than a single man could use. On the other hand, he could sell them. He snickered to himself. This was a farming community. Just about everyone had their own gardens. And everyone would be pulling their winter squash and storing them in their root cellars. He'd have to take a trip to Knoxville if he wanted to make any real profit selling his produce. The better part of wisdom would be to simply give away as much as possible. The Hubbard squash in particular, known to have a pantry life of up to six months, could be a real blessing as a gift to a few of the elderly in town. His mind drifted to Mrs. Miller and what she could make with them. Pleased with the solution, he loaded his wheelbarrow with various squashes and headed over to Mrs. Miller's. He could smell her apple pies before he turned the corner to her street.

The line outside her house wasn't too long. Hopefully she hadn't run out of pie. He glanced down at the wheelbarrow full of Hubbard, acorn, American turban, and autumnal marrow squashes. The Hubbard, also known as the Marblehead squash, was by far the largest. One of those could feed an army. Perhaps he should bring a couple to the university's cook.

Daniel joined the line behind the others.

"Whatcha got there, Professor?" one of the students in line asked.

"Bartering?" asked another.

"Did you grow these?" Edward Clancy asked.

"Yes, Edward," Daniel replied. "Various squashes," he answered John, and, "No, I'm not looking to trade," he said to the third. "I'm giving them to Mrs. Miller, if she would like them."

"What's this large one?" Edward's major was agriculture.

"The old name is Marblehead squash, but the name growing in popularity is the Hubbard, taken from the woman in Marblehead who grew the first ones in the United States."

"It's huge." Edward reached over and touched the large blue Hubbard squash. "These are all winter squash varieties. The

Hubbard can last for six months after harvesting if kept in a cool root cellar."

Edward reached over to another. "What's this one?"

"Autumnal marrow, another variety from back east, actually from Boston. It is similar to the Hubbard but smaller. The outer skin is thinner, and there's another layer, another skin if you will, that is thicker and has a dark orange color."

"Are you cross-pollinating them?" Edward asked as they all took a step forward.

Daniel glanced toward the front of the line. There were at least three more in front of Edward.

"No, I'm studying the effects of different soils and fertilizers on the squash and other vegetables."

Edward nodded. "Thesis?"

"Yes. What about your studies?"

"Progressing well. I'd be interested in your findings for your thesis. I'm leaning toward cross-pollinating for heartier plants. For example, how can I alter a squash to be more tolerant in drought areas, and what would be the difference needed for the opposite end of the environmental spectrum?"

Edward pointed toward the blue Hubbard. "What do you think, twenty pounds?"

"At least. I love the Hubbard for the texture and quantity."

"Interesting. . ." The line moved forward again. "But the economics of getting them to market isn't really practical, is it? I mean, it would seem to me that its sheer size alone would make it a better squash for a manufacturing plant to process and can for the market, don't you agree?"

"They would be hard to sell at the general store," Daniel

admitted. "But for the home farmer, one Hubbard can produce what five or six other winter squashes can."

Edward chuckled. "What would you do with that much squash?"

They'd reached their turn in line for the baked goods, where Mrs. Miller interrupted with a smile, "I'd bake pies and breads. Are those for me?"

"As much as you'd like," Daniel replied.

"Oh my word," Helen chimed in. "What is that?"

Daniel laughed. "Blue Hubbard squash."

"And they're delicious," Edna Miller said. "Daniel, would you please bring what you're giving me into the kitchen?"

"Can you use all of them?"

Mrs. Miller leaned over and examined the full wheelbarrow. She straightened. "I believe I can. I'll be happy to share with some of my friends what I can't use or store."

"Wonderful. Can I get a free pie out of it?"

Mrs. Miller swatted him with a towel. "You won't have to pay for the rest of the year."

Daniel smiled and turned to Edward. "Would you mind giving me a hand bringing these into Mrs. Miller's house?"

"Be my pleasure. Please save me a sweet roll and one of those muffins. I didn't bring a bowl for the potpie. Smells great though." Edward chuckled.

"I'll have them waiting for you. Bring the squashes around back, Professor."

"Yes, ma'am." Daniel steered the wheelbarrow around to the side of the house and followed the well-worn pathway. Her plants needed some trimming. He knew Edna Miller's children should be helping out, but they had their own needs. Mrs. Miller's time was put into baking each day for the students. She probably didn't have the energy to care for all her plants.

As he pulled the wheelbarrow to a halt, Miss Jones opened the back door and banged him in the head.

⚭ Chapter 3 ⚭

*H*elen couldn't believe it. Her second encounter with the professor and she banged into him—again! Not with her head this time, but rather the door. "I am so sorry, Professor. Are you all right?"

He rubbed his head. "I'm fine, thank you." He reached down into the wheelbarrow to lift the strange-looking squash. She'd never seen one so big before. Pumpkins, maybe, but never anything like this, and bluish in color, no less.

A young man standing next to the professor extended his hand toward her. "Hello, I'm Edward Clancy."

She supposed he was close to her in age, yet for some reason he seemed much younger. "Helen Jones," she said, receiving his handshake. "Pleasure to meet you. Did you help the professor grow these?"

"No, ma'am. I'm further along in my studies. I'll be graduating this spring with my master's."

"Oh." *Then he must be around my age, possibly older.*

"Let's not pester Miss Jones much longer, and put these in Mrs. Miller's kitchen."

"Yes, sir." Edward Clancy picked up a squash in each hand and headed into the kitchen.

Helen slipped out the door, picked up a few acorn squashes, and carried them in. She nearly bumped into Professor Moore again. She glanced up in time to see his approach. He held the door open for her. Edward Clancy squeezed past before she stepped in. Within three minutes the wheelbarrow was empty.

"I'm going to get my goodies before they're all gone, Professor." Edward tilted his head toward Helen. "Good night, Miss Jones."

"Good night. Thank you for your help."

"You're welcome." His smile beamed from ear to ear.

Professor Moore wagged his head back and forth and sighed.

"Is there a problem, Professor?"

"No, sorry. How are you, Miss Jones? How are your students adjusting?"

"Fine, thank you. All things considered, I believe they are doing fairly well. I've been evaluating where each of them is in their studies. They lost an entire year of schooling. Several families tried to keep up with their children's studies, some more than others. But overall, I believe we shall have an excellent year."

"Wonderful. I have two who are about to flunk out. I suspect they may not be able to read very well."

"Oh dear. How could they enter college. . ." She let her words trail off, reminding herself once again to hold her tongue.

Professor Moore shrugged. "I don't know. However, it is fairly easy to listen carefully and pretend to read. Each of the answers they got wrong on tests were directly related to their reading assignments. I found another student also having trouble writing his papers, but it turns out he's left-handed and was taught to use his right hand, which slowed him down."

"Interesting. I had a teacher when I was young who tried to make one of the boys in school do the same thing. Eventually, she gave up, and he excelled."

Professor Moore smiled. "Well, I must get going." He took a few steps toward the front of the house. "Oh." He pivoted around. "Would you ask Mrs. Miller to save the seeds?"

"I'd be happy to. Do you sell seeds?"

"No. I am working on various planting methods. . . . Actually, I believe I already mentioned what I was doing with these squashes."

"Not to me, Professor," Helen said.

"Daniel, call me Daniel. We are peers, are we not?"

Helen nodded. "Yes."

"I'm working on my doctoral thesis. I'm comparing various types of organic fertilizers and chemical fertilizers and how each affects plant growth. So each plant has at least three within one type of study. And with three plants per study, multiplied by four studies per. . . Well, let's just say I have a lot of squash."

Helen smiled. "I can see. So what are you going to do with the seeds?"

"I'll save and label them. All of these were from the cow manure plots, all natural, if you will."

"I may not want to know."

"It's a great fertilizer. The only problem is how to have enough manure for the large agricultural farms. Limited fertilizer means they have to split the farm's production between dairy and growing vegetables. Most commercial farmers concentrate on one particular area. I'm not certain it is economically sustainable. The squashes that had the chemical fertilizers grew just as large. However, I'm still working on the figures."

"Ah, your thesis." Helen smiled, glad it wasn't her work. She'd go loony categorizing all those numbers.

"That's right. I take it you're not a planter?"

"No, not really. Mother had a small vegetable patch and flower garden where we lived. After she passed, I didn't have time for gardening in addition to caring for the house and attending to my studies. Father didn't have the heart to continue with the gardens either."

"I'm sorry to hear about your mother," he said.

An awkward silence dropped between them, as if a curtain closed and the audience was unsure if it was the end of the play or not. "Thank you. I should get back to helping Mrs. Miller."

He nodded and headed off again toward the front of the house. Helen shuffled into the kitchen and from there to the front door, where Edna had the last of her supplies laid out for the hungry customers. It was the second day of her lamb potpie, and it was just as big a hit as it had been the day before.

Daniel came up to the doorway. "What would you like, Professor?" Edna asked.

"Anything. I'm starving."

Edna served him a double portion of potpie on one of her own dishes. "You can bring the dish back." She added two rolls and two muffins. "Tomorrow I'll have a squash pie for you."

"I'm looking forward to it." He laid a dollar on the table.

"No, no! I told you, you'll be eating for free for the rest of the year. Thank you." She handed the dollar back to him.

He placed his order back down on the shelf of the Dutch door and put the dollar in his front pocket. "Thank you," he said, scooping up his dinner and waving as he walked away.

The rest of the crowd was served, and they closed up shop. Edna walked into her kitchen, greeted by a pile of assorted squash. "Oh my, we have work to do."

Daniel fought his desire to get to know the intriguing Miss Jones. In fact, he continued to think of her as Miss Jones to maintain that formal sense of distance between them, and besides, she'd not given him permission to use her first name. The next day he walked past the schoolhouse, where she welcomed the children in for the day from the front step. He waved and she returned the gesture.

After a full day of teaching, he headed home. The garden needed attention and he was behind on the records for his thesis. *Perhaps I should hire a student to give me a hand.* The thought occurred to him as he walked past the schoolhouse. He slowed his normally brisk pace. Miss Jones had the front door wide open. It was long past the hour of teaching. *What's going on?*

He walked up the stairs and stared into the classroom. The rows of desks were empty. Miss Jones stood at the chalkboard drawing a flower. On another board were spelling words and addition and subtraction tables. She turned. Her hair hung down to her shoulders. She saw him and immediately scrabbled at her hair to put it back in a bun. "Sorry, I wasn't expecting anyone."

He swallowed, stifling his immediate response to her beauty. He proceeded with an explanation. "I saw the door open and—"

"Yes, I'm sorry, it was a warm day today. I thought the building could use an airing out."

"There's no need to apologize to me, Miss Jones. I understand. You're fine. I—I mean," he stammered, "I mean, you're doing fine."

"I'm trying to decide what book I should read to the students. If I can gather math problems from the story, as well as showcase the sciences, vocabulary words, etc., it will make the rest of their learning much more interesting. At least, that's my hope."

Daniel smiled. "I always loved *Around the World in Eighty Days*, but I doubt the students are ready for French."

"Actually, I thought about that one as well, and I have a translated copy. It would give us a fascinating approach to the study of world geography, various cultures, transportation. . .so many things."

"Absolutely. And for your advanced students, you could even begin teaching French."

Helen moved over to her desk and sat down. Daniel grabbed a wooden chair and pulled it alongside as she rummaged through some neatly arranged papers. "This gal," she said, lifting one sheet, "Emma Waters, she's my most advanced student. She's in sixth grade, according to the records, but I believe she's possibly around ninth grade in her abilities." She reached for another. "Then there is Jesse Harrison. He's been placed in fifth grade, but he really should be around second grade. I believe he might have either a visual or learning issue. I just need more time to determine what the problem might be. "Here," she said, handing

Daniel the paper. "Look at his handwriting."

"Hmm, I have a student who writes with a heavy hand like this. I mentioned him last evening. He was taught to use his right hand even though he's naturally left-handed."

"I'll check on that. I hope that's all it is. It isn't that he doesn't try. He does try. It just seems that nothing comes quickly for him."

Daniel nodded. If only Rusty Burger had had a teacher in his younger days to encourage him to use his left hand. Perhaps Helen could help this Jesse. He prayed it was so. "There's always a Mark Twain tale," he suggested. "I haven't read any of his books myself, but I've heard they are very entertaining."

"Perhaps. . . ." She glanced around the room and toward the door.

Changing the subject, he brought up his squash. "There's a pig farmer on the other side of town, Buddy Kyle. I'm going to take the rest of my extra squash over to his place. I figure what they don't want their pigs will eat."

"Just how many did you grow?"

"More than I should, I suppose, but I wanted to run a fair test. That will make my statistics more accurate." Daniel stood. He enjoyed speaking with Miss Jones too much. He should get back to his studies, and he did need to finish his doctoral thesis.

"By the way, I have a copy of *Around the World in Eighty Days* in French, if you could use it," he offered.

"Thank you, I might take you up on that. But did you mean *Le tour du monde en quatre-vingts jours?*"

Daniel laughed. "How many years?"

"Since I was seven. You?"

"Ah, I was twelve."

They conversed in French for a few moments, until he broke it off politely and stepped back. "Pardon, mademoiselle, *à bientôt*."

"À bientôt."

Daniel hustled out of the building. He closed his eyes for a moment, wondering why on earth she shared a love for the French language same as he. . .and stumbled on the stairs. *Pay attention.*

"At least I didn't cause that one!" Helen called out from inside the schoolhouse.

Daniel smiled sheepishly and waved good-bye. She had indeed caused the misstep, but he wouldn't be telling her that.

Helen couldn't believe the interest Daniel took in her work, and was even more surprised that he liked the idea of using a novel to help teach other subjects. Beyond all of that, however, he loved French, and he too had read *Le tour du monde en quatre-vingts jours.* And while she thought an excellent job had been done on the translation of the novel into English, there was nothing like reading the story in the author's own language.

She'd only been in town for a few short weeks, and already her mind was captivated by Professor Daniel Moore. She was here to teach. She certainly wasn't ready for a romance. And she wasn't about to give up her teaching career in order to marry. After all these years of preparation, how could she?

Helen drew those thoughts to a close, finished the drawing of the flower on the chalkboard, and then returned to her desk and continued working on the lesson plan for the following Monday. Thoughts of Daniel's work crept back in. All that delicious squash would get boring after a while, and yet he had many times what he'd brought over still at his home garden. Unbelievable!

She thought about teaching the science of growing things. Nothing would be better than to have the children plant seeds and watch them grow. She should ask Daniel what, if anything, they could grow this late in the year. There had to be something. But winter would be coming soon. She made a mental note to ask him the next time she saw him.

Home for the evening, she helped Edna with her tasty treats. The squash pies were a hit. She sold out of them before an hour was up. Thankfully, she had also made some squash muffins with raisins, as well as her standard fare of fluffy bread rolls.

"How was your day, dear?" Edna asked as they sat down at the kitchen table for dinner.

"Fine, thank you. I stayed late to prepare the blackboards for Monday morning classes."

"Ah. Oh, by the way, I invited Professor Moore over for dinner tomorrow night. I want to thank him for his kind gift of squash. I don't mind telling you though, I will be glad once it is all canned or put away. I'll be squashed out after all this."

Helen chuckled. "What can I do to help you tomorrow? I won't be in school, and I don't have any work I need to catch up on."

"I thought we could make something different than lamb for tomorrow. Have you ever made pasta?"

"No, but I'm willing to learn."

Edna reached over and patted Helen's hand. "Wonderful. I'll teach you in the morning. I had some fresh tomatoes, onions, and peppers given to me today. We could make a wonderful sauce. I wonder if the professor grew any zucchini squash."

"I'm not sure. Who gave you the tomatoes?"

Edna giggled. "Professor Moore. I just love his doctoral thesis. I end up with some of the nicest vegetables."

"I'd love to see his garden. It must be huge."

"From what I understand, he turned his backyard, side yards, and front yards into gardens. Then he rented another space from someone else."

"Wow, and he still has time for his teaching."

Edna smiled then sobered. "He's a dedicated teacher. Much like you, dear."

"Thank you," Helen said. "I hope the parents and the school board see that."

"They will, dear." Edna patted her hand again and cleared the table of her dinner dishes. "I feel like a walk. Would you like to join me?"

"Sure. I'll clean the dishes and—"

"No, we can do them once we get back. The sun will be setting soon."

"Yes, ma'am." Helen finished off her lamb potpie. She loved the dish, but also had to admit she was looking forward to something different tomorrow.

They were soon out the front door and walking down the street, heading away from town. "Where are we going?" Helen asked.

"I need to see a friend."

Helen was still trying to get used to all of Edna's ways. She was a loving and caring person. She also didn't put up with any sass. Helen hoped and prayed she would grow up as mellow and strong as Edna Miller.

They turned the corner. Helen scanned the unfamiliar street. In two seconds, she knew exactly which friend Edna was going to see. The front yard left no question as to whose house it was. Edna marched up to the front door and knocked.

No answer. She waited a moment longer and knocked again.

"Come on, Edna," Helen said. "Professor Moore mustn't be home."

Edna sighed. "I hoped he would have some zucchini. It would be excellent in our sauce."

Relief washed over Helen. She felt certain Edna was trying to play matchmaker. Grateful the knock went unanswered, Helen offered, "I'll be happy to come back in the morning and see if he has some."

"Thank you, dear. These old bones don't have it in them to take another walk this far again tomorrow."

Helen helped Edna down the stairs. "Let's walk back at a gentler pace."

Edna nodded. Helen prayed they weren't walking too far for Edna. She was a spry old lady, but she'd worked hard all day preparing those squashes and making all those pies and muffins, not to mention their supper.

"Edna? Helen?" Daniel called out. "Is something the matter?"

∾ Chapter 4 ∾

Daniel couldn't believe the two women were at his house. Helen wasn't a stretch, except that she didn't know where he lived, but Edna Miller didn't take long walks, and she certainly shouldn't. "Are you two all right?"

"Fine. May I rest a spell?" Edna asked.

"Of course, let me get you a chair." He hustled out to the backyard and carried a wooden yard chair out to the driveway, which he'd given serious thought to turning into another plot. The landlord, he'd learned, was grateful he hadn't. Daniel had promised to regrow the grass in the front and side yards after his thesis was done.

He brought the chair to Edna, and while she sat down, he looked to Helen to see if she could explain this sudden visit. Helen shrugged. Interesting, he thought, that she could read his nonverbal communication so well.

"Pardon our familiarity in coming by without an invitation," Edna began.

"You're always welcome, Edna."

"Thank you. I don't want to seem ungrateful for all that you have already given me, but I was wondering if you might have any zucchini?"

"I'm afraid not. Those were done much earlier in the season."

"Ah," Edna sighed.

"Why? If you don't mind me asking." Daniel knelt down beside the chair.

"I'm planning on making some tomato or marinara sauce and, well, zucchini makes a wonderful addition."

"I see." Daniel could see Edna was tired. "Can I help with the canning? Perhaps I can arrange to have a couple students help?"

"Oh my. I don't know if the kitchen is big enough for so many people."

"What if you told us what to do?" Helen suggested.

"I suppose I could use the help. All that canning. . ."

"Exactly. Do you have enough canning jars?"

"No, I suppose not."

"I have a few in the house. Let me see what I can do. I'll be at your place by ten in the morning. Will that be all right?"

"I don't know—"

"Edna," Helen interjected, "why not let Professor Moore help? You could use a break. You've been working hard all day and there are still quite a few squashes to process." She knelt down on Edna's other side and patted her hand. "Let us help you."

"Very well. I didn't come for help, only zucchini."

Helen giggled, a light and sparkling sound.

"Nor did you ask for a wheelbarrow full of squash," Daniel

said. "I have some additional vegetables for the root cellar. I'll bring them over next week."

Edna sat up straighter. "What kind?"

Daniel laughed. He and Helen stood at the same time. Her green eyes sparkled, and she silently mouthed, "Thank you."

He nodded. "Are you up for walking home?"

"Yes, I do believe I am. But you didn't answer my question. What kind of vegetables?"

"Let's see. . .I have some onions, potatoes, sweet potatoes, parsnips, and rutabagas, to name a few." He helped Edna stand. "Would you mind if I escort you beautiful ladies home?" he asked her, hoping Helen wouldn't think he was being too forward.

If he was going to get some help for Edna Miller, he would need to act fast. He doubted he would find too many students interested in cooking and canning squash. Then it hit him— Buddy Kyle's wife might be willing to help. He decided to head over there this evening after he escorted Edna and Helen home.

The walk to Edna's was slow but pleasant. The sun was setting on the horizon as they approached her house. He would need to run to Buddy's if he was going to get there before they turned in for the night.

"Good night, ladies. I'll see you in the morning."

"Thank you, Daniel." Edna winked. "You remind me of my grandson Bentley."

"Thank you, Edna." He bowed and cast a look toward Helen. "Good night, Miss Jones."

"Good night," Helen replied, and held the door as Edna stiffly walked in. He thanked the Lord for Helen Jones. She was not only a benefit to the children of the community but also a benefit to Edna Miller. The woman was getting on in years and no doubt would be moving in with one of her sons soon. For the time being, it was good that she had someone living with her.

He gave a simple nod of the head and walked as quickly as possible toward the train station, then picked up his pace and jogged over to Buddy Kyle's house. It would be dark before he got home, and he hadn't brought a hand lamp to guide his way.

Daniel rushed through his morning chores. Normally his Saturdays were spent tending the garden and working on his thesis. Today would be different. He'd bartered with the Kyles for three wheelbarrows of squash for a few hours of Wonda's help at Edna Miller's house. He glanced up at the wall clock. Wonda would be joining him at Edna's by ten o'clock. He figured one middle-aged woman who knew her way around a kitchen and canning would be more helpful than a handful of young college men. Before he stopped at Edna's, he ran to the mercantile and purchased four cases of quart-sized canning jars and one case of pint-sized canning jars. He figured there would be times when cooking for two would be preferable for Edna and Helen.

He arrived at Edna's precisely at ten, just as Wonda Kyle was walking up the road toward Edna's house. He knew some folks would find it intolerable to let a Negro woman come into the home of a white person, but he knew that Edna would have no problem with it. They arrived outside the home at nearly the same moment, and he knocked on the door. Shortly after, Helen opened it. "Good morning," she greeted them cheerfully, as her eyes caught a glimpse of Wonda, who stood behind Daniel.

"This is Wonda Kyle," Daniel announced. "Her husband raises the best pork in the entire county."

Helen extended her hand. "Good morning."

Wonda paused, then stepped cautiously around Daniel and extended her hand as well. "Come on in," Helen said to her. "I assume the professor asked you to help."

"Yes'm. I's come. . ."

Daniel interrupted Wonda as they entered the house. "No need to hide your intelligence in this home, Wonda."

Wonda nodded. "I'm happy to help."

Helen smiled. "And we're glad to have you. I canned very little while my mother was alive. I've learned more in the past couple of days than in my entire life."

Wonda smiled. Her bright white teeth, offset by her coffee-colored skin, brightened the entire room.

Within minutes Daniel found himself up to his elbows in soapy water as he washed and prepared the jars for canning. Wonda and Helen were peeling and chopping up the squash. Edna sat at the kitchen table for a few minutes, then decided to relocate to one of her comfy chairs in the parlor and put her feet up. Helen glanced over at Daniel, her green eyes sparkling as she gave him a reassuring nod. Bringing Wonda to help had been a good choice.

As the morning progressed, Helen learned that Wonda was her counterpart to the Negro community. Wonda's sister had even gone to college and was now a doctor serving out west in New Mexico. Three teachers spending the day canning couldn't have been pegged any higher as one of the best days of her life. They talked lesson plans, and she shared her plan of teaching various subjects using *Around the World in Eighty Days* as a backdrop for all the studies.

"What a marvelous idea," Wonda said. "And to teach French using the book as well. I'm afraid I'm not fluent in French."

"I'd be happy to teach you," Helen offered.

"*Moi aussi*," Daniel added.

"Me too," Helen translated.

"I assumed," Wonda said, offering her bright smile. "I'm afraid, however," she said, drying off her hands, "that I need to get home and put together our dinner."

Edna walked in. "Please, take a quart or two of the squash."

Wonda giggled. "Thank you, Mrs. Miller, but the professor here brought three wheelbarrows full of squash to our house. I have plenty."

"Oh dear," Edna said, looking sideways at Daniel then back to Wonda. "You have my prayers."

"Thank you, but we also have pigs that will eat what we can't save or can."

"Oh good. That's a lot of work."

"It is, but we'll share with our friends and family. I was happy to taste that blue Hubbard squash here so I can tell the folks how good it is and how to cook it."

Edna smiled. "Glad I could impart some wisdom about those huge squashes. Speaking of which. . ." Edna turned around and handed Daniel four small paper bags. "Here are the seeds from the ones I cooked and cleaned yesterday."

"Thank you." Daniel wiped his hands and took the proffered bags.

Wonda left after exchanging hugs and thank-yous. Daniel made his way to the front door as well. "Thank you for your help, Daniel," Edna said as she eased back in her chair.

"You're welcome. Next time I'll bring the vegetables in smaller amounts."

Edna smiled.

"I'd appreciate that," Helen quipped.

Everyone chuckled.

"Thank you," Helen said, "for introducing me to Wonda Kyle. I'm happy to know there is a school for the Negroes."

He placed a hand in the air, motioning for her to stop. He directed a glance over at Edna, who had fallen asleep.

Helen exited the house with Daniel, careful not to snap the door shut, so she could continue. He spoke before she could. "I agree with you," he said, "but we have to keep our knowledge of Wonda's education and teaching hidden. There are some in these parts who would burn down their barn, possibly their home, if they knew the children were being educated. I don't agree with them at all, but we have a responsibility to keep their secret and keep them safe. Having Wonda's help, her appearing to do servant-type work, is socially acceptable. But if you were to go to her home simply to visit. . . Well, let's just say you could be putting her life in harm's way. There's a reason she speaks in public as if she's uneducated."

"So are you saying that Willy, who works at the mercantile, can speak perfect grammar?"

"Probably. He is Wonda and Buddy's oldest son."

"Oh, I'm so glad you told me. I was about to march up to the school board and demand—" Another example, she quickly realized, where she would have spoken without praying or thinking something through.

"I suspected as much. I'm not going to try to stop you from teaching Wonda French, if that is something she would like to learn. But if you do, please be careful. Having her come here to Edna's to help with the cooking might be a way to teach without others knowing." Daniel shrugged. "I don't know." He reached for her shoulders and peered into her eyes. "Pray, Helen. Ask the Lord for guidance. There is always a way."

"Thank you, Daniel. I mean that. The hardest lesson of my life is learning to keep my tongue silent and wait on the Lord. I appreciate the godly counsel."

"You're welcome. Now, I must get home. I have a ton of work I need to do."

"Good-bye, Daniel."

"Good-bye, Helen."

She watched him walk down the road toward his home. He was a good man, a wise man. As much as she disliked bigotry and prejudice, she knew she couldn't single-handedly fix all the wrongs in this world. However, if Wonda would like Helen to teach her French, or any other subject, she would do it. She marched back into the house and found Edna reading. "I thought you were asleep."

"No. . ."

"Edna?"

"Yes, dear?"

"Mrs. Miller," she tried again, hoping to sound a little more forceful, "I don't want you to think me ungrateful, but I have to ask you, please, don't try to play matchmaker with Daniel and me."

Edna shrugged. "Whatever gave you that impression?"

"The walk last night. . .pretending to be asleep just now. He's a nice man, and he's quite handsome, but I need to concentrate on my teaching, and he needs to focus on his doctoral thesis. Now isn't the time to get romantically involved."

"Yes, dear. Whatever you say." Edna glanced back down at her Bible.

Helen rolled her eyes and went to her room. It was time to turn her attention to converting *Around the World in Eighty Days* into lesson plans.

The next three weeks went by without a hitch. Daniel didn't bring over too many vegetables again. She doubted he even had any more, as temperatures were starting to get down into the forties at night.

They saw each other every morning as he walked to college and she held the door open for her students. She had ordered three primers to learn French, one for herself, one for Emma Waters, and one for Wonda, who came by every Saturday morning to help Edna in the kitchen, all on pretense, of course. Wonda's gift for language was apparent, and her progress in completing the lessons was two to three times ahead of young Emma.

The students were enraptured when Helen read the story to them each day. They soon realized that some of their spelling words came from the book. Helen also utilized a map of the world to help the students trace the travels of Phileas Fogg and

Passepartout. She even worked in several math problems based on the story. Within a few days of her reading the story aloud, parents began to show up with their younger children. Everyone seemed enthralled with the story. Even a professor's wife from the college came over.

By the end of October, the children had decided to attend the annual harvest party dressed in exotic European and Asian costumes inspired by the book. The mercantile had ordered a case of *Around the World in Eighty Days*, as families and relatives of the students all wanted to read the novel. The only problem came when Mr. Kroger found out he'd ordered the books in French. Helen purchased two, but the rest had to be sent back and English translations reordered.

"Miss Jones." Billy Williams stood at her desk.

She'd already dismissed the children for the day. "Yes, Billy, how may I help you?"

He plopped his math paper on her desk. "I don't understand this."

Helen glanced at the paper. Billy was six and learning simple addition and subtraction.

"What is it that you don't understand?"

"These." He pointed to the roughly scribbled numerals on his paper.

"You mean the numbers?"

"Yes'm." He nodded his head.

Helen had assumed he knew his numbers because he could recite them. "Ah, so you don't know which symbol represents which number."

He shook his head. "No, ma'am, I don't."

"Let me help you." She drew the numerals from one to ten on the board. She pointed to the one. "This is the symbol for the number one." She drew an apple below the number. "This is the number two." She drew two apples below that number then pointed to each and counted, "One, two." She repeated the process up to the number ten.

"So these are letters for numbers."

Helen chuckled. "Yes, Billy. Should I write this on a paper for you to take home?"

"No, ma'am. I understand now." He pointed to his paper. "Two plus two equals four, right?"

"Right, that's very good."

Billy beamed. "Good-bye, Miss Jones. I gotta show my mom."

She watched Billy run out the door and paused for a moment. This was what she loved most about teaching. A moment later, Daniel appeared in the doorway of the school, silhouetted by the setting sun. "Good afternoon," he said.

Her heart fluttered. She knew she was falling in love with Daniel. Not a single day passed without at least a dozen thoughts of him coming to the surface. But she couldn't act on those thoughts. "Good afternoon, Professor. How may I help you?"

"I just wanted to let you know that the college stopped Mr. Kroger from sending back the French copies of *Le tour du monde en quatre-vingts jours*. It will be used in next semester's advanced French class."

Helen chuckled. "You should have seen the crowd of parents and younger siblings here this morning. You would think I was handing out the latest news from President McKinley."

"Helen." His voice softened and he stepped farther into the

schoolhouse. "You've touched the community. Everyone is asking about Phileas Fogg and Passepartout and where they might be going next. You did that, no one else. You were called here for a purpose."

Her heart began to race. She placed a hand on her desk and pushed herself up from her chair. "Thank you, you're very kind. How is your thesis coming?"

"It's done. I submitted it last week." He took a step closer.

She stiffened. Her attraction to Daniel Moore had grown each day, yet nothing had been said or done between them since working together in Edna's kitchen. Why the attraction?

Daniel had crossed the length of the schoolroom floor but stopped himself from stepping right up to Helen at her desk. Instead, he stepped back and leaned against one of the student desks in the front row. He crossed his arms, guarding himself from his own desires. He loved her work ethic. He loved how she dealt with the students, and he loved how she cared for Edna. But he wasn't going to get involved in a relationship. Not now. Possibly after he was awarded his doctoral degree and after he knew what his future held, if he'd be staying in the area or moving on to a larger university.

"Congratulations." She smiled and looked down at the papers on her desk.

"What's your plan for the students for the holidays?"

"For Thanksgiving, we're creating a cornucopia. Each student will make a vegetable, nut, or fruit out of paper or papier-mâché and will put their name on it. The student will attach what they've made to a board inside the cornucopia."

"Why their names?" He envied her creativity and zest for teaching young children.

"Ah, that's so I can point out how each one of them is a part of God's overall plan, and how we should be thankful for the special people in our lives."

He smiled. "Marvelous. I never would have thought of something like that. I do well with adult students, but children. . ." He shook his head. "I don't understand them."

"Probably because you think with your scientific mind. I know you enjoy literature, but you enjoy science much more."

"Guilty, I'm afraid."

"What was your favorite book or story as a child?"

"Hmm, I don't recall. I don't believe I was ever read to as a child."

"What? You're joking. Not even in school?"

"Nope." Prior to this encounter, the thought had never occurred to him that there might be anything different or unusual about his upbringing. "We were read to from our primers, but we were to follow along, to read those words ourselves so we could recognize them."

She reached down behind the desk and rummaged through a satchel. She pulled out a thick book with a dark blue cover and gold etchings. "Did you read this?"

"*Treasure Island*? It wasn't assigned reading."

She slid the book closer. "Go ahead and take it. If you liked *Le tour du monde en quatre-vingts jours*, I think you'll enjoy this."

He held the blue cloth-bound book with golden illustrations and letters. "I don't know that I have time for light reading."

"Why not? You said you were through with your thesis. What else are you working on?"

He could feel the rumble in his chest. "You've got me there. It is a children's book, is it not?"

Her lips turned up gently on the right side in her quirky smile. She often did that when she felt she had the upper hand. And perhaps she did. He glanced down at the book again. "Why would I like this?"

"Granted, it is a children's story. But it's an adventure. I don't want to spoil it for you. I believe that reading adventure stories, even those written for children, gives us a chance to relax and take our minds off of our present-day troubles. Beyond that, they stir our imaginations and bring out our creativity."

He paused and glanced into her green eyes, the color of emeralds. "Are you troubled, Miss Jones?"

She sighed and looked down at her feet. "This job will soon be over, and I will need to find another."

"Do you not like it here?"

"Yes, of course I do. But, if you'll remember, I was hired as a temporary teacher."

"Ah, yes." He glanced toward the window. The trees were turning bright orange and red. His gaze fell back on her. "Would you care to walk with me, Miss Jones?"

She tilted her head. "Let me gather my work. You may escort me home."

He nodded. What was he doing, inviting temptation to walk with him? He was attracted to her, of that he had little doubt. But her love was teaching, and if she wanted to continue to teach, she could not marry. Miss Jones would lose her ability to teach these students if she were to marry him. Daniel pushed off from the desk and stood up straight. Where had that thought—marriage—come from? He had merely asked to escort her home. He had wanted to encourage her, not ask her to marry him. They hadn't even courted. And he wouldn't ask. She would be sacrificing too much. Besides, she was a marvelous teacher. He couldn't do that to her or the children.

She loaded a bundle of papers and books into her satchel. "I'm ready."

"May I carry that for you?" he offered.

"Thank you, but I'm fine."

"You are capable, of course, but I would not be a gentleman if I did not carry your burden."

Helen giggled—that wonderful, warming giggle—and handed him the satchel. He ushered her forward with a sweep of his free hand. "Have you started applying to other school districts?"

"No. I should, but I'm enjoying my life here."

"Perhaps you should talk with the school board to see if they would reconsider."

She shook her head. "I couldn't do that. They've already sent me a letter questioning my teaching style, especially for allowing parents and younger children to come in and disturb the classroom for the reading of *Around the World in Eighty Days*. Even though the parents were delighted with that, it appears that nothing I do will be acceptable to the board. So I will continue to go on each day as I have until the year is over. I know this job is temporary." She sighed. "I knew teaching as a profession was temporary. Women today are not allowed to work once they are married, especially in teaching positions. I see the day coming when that will no longer be the case, but the politics of change are slow. Just look at the segregation issue here, for example. I am wondering if my father was right and that I was wasting my time with an education."

He reached out then held back. "I understand your frustration, and I agree in principle with what you are saying, but I also know that I would need my wife to stay at home to care for and protect our children while I am at work. But prior to children or, perhaps, after children, an occupation might be acceptable."

She laughed. "I can't imagine it. Can you?"

"If I understand what I'm hearing from the women's suffrage movement, I can imagine it." He began leading the way to Mrs. Miller's house. He still thought of the place as Edna's, and not as Miss Jones's home. She truly didn't have a part in this community. He understood her concerns. Her job was temporary. She didn't have a home. She didn't have a husband. And what male would be able to accept a woman as vibrant and intelligent as Helen Jones?

He could, he supposed. And yet he couldn't. He couldn't feel responsible for ending her career. He could be a friend, and he would continue to be that for her. "But it will take time."

"That is my point. Time. It seems to be working against me. I will be returning to my father's house come summer, with no prospects for work. I'll be facing an endless line of suitors, from the very old and fat to the young men who simply want a slave in their kitchen."

"We do not know the ways of God, but I doubt He has such a torturous life planned for you."

She glanced up at him. His heart cinched. "Thank you. I do feel glum from time to time. But God has chosen for me to live now, in this time, and He has given me these gifts. He knows our future."

"Amen." They approached Edna's house. The line outside her home was as long as usual.

"Thank you for escorting me. I'd better go in and give Edna a hand."

He handed over her satchel and took his place in line. "Good day, Miss Jones."

"Good day, Professor."

He stepped forward as the line moved. Edward Clancy stepped away from the doorway with his pick for the day. "Good afternoon, Mr. Clancy," Daniel called out. "What does Mrs. Miller have for us today?"

"Apple fritters."

"Yum," Daniel replied.

"They sure are." Edward took another bite. He came over and leaned in confidentially. "She could charge double and make a real profit. But I'm not telling her. I like how affordable these treats are."

"Perhaps that is why her customers keep returning. Know the market. Know what your customers can afford. She always runs out, or at least most of the time. So she doesn't have waste."

"True, there are economic factors in what you suggest."

"Just a thought. When you are thinking about your future, about making a profit in the food market, remember to keep pricing down to the minimum, as well as keeping your production prices down, so that people can afford to pay."

Edward nodded. "I thought economics wasn't your strong suit."

"It's not. But a good student knows many, if not most, of the factors surrounding their primary area of interest. And food, whether raising it, selling it, or supplying it for the future, is all part of the agricultural field, is it not?"

"It is. I always learn something new when I'm around you, Professor Moore. Have a good night. I have some work to do back at the dorm."

"Good night, Mr. Clancy."

"Good night," he said, and headed back toward the university.

By the time Daniel reached the doorway, Edna's apple fritters were all gone. Daniel sighed. He placed his hand on the Dutch door and leaned in. "All gone?"

"Except for you, Daniel. Come in and close the door behind you."

He turned to the line. "There's nothing left," he announced. The three young men behind him groaned, turned around, and headed back toward the school. Daniel slipped inside. Helen had taken her hair down. His stomach flipped. She was gorgeous. It was all he could do to keep from reaching out to touch her silken reddish-brown hair.

∾ Chapter 5 ∾

*H*elen swept up her hair to tie it back. She didn't realize Edna would invite Daniel in. He stared at her as if she'd grown two heads.

"Pardon me, Miss Jones. Edna, what did you need?" He stepped past her and headed into the kitchen to follow Edna.

Helen's hands shook. Daniel had been staring at her with such intensity she nearly collapsed under her own weight. How could he affect her so? Her growing attraction to him compared with what she'd read about a volcanic eruption. She shook off the foolish thought. She caught a glimpse of him in the kitchen, of Edna handing him a box and pointing to a ladder. Helen retreated to her room. She needed to put distance between her and Daniel. Nothing could develop between them. She would lose her job, and at that point she would lose her mind. She closed her eyes and leaned against her bedroom door. "Dear Lord, what's come over me?"

Helen fought her growing attraction through the holidays, thankful that Daniel had gone home for the Christmas break, as she had. She knew his parents lived in western Tennessee, while her father lived in Virginia. Although her father was concerned that she didn't have a contract, he was nevertheless happy to see her. He also arranged a few not-so-subtle encounters with single gentlemen from the community. She'd gone to lunch with one and entertained another in the parlor of her father's home.

Neither man compared to Daniel Moore. He'd been in her thoughts day and night for the past five weeks. She couldn't shake his chocolate-brown eyes shimmering with desire. No question about it, when he'd seen her with her hair hanging down, he'd been smitten. Oddly enough, he had not stopped in again, not even when Mrs. Miller asked for help. He'd simply gotten a student to help. His distance caused more grief for Helen.

The holiday season drew to a close, and Helen kissed her father good-bye and boarded the train back to Warren. From her seat on the train she saw him standing beside Kathryn Granger, whom he would be marrying in the spring, no doubt. They seemed like a good pairing, but. . . She couldn't help but feel she was being replaced. Then again, it was a good thing. The Bible spoke about a man not living alone, that he who findeth a wife findeth a good thing.

Wife? She closed her eyes and thought about that. For the first time in her life, she thought about what it would mean to be a wife, to partner with a man, to be his helpmate. And the only man she could picture being a helpmate to was Daniel Moore.

She opened her eyes. "Daniel?"

He smiled. "Helen, it's good to see you."

"What are you doing boarding a train in Virginia? I thought your parents lived in Tennessee."

"They do. May I sit down?" He motioned to the seat beside her.

"Of course, please do."

"My grandmother Iris took ill, and our family spent Christmas with her." His voice caught. "She's gone on to glory now."

"Oh Daniel, I'm so sorry." She reached over and took his hand.

He glanced at their hands knitted together. Helen's heart thumped wildly in her chest. He squeezed her hand and released it. "Thank you. She was ready to go home and join my grandfather. He passed last year."

Helen nodded and clasped her hands together. She wouldn't be so bold again.

"I want to thank you for *Treasure Island*. It was a delightful read. Do you have any other works by Robert Stevenson?"

"No, I'm afraid not. But I did pack up a carton of books to bring back to Warren. I haven't decided what will be the next book for my lesson plans, but I'm leaning toward *The Adventures of Tom Sawyer*. Have you read it?"

He shook his head then shrugged. "As you said before, I have a limited knowledge of books. It's odd, really. Both of my parents read. But my father tended to read scientific journals, and Mother loves cooking and gardening books."

"All work, no play."

"Precisely. It helped me earn my PhD by the age of twenty-six. It would have been sooner if I hadn't had to help out my grandfather, my mother's father, in Franklin, Tennessee. However, it was by helping him that I found my passion for gardening and growing things. While I would have loved to earn my degree by the time I was twenty-four, I don't regret helping my grandparents. Grandma Iris was my dad's mother. Father has a business in Nashville. Both of my brothers, John Jr. and James, are married and working at the family business. You might say I'm the odd one. But in fact, I favor my mother's side of the family with my interest in gardening and maintaining the land the Lord has given us. Oh, I'm sorry."

"For what?"

"Talking too much. It was hard losing Grandma Iris. The harder part though was being told that I'm wasting my life. Farming, apparently, is not commercially viable." Daniel snickered.

"But it *is* vitally important, just like teaching. The pay is horrible, but the profits of seeing the children capture a new concept, watching them learn something new. . ."

Daniel groaned. "Precisely. My father doesn't see that. In a way, Edward Clancy reminds me of a younger version of my father. I'm hoping to have Edward rethink his ideas of profit to the exclusion of running the small farmer out of business." He smiled at her. "What about you? How was your Christmas visit?"

"Father's entertaining an engagement. She's a nice woman. I pray the best for them. And he set me up with two potential suitors. Neither one of them measured up."

"Measured up?"

Oh no, did I really say that? "What I mean is they just didn't spark my interest."

Daniel nodded. She prayed he wouldn't bring it up again.

"I would never presume myself on anyone."

Helen giggled. "No, you would not." She glanced out the window to avoid staring at her handsome neighbor.

The conductor came by and took their tickets. "You're getting off at Knoxville and continuing on to Nashville?"

"Yes," Daniel said.

"That'll be our second stop."

"Thank you," Daniel replied.

The conductor took her ticket. "You'll be changing trains in Knoxville."

"Yes, sir."

The conductor handed them back their tickets. An hour into the trip, Daniel started to fall asleep. His masculine scent wafted toward her as he nodded off. His head fell on her shoulder. Surprisingly, she found the closeness refreshing. He turned in his seat, wrapped his arm around her waist, and nuzzled his head against her. "Helen," he murmured.

She closed her eyes. Her heart raced. Her blood pumped so hard she was hearing the beats in her eardrums. She reached up to his hair and pushed it from his face. "Daniel," she whispered.

He smiled.

"Daniel," she whispered again a bit louder. "Please, wake up."

His eyes flickered open, closed, then opened again. Shock settled on his face as he realized where he was and what he was doing. He jerked and stood up. "I'm so sorry. I'm so, so sorry."

"Sit down," she hissed, grabbing his wrist and pulling him down, "before everyone stares at us."

"Please forgive me." He settled back down in the seat beside her.

"You were asleep. You didn't know what you were doing."

"Yes, but. . ." He glanced away. "I can't believe. . . I'm so sorry, forgive me."

"Hush, Daniel, it's fine. You're forgiven."

His face was redder than a rose. "You're so beautiful, so pure. I never would have taken such liberties."

She grabbed his hand. "Daniel," she whispered. Her voice was husky. She wanted to be wrapped in his arms. "You are a man of honor. It was purely an accident. Although. . .you did call out my name."

"I did?"

She nodded.

He closed his eyes as his face grew a deeper shade of red. "I'm sorry. You've been a part of my dreams for quite a while. I promised myself I would not set my sights on you. I promised I would not do anything to take you away from your career of teaching. It wouldn't be right. You're such a good teacher. The students love you, and I daresay most of the parents do as well."

Was she hearing him right? Had he been thinking about her the way she'd been thinking about him? Could it be? "Oh Daniel." She leaned into him and kissed him. She knew she shouldn't but couldn't help herself. She pulled back and lightly stroked his full beard. "I've thought about you as well. Those two men my father tried to set me up with could not hold a candle to you. You're a wonderful man, and I'm honored to know you."

"But your career?"

"Will be over, come June."

He leaned into her and kissed her this time. She melted in his arms. How could something so simple be so complex and wonderful all at the same time?

The conductor came by and cleared his throat.

They released each other and settled back in their seats. "We will need to be careful in Warren," Daniel said. "I'm only allowed to court a woman once a week. If we meet at Mrs. Miller's house, she must always be present. And we can't confide in her. As much as I love Edna, she's been known to spread a tale or two. Not on purpose. But when she starts talking, well. . .she lets some information slip."

"I've noticed that as well. But if you officially court me, she will know."

"True. I would wish to see you more than once a week."

"Do you know your schedule for the spring semester?"

"Yes. What are you thinking?"

"What if you come and offer a class once or twice a week to my students? We can use the time to plan lessons together as well as get to know one another without the world watching."

"Hmm. I'm not good with children."

"Perhaps not, but I am. Between us we should give the children an enjoyable lesson."

"Some sort of botany lesson?"

"Sure, why not? We'll both be busy with our teaching requirements. But this could work. We could develop a lesson plan."

He nuzzled into her neck. "A lesson in love?"

She giggled and swatted him. "No."

He sat back and took her hand. "What kind of plants are mentioned in that Tom Sawyer book?"

"Well, it's set on the Mississippi River. I suppose there are a great variety of plants."

"I'll look them up. Perhaps we can grow some seeds and then dissect the plants. I have a microscope the students could look through."

Helen squeezed his hand. "I like it. However, I'm really interested in finding out more about you."

Daniel couldn't believe his good fortune and that his dreams of Helen were becoming real.

Thankful he hadn't scared her off, he was concerned about how they could proceed as a courting couple. His contract was clear: one evening per week was allowed for courting. Granted, their idea of a botany class could cause some of the university board to question his integrity, but he should be fine. The only other option would be to marry her right away. But it was too soon for that. Not to mention, the town would be out a teacher for their students.

"Are you certain you want to continue a relationship with me? I mean, you will lose your job. . . ."

She placed her silky soft finger against his lips. "I'm certain. I do love teaching, but I also care for you. If things are to move forward with us, what would our future hold? Where do you see yourself in five years?"

"Interesting questions. Prior to you, I was headed to one of the larger universities. Would you consider moving with me?"

"Not if we aren't married, no."

He could feel the heat rise to his cheeks again. "Of course I meant if we were married."

"I would go wherever my husband goes. However, we would

have to discuss the matter. I cannot abide a man who makes blanket decisions and doesn't let his helpmate be a part of the conversation."

"I would not make a move without discussing it with my wife."

"Daniel, why are we discussing such far-off decisions?"

He smiled. She returned the smile. "Because we have both arrived at the same decision at the same time, knowing that if we are to yield to our attraction, there will be serious consequences."

"True."

"And I would not have been so forward with you if I hadn't already thought about you becoming my wife. Have you considered such a possibility?"

Helen groaned. "Yes, unfortunately. Wait, I don't mean that the way it sounds. I fantasized about us becoming a couple, falling in love, marriage, babies, of course, but—"

"It would mean the end of your career. I understand. I didn't approach you, for those very reasons. But we've gone beyond 'approaching one another' by sharing those kisses. I don't regret it, but there will be issues for us to deal with. Timing, courting, etc."

"Yes. I would not feel right hiding our relationship."

"Nor would I. However, it will be hard to limit our time with one another to once a week."

"Six months is a mighty long time," she agreed.

Daniel held her hand. "With God's grace we shall work this out. Can you make yourself available for Saturdays? That will be our day, once a week, you and I."

"Yes, I like that. Saturdays will be ours."

"I will come by once a day on my way to the university, and

we can exchange a few words before classes begin. That shouldn't be a problem."

Helen giggled. "Knowing the school board as we do, I imagine it will be."

Daniel sighed. "You're probably right. We'll be careful. We have to be. I will begin escorting you and Edna to church on Sunday mornings."

"That would be wonderful. But we should sit with Mrs. Miller, one on either side of her. That should help with the school board."

"Agreed. I would prefer you by my side, but. . ."

"As would I."

Daniel wrapped her in his embrace and held on as the train rolled down the tracks. He couldn't believe how much his life had changed in a few short months. He hadn't been looking for a wife, and yet the Lord had put this wonderful woman onto his path. His mind swirled with thoughts of the future. He wanted to ask about children and starting a family, but they needed more time. They could marry the day after school ended for the summer. . . . But how could he ask about a marriage date when he hadn't proposed! They hadn't even gone out with each other. Still, his mind filled with all the possible places they could go on their special day. If he was only allowed one day, he would make the most of it.

Helen exited the train with Daniel following close behind. A part of her didn't want to continue on to Warren. Another part of her was excited to get to know Daniel. It felt odd to work so long for a degree in order to teach, and then not be able to because she had fallen in love. She understood her duties at home would take a lot of time, but felt confident she could do both. The school board, however, would never make an exception and allow a married woman to teach. Could she honestly give it up?

"Daniel." She turned to speak with him. "I know you will think I'm fickle, but I am having doubts about leaving my career behind. I've worked so hard for my degree."

It was hard for her to see his facial changes behind his beard. He closed his eyes for a moment then gave a single nod of his head. "We shall wait. I will not reveal to the university our intention to court. When you are comfortable, or if you are ever comfortable about giving up your career, I'll be waiting." He glanced around the area. He extended his hand. "It was a pleasure seeing you, Miss Jones."

"What?" He shook his head with a glance over to their right. One of the school board members, Mr. Markle, waited on the station's loading dock. "Pleasure meeting you, Professor Moore." She grabbed her valise and headed toward the train station to determine which train she would be taking for the final leg of her journey back to Warren.

Daniel didn't follow her in. After her inquiry, she exited the station and found him engaged in conversation with Mr. Markle. Her stomach twisted in knots thinking about Daniel, the train ride, the kisses they shared, and the conversation that followed. In his arms, it was easy to walk away from teaching. Apart from him, it was more difficult. *What should I do, Lord?*

A couple of days earlier her fantasies had leaned toward a simple life with Daniel as her husband. Now she was fighting those desires to maintain something she had worked so hard for, something she enjoyed. But was it her life?

She glanced back at Daniel. He nodded and gave her a slight wave as he headed back into the train. He was going on to Nashville. He would return to Warren later. He hoped to teach at a larger university someday. It made sense—better pay, more opportunities. But Warren would seem lonely after he was gone.

"Miss Jones!" Mr. Markle made his way over to her. He was wearing a dark suit with a light-colored vest.

"Mr. Markle," she replied. "Visiting family?"

"Yes and no, I'm afraid. Mostly business. Professor Moore says you are coming back from your father's."

"Yes, sir. We had a lovely holiday together."

"Wonderful. Well, I wanted to extend my appreciation for your reading of Jules Verne's book, *Around the World in Eighty Days*. Quite enjoyable. The whole community really enjoyed it. I heard there was standing room only during your reading time with the children."

"Yes, sir."

"Wonderful. Perhaps now we can get the local families behind a better education budget."

That is certainly needed. "That would be nice."

"I'm wondering if you would consider signing a contract for next year? I don't have the authority to offer it to you at this point, but I would like to bring it to the board's attention, if you are interested."

"For the same pay?"

Mr. Markle blushed.

"I'm afraid I can't afford to rent my own place on such a

meager salary." Helen swallowed, not sure if she should continue, but decided to go ahead anyway. "The school board would have to do better for me to consider staying on another year." Not that she could imagine staying in Warren, having such feelings for Daniel. Of course, he might be leaving for greener pastures by the fall.

Mr. Markle coughed. "I think we might be able to improve your wages. As I said, I cannot speak for the entire board."

"I understand. My father would like me to return to Virginia and has sought out a teaching position for me there as well."

He gave a curt nod. "I will speak with the board."

"Thank you, Mr. Markle. I have enjoyed teaching in Warren."

"What is the next novel you'll be reading from?"

"Mark Twain's *The Adventures of Tom Sawyer*. I might have the children whitewash the fence around the church as a class project."

Mr. Markle chuckled. "Oh, Pastor Stevens would enjoy that." He glanced at his pocket watch. "I must be going. It was a pleasure to see you, Miss Jones. Have a pleasant trip back home."

"Thank you, and you as well."

Helen prayed she would not be sharing the same train as Mr. Markle. She needed the time to rest, pray, and try to decide her future. Did she want a future of aloneness? Did she want a husband and children?

Two hours later she was back in Warren, in her room at Edna Miller's house, and still had no answers. Edna, who had said she might stay visiting with family until the end of February, had not returned. At the moment, Helen wished that were not the case. She rattled around the empty house alone, so alone. Her stomach knotted. No matter how much she prayed and tried to think about the Lord and more pleasant things, she could not relax and find peace. Instead she found boredom and loneliness.

The weeks passed and Helen remained alone in Edna Miller's house. The university students had come the first couple of days after Helen's return, only to discover Edna was not back from her family visit to cook for them. They no longer came to check.

Helen watched every morning for Daniel but had only seen him a couple of mornings each week. He nodded as he passed by but never stopped. He never approached her about doing the Tom Sawyer botany lesson. Instead, she worked out her own curriculum. She ordered pansy seeds from Mr. Kroger down at the mercantile to represent the flower Tom buttoned in his jacket next to his heart after meeting Amy Lawrence. Helen wanted to do the same. She missed Daniel more than she expected to. She closed her eyes and wiped the tears from them as she settled down for the night. *Father, I'm so lonely. Where is Edna? Why won't Daniel even speak with me? I guess I understand that he's waiting on me, but what do I do?*

∾ Chapter 6 ∾

*M*emories of their intimate moments still stirred Daniel's soul. Helen had started her readings of Tom Sawyer, and word spread through the local grapevine. Daniel read the book over the weekend and loved it. He was beginning to discover how much literature he'd never read due to his singular focus on science. If only Markle hadn't been at the station that day, he might have been able to persuade her to reconsider. But Helen wanted to continue with her career. He understood, since he'd worked so hard for his own degrees. It would be a very hard decision for him to give up his career in order to marry.

Irving College began receiving requests from some of the larger universities for recommendations of Daniel's performance as an instructor. The college administration decided to offer Daniel a salary increase but knew they couldn't compete with the larger universities. And Mr. Markle had confided in him that the community school board was considering offering Helen a larger salary and a contract for the following year. He hadn't spoken to her since seeing her on the train and since she'd turned a hundred and eighty degrees from their discussion of courtship. Her situation didn't seem fair, but it also wasn't right for a woman to work outside the home. Someone had to be there to raise the children. Children—he'd never found himself too interested in them. That is, until he spent time around the schoolhouse and saw the excitement in the children's faces as they learned from Helen Jones.

He closed his eyes and calmed his aching heart. He wanted to approach her—

"Professor Moore!" One of his first-hour students came running into his office. "Professor, Mrs. Miller is back, and she's been baking up a storm."

Daniel laughed. "Relax, John, she'll have plenty."

"I hope so. I've been starving for weeks." He tapped the inside of the door casing. "I've got to tell the others."

"You go do. . ." Daniel's words trailed off as John's footfalls echoed down the hallway. Daniel's stomach gurgled. He'd been missing Edna's fine cooking as well. But as much as he would love to partake, he wouldn't be going there. He didn't want to push Helen. He would wait for her, but not too long. He had to decide whether he would stay or go by the end of March. He went back to the papers in front of him.

I could go for a squash pie right about now though. He shrugged off the thought. He couldn't intrude on Helen. He still wasn't certain he wouldn't grab her and kiss her. His arms ached to embrace her. *Father, guide us.*

His next class started filing in. One by one the students took their seats, each nodding as they caught a glimpse of Daniel. He smiled. He couldn't think about Helen. He couldn't even think about Mrs. Miller's treats. It was his last class for the day. "Good afternoon," he began. "Today we're going to. . ."

Thankful the hour session went by quickly, he gathered his papers.

"Professor Moore?"

He looked up. "Mr. Knowles. How can I help you?" Thomas Knowles stood about six feet tall with blond hair and blue eyes.

"Did you hear that Mrs. Miller is back?" he hedged.

Daniel chuckled. "Yes, what's today's special?"

"I don't know, sir. I don't have the extra money right now." Thomas looked down at the floor. "I'll be leaving at the end of this semester."

"Finances?"

Thomas nodded. "I married over the Christmas break. My folks know, but hers don't. I'm actually wondering if you need any help with your backyard farm so I can earn a little extra."

Daniel thought for a moment. "I don't have any work at the moment, but I'll let you know if I do or if I hear that someone else does."

"Thank you, Professor."

"Can I ask why her parents don't know that you've married?"

"We eloped. She's living with her parents rather than move into my old room that I share with my brother. If her parents knew, they might kick her out."

"Ah, I see." Truthfully, he wondered if they'd been caught up with passion and hadn't thought through their choices.

"Pa said she could move in, but she has a room to herself at her home, and her folks aren't keen on her marrying a man with a college education."

"If you drop out at the end of the semester, you won't have a degree."

"True. I'm a farmer. I'll raise pigs on my pa's land, and we'll build our house on the land."

Maybe they have thought through their future, Daniel thought. "What brought you to Irving?"

Thomas sighed. "I thought I might go into agricultural business. Help my dad and other farmers sell their animals and corn at a higher rate like the cattlemen do out west. Probably not feasible, but that was my goal."

"Interesting. Have you met Edward Clancy? He's a senior. Talk with him about your co-op."

"Co-op, sir?" Thomas's face contorted.

"What you are describing is what some farmers are doing as a cooperative effort. Mr. Clancy should be able to give you some pointers, and he might be a good contact for your future sales."

"Thank you, sir. I'll look him up."

"Check Mrs. Miller's. He's a regular customer."

Thomas chuckled. "I think half the student body is, sir."

"You're probably right, Mr. Knowles. Have a good day, and congratulations on your marriage."

Thomas beamed. "Thank you." He walked out the door.

Maybe if he and Helen had met while they were both starting their college careers, they would have fallen in love, eloped, and wouldn't be having this issue right now. Of course, with their six-year age difference, he was already finishing his master's when she entered college. Which would have put her in seventh or eighth grade when he started college. Daniel moaned. He had to stop thinking about her every moment of the day.

He gathered the papers on his desk and headed home. Perhaps there he could put balance back into his life. Maybe it would be for the best if he took a position at a different university.

With Mrs. Miller again setting up shop, Helen hoped Daniel would come by. But with the last of the goodies gone, he still hadn't shown.

"My, my, those boys were hungry today," Edna said as she closed the door.

Helen smiled. "You were gone for a long time."

"Nonsense. It was only an extra ten days."

"Ten days too many, I suspect. They love your goodies."

"It does help. I don't need much these days, but the extra my baking brings in gives me independence. My children are concerned. They think I work too much. What they don't understand is that making those goodies and feeding those boys makes me happy. And keeps me out of trouble," she added with a twinkle in her eye. "I don't know what I'd do with myself sitting around all day. On the other hand, it was wonderful seeing those grandbabies and great-grandbabies. Who aren't so little anymore. In fact. . ." Edna picked up the empty tray and walked toward the kitchen.

Helen picked up another and followed.

"My youngest granddaughter is getting married in the spring."

"Congratulations."

"I got a good eyeful of that man. He's all right. Could use a little growing up, but I suppose we all could when we were that age. He loves my Chrissy so much, and she loves him. That's all that's important."

"True," Helen admitted. And yet she couldn't accept that philosophy for herself. She had a choice to make. Did she want to continue being a schoolteacher, or did she want to become involved with Daniel, get married, and lose her ability to teach? "Who makes up these rules?" she mumbled.

"What rules?" Edna asked.

"Women not being able to teach once they are married."

"Daniel?"

Helen nodded. "I don't know if I have permanent feelings for him. But if we start to court, I can cancel my teaching next year."

"True. You could court for a year—most do."

A nervous chuckle escaped her lips. "Not in this town. You and I both know I'm only teaching here now because the town was desperate. If Daniel and I were to court, they would not ask me to teach next year."

"I see your point." Edna filled the sink with soapy water.

"Daniel is applying to other universities. He might not be here next year."

"Ah, so all your education would be used for only one year."

Helen nodded. "I like him, I really do, but. . ."

Edna tapped Helen's hand with her warm, soapy one. "Give it to the Lord, dear."

She'd been trying to do that for weeks, but the feelings inside were murky, even muddier than immediately after she and Daniel shared those sizzling kisses on the train. Was being a wife such a lower position than being a schoolteacher? Helen glanced at Edna. "Did you ever work outside the home?"

"No, still don't." She winked.

Helen laughed. "I suppose you don't."

"Here's the problem. Today we are fighting for women's rights. And we should have rights. The right to vote, to work, all sorts of things. However, with the push for those rights, an underlying problem is developing. Women are being told that to be a wife and mother is inferior work. To be a schoolteacher, for example, is a higher calling. Granted, it is a high calling. But there is nothing higher than being the helpmate to the man God puts in your life. Nor is there a higher responsibility than to raise our children. That's what is being pushed aside. Most would never say it out loud, but it is there. Young women like yourself don't see the honor of becoming a wife and mother."

"I'm not saying—"

Edna raised a finger. "I didn't say you were dishonoring women who choose to become wives and mothers. I am saying you are probably not seeing the honor of becoming one. It's like crossing that stage and receiving your diploma. It says you did a good job. A wife and mother's diploma is a content, healthy husband and family."

Helen leaned her backside against the counter. Did she look condescendingly on women who chose to stay at home? Did she see them as inferior? Nothing could be further from the truth. Her own mother had been a hardworking woman, constantly busy, and yet food was on the table, the house clean, and the family engaged socially prior to her mother's passing. Father never hosted such events after her passing. *Hmm. . .*

Am I missing something?

"Read the thirty-first proverb. Lemuel's mother lays out what the ideal woman would be for a king, not that any of us could ever meet all her standards." Edna chuckled. She finished washing the trays, then went to the oven and pulled out a beautiful ham baked with apples that infused the room with wonderful aromas.

"Wow, I knew I was smelling something good! I thought it was apple pie for tomorrow."

Edna smiled. "This ham will feed us for a week. I have quite a few ham recipes."

Helen rubbed her hands together. "I look forward to trying each and every one of them."

"Good, because I'm inviting Daniel for dinner tomorrow night."

Helen closed her eyes. The room seemed to swim. She still wasn't ready to face him, not yet. Not until she knew her own heart.

Daniel picked up a note from the living room floor that had been passed through the brass mail slot. He smiled, looking at the delicate scrawl that showed the age of the person who had written it. "Edna." He flipped the envelope over and broke the wax seal.

The body of the letter was written on the inside of the envelope, meaning the envelope and sheet of paper were the same. He flipped it over and saw that it was decorated on the outside to be used as a mailing envelope.

Dear Daniel,

*Would you please consider being my guest for dinner
tomorrow evening? I've been gone for such a long time, and
it would do my heart good to see you.*

*Sincerely,
Edna Miller*

Daniel sat down and penned a quick response.

Dear Edna,

*I would be honored to be your dinner guest tomorrow
evening.*

*Sincerely,
Daniel Moore, PhD*

It was still new to write "PhD" after his name. But it meant
a lot. It stood for so many years of hard work. He closed his
eyes. The same would be true for Helen as well. She hadn't gone
through the eight years of education that he had, but she had
worked hard to earn her degree. Perhaps their timing just wasn't
right.

He fingered the finished letter, stood up, and put his coat
back on. He would deliver his response in person. After hustling
through the snow-laden streets, he approached Edna's house
and noted that all the lights were dimmed. He slipped his note
through the mail slot and returned home. Tomorrow he would
give his suggestion to Helen, hoping they would be able to continue with a relationship. He would pray it through tonight and
tomorrow before he presented his idea to her.

The day dragged on as Daniel went about his classes. Nothing noteworthy happened. No one came for advice; no one decided to quit their education. It had been a peaceful day. The knot in his stomach twisted again. He was certain he'd come up with an idea that would allow him to spend time with Helen while giving her another year to teach before they married. One thing was certain: he would be marrying Helen Jones. It might not be this year, but hopefully the next. The question that remained was, would Helen be comfortable with the arrangement, or would she prefer to remain teaching and single longer? He knew he could wait another year and a half, but not marrying would be a hindrance to his career. Most universities wanted a stable family man working for them. An engaged man would pass the test for a year, but no longer.

These thoughts bothered him too. He wasn't trying to put his career over the choices that he and Helen would need to make, but his career would provide for their needs.

He stopped himself. He was overthinking things. He still hadn't spoken with Helen. He didn't know her thoughts, or whether the kisses on the train invaded her mind as they did his. He couldn't imagine they didn't, but then again. . .she had walked away from him.

Of course, he hadn't approached her. Daniel groaned in frustration. He had to stop dwelling on such matters. He could not live for a year and a half like this. No, he needed to gain control, work through his emotions, and allow Helen to make up her own mind. He would approach her with his suggestion and let her choose whether to move forward or not. It was the best he could do, the honorable thing to do. *"Charity suffereth long, and is kind."* He sighed as the familiar verse came to mind.

Father, give me peace and help me love Helen in a proper way.

Later that evening he buffed the tops of his black shoes against the calves of his trousers. He'd spent more time grooming his hair and beard than normal. He lifted his hand to knock just as the door was flung open. "Good evening, Professor Moore." Daniel blinked. He hadn't realized Edna Miller had invited others.

~ Chapter 7 ~

From a few feet away, Helen saw the shock on Daniel's face. She knew he wasn't expecting this small dinner party of six.

"Good evening, Marcus." Daniel extended his hand. "Pleasure to see you."

Marcus, one of Edna's many nephews, shook Daniel's hand. "Good to see you as well. Auntie Edna has told me that you completed your PhD."

"Yes, I have. And how are you? Your studies?"

"I am passing. Science is a bit of a bore." Marcus winked.

Daniel laughed.

Helen relaxed. She was glad that Daniel knew Marcus, which meant he knew Marcus's parents as well. They were strangers to her but apparently not to Daniel. Edna had invited them when she was at her son's for Christmas. They traveled six hours to visit and would be staying overnight in Edna's home. Exactly which rooms, Helen didn't know, but she feared her room might be occupied.

"Daniel, I'm so glad you could come," Edna said, carrying in a tray with delicious treats on it.

"Thank you for the invitation. I'm honored. You should have told me your family would be in town."

Edna blushed. "I was hoping to impose upon you."

Daniel looked down at Edna and held her gaze. "And?"

"Would you be willing to let Marcus stay at your place tonight? He said he wouldn't mind sleeping on the sofa, but—"

"He's more than welcome," Daniel interrupted.

Helen found herself wanting to get closer to Daniel. She wanted to sit on the sofa and have him sit beside her. Instead, he stepped over to Marcus, slapped him on the back, and exchanged pleasantries about rooming together.

Helen felt the separation from Daniel more vividly than after the first time he simply waved to her and kept on walking. Unfortunately, tonight was not the night to speak with him. At first, she'd been glad that Edna had invited others, but now she wanted time alone with him. They needed to talk, or at least she needed to talk. But how? About what? Her thoughts still hadn't changed. She still wanted to be a teacher. Goodness, why was this so difficult?

The evening passed with enjoyable conversation. Edna did her part to try to include her, but Helen knew she was the odd man out in the room. She excused herself as soon as it seemed proper and went to her room. She went over her lesson plans for Tom Sawyer. The pansy seeds she ordered had come in. They would be planting them later, when they got to the chapter where Tom gave pansies to Amy Lawrence. She would remind the children of the story as they watched them grow and blossom. Whitewashing the fence at the church would happen once the temperatures rose.

There was movement in the hall outside her bedroom. A shadow crossed beneath the door. A small white piece of paper appeared. Helen walked over and picked it up.

> *Helen, would you meet me at the schoolhouse before church on Sunday morning?*
>
> *Daniel*

A smile rose on Helen's cheeks. She closed her eyes. *Thank You, Lord.* It was time. The trouble was, could she wait a day and a half to speak with Daniel?

She went back to her desk, put the note aside, and turned up the light on the oil lamp. The lesson plans for the next week would not get done by themselves.

Hours later, Helen yawned as she glanced at the wall clock. "Oh dear." She put her work away and undressed for bed. It was midnight, much later than she normally stayed up.

Sunday morning came without any further contact from Daniel. She followed his instructions and met him at the schoolhouse. She arrived as early as possible, bringing her lesson plans and placing them on her desk. The schoolhouse had changed so much since her first day.

"Good morning, Helen." Daniel's voice sent shivers down her spine.

She turned to face him. His brown hair and beard seemed

regal this morning. "Good morning, Daniel."

"Thank you for coming." He stood by the open doorway. "I don't want to expose you to undue scrutiny, so I'll remain here. Helen, I understand your desire to keep teaching. And I'm willing to wait for you. Can we correspond by letter?"

She stepped toward him. He held out his hand, stopping her from moving forward. "What are you asking, Daniel?"

"I've put my thoughts down in this letter." He pulled an envelope from his chest pocket. "Basically, it comes down to this. I can't stop thinking about you, and I want to court you. We can get engaged for a year, at the end of this school year, without anyone thinking poorly of you. That will give you the rest of this year and all of next to teach. I know I'm being forward here, but we don't have much time. The letter will explain in further detail, and I would like for you to add any suggestions of your own. These are my thoughts on how we can get to know one another without threatening either one of our careers. I think it is doable. However, I won't be able to continue longer than a year. We will have to marry or end our relationship. My job would be in jeopardy if we did not marry within a year from our formal engagement." He stepped back. "I'm sorry. I'm not giving you any time to speak or think about all of this. Please, read the letter. I hope that will explain it better."

"Daniel—"

"Read the letter, Helen." Daniel slipped out and closed the door behind him.

Helen sat down and opened the letter. She scanned it then read it again. His plan had merit. Would she be content to marry, having taught for only two years?

Then again, could she keep from giving in to her feelings for Daniel to be her husband for more than a year and a half? He suggested they court until the end of the school year and, if she were agreeable, they would get engaged during the summer. He would go on to teach at one of the universities he'd applied for. They would continue to correspond by letter. It would be a very long school year if he moved away. She understood he would be making better money, and it would be helpful for his career and future endeavors, but not seeing him for an entire year. . . Helen sighed.

She put the letter back into the envelope and then into her purse. The church bells were ringing, calling everyone to worship. She would have a lot to pray about. She was touched by his letter. He understood the hardship it meant to give up her career.

Once again, Edna's words about not seeing the high honor it was to be a wife and mother came to mind. Had she really been thinking women who chose that path had compromised their talents and abilities? *Father, help me see the truth.*

Daniel stole a few glances at Helen in her pew. Her uncomfortable posture said she had read his letter and she was thinking about it. He couldn't ask for more. He hoped she would see his love in his willingness to give her additional time to be a teacher. He rubbed his hands together, worried she might see him as being too forward or assuming too much. It was such a fine line to promise one's love and not overstep. The few words and moments they had shared on the train were not enough to build a foundation on. But letters could provide the answer. What they were doing now wasn't working.

The final hymn began. Daniel stood with the rest of the congregation. He hadn't heard much of the sermon. Something about allowing God to be the priority in our lives, which he couldn't agree with more. Was he putting Helen above the Lord? She certainly invaded his mind more than thoughts about the Lord. Then again, he bathed all of those thoughts in prayer. He snickered to himself. Perhaps she was actually making him think more about the Lord, about putting Him first in a possible relationship with her.

Lord, I need a distraction.

Helen nodded as she walked past him down the aisle and out of the church.

He responded with a nod instead of stepping out and escorting her from the sanctuary. He allowed many to pass before stepping into the flow of exiting parishioners. He squinted as he exited the church onto the front steps.

"Yoo-hoo, Professor Moore?" Edna sang out, waving him over. "Would you do us the honor of having dinner with us today? I made ham and brown beans with corn bread."

Her words churned his stomach. He wasn't one to pass up a home-cooked meal. He glanced over to Helen. She gave a slight nod of acceptance. "I'd be honored to."

"Marvelous! I asked the reverend to come too. Unfortunately, he will not be able to join us this afternoon."

"May I escort you lovely ladies home?" Daniel held out his elbow for Edna. Edna took it and Helen fell in step behind them.

"One day you two will not have to do this." Edna smiled and waved to some of her friends.

"Edna!" Helen scolded in a whisper.

"Nonsense. You two have some talking to do. I'll be in the house, but you two need to settle things without the entire town watching," Edna said.

Daniel placed his hand on Edna's hand holding his elbow. "Thank you."

"You're welcome."

They made it through town and to Edna's house at a slow pace, though still faster than normal for Edna. Once inside she said, "I'm going to the kitchen to finish fixing dinner. You two speak to one another. And keep away from the windows. No telling who might just"—Edna finger-quoted the words—"happen by."

"Yes, ma'am, thank you."

Daniel turned to Helen. He extended his arms, and she stepped into them. All the worries and fears washed away. He felt at peace and one with Helen. He knew beyond any reasonable doubt that Helen was the one God designed for him. He leaned down and kissed the top of her reddish-brown hair. "Helen," he whispered.

"Daniel," she whispered to his chest. "I've missed you."

"And I you. What do you think of my suggestions?" He led her to the front sitting room and sat her down on the edge of the sofa farthest from the front window. He took the chair beside her.

"Your suggestion of writing letters to get to know one another is wise. But how are we courting if we are only sending letters?"

He smiled, his heart full and encouraged. "For the remainder of the school year we shall court once a week. I'm allowed that within my contract. In the fall I shall leave for one of the other universities and we can only correspond by letter. That will be difficult but necessary."

"Necessary? Why?"

"For you to continue teaching," he said.

"I understand the opportunities afforded you to teach at a larger university, but. . ."

Daniel's heart stopped.

"Do you have to leave? Is it that much more money or prestige?"

"Yes and no. It is important for my career, yes. Would it hurt my career to wait an additional year? Not really. What are you asking?"

Helen trembled. She'd been wrestling all through the church service with Daniel's suggestions for a possible future for the two of them. A large part of her loved that he was giving her another year to teach. Another part of her was wondering if it was worth it to wait. In so many ways it would be easier to stop teaching and simply marry Daniel. "I'm not sure. I only read your letter a couple of hours ago. I will need time to process it."

"Understood."

"On the other hand, people are going to suspect something if Edna keeps inviting you over."

"Which is why I suggested a formal courtship."

"Yes, but that would limit how often we could spend time

with one another. And you know this school board will be watching me."

"No matter what we do, they will be watching both of us. The only way to see more of each other would be to elope and get married, but then you would lose your job, and I can't be a part of that."

"Daniel." She reached over and took his hand. "A year and a half—that's a long time to wait for me."

"Merely time, my love. We're both young. We can wait."

She released his hand and said, "I need more time to think and pray about this. I know it is foolish to hold on to a dream of teaching when I know the laws won't be changing anytime soon. Perhaps one day a woman can teach and be married. I hope so. I worked hard for my degree. On the other hand, I don't want to be apart from you, to not see you for an entire school year. . ." Her words trailed off.

He got up and knelt before her. He captured her hands and heart. "Pray with me, Helen. The Bible says that charity 'beareth all things, believeth all things, hopeth all things, endureth all things.' If our feelings for one another are from the Lord, then we shall overcome this obstacle."

She focused on his chocolate-brown eyes. So warm and trustworthy. His soul, his love, his hope shone through them. "Yes, thank you. The Lord will see us through, and I wouldn't want to live my life with a man whom God has not designed for me."

Daniel prayed. "Father, we give our desires over to You. You know what is the best path for Helen and me to take. Show us Your way and not our own. In Jesus' name, amen."

"Amen," Helen echoed.

"Amen," Edna said. "Dinner is served."

Daniel stood up and escorted Helen to the kitchen table. She smiled at the array of fancy china.

Edna pointed to the chair at the head of the table. "Daniel."

"Thank you. May I?" He held out a chair for Edna. She sat down. He then moved to the other vacant seat and held it out for Helen. Helen sat, and he placed his hand on her shoulder and gave it a gentle squeeze.

Edna bowed her head as Daniel sat down. Helen did likewise, grateful she and Daniel had been able to talk of their attraction and future together. *Thank You, Father.*

"Shall we pray?" Edna said. "Father, thank You for Your blessings. Guide these two young people and help them see Your path. In Jesus' name, amen."

"Amen," Helen and Daniel repeated.

The meal was fabulous, as if anything Edna cooked wouldn't be. Light conversation continued with Edna throughout the meal. She excused herself as Daniel and Helen cleaned up the dishes. As she finished washing the last dish, Daniel came up beside her and wrapped her in his arms. "I'm so happy. I've been miserable since. . ."

She twisted into his arms. "I'm sorry."

"No, I understand. I know how hard it would be for me if I had to give up my career to follow my heart."

She glanced up at his sweet lips and closed her eyes. Daniel did what she'd hoped and kissed her. Warmth and love filled her. With all the strength she could muster, she pushed away and stepped back. "Thank you for understanding." She drew in her breath, held it for a second, and asked, "What if I don't want to give up teaching at the end of next year?"

He turned to the window. "Then I would have to cancel our engagement. Not that I would wish to." He spun around and faced her again. "But I would have to for the sake of my contracts. And honestly, if you decide your career is of more importance than our relationship, we should end this right now."

Helen sucked in a gasp of air. She expected as much, but to hear his words. . .

"Helen, I don't say this to corner you into a commitment. I state this as a fact. I will need a wife, and if we are not getting married within a year of our engagement, then I shall have to look for another bride. It is not what my heart wants, but it is what the university will be expecting of me. A married professor is a stable professor."

Helen nodded. Her mind spun with the ramifications of the possible finality of her decision. And yet she knew she loved Daniel. The question for her to ask herself was, did she love him more than her career? Would she harbor resentment if she married him and never had the opportunity to teach again? Were love and family more important than a passion for a career in teaching?

Daniel reached out and took hold of her shoulders. "I've been praying about this for weeks, thus the proposal in the letter. You need time to pray it through. Why don't we court for a few weeks and see what develops?"

Helen gave him a halfhearted smile, her body betraying her mind. She wanted to be back in his arms. The thought of not having him in her life frightened her, but the thought of not being a schoolteacher ever again tore at her heart. If she hadn't had such a good first year, she might not feel this way. But now she knew that she was a good teacher, and excited for her students to learn.

He pulled her into his embrace. "I love you, Helen, and I wish I could say I could wait five or ten years, but I can't. Even if my career didn't expect me to have a wife, I want a wife. I want to have a helpmate and a mother for my children. I hope it will be you. But I shall wait on you to decide."

She sighed and tapped his chest. "Thank you. I'm sorry this is such a difficult choice."

He smiled. She loved his smile. "I'm glad it is difficult. That means you care and are considering this arrangement."

She balled her hand on his chest and smacked him.

"Uff," he gasped. He looked down at her with a look she hadn't seen since her father had scolded and teased her at the same time. "Helen."

She laughed.

Edna called out, "Come join me in the sitting room."

"Coming," Helen answered, and led Daniel to the front parlor. No man had ever garnered so much of her thoughts and emotions. Even her relationship with Michael, her old beau, hadn't taken up this much of her energy or passion. Daniel was right in not wanting to wait for years, and he was generous in offering to let her teach for an additional year before they married. What was holding her back? Why couldn't she just say yes and marry him after this school year ended or after the next?

∾ Chapter 8 ∾

*D*aniel held down his emotions. He couldn't give in to his feelings and kiss her senseless until she agreed to his recommendations. On the other hand, if she did agree, he would have to endure a year and a half of torture waiting for them to become man and wife. Edna had provided the perfect place for them to have this intimate conversation, but after the meal he extended his thanks and apologies. Staying too long would have the school board questioning not only Helen's behavior, but his own. And no doubt Mr. Markle had caught the exchange of glances with Helen during the church service. He was an ultra-conservative man but also a fair man. He would have them married before the end of the school year if he knew about their passionate kisses.

At home, Daniel went over his lessons. The following week would be the winter break and he planned on seeing his parents in Nashville. He penned a letter telling Helen of his schedule.

The next day when he returned home from the university, he found a note.

Dear Daniel,

I'm sorry I am having trouble with this decision. I do care about you deeply. When you return, I hope to have an answer for you. God's blessings on you and your family.

Sincerely,
Helen

Daniel took in a deep, cleansing breath and continued with his work. Anytime his mind wandered to Helen, he would pray for her and try to go about his business without further distraction.

Visiting his parents proved to be dull. His father and brothers were working, and his mother was busy with her social engagements. He felt out of place, even though he loved his family and his family loved him. He felt their love yet still felt disjointed from them. He returned to Warren more tired than refreshed, retreating to his home office to look over the school lessons for the rest of the semester.

A knock on the door brought him from his unproductive musings. A hope that Helen would be standing there was quickly dashed by the appearance of Thomas Knowles and a woman, presumably his wife. "Mr. Knowles, ma'am. How can I help you?"

"Professor, may we come in?" Thomas asked. "This is my wife, Diana."

"Pleasure to meet you, Diana. Come on in. What can I do for you?"

Thomas led his wife to the sofa. He turned and faced Daniel. "Professor, I'm in a bit of a quagmire."

Daniel signaled for Thomas to sit down. Thomas sat beside his wife and she reached out to hold his hand. "What seems to be the problem, Thomas?"

"Diana's parents found out we are married, 'cept they don't believe us. We showed 'em the marriage license, but it didn't make any difference. Her father threw it in my face and told us to leave."

"I'm so sorry. Are you both all right?" Daniel asked, turning a scrutinizing gaze upon Diana for any evidence of abuse.

"Fine, sir." Thomas cleared his throat. "The problem is we have nowhere to live. I don't want to lose the money I've spent on my schooling, and I don't have a way to earn enough to rent a house here for Diana and myself."

Daniel leaned back in his chair. "I see. That is a problem."

"Yes, sir. You're the only professor I thought of who might be able to help."

"I don't know how. When did your father kick you out?" Daniel asked Diana.

"Two days ago," Diana said.

"Where did you spend the night?"

"The first night at my folks' place. The second night we slept on the train as we traveled here. As I said before, my folks said Diana can live there, but—"

"The house is crowded," Daniel finished for him.

"Yes, sir. We came on the train to Warren, but there isn't any place for us to live."

"I imagine that is a problem." Daniel stood up and paced. He always did problem solving better on his feet. "Where were you hoping to spend the night tonight?"

"I have a tent, but—"

"That won't do this time of year." Daniel stopped pacing in

front of them. "I have a spare room. You can stay there until a reasonable solution can be reached."

Tears filled Diana's eyes.

"Are you certain, Professor?" Thomas asked.

"Of course. Please make yourself at home. Let me show you to your room."

Daniel spent the next two hours helping Thomas and Diana settle in, making up the spare room, setting out linens for them, and fixing them some dinner. He also showed them where items in the kitchen could be found, including the few canned goods he did have and the stock of hams hanging in the basement.

Just before bed he found a note at his door. He rushed into his study. His heart thudded in his chest. Would Thomas and Diana find out about his letters with Helen? Would their presence in the house be a problem for her? He opened her letter, breaking the wax seal.

Dear Daniel,

I have missed you. I hope you had a wonderful visit with your family. I have come to a conclusion about our relationship. Would you do me the honor of coming to dinner tomorrow evening?

With great affection,
Helen

Daniel smiled. He penned a note and rushed out to deliver it to Helen. He slipped it through the brass letter opening and hustled back home.

Thomas and Diana had retired for the evening. He breathed a sigh of relief. He wouldn't lie about his whereabouts, but he prayed he wouldn't expose Helen and their budding romance.

"Daniel, it's good to see you," Edna said as she opened the door to him. "I'm so glad you could accept the invitation," she added, closing the door.

"Thank you."

"Word has it you have houseguests."

Daniel snickered. "News does travel fast. Yes, one of my students and his wife."

"There's a story there, no doubt. You'll have to tell me later. Helen would like to see you."

He stepped into the kitchen where Helen, wrapped in an apron, leaned over a pot on the stove. "Hi." She smiled. "I'm glad you came."

"Excuse me," Edna said as she walked to the front room.

Helen put down the wooden spoon and faced him. He scooped her into his arms. "I've missed you." Her kiss branded him. His lips seared against hers. *Lord, give me strength to wait another fifteen months or so.*

Helen sighed against his chest. "I missed you too." She stepped away. "I don't want to keep you waiting for my decision, Daniel, but I want you to know how I made it."

She clasped her hands in front of her. "After you left here that Sunday, I rose early each morning and prayed for the Lord to tell me His will for me. And I wrestled with the question, 'Do I love teaching more than I do Daniel and having a family with him?'"

He looked stunned, and she took a shuddering breath. "A few days after you left on your break, I was standing at the blackboard writing the spelling words for the following day, and I suddenly saw myself with you and four small children." She smiled shyly at him. "I could hardly breathe." Her smile faded, and her eyes focused over his shoulder. "Then I saw myself as an older woman, gray hair, wrinkled hands, writing on the blackboard. When I looked behind me, the desks were filled with young students, eager to learn."

She shook her head, as if coming back to the present. "I distinctly felt the Lord saying in my heart, "It's your choice." She took a deep breath. "Daniel, I gave the school board my notice that I won't be teaching in the fall."

"What? Why?"

Helen chuckled. "Because I enjoy teaching. But I love you. And although we might be within our rights to have a prolonged engagement, I can't see myself. . .correction, I can't see *us* being so far apart."

"Are you suggesting—" Daniel's hand shook as he reached out.

She clasped his hand and looked into his chocolate-brown eyes. "That we get married after the school year is over? Yes."

Daniel's smile filled his face. "Don't misunderstand me, but why? We could get engaged—"

She leaned into him and put a finger to his lips. Her heart pounded. She stood up on her toes and kissed him. He wrapped his arms around her and held her tight and deepened the kiss.

She broke away, and he loosened his hold. "That's why." She blushed.

His smile widened. "I shall announce our engagement in the morning."

She slipped from his arms and took a bundle of letters from the countertop.

"What are those?" he asked.

"Our wedding announcements," she said with a wink.

He examined the perfectly printed handwritten cards. A pressed pansy was on the corner of each. "There are enough for my father, your parents and brothers, and your school board as well as mine," she said, and returned to the pan on the stove. "Tell me about your houseguests."

Daniel chuckled. "Thomas married Diana over the Christmas break. Her parents didn't know. They have a problem with Thomas seeking a higher education. His parents were fine with them getting married, but their house is overcrowded. Thomas didn't want to lose the money he'd spent on the semester, so he brought her here because when her folks found out, they kicked her out of their house."

"Oh, how horrible. She must be hurting."

"I imagine so. Needless to say, they are staying in my spare room until they find a solution to their problem. It is only eight weeks until the end of the university's school year."

"True. And that means you'll be busy getting ready for our wedding while I finish out my school year."

"Sounds like gardening would be easier," he teased.

"Probably. However, I'm hoping to have a small, intimate wedding. We'll invite our parents, your brothers, the school boards, and Edna, of course. Who else?"

"Don't know, apart from the pastor and his family."

"That sounds perfect. Small, intimate. . ."

He came up beside her. "I love you, Helen."

She turned and faced him. "I love you too, Daniel."

"Are you certain about no longer teaching? I can wait another year."

She nuzzled her head on his shoulder. "I'm certain. I'll teach again, after we start having children."

Daniel rumbled with laughter. "Of that, my dear, I am certain. I'll be there for story hour. There are so many books I haven't read yet."

She smiled. Her heart was full. She was beginning to learn the biggest lesson of her life—one on love, and how to give and take within a marriage.

Epilogue

*H*elen tried to stand still while Edna worked on all the buttons of her wedding dress. Why on earth her mother picked such a dress, she didn't know. But her father had sent it after he received news of her and Daniel's wedding. It was an honor to wear the dress, just a pain to stand still for so long.

"Daniel's going to have fun trying to get all of this unfastened," Edna quipped.

"It's time, Helen," her father said through a closed door.

"Just about done," Helen answered. "It's all these buttons."

Her father snickered from behind the closed door. "I remember," he mumbled.

"Finally," Edna said. "That was the last one."

"Thank you, Edna. Thank you for everything."

"You're welcome, dear. And I'm so glad Daniel decided to stay here at the university. You'll still be around."

"I am too." Helen hugged her good friend. Decades separated them in age, but their hearts were bound together in the Lord and His plans for their lives. She'd learned so much from Edna. "Come in, Daddy."

Her father entered, handsomely dressed in a sharp black suit and perfectly framed by the fluted white doorframe. "Oh my gracious, you look just like your mother. She was so beautiful I had a hard time standing up when she came down the aisle."

Helen smiled.

He held out his elbow and escorted her out of the pastor's office and into the vestibule. Edna hustled down the aisle before them. The pastor's wife began playing the piano.

"Are you certain, Helen?"

"Yes, Dad. He's a good man."

He patted the top of her hand. "Good. I couldn't ask for anything more. Shall we?"

She nodded.

They stepped through the vestibule and turned down the aisle. Daniel stood tall, his brothers standing beside him. The small gathering had turned into a much grander affair. Several members of the local school board were there, as well as several professors and their families from the university. Daniel's smile glowed brighter as she focused on him, on the love they were beginning to share. As Daniel put it, they were beginning their lesson in love.

She giggled, remembering it.

Daniel winked.

She might no longer be able to teach other people's children in a formal way, but she would be giving private lessons to some of her former students, since Warren hadn't found a schoolteacher yet for the upcoming year. One day politics might change, but for now she was content to join her life with her husband's and begin the mystery of love.

Her father took her hand and placed it in Daniel's. Within moments they would be pronounced man and wife, and they would be one, forever and always.

Joy filled Helen's heart. Daniel's eyes sparkled. Yes, it would be a great lesson in love.

Lynn A. Coleman is an award-winning and bestselling author of *Key West* and other books. She began her writing and speaking career with how to utilize the internet. Since October 1998, when her first fiction novel sold, she has sold forty-five books and novellas. Lynn is also the founder of American Christian Fiction Writers Inc. and served as the group's first president for two years as well as spending two years on the advisory board. One of her primary reasons for starting ACFW was to help writers develop their writing skills and encourage others to go deeper in their relationship with God. "God has given me a gift, but it is my responsibility to develop that gift," she says. Some of her other interests are photography, camping, cooking, and boating. Having grown up on Martha's Vineyard, she finds water to be very exciting and soothing. She can sit and watch the waves for hours. If time permitted, she would like to travel. She makes her home in Keystone Heights, Florida, where her husband of forty-six years serves as pastor of Friendship Bible Church. Together they are blessed with three children, two living and one in glory, eight grandchildren, and one great-grandchild.

Coming Soon. . .

Blacksmith Brides (Releasing May 2020!)
Come along to the local forge and meet men of steel who were the backbone of local industry. Can four blacksmiths be softened by romance? Meg in 1774, Elowyn in 1798, Esther in 1861, and Leah in 1870 must bend or break when faced with her own fears of falling in love with a strong and determined man of the forge.

Paperback / 978-1-64352-422-1/ $14.99

Carousel Dreams (Releasing June 2020!)
Experience the early history of four iconic carousels—Oak Bluffs in 1889 Martha's Vineyard, Crescent Park in 1895 Rhode Island, Conneaut Lake in 1910 Pennsylvania, and Balboa Park in 1922 California—that draw together four couples in whirling romances full of music and charm.

Paperback / 978-1-64352-470-2/ $14.99